Praise for *The Informationist*

"Smart, sexy, fast-paced—a turbo-charged debut with a protagonist as deadly as she is irresistible."

—Vince Flynn, *New York Times* bestselling author of *American Assassin*

"A breathless, international thrill ride as Vanessa lies, kills, and uses her incredible gift for getting what she wants. But underneath all the action is an even more powerful story of a woman trying to make peace with her personal demons."

—*Family Circle*

"A terrific thriller with piercing tension, chest-tightening adventure, and a one-of-a-kind heroine I've continued to think about long after finishing the last page. Taylor Stevens is a born storyteller. I couldn't put *The Informationist* down."

—Michael Palmer, author of *The Last Surgeon*

"A fast-paced thriller . . . with bestseller written all over it."

—*Vogue*

"[Stevens] writes with the confidence of one who knows she's hit on a winning series character who has the world at her beck and call."

—*Los Angeles Times*

"With its breakneck pacing set against the simmering violence of Central Africa, *The Informationist* is a thriller of the highest caliber. Michael Munroe is a heroine you've never seen before—a shape-shifter who's sharp, fast, and deadly, but still vulnerable to her own demons. Powered by intricate plotting that leads to a climax on a grand scale, this novel announces Taylor Stevens as a writer to watch."

—Colin Harrison, author of *The Finder*

"Extraordinary . . . No one has written a more exhilarating, adroit, and stylish debut for a suspense series since Raymond Chandler introduced Philip Marlowe in *The Big Sleep* back in 1939."

—*Daily Beast*

"A globe-trotting thriller . . . *The Informationist* is an accessible, crisply told tale."

—*NYTimes.com*

"A dazzling new thriller."

—*Daily News* (New York)

"[Vanessa Munroe is] the book world's newest tough-girl action hero."

—*New York Post*

"An international thriller featuring a most unusual hero."

—*Fort Worth Star-Telegram*

"An irresistible, gorgeously written thriller . . . impossible to put down . . . Hollywood, let the casting wars begin."

—*Dallas Morning News*

"A page-turning thriller . . . Stevens has created a character who, possibly like herself, may not always know what dangers lay in front of her or how she'll come out ahead, but it's our pleasure to travel these strange, exciting roads with her."

—*Huffington Post*

"Taylor Stevens in her first novel has achieved the gripping story telling technique of many acclaimed authors."

—*Paramus Post*

"Stevens's blazingly brilliant debut introduces a great new action heroine, Vanessa Michael Munroe, who doesn't need to kick over a hornet's nest to get attention, though her feral, take-no-prisoners attitude reflects the fire of Stieg Larsson's Lisbeth Salander."

—*Publishers Weekly* (starred and boxed review)

"Stevens has penned a fast-paced, gripping, edgy mystery with a heroine whom even Lisbeth Salander would admire."

—*Library Journal* (starred review)

"Dazzling . . . Munroe is a model of an emerging action heroine: like Stieg Larsson's Lisbeth Salander, not a guy in a girl suit but not one to whimper in the corner, either."

—*Booklist*

"Stevens debuts with a tightly written thriller . . . the writing is stellar, the heroine grittier than Lara Croft and the African setting so vivid that readers can smell the jungle and feel the heat—a gifted debut with much promise."

—*Kirkus Reviews*

also by Taylor Stevens

tHe INNOCeNt

taYLOR steveNS

tHe

informationist

a thriller

Broadway Paperbacks

NEW YORK

Copyright © 2011 by Taylor Stevens
Excerpt from *The Innocent* copyright © 2011 by Taylor Stevens

All rights reserved.
Published in the United States by Broadway Paperbacks, an imprint of the
Crown Publishing Group, a division of Random House, Inc., New York.
www.crownpublishing.com

Broadway Paperbacks and its logo, a letter B bisected on the diagonal, are
trademarks of Random House, Inc.

This book contains an excerpt from the forthcoming book *The Innocent* by
Taylor Stevens. This excerpt has been set for this edition only and may not
reflect the final content of the forthcoming edition.

Originally published in hardcover in the United States by Crown Publishers,
an imprint of the Crown Publishing Group, a division of Random House, Inc.,
New York, in 2011.

Library of Congress Cataloging-in-Publication Data is available on request.

ISBN 978-0-307-71710-8
eISBN 978-0-307-71711-5

Printed in the United States of America

Book design by Lynne Amft
Cover design by Brian Moore
Cover photographs by Jen Butcher

10 9 8 7 6 5 4 3 2 1

First Paperback Edition

To my fellow childhood survivors — you know who you are

West Central Africa
Four years ago

T his is where he would die.

On the ground, palms flat to the earth, fighting against thirst and the urge to drink from a mud-filled puddle. Blood was in his hair, on his clothes, and, beneath dirt and grime, it painted his face. It wasn't his blood. And he could still taste it.

They would find him. Kill him. They would cut him to pieces just as they had Mel, maybe Emily, too. He ached to know that she was still alive and heard only the quiet noise of the deep forest broken by the strike of machetes against foliage.

Filtered light escaped the rain forest's canopy, playing tricks with shadows. The sound of the blades carried long in the stillness, bouncing, making it difficult to gauge direction.

Even if he did escape his pursuers, he wouldn't survive a night in the jungle. He needed to move, to run, to continue east until he crossed the border, though he no longer had a bearing on where that was. He willed himself to his knees, struggled to his feet, and spun, disoriented and dizzy, searching for the way out.

The machetes were closer now, followed by shouting not far behind. He propelled himself forward, his lungs on fire and his eyes burning.

Time had lost meaning long ago. In the dimming light, jungle plants loomed large and ominous. Was this hallucination?

Another shout, closer still. His legs buckled, and he fell to the ground, cursing himself for the noise he made. He wrestled out of the backpack; it wasn't worth his life.

Hope came with the low grumble of dilapidated jeeps vibrating through the undergrowth. The road was a marker pointing toward escape, and now he would find it. He crouched, then peered above the leafy cover, implored providence for no snakes, and ran, following the sound. Without the pack he moved faster, should have thought of it sooner.

A chorus of voices erupted a hundred meters behind. They'd found the pack. *Carry on your body what you cannot afford to lose.* Wise advice from a cousin who had spent time in this godforsaken wilderness. He had bought time, minutes—maybe his life—by dumping it.

There was a shaft of light twenty meters ahead. Instinctively he moved toward it. It wasn't the road but a village, small and silent. He scanned the deserted scene for the one thing he wanted more than all else and found it in a corroded oil barrel. An assortment of water insects made their home along the surface, and mosquito larvae skirted about the bottom like miniature mermaids. He drank greedily, risking what disease the barrel had to offer; if he was lucky, it would be curable.

A jeep drew nearer, and he retreated to the shadows and lay hidden within the foliage. Soldiers spilled from the vehicle and spread between the baked-mud structures, shattering slatted doors and windows before leaving. He understood now why the village was deserted.

Another fifteen minutes until total darkness. He followed along the edge of the village track to the road, listening intently. The jeeps were gone, and for a moment there was no sound of his pursuers. He stepped from cover onto the main strip and heard Emily yell his name. She was far down the road, running, stumbling, soldiers close behind. They hit her, and she crumpled like a rag doll.

He stood in shock, trembling, and in the darkness watched the machetes fall, glinting in the moonlight. He wanted to scream, he wanted to kill to protect her. Instead he turned east, toward the checkpoint less than twenty meters away, and ran.

CHAPTER 1

Ankara, Turkey

Vanessa Michael Munroe inhaled, slow and measured, focused entirely on the curb of the street opposite.

She'd timed the motorcade from Balgat to the edges of Kizilay Square and stood now, motionless, watching from a shadowed notch while the target group exited the vehicles and progressed down a wide, shallow stairwell. Two men. Five women. Four bodyguards. A few more minutes and the mark would arrive.

Multistoried glass buildings reflected neon onto broad streets still alive with late-evening pedestrian traffic. Bodies brushed past, seemingly unaware of her presence or of how her eyes tracked movement in the dark.

She glanced at her watch.

A Mercedes pulled to a stop across the way, and she straightened as the solitary figure stepped from the backseat. He walked casually toward the entrance, and when he was fully out of sight, she followed, down the stairwell to the Anatolia: private of all private clubs, Ankara's holy of holies, where together the wealthy and powerful fattened the cogs of democracy.

At the door she flashed the business card that had taken two weeks of greased palms and clandestine meetings to acquire.

In acknowledgment the doorman nodded and said, "Sir."

Munroe replied with a nod, slipped a knot of cash into his hand, and entered into the din of smoke and music. She moved beyond the hive of secluded booths, past the bar with its half-filled line of stools, through the corridor that led to the restrooms and, finally, the "staff only" door.

Inside was not much more than a closet, and here she shed the Armani suit, the Italian shoes, and the trappings of the male persona.

It was unfortunate that she was known as a man to the contact she'd used to gain access, when tonight of all nights she needed to be a hundred percent woman. From her chest she shrugged down the sheath that would function as a figure-hugging dress and slid thin lacy sandals from the lining of the jacket onto her feet. She pulled a mini clutch from the suit pocket and then, checking that the hallway was empty, stepped into the restroom to finish the transformation with makeup and hair.

Back in the main room, the motorcade's bodyguards stood as homing beacons, and she walked, with long and languid strides, in their direction. Time slowed. Four seconds. Four seconds of direct eye contact with the mark and then the slightest hint of a smile as she averted her eyes and continued past.

She placed herself at the end of the bar, alone, face turned away, body turned toward him. Ordered a drink. And demurely toying with the chained medallion at her throat, she waited.

This final step and the job would be complete.

She'd estimated ten minutes, but the invitation to join the party came within three. The bodyguard who delivered the message escorted her to the table, and there, with only the briefest round of introductions, coy smiles, and furtive glances, she slipped into the evening's role—seeking, hunting, prodding, all in the guise of the bimbo's game.

The charade lasted into the early morning, when, having gotten what she wanted, she pleaded exhaustion and excused herself from the group.

The mark followed her from the club to the street and, in the glow of the neon lights, offered a ride that she declined with a smile.

He called for his car, and as she began to walk away, he came after her, fingers gripping her arm.

She pulled away. His grip tightened, and she inhaled deeply, forcing a veneer of calm. Her vision shifted to gray. Her eyes moved from his face to the veins on his neck, so easily slit, to his throat, so easily crushed, and back again. With blood pounding in her ears, she fought down the urge to kill him.

Against instinct she maintained the smile and sweetly said, "Let's have another drink."

The Mercedes pulled to the curb. The mark opened the rear door and, before the chauffeur had a chance to step out, shoved Munroe into the backseat. He climbed in after her and slammed the door. Ordered the chauffeur to drive and then pointed in a brisk movement toward the minibar. "Have your drink," he said.

With a flirtatious smile, she looked over her shoulder, seeing but not seeing. It was the smile of death and destruction, a disguise to the fire of bloodlust now coursing through her veins. She struggled to maintain reason. Focus. Subduing the urge, she reached for the bottle of Jack with one hand, her clutch with the other, and said, "Drink with me."

Reacting to her calm, and with the unspoken promise of sex to come, he relaxed and took the drink she offered. She dipped her fingers into it and then pressed them to his mouth. She repeated the gesture, playfully, teasing the Rohypnol into his system until the glass had been emptied, and when it had been done, she staved him off until the drug took effect. She told the chauffeur to take the man home and, without resistance, stepped out of the car.

In the cool of the predawn, she breathed deeply to clear her head. And then she began to walk, oblivious to time, aware only of the lightening sky and eventually the morning call to prayer that sounded from the minarets across the city.

It was fully light when she arrived at the apartment that had served as home for the last nine months.

The place was shuttered and dark, and she flipped on the light. A bare low-wattage bulb hung suspended from the ceiling, revealing a one-room apartment with more floor space devoted to cluttered stacks of books, file folders, and computers with their attendant wires and paraphernalia than to either the desk or the couch that doubled as a bed. Beyond that, the place was empty.

She removed the medallion from around her neck and paused, momentarily distracted by the blinking red light at the foot of the couch.

Then, with the medallion flat between her palms, she twisted it and removed a microcard from the opened halves. She sat in front of the computer, slid the card into a reader, and, with the data downloading, reached for the answering machine.

The voice on the recording was like champagne: Kate Breeden at high noon. "Michael, darling, I know you're still wrapping up and aren't expecting another assignment for a while, but I've received an unusual request. Call me."

Munroe sat on the couch, replayed the recording, leaned her forehead onto her arms, and closed her eyes. Exhaustion from the day's work weighed heavily, and she lay back, eyes glazed in the direction of the monitor and the download status. She glanced at her watch. Just after ten in Dallas. She waited a moment, then straightened, and bracing for what was to come, picked up the handset, and dialed.

The effervescence in the voice on the other end brought the crack of a smile, and Munroe said, "I just got your message."

"I know that you aren't looking for new work for a few months," Kate said, "but this is an exception. The client is Richard Burbank."

Munroe paused. The name was familiar. "Houston oil?"

"That's him."

She sighed. "Okay, fax me the documents, I'll take a look."

There was an awkward silence, and then Breeden said, "For a hundred thousand dollars, would you be willing to meet in person?"

"In Ankara?"

"Houston."

Munroe said nothing. Simply let the silence of the moment consume her.

Breeden spoke again. "It's been two years, Michael. Consider it a good omen. Come on home."

"Is it worth it?"

"You can always go back."

Munroe nodded to empty space, to the inevitable that she'd so far managed to postpone, and said, "Give me a week to wrap things up." She dropped the phone into the cradle, lay back on the couch, and with an arm draped over her eyes inhaled long and deep.

There would be no sleep today.

. . .

FOR THE FOURTH time in as many minutes, Munroe checked her watch, then the length of the line ahead.

Stamps hammered into passports. The irregular beat created a distracting rhythm, a cadence that patterned the background of her thoughts.

She was going home.

Home. Whatever *that* was supposed to mean.

Home. After two years of shifting time zones and Third World countries, of living a nonstop clash of cultures through places alien and alive. These had been worlds she could feel and understand—unlike home.

Teeth clenched, Munroe shut her eyes and exhaled softly, tilted her head upward and took in another drink of air.

One more person moved through passport control and the line crept forward a few inches. She drew another breath, an attempt to invoke a temporary calm, to relieve anxiety that had been building over the last few hours, and with that breath the tumult inside her head increased volume.

The land shall be emptied, and utterly spoiled . . .

The transit had shifted through two sunrises and a sunset. Her body said 3:00 in the afternoon yesterday, and the clock on the far wall said 6:48 in the morning.

. . . The haughty people of the earth do languish . . .

Another subtle glance at the time. Another breath. A few more inches forward. She hovered on the brink of panic, keeping it at bay one breath at a time.

Home.

. . . The earth is defiled under its inhabitants . . .

Minutes passed, the line remained stationary, and her focus turned to the front, where the man facing the immigration officer stumbled through a few words of English, unable to answer the basic questions asked of him. Six feet tall, with perfect posture and jet-black hair, he carried a hard-shell briefcase and wore a dark maroon trench coat.

Another three minutes that felt like a painful thirty, and the immigration officer sent the Trench Coat to a separate room at the end of the hall.

... They have transgressed the laws, changed the ordinance ...

She tracked his path and pushed her bag forward with her foot.

... Therefore has the curse devoured the earth ...

Each of his steps brought back the dread of her first entry into the United States. Similar doors and a similar experience—how much could have changed in nine years?

... and they that dwell therein are desolate ...

The Trench Coat was now a silhouette behind a translucent window. She checked her watch. One more person in line. One more minute.

... The mirth of tabrets ceases ...

She stood in front of the booth, passport and papers in hand, the mental noise now reduced to a whisper beneath the surface. Perfunctory questions, perfunctory answers. The officer stamped the passport and handed it back to her.

... The noise of those that rejoice ends ...

She had no luggage and nothing to declare, and with a final glance at the Trench Coat's shadow, she left the area through opaque sliding doors that opened to a waiting crowd. She scanned the faces, wondering which, among the expectant eyes and attentive glances, waited for him.

... Strong drink will be bitter to those that drink it ...

On a far wall was a telephone bank, and she walked toward it.

... The city of confusion is broken down ...

She dialed and then angled herself so that she could watch the opaque doors.

... All joy is darkened, the mirth of the land is gone ...

Passengers exited sporadically, smiling as they made contact with loved ones who stood waiting. That was how it should be coming home, not sending packages and gifts ahead to estranged family and a few strangers called friends, dreading the reconnection that must inevitably take place.

Kate's answering machine picked up, and Munroe disconnected without leaving a message. The Trench Coat exited the glass doors.

... In the city is left desolation, and the gate is smitten with destruction ...

He was alone. There was no girlfriend with flowers or any happy faces waiting—not even a somber suit holding a placard with his name.

He passed within a few feet of where Munroe stood, and her eyes followed. On impulse she picked up her bag and trailed him to the ground level, keeping just close enough to avoid losing him in the crowds.

The Trench Coat boarded the shuttle for the Marriott, and she stepped on behind him. He nodded once in her direction and paid no attention beyond that. Dressed as she was, it was to be expected. Cropped hair, lightweight cargo pants, a linen shirt that had once been white, and thick-soled leather boots: to all but the most observant, she was every bit as male as he.

At the hotel Munroe trailed to the front desk and stood in line. Noah Johnson. Room 319. Such an American name, and yet he struggled with rudimentary English. She knew the accent: the French of high-society Morocco.

When he had finally completed check-in, she booked a room, then placed several calls, and finally, getting past Kate Breeden's voice mail, arranged to meet for dinner at the hotel's restaurant.

OUTSIDE, MUNROE HAILED a taxi and twenty minutes later stood in a parking lot on a semideserted industrial strip. Far down the street on either side and in both directions were squat cement structures, businesses divided one from the next by narrow windows and truck bays.

Munroe watched the cab drive away and then climbed the steps that led to the closest door. The signage scripted in large metallic block letters read LOGAN'S.

The front door was locked. She pressed her face to the glass and, seeing no light, rapped on it. A few minutes passed, a light came on from the back, and Logan approached in sweats, barefoot and with a sheepish grin on his face. He unlocked the door and let her in, and then, scanning her up and down, said, "You look like shit."

She dropped the duffel bag on the entrance floor and let the door close. "Glad to see you, too," she said.

His smile broke first, and they both laughed. He wrapped his arms around her shoulders in a hug and then held her at arm's length. "Welcome back," he said. "God, it's good to see you. How was the trip?"

"Long and tedious."

"If you want to crash, the couch is available."

"Thanks but no thanks," she said. "I'm going against the jet lag."

"Coffee, then?" He turned toward the small kitchen. "I'm just getting a pot on."

"Caffeine I could use. Thick and black."

Nothing he could conjure in his kitchen would come close to Turkish coffee; the caffeine withdrawals would follow on the heels of the anxiety and jet lag. One hurdle at a time.

The office portion of the building had four rooms. Logan used one as an office, another as a conference room, and the third and fourth as living quarters. In the back the warehouse doubled as repair shop and storage area. He wasn't supposed to be living in the building, but he paid his rent on time and thus far no one had complained to the property managers. The arrangement had been going on as far back as Munroe had known him—that muggy summer night seven years before, when prejudice in a hole-in-the-wall bikers' bar had turned to violence and she'd thrown in her lot with the underdog. They'd laughed when it was over, sitting by the edge of the road, under the blackened sky, making introductions like star-crossed soul mates.

Munroe walked the hallway slowly, following a row of poster-size frames that adorned the walls, stopping for a moment in front of each. Most contained photos of motorcycles on a speedway, Logan in the races he competed in, split-second snapshots of his professional life.

Logan was thirty-three with dusty blond hair, green eyes, and an innocent smile that placed him closer to twenty-five. Over the years the impression of childish innocence he gave had drawn in a succession of boyfriends who each in turn had discovered the reality of a dark and hardened soul.

Logan had been on his own since he was fifteen, had started by scraping together an existence fixing cars and motorcycles part-time from a repair shop owned by his best friend's father. Everything he had he'd earned by clawing his way to it one exacting day after another, and he was, by Munroe's judgment, the closest being she'd found to perfection in the nine years since she first set foot on American soil.

Logan joined her in front of the last frame and handed her a steaming mug. She nodded thanks, and they stood in comfortable silence for quite a while. "Two years is a long time," he said finally. "There's a lot to catch up on, Michael." He turned toward the back door. "You ready?"

She didn't move and in a voice laced with confession said, "I might be taking another assignment."

He stopped.

"It's why I've come back."

Logan studied her. "I'm surprised you're even giving it consideration. I thought you'd told Kate to turn down all incoming requests."

Munroe nodded.

"You already know what I think," he said. If he was upset, he hid it well. "If you decide to take it, I'll be there to back you up."

She smiled, reached for his hand, and in his palm placed the medallion. "It was perfect," she said. "Thanks."

He nodded and with a half grin said, "I'll add it to the collection." He put his arm around her shoulders. "Come on, let's go."

They exited the office and living area through the back door that opened to the warehouse and workshop, and halfway to the end of the building they stopped. Munroe reached into a set of stacked plastic drawers, retrieving a backpack and a few personal items while Logan let down a ramp and rolled the Ducati from its storage space.

The bike was sleek black-on-black, a thing of pure beauty, and Munroe smiled as she ran her fingers over the custom race fairings. "I've taken good care of her," Logan said. "Took her out for a spin last week just to make sure everything's tweaked and peaked."

If it were possible to love a machine, Munroe loved this one. It symbolized power, life broken into split-second intervals, calculated risk. Few things were capable of providing the same adrenaline rush that the horses between her legs delivered as they tore down the roads at over 150 miles an hour. The rush had become a form of self-medicating, a narcotic sweeter than drugs or alcohol, just as addictive and equally destructive.

Three years prior she'd totaled the bike's predecessor. Shattered bones and a head injury had kept her in a hospital for several months, and when released she'd taken a taxi direct from the hospital to the dealership to pick up a new machine.

Munroe straddled the bike, sighed, and turned the ignition. She felt the surge of adrenaline and smiled. This was home: running along a razor's edge of self-induced terror, calculating mortality against probability.

Assignments were the reprieve. When she was abroad, although she would do whatever was necessary to get the job done, there was a degree of normalcy, sanity, purpose, and the destructive forces propelling her to gamble with her life were dormant.

Munroe nodded a helmeted good-bye to Logan and, with the screaming whine of the engine, shot forward. Returning home was an eventuality, but if she planned to stay alive, perhaps not all that smart.

IT WAS EARLY evening when she returned to the hotel. She had spent the day at the spa, had been soaked and wrapped, peeled and painted; they had given her back her dignity and femininity, and she had loved every moment.

She now wore clothes that hugged her body, accentuating long legs and model height. Hers was an androgynous figure—boyish, sleek, and angular—and she walked through the lobby with a sensual stride, subtly provocative, fully aware of the surreptitious glances coming from the mostly male guests.

. . . When I would comfort myself against sorrow, my heart is faint . . .

The attention amused her, and she took her time.

. . . I hurt; I am black; astonishment has taken hold . . .

Now, on her eighth trip back to the United States, each return more of the same and with anxiety continuing to crest wave upon wave, it was time to find a distraction. A challenge. A game.

He was in Room 319. But first there was business to attend to. Munroe glanced at the clock. Breeden would already be waiting.

SIX YEARS AGO Kate Breeden had a thriving law practice in downtown Austin and was married, with a daughter in junior high, an eight-hundred-thousand-dollar home, three luxury cars, and yearly trips to faraway places. Then came the messy divorce.

The house, the cars, the vacation and investment properties were all sold off, and Texas's community-property law split twenty years of earning down the middle. Her daughter chose to live with the ex-husband, and Breeden took what was left, put it into an investment fund, packed up, and moved to Dallas to start over.

They'd met on the Southern Methodist University campus, where Breeden had returned for an M.B.A. and Munroe was in her sophomore year. The relationship began as a cautious mother-and-daughter surrogacy at a time when people still called Munroe by her given name.

When she'd received the unusual job offer that would require interrupting her studies in order to make a trip to Morocco, Breeden was the one she'd gone to for advice.

Breeden now owned a successful marketing consulting firm and practiced law on the side for a few select clients. She was Munroe's buffer between everyday life and life on assignment. In the months and sometimes years that Munroe was out of the country, Breeden paid the bills, kept the accounts open, and forwarded pressing matters. Breeden was warm and friendly and absolutely ruthless. She'd screw a person over with a polite smile—cozy up and bury them alive—and for that reason Breeden was an ally: She was safe.

Breeden was a bottle-dyed blonde with shoulder-length hair and heavy bangs that flattered almond-shaped eyes. Munroe found her at a corner table looking over a stack of paperwork and sipping red wine. Breeden made eye contact, rose with an enormous smile, and grasped Munroe's hands warmly. "Michael," she said with trademark breathlessness, "you look so well. Turkey was good to you!"

"The Four Seasons did this to me," Munroe said, taking a seat, "but I did love Turkey."

"Have you completely wrapped that one up?"

"A few minor details and then I'll be finished." Munroe dug into a roll, spread the butter on thickly, and then politely motioned for the documents.

Breeden passed them across the table. After a few minutes of flipping through pages, Munroe said, "This doesn't seem like something I'd handle." She smiled. "Is that what you meant by 'exception'?"

"It's the easy money," Breeden said. Munroe paused, and Breeden continued. "When Burbank's daughter disappeared in Africa about four years ago, he hired the best international investigators and, when that proved futile, mercenaries. So far, nothing."

"Why come to me?"

"He's seen your work, says this is just another form of information."

"It could be." Munroe shrugged. "But that's money hard earned, nothing easy about it."

"When I got the call, I spoke with Burbank himself—no middlemen or corporate strategists. He's offering that hundred thousand just for the meeting, regardless of your answer. He wants to present the case to you personally."

Munroe let out a low whistle.

"I did explain that he was probably wasting both his time and his money. But there are worse ways to earn a hundred grand than overlooking the Houston skyline for a day."

Munroe pressed her thumb to the bridge of her nose and sighed. "I really don't know, Kate. Once I hear the details, I might want to take it, and we both know that whether I wish it or not, I need a break . . ." Her voice trailed off.

"I'll call Burbank in the morning," Breeden said. "I'll let him know you've declined."

Munroe's eyes fell to the documents. "I haven't declined yet," she said. "I made the trip, didn't I?" She reached for the papers and thumbed through them again. "Is this everything?"

"Officially, yes."

"Have you read it all?"

"Yes."

"What about unofficially?"

"In the dossiers are personal bits and pieces centering on Elizabeth Burbank. It seems that at or around the same time the first teams were setting out to track down Emily, she had a nervous breakdown and had to be hospitalized. She was in and out of retreats for a year before she passed away. Suicide."

Breeden took a sip of water. "For the family it was fortune followed by tragedy. Less than two months before Elizabeth's death, Burbank's drilling venture off the coast of West Africa struck oil and the stock in his company went through the ceiling. He became an overnight multi-millionaire and since then, through careful investment of capital, has become a billionaire several times over."

She paused, and Munroe motioned for her to continue.

"Prior to this the family wasn't hurting by any means. Richard Burbank had done well in life through high-risk enterprises that paid off, and he also married well both times. Elizabeth came from old money, ran with the Houston elite, so it's safe to say that they were already well-off before the oil windfall. Elizabeth was Richard's second marriage— Emily, the girl who's missing, is Elizabeth's daughter from a previous marriage. Richard legally adopted her when she was seventeen. It was right around their ten-year anniversary. He and Elizabeth held a recommitment ceremony, and he let Emily choose a charity for a big donation in their honor."

The waiter approached with the meal, and Breeden stopped. Munroe flicked the napkin over her lap and inhaled the aroma coming off her plate. "So," she said, "he's a philanthropist. What else? What's he like as a person?"

"It's hard to say," Breeden replied. "My impression while on the phone is that he's no-nonsense, he gets what he wants. There isn't a lot of press coverage on him prior to the oil discovery. His company, Titan Exploration, has been publicly traded for almost seven years, but there's little mention of Burbank other than to point out that he's the founder and a major stockholder. He seems to be somewhat camera shy."

Munroe nodded and chewed. She cleared her throat. "For a hundred grand, I'll listen to what he has to say. But make sure he knows that I'm coming for the money and out of pure curiosity."

"I believe he'll want to see you as soon as possible."

"Try to arrange it a few days from now—give me some time to catch my breath."

"How are things this time around?" Breeden asked.

"Hasn't changed much. I deal." Munroe put down the knife and fork. Discussing the insanity inside her head was out of the question; it was a private hell best lived alone. "I'm fine," she said.

Breeden pulled out a cell phone. "Before I forget." She handed it to Munroe. "So I don't have to hunt you down. Number's on the back, charger's in the briefcase. I'll call you as soon as I've got the appointment sorted out."

The meal over, Munroe returned to her room, disassembled the file, glanced through the pages, and at some point in the middle became intrigued. When she found herself losing track of time, she set the alarm clock and went back to the beginning, starting with the summary from the official files.

Whoever had written this document described the Africa that she knew well and had long given up trying to forget. Munroe became lost in the pages until the alarm buzzed a reminder that something needed attention. *Noah Johnson.*

He would be the distraction du jour, the assignment of the night. She shuffled the papers into a semblance of order and tossed them on the desk. She leaned her head back, closed her eyes, and pulled in a deep breath, followed it with several more—a shift from one work mode into the next.

She found him at the bar, staring into his drink. Even from a distance, he was beautiful, and if he hadn't been so immersed in his own thoughts, he might have noticed the glances from several women nearby. Munroe sat at the opposite end of the bar, ordered a drink, and requested that a second of what he was having be taken to him.

When the glass arrived, he looked up and then in her direction as the bartender pointed her way. She leaned beyond the couple blocking his view and gave a slight wave. He smiled, picked up the glass, and walked toward her. *"Bonsoir,"* he said, and seated himself on the adjacent stool, then raised his glass in thanks.

Experience predicated that he, like most men after a few drinks and faced with a beautiful woman showing interest, would be unable to help himself. Getting him into bed was beside the point; the challenge was in possession, to crawl inside his head so deeply that he wouldn't want her out.

She replied in French and in the small talk listened for his personality, filtering options through his answers. When the pieces became a composite whole, she would shift into characteristics that would most easily enchant—whatever the particular role necessitated in order to acquire the end goal. Bimbo, coquette, siren—name it and become it.

His answers were unexpected and made her laugh, not the laugh of an actress but one that was genuine, real. And that he carried his own streak of adrenaline hunger didn't hurt.

Discovering that work had taken her to Morocco, he flashed a teasing smile and switched from French to Arabic: *"Hal tatakalam al-Arabia?"*

She grinned and whispered, *"Tabaan."*

Their conversation undulated, it swelled and lingered. His personality was beyond what she'd anticipated—closer to her own than any distraction she'd yet sought out. Perhaps this hunt would be the easiest of all. No games, no roles, just a sanitized version of who she really was.

Desiring more privacy than the bar and lounge provided, Munroe said, "You want to find the Jacuzzi with me?"

"I'd love to," he said, "but I don't have a bathing suit."

She moved closer to his ear. "Neither do I, but if you wear your underwear and act like you own the place, nobody will ever notice."

He laughed, a deep, hearty laugh, spontaneous and alive. He gulped down the remainder of his drink and placed the glass on the bar counter. "I think I like you, Lady Munroe." He stood. "Where is this Jacuzzi?"

The hot tub was situated in an alcove away from the main pool, and when they'd found it, Munroe shed her clothes and slid into the foaming water. Noah studied her for a moment and then, without breaking eye contact, draped his shirt over a nearby pool chair and slid in beside her. "These," he said, tracing his finger along one of the many white slivers etched into her body. "Are the scars also part of your job?"

She began to say something, then hesitated and stopped. "Those," she said finally, "are a story for another time." It wasn't the usual bullshit about car accidents and glass, and it avoided a truth she had no desire to relive.

chapter 2

To: *Katherine Breeden*
From: *Miles Bradford*
Subject: *Emily Burbank—Disappearance/Investigation*

Ms. Breeden:

On behalf of Richard Burbank and for the purpose of review by your client Michael Munroe, I am sending the complete collection of documents related to Emily Burbank's disappearance.

In addition to the summaries that follow below, attached are six PDF files that include copies of all communication from Ms. Burbank prior to her disappearance, government records and documents, as well as reports and transcripts (including translations) from private investigations, in total 238 pages.

Sincerely,
Miles Bradford
Capstone Security Consulting

BACKGROUND SUMMARY

Namibia: Wild, vast, spectacularly beautiful, and home to some of Africa's best animal preserves. It is sparsely populated, outlined by the Namib Desert on the Atlantic coast and the Kalahari Desert on the eastern border. The country is, by African standards, safe and modern, the government stable, and the infrastructure solid. It is not the first place on the continent to come to mind when a foreigner disappears, but an Internet café in the capital of Windhoek became Emily Burbank's last known place of contact.

Nearly five months separated Emily's arrival in Africa from her disappearance. The journey began in South Africa as an overland safari. The tour by open-air truck lasted thirty days and passed through six countries on its way through the south and east of Africa, ending in Nairobi, Kenya.

Originally scheduled to return to Johannesburg by air, Emily remained in East Africa with two men from the overland tour, Kristof Berger (German, later determined to be 22 years of age) and Mel Shore (Australian, 31). Of this decision, Emily wrote, "We want to skip the game parks and visit towns and villages off the beaten trail and, if we can, spend time living with the local population in some of the rural areas we've already passed through. Don't worry about me, I'm fine. Kris and Mel are great, and we keep an eye out for each other." (See addendum for original copy.)

Two months separated this e-mail from the next contact, which came by way of a phone call out of Dar es Salaam, Tanzania. There is no record of this conversation; it was later relayed by Elizabeth Burbank. The trio still traveled together, the lapse in communication due to their having spent over a month living in a Masai village outside of the Serengeti, where they had been without electricity and the closest telephone over a day's walk away. That stay had ended when Emily developed a fever and her traveling companions took her to a Catholic mission for malaria treatment. At the time of the call, Emily had fully recovered and the trio was about to begin the overland return to Johannesburg.

E-mail from Emily arrived at regular intervals: Lusaka, Livingstone, Gaborone, and finally Johannesburg, each a brief note providing detail on location and the next segment of travel.

Several days before her scheduled return to the United States, Emily gave notice of her decision to remain in Africa for an additional two months. Her plans would then route her through Europe, where she would spend a few weeks traveling the Balkans with Kristof before returning home.

In communications that followed, Elizabeth agreed to send Emily money for Europe if her time in Africa was limited to one month and, upon receiving Emily's consent, wired four thousand dollars.

Emily wrote from Windhoek a week later. Together with a small amount of descriptive detail on the trip and the promise to notify her family as soon as she knew where they would go next, Emily provided Kristof Berger's address in Langen, Germany, requesting that her mother post a few items so that they would be waiting when she arrived.

This was the last communication received from Emily Burbank.

When Emily did not contact her family and failed to return home on the established date, the Burbanks contacted South African Airways in an attempt to discover if Emily had departed Africa for Europe. The airline had no record of Emily's boarding the flight out of Johannesburg or the connecting flight in Europe and, citing security factors, was unable to provide information on either Kristof Berger or Mel Shore. The Burbanks filed a missing-persons report with their local police department and contacted the Department of State.

INVESTIGATIONS SUMMARY

From the onset it has been understood that the chances of locating Emily are slim. Emily had set a precedent for traveling to remote areas, and although it is assumed that she would have notified her family before leaving Namibia, it is not certain; therefore the actual location of her disappearance is open to speculation. Additionally, little is known about her traveling companions and the relationship among the three. Permutations are many, and the investigations that followed centered not only on locating Emily but also on locating the men who traveled with her.

Phase One: The initial phase of the investigation branched immediately in three directions.

Namibia: The U.S. Department of State, the U.S. embassy in Windhoek, and local law enforcement worked jointly to trace the movements of the trio throughout the capital. After outlining three days of stay, the trail ended cold. Beyond being able to ascertain that Emily Burbank and her traveling companions had indeed been in the capital, no additional information was forthcoming. From this first phase, the following is worth noting:

At the hostel in which they stayed, the proprietor heard them discussing Luanda (Angola), and at a restaurant the trio frequented, a waiter recalled Kristof Berger inquiring extensively about the Caprivi Strip and road conditions to Ruacana on the border of Angola. Another waiter said he had heard them discuss Libreville (Gabon).

Kristof Berger: Using the address Emily provided, a second team was sent to Germany to locate Kristof Berger's mother. When shown photos of Emily, the woman denied having seen her, and when the line of questioning turned to Kristof, she terminated the conversation.

Working through the Langen Rathaus, the team was able to confirm that Kristof had returned to Germany, and it is worth noting that the date of Kristof's return to Europe does not coincide with the flight details Emily provided her parents. Repeated attempts to locate him proved futile.

Mel Shore: Emily's letters home had provided only scattered pieces of information about Mel Shore, and through these his name, age, and nationality are assumed. Beyond this, little is known of the man, and all attempts to locate his city of origin or family members have failed.

Phase Two: Local law enforcement worked to establish a basis for Emily Burbank's remaining in or leaving Namibia. The only intra-African airlines flying out of Windhoek that retained searchable records were South African Airways and Air Namibia, neither of which held any listing of Emily. That the trio had caught a bush plane or traveled out of Namibia by road could not be ruled out.

Based on information provided in phase one, the investigation transferred to Ruacana and then to the cities through the Caprivi Strip, a narrow stretch of lush land sandwiched between Botswana and Zambia. The investigators were not able to locate anyone who recalled the young travelers.

All indications pointed to the group's having left Namibia, but no record of their having done so existed. At this phase active searching within Namibia stopped.

Phase Three: The Burbank family sent a team of lawyers to the U.S. embassies in Luanda, Pretoria, and Gaborone. Similar visits to the German and Australian embassies were made on the chance that information on Kristof Berger and Mel Shore could be garnered. The embassies had received no reports of missing citizens and were unable to help.

Phases one through three lasted the better part of eight months and concluded when no definitive information on Emily Burbank or either of her two traveling companions could be unearthed.

Phase Four: Roughly a year after Emily's disappearance, the package that Elizabeth Burbank had mailed to Emily in care of Kristof at his address was received back in Houston, unopened, marked "return to sender." Once again a team was dispatched to Europe, and Kristof was eventually located at Klinik Hohe Mark. Chronologically, Kristof's first admission appears to be shortly after his return from Africa. Medical records show that he suffered a mental breakdown, initially responded well to treatment, and was released after six months. He was returned that same month and has since been a permanent resident.

The investigative team was able to speak with him, but he wasn't lucid and what responses he gave had no bearing on the conversation or the questions asked of him. Transcripts and translations are included in the supporting documents.

Unable to learn anything from Kristof, the team once again attempted to speak with Frau Berger. Offered a substantial sum of money, the woman agreed to listen to their questions. When again shown photographs of Emily Burbank, Frau Berger did not recognize her, nor could she provide details on where Kristof had been while in Africa or whom he had befriended while traveling. She merely confirmed the date that Kirstof had returned and admitted to the date he had entered the institution.

Suspecting that Frau Berger knew more than she was revealing and seeing the state of the woman's home, the investigating team offered an additional sum of money should she recall further details, and with that, Frau Berger again terminated the conversation.

Phase Five: In Namibia, where the first and second phases ended, a group of former military personnel attempted to track Emily's path out of the country. Over a four-month period, they reviewed exit records at every staffed land-border crossing in Namibia and spoke with every official available; given that they were generously dispersing "bonuses," they also spoke with many who were not officials. In the end there was no record of Emily's having left Namibia.

Phase Six: In e-mails home and in conversations with Elizabeth Burbank, Emily had indicated plans to remain in Africa to travel through countries not yet visited. Geographically, the only direction the group could go to fulfill this plan would have been north.

No visas were issued to Emily or to either of her companions from the Angolan, Congolese, or Gabonese embassies in Windhoek. Visas for these countries could have been applied for elsewhere on the conti-nent, or the trio, now familiar with the protocols of African border transit, may have attempted to purchase visas while border crossing.

Although Angola borders Namibia to the north, those who knew Emily had difficulty believing that she would enter the country. Entering Angola overland as a tourist was not considered possible at the time and is still inadvisable due to the decades of conflict. However, there was the possibility that the trio had flown to Luanda as a stop point to head far-ther north. Congo and Gabon also posed question marks, as they are expensive to travel to, in terms of the transportation costs as well as visas, food, and shelter.

Language was an additional consideration. Unlike South and East Africa, where English is widely spoken, along the west coast of Africa, French is the primary language. Emily did speak rudimentary French, and it had by this point been confirmed through Kristof Berger's school records that he, too, spoke French. Nothing is known about Mel Shore.

The search team split in three and traveled to Angola, Gabon, and Congo. As with the previous phases of the investigation, this venture ended with no additional information.

Munroe turned the page and jotted another note on the addendum. All things considered, the extensiveness of the search was impressive, and the family had committed a sizable chunk of resources to it. But there were questions the history did not answer.

Papers were strewn around her. The coffee cup on the bedside table had been filled and refilled several times and, in spite of precautions, had left a ring on the furniture.

Munroe picked up the mug—time for another. It was nearly eight in the evening. Noah would be back soon; he wouldn't be able to help returning to her. She poured another cup of coffee.

The details of the case ran through her head, and with them came the memories. It was another life, another world, untamed and vast, where stretches of two-lane tarmac ran veinlike through sub-Saharan emptiness, and buses—old, rusted, and belching black smoke—pumped the blood of humanity along the way.

It was a world where urban areas were intractable masses, indelible human footprints that rose out of the landscape fusing modernity with the castoffs and refuse of Europe and Asia, where even the new was old before its time, and where hot running water and stable electricity were still considered luxuries to most.

Munroe took a sip of the tepid liquid and let out an involuntary snort. No wonder each investigation turned up nothing. The continent was vast, records nonexistent, and evidence scarce. Finding the girl was highly improbable.

But the challenge was seductive, and its alluring tendrils wrapped themselves around her mind like the ethereal threads of a spider's web.

A gentle knock at the door jolted her from her thoughts. She opened the door, and Noah greeted her with a kiss and handed her a small white rose. She tucked the flower behind her ear, and he looked past her to the documents spread out on the bed. In French he said, "Are you busy? Should I come back another time?"

She tugged on his shirt collar, drew him close, and kissed him. "No. Give me a minute to put this in order. There's something I want to show you."

Outside, Munroe pulled away the sleeve that protected the bike from the elements and curious hands, and Noah knelt down beside it and brushed his fingers across the sleek body.

"From one enthusiast to another, I thought you could appreciate it." He smiled. "I do."

They headed to lower Greenville, where they found a dance club and spent several hours moving around the floor oblivious to everything and everyone around them, engrossed in the rhythm and in the closeness of their bodies. By the time they got back to the hotel, it was nearly three in the morning.

The days that followed brought a similar pattern. Noah would be gone before she was fully awake, and in his absence she perused and deliberated over the information provided in the Burbank files. When he returned, they would take the bike out.

She showed him Dallas, took him to the places she rarely found the time to go to, and when they had experienced all that they could, they would return to the quiet of the room and the satisfaction of exploring each other's bodies. Being with him brought peace; the edge of anxiety that had been stalking her since her arrival ebbed, and inside her head the demons were sleeping.

IT WAS THE fourth morning, and for the first time Munroe woke with Noah in her bed. She ran her fingers over his chest, and he reached for her hand, rolled to his side, and kissed the top of her head.

Munroe switched on her phone, and waiting was a message from Breeden. She got up to jot a few numbers and then crawled back into bed and snuggled against Noah's chest. "When is your flight?" she whispered.

"Tomorrow evening."

"I leave for Houston early tomorrow," she said.

Silent for a moment, he said, "We still have tonight." There was genuine sadness in his voice and, worse, she felt it too. He was meant to be a challenge, a conquest to numb the torment of anxiety, not to seep into the crevices of her mind. "I'll be back at eight," he said. "Have dinner with me?"

"Of course," she whispered and kissed him, and then as a way of escape climbed out of bed for the shower.

WHEN HE HAD gone, Munroe sat cross-legged on the bed with dossiers on Richard, Elizabeth, and Emily Burbank lined up in front of her. The dossiers—assembled by Breeden or whoever Breeden had hired to put them together—were standard practice, critical to an assignment. Every potential employer had a private motivation for pulling her into a project, and that motivation didn't always coincide with what she was officially told.

Munroe searched the dossiers for information to better understand the background, and after having spent the greater part of the day finding nothing more than what amounted to high-society gossip, she tossed them aside.

She left the hotel just before six and headed north on the bike, no destination in mind, only the desire to burn fuel and, through a surge of speed, purge the demons that had begun to stir. The adrenaline worked as a nostrum, an appeasement, a small sacrifice to the gods in exchange for a few hours of peace.

Three hours later, with nearly three hundred miles added to the odometer, Munroe returned to the hotel. When she entered the room, Noah greeted her with a full bouquet of flowers—no accusatory questions about why she'd kept him waiting, only a kiss and the fragrance of the roses. She smiled and reciprocated his kiss. Both were gestures of rote, neither calculated nor genuine. Internally, she was shutting down.

He produced a bottle of wine and poured a glass. "Are you still going to Houston tomorrow?"

She took the glass, kissed him again, and set it aside. "I'll leave at six or seven," she said. She shrugged out of her jeans. "Let me shower, and then we can go."

He stroked her cheek and ran his fingers through her hair, then sat on the edge of the bed and pulled her, half naked, to his lap. His hands slid around her waist. "Come with me to Morocco."

The invitation should have signaled triumph, official notice that the challenge was over, that it was time to go. She slipped off his lap and stood by the window, staring at the city lights in the distance and hating most that she wanted what he offered.

It wasn't the first time a conquest had made such a request or similar words had been spoken, but it was the first that she'd felt a twinge of longing—that desire to fly off into the proverbial sunset for however long it might last.

"I'm not saying that I don't want it," she said. "I just can't do it." Silent for a moment, she returned from the window, climbed onto the bed, and placed a knee on either side of his legs. She held his face to her chest and kissed the top of his head.

He held her tight and then with a deep breath stood, pulling her up with him. "I need to go," he said.

From his wallet he extracted a business card. "So that you can find me—in case you change your mind." He placed it on the desk and, without looking back, left the room.

The door closed, a resounding thud in the silence. Munroe picked up the wineglass, swished the liquid in a gentle circle, ran her thumb against the stem. It was so delicate, would be so easy to snap, and she waited for the urge to do so. No reaction. Numb. The internal shutdown was complete. She placed the glass back on the desk, lay on the bed with her hands behind her head, and, as she knew they would, waited for the demons to rise.

CHAPTER 3

Walker County, Texas

The sky was dark, tinged by the murky haze of city lights, of civilization and pollution. The weather had warmed; even in the predawn, Munroe could feel it, and if the temperature was rising, she would welcome it. The roads were empty, and at 150 miles an hour the wind had a way of rushing through a person.

At three in the morning, she'd tossed the documents from the Burbank case into a backpack and left the hotel. Her head was filled with a cacophony of ancient words and the accompanying attacks of anxiety that prevented sleep. She would ride through the night, and in the dark and the silence her head would clear.

She traveled the winding Texas backcountry, endless lane dividers blending into a solid line, time calculated by the changing colors of the sky and a tugging ache that lurked at the periphery of her consciousness, the result of hours spent on a machine built for speed rather than comfort.

The meeting was set for ten, and now at nine-thirty she moved with the flow of traffic through the tail end of the morning rush hour into the matrix of Houston's downtown. She found parking and then, gazing up at the building, ruffled her short hair free of the shape of the helmet.

She stretched and pulled the kinks out of her shoulders, locked the helmet onto the bike, and unzipped the riding jacket. Underneath she wore a tight T-shirt, and the combination of the shirt, blue jeans, and thick-soled boots gave her the appearance of having recently stepped out of the cab of an eighteen-wheeler. Like every decision she made, the choice in clothing was calculated, a statement to the client, a silent "fuck you" to a succession of men in suits who aggressively jockeyed to have their assignments accepted.

To them she provided no decorum, abided by no protocol, and each in turn would accept this because they all wanted the information she would procure that had the potential to turn meager profits into gold.

It hadn't started out that way. The first assignment had been a fluke and had come at a time when she considered herself marred for life, unhirable in the traditional sense and wondering how to pay off amassed student loans in her own lifetime.

During sophomore year of college, in a period of drink- and drug-induced haze, with the deadline of a research assignment for her comparative-politics class looming, she pulled an all-nighter with a beat-up laptop and four pots of coffee, fabricating a report using Cameroon as her target of study. The sources were fudged, but the information, based on past personal observations, logical conclusions, and in-depth understanding of the demographics, was highly accurate.

The relief of having completed the assignment segued to dread when instead of a grade she received a request from the professor to discuss the paper. He had, as it turned out, taken the liberty of passing her report to a colleague, who after reading it had asked to meet her.

The colleague was an economist for the International Monetary Fund working in the IMF's African Area, and he in turn introduced Munroe to one of his business partners, a man named Julian Reid. Although it was evident to those who read the report that the material had not been pulled from genuine sources, the analyses and conclusions had piqued their curiosity. Over lunch Reid inquired as to the chances of having her prepare a similar report on another country. He and his partners, he explained, were planning to begin a venture in Morocco, and although the country was fairly stable politically and economically, what they didn't have was someone on the inside with an innate understanding of the place, the customs, the subtleties, and a map, for lack of a better term, of how to navigate the political hierarchy with its graft and jockeying for power. It was such underlying information in her report on Cameroon that had caught the eye of those who'd read it. Could she, he wanted to know, replicate the research in a different scenario?

That was how it began.

Morocco was the first assignment; it had taken eight months, and those eight months transformed the direction of her life. The drugs stopped, the drink dried up, the intense focus of the work brought peace, and that one assignment carried her finances into the black. Next was a two-month period in Uruguay on behalf of the IMF. By the time the third project, in Vietnam, had been completed, word had begun to spread. With each assignment her reputation for extracting impossibly accurate information grew, and it was only a matter of time before the law of supply and demand took over. The value of her services increased exponentially, and so did the paychecks. No one questioned how she came by the information or what she had to do to get it; they simply paid.

Now came the possibility of an assignment far outside the area of her expertise, and for that reason it intrigued her—that, and the fact that she had not returned to the continent of her birth since abruptly departing it nine years ago. Munroe pushed the memories away, joined Kate Breeden in the lobby of the building, and in silence rode the elevator to the thirty-eighth floor, where the doors opened onto a wide reception area.

The halls were carpeted, the wooden office doors richly paneled, and the atmosphere hushed and reverent. Titan Exploration was a fascinating specimen of the acme of corporate America, and Munroe observed the goings-on with detached curiosity while she followed Burbank's assistant across expensive rugs and through well-lit hallways.

With its internal politics and sedate proprieties, the corporate world was as foreign as any of the countries she'd traveled, and it comprised a distinct culture she had yet to internalize. Over the years she'd made several attempts to live as "normal" people did, holding standard jobs and maintaining a permanent residence, each try a more miserable failure than the one before it. The longest stretch of employment had been eight weeks as a bean counter at an auditing firm. It had come to a quick end when the idea of killing the department manager became palpable. Insecure and inept, the woman had been a tyrant set out to destroy talent before it replaced her, and few would have wept over her passing. But when ideas of how to do it and get away with it danced through Munroe's head, she had known it was time to get out. And that was the good job.

The assistant brought them to a corner office, knocked gently, and opened the door. Thirty feet of empty space unfurled between the door and Burbank's desk. The front of the office held a sitting area with a wet bar; framed autographed photos lined the right wall. The left and back walls were solid glass, with a spectacular view of the downtown Houston area.

Burbank sat on the edge of an oversize mahogany desk in front of the wall of windows, a phone to his ear, one leg firmly on the floor, the other dangling over the corner of the desk, and he was in the middle of a heated conversation. He paused, beckoned to Breeden and Munroe, and then curtly dismissed whoever was on the other end of the line.

Burbank was Munroe's height, tanned, fit, and impeccably dressed in a tailored black suit with a pale pinstriped shirt and a pink tie. Silver around his temples framed eyes the gray-blue of a winter sky. He radiated tangible energy and genuine charm.

Munroe sat in one of the two chairs facing Burbank's desk and immediately regretted having done so. The chair was plush and comfortable, and she sank into it several inches so that her eye level was closer to Burbank's chest than to his face, forcing her to look up at him.

When the silence in the room became uncomfortably long, Burbank smiled at Munroe and finally said, "Thank you so much for coming. I really do appreciate your taking the time to hear me out and at least consider the job that I need done."

Munroe stared out beyond him through the windows and, with a look of boredom and her voice monotone, said only, "I came for the money."

Burbank laughed, and he placed his hands together. "I trust that the transfer went through smoothly and that everything is in order?" Breeden nodded, and Burbank continued. "Have you had a chance to look over the material I provided?"

"Yes, I have," Munroe said.

"Good, good," he said, nodding as he spoke, and then he paused as if cutting himself off in the middle of a thought. "You know, I'm not really sure what to call you—do you prefer Michael, Ms. Munroe, Vanessa, or is there perhaps another moniker you've taken?" The words were almost sarcastic, but his tone was sincere. He had done his research and was letting her know.

"Most of my clients call me Michael," she replied.

"Fine, Michael it is." Burbank paused and looked out the window at the skyline, then rubbed a finger against his mouth. "Michael," he said, "I know you don't have children, but perhaps you can understand the pain of uncertainty and the lack of closure that come from simply not knowing what happened to a child.

"Emily is the brightest and most lovable daughter a parent could wish for, and I thank God every day for bringing her and her mother into my life." He pulled a photo out of his wallet and handed it to Munroe.

"That's Emily's high-school graduation picture," he said.

Munroe nodded. As in the file photos, Emily was a petite girl with straight, long blond hair and brown eyes made stunning by deep, dark lashes.

"When Emily decided to go to South Africa, I was against it. I didn't feel it safe for her to travel alone. She insisted that she *wasn't* alone, and she was right in a sense—the whole expedition traveled as a group. I think you know what I mean, though. But she was eighteen, old enough to start making her own decisions. I didn't think it was a good one, but her mother felt that the overland adventure would give Emily a chance to come into her own, and I really did not have a lot of say in the matter.

"Emily is a tiny girl and soft-spoken, but she has a very determined personality. When she wanted something she found a way to get it, and this was no exception.

"As I'm sure you've read in the file, shortly before Emily was scheduled to travel to Europe, she disappeared. It's been four years now, Michael." Burbank's voice cracked. He stopped and caught his breath, and after a long silence began again. "Between the private investigators and security experts, I have spent a small fortune. I have been through hell trying to deal with government agencies that know nothing." He paused again, his breathing deep and measured. "Honestly," he continued, "I have little hope of finding her alive after all this time. But I do want to understand what happened, to know if there is any way that I can make wrongs right, to right them on her behalf." A sense of heaviness filled the room. "I need to find her, Michael."

Munroe waited and then said, "I'm sorry that you've had to go through this." She spoke slowly, mirroring Burbank's pattern of speech and choosing words that would convey meaning without causing pain. "I do understand the agony of losing someone you love for reasons that make absolutely no sense. But what I don't understand is why you want to hire me. I don't do this. I don't travel the world trying to find missing people and I don't think I can help you."

"No, you don't find missing people." Burbank sighed. "But you do have the skill set to survive and blend in with any culture that you come into contact with. Even more, you know how to ask the right questions of the right people to get the answers you need." He pulled a folder from his desk and slid it to her.

It was nearly an inch thick, a thorough encapsulation of the past nine years of her life. With an air of indifference, Munroe leafed through the pages. After the documents came the photos: of her family, of her on each of the three Ducatis she had owned, of Logan's shop, of Logan and his then boyfriend, and several from college that she wished had never been taken. Munroe stopped when she came to a high-resolution blowup—a still lifted from Internet footage of one of the many BASE jumps she'd made at Kjerag in Norway. The bastard had been meticulous. Medical records, school records, and her driving record with its long list of speeding tickets. The file included conversations and details recounted by people who knew her when she had just entered the country. But except for a few notations on her childhood, prior to her arrival in the United States, the file had nothing. The way it should be.

Munroe tossed the file on the desk. "You get a B-plus on your homework assignment," she said with a yawn. "I hope you're not expecting that to be some form of blackmail to convince me to take the case, because there's nothing in there that bothers me."

"Blackmail? Goodness no," he said. "I have nothing to gain from forcing you into a job you don't want to take—surely the results would be less than ideal. No, Michael, I had that file put together so I would have a thorough understanding of what you were capable of. I also wanted you to know that I had done my research before presenting the offer I am about to make."

Munroe said nothing, and the room went silent. When it was apparent that Burbank was waiting for a reaction or an indication of interest, she yawned again and slid deeper into the chair, resting her head on the back of it and stretching her legs out in front.

Burbank clasped his hands together and leaned forward on the desk. "I'm prepared to offer you a contract of two and a half million dollars as a final attempt to locate my daughter."

She tilted her head to the side, raised an eyebrow, and continued to say nothing.

"Michael, I need closure. I cannot sit around day after day for the rest of my life just waiting and hoping that someday someone will bring me news. You are the best at what you do. You have never gone on an assignment and failed to deliver. I know that if you agree to this assignment, you will deliver. And maybe that's partially what I'm afraid of. I'm afraid that you'll choose not to do it because you don't think you can deliver, and that's why I'm willing to pay you two-point-five million for giving it your very best effort. I don't know how long it would take before you ran up against a dead end. We've been at it four years. If you give me a year, that's all I ask, even if you don't get any further than we have."

"So you're willing to take a two-and-a-half-million-dollar risk on the remote chance that I might get further than you have?"

"If you want to put it that way, then yes, although I don't see it as a risk." He swept his hand around the office. "Obviously, money is not my greatest concern. I have enough to last me several lifetimes. What I don't have is closure. I can't handle not knowing—and possibly not *ever* knowing—what happened to my daughter, and time is running out. Each day that passes without bringing new information further seals the outcome. I've read some of the reports you've put together. You snatch information out of what seems to be thin air. I believe with utmost certainty that if you say my daughter is dead, that she is dead, and if she is alive, that you are the one who can find her. And if you tell me that the trail has ended and there is no hope of going further, I will know that all that can be done has been done."

Munroe pulled herself up in the chair and leaned forward across the desk so that her eyes were level with his. "That's it? I promise to do my best and you hand over payment? What if I signed your contract, took a yearlong vacation in Africa, and simply said that I tried?"

Burbank smiled and held her gaze. He waited a few seconds before answering, as though choosing his words carefully. "If I've come to understand you correctly," he said, "I don't think you would even consider that as an option—you have your reputation at stake. However, I am also a businessman—I protect my investments. I would expect to receive progress updates from you on a frequent if not regular basis, and I retain the right to send one of my people to assist you if I deem it necessary."

"You do realize," Munroe remonstrated, "that I have never been babysat on a job before, and I have no desire to start now. I work alone, Mr. Burbank, and I very carefully select the people who help me. If I should choose to accept your assignment, what makes you think your 'people' are qualified? If they were, you wouldn't need me."

Burbank reached into his desk and withdrew a second folder. "This is Miles Bradford," he said. "I trust him with my life. He has been with me through hell and back, and it was he who recommended you to me. Miles is no stranger to Africa, and although it wasn't mentioned in the background documents, Miles was on the investigative team that traveled from Windhoek to Brazzaville, Congo. You are free to research him yourself. If you feel he's unqualified, let me know and you can have your pick of the people within my organization whom I would trust with this."

Munroe glanced briefly through the file and then took her own file off Burbank's desk and handed them both to Breeden. "All right, Mr. Burbank," she said. "I will think about your offer. After I've reread the information on your daughter's case, then read the information on Miles Bradford and the dossier you have on me, I'll get back to you. You should hear from me through Ms. Breeden within seventy-two hours."

"Thank you, Michael," Burbank said, his voice softer. "That's all I ask."

THERE WAS SILENCE in the elevator on the way to the lobby. Breeden tapped on the thick files and said, "I'll drop these off at your hotel as soon as I get back into town."

"Don't bother," Munroe said. "I'm not planning to read them anytime soon. I just wanted to have copies handy. When's your flight?"

Breeden glanced at her watch. "About three hours."

"Let's get some coffee."

"Does that mean you're considering Burbank's offer?"

"Perhaps."

Two blocks down the street, they found a coffee shop, cozy and quaint, and when the caffeine had for the most part been quaffed and all that remained of the scones and muffins were a few crumbs that had tumbled onto the table, Munroe shifted the conversation back to the offer Burbank had made. "I'm going to take the job," she said. "If Burbank will agree to several concessions."

Breeden put down her mug and pulled a handheld from her purse.

"I want the two-point-five million up front," Munroe said, "plus expenses." She paused for a moment and tapped her fingers on the table in a rhythmic pattern that resembled Morse code. "If I can deliver hard evidence on the facts surrounding his daughter's disappearance," she continued, "then I want an additional two-point-five upon delivery, and I want to work alone—no tagalongs. I may have a few more stipulations, but the tagalong is the only one he's going to balk at. Wait at least seventy hours before you submit the terms—I want to buy time to change my mind."

Breeden nodded and jotted notes.

"I also want the names and numbers of every person involved in any investigation that has ever been done into Emily's disappearance. I have questions that weren't answered by the information Burbank sent you."

Breeden finished tapping on the handheld, tilted her head, and whispered, "I would really love to know what made you decide to take the assignment."

"Because I think I can get further than they have."

"And the money's good."

Munroe smiled. "A year of my life is a year I'll never get back. But there was something in the file that needled me, something I couldn't put my finger on until the ride down. Every time people have gone in search of Emily, they've always started where she disappeared. I think the answer lies in Europe."

"With the guy—oh, what's his name? The boy that's in the institution?"

"Yes, with him. He was there. He should know what happened."

"But people have tried talking with him. He makes no sense."

Munroe nodded slowly. "I realize that." She drew a long sip from a glass of water. "Perhaps they weren't speaking his language."

THE RETURN TO Dallas brought Munroe to the hotel by midafternoon, and Noah's business card, still on the desk where he'd left it, was the first thing she saw as she entered the room. She dropped the backpack and helmet on the bed and moved to the card, picked it up, and flicked it against her hand. His name and business address stared out at her. The clock by the bed read four-thirty—still time to see him before his flight.

In the silence of the room, the pressure in her chest began to build. The voices were there, low and quiet but still with her.

. . . *Why do the heathen rage* . . .

She ran her fingers over the top of the card, the raised ink, braille through her fingertips, translated memories of his face.

. . . *The kings of the earth set themselves and the rulers take council* . . .

She let the card fall into the garbage can.

Time to go.

She gathered her few belongings and tossed them into the backpack; she would drop them off with Logan on her way out of town. She'd contact Breeden before the self-imposed deadline expired, then ride until exhausted and find someplace to collapse for the night. On impulse she headed for Colorado Springs, cutting across the vast, cold emptiness of North Texas.

It was on the outskirts of Amarillo, shortly before midnight, that she stopped for fuel. The station was poorly lit, and only after getting off the bike and removing the helmet did she see the small group of young men in the shadows. They sat on the tailgate of an old Ford pickup. The smell of cigarettes wafted in her direction, and she could hear in their voices the bravado that comes when alcohol is mixed with youthful inexperience. She ignored them and unscrewed the cap on the fuel tank.

When she removed her wallet, the conversation that carried on the air shifted in tone. She kept her back to the truck and swiped the credit card. Voices hushed. The tailgate creaked. She closed her eyes and relaxed, ready for what she sensed was coming. Adrenaline flowed, and euphoria followed. Irregular footsteps. Metal on metal. A hand reached for her shoulder, and with celerity she grabbed the owner's wrist and forced his arm backward until she felt the snap, and in that same second slammed a fist into his abdomen. When he doubled over, she picked up his knife from the ground.

"That was a warning," she said, and fought the urge to pummel him. He was eighteen, maybe nineteen, his face tinged with the rosy pink flush of youth and alcohol, his chin sporting patches of stubble. She ignored the feel of the knife in her hand as it screamed to be used, pulled him up by the hair, and shoved him in the direction of the others who had begun to rise off the back of the tailgate. She saw the faint glimmer of a gun and instinctively handled the knife, measuring the weight and balance of it.

"If any of you want a piece of me, you're welcome to it," she said. "I could use a good fight right now. And you better be a hell of a shot, because I will slice you to pieces before you empty the chamber."

She saw their uncertainty and ignored the swearing and threats; underneath the noise she could hear fear and knew that the fight was already over. She turned her back to them and continued the process of fueling the motorcycle.

Two hours north she found a cheap motel, where she slept for a few hours before voices from the past once again called through slumber and brought her awake.

Three days out of Dallas, Munroe contacted Breeden to confirm that she would take the assignment and faxed the last of the stipulations. Two days later, while passing through Sacramento, the reply arrived on her voice mail. By arrangement Breeden faxed the contract to the nearest UPS store. The document was less than four pages, and although Breeden would already have gone over the details, studying the fine print was a routine that Munroe would not violate. Burbank had accepted all her stipulations save one: He would not vacillate on his right to send a companion on the assignment if he felt it necessary.

For five million she could put up with the possibility of being babysat; worst case, she'd conveniently lose the sitter. She faxed the signed copy to Burbank's office and overnighted the original to Breeden.

Within minutes of her having done so, the driving edge of anger and anxiety ebbed, and calm overtook her. She checked into a motel and slept for fifteen hours.

CHAPTER 4

Frankfurt, Germany

Hands deep in her coat pockets, Munroe strode toward Zeil, Frankfurt's downtown walking street, and toward the steps that led to the underground rails. It was November cold, and the streets were bare and windblown. Autumn leaves danced on the gusts, and the aromas of coffee from the cafés and chestnuts roasting at open-air stalls lifted on the breeze, exciting the senses.

She stood at the subway entrance and, a predator catching the first whiff of prey, filled her lungs with the crisp taste of winter.

After nearly a month of background preparation, she was ready to pick up the scent of a trail that had vanished and, if things went according to plan, to take the investigation where others before her had searched and failed.

She'd arrived in Frankfurt the day before yesterday. Her hotel was near the city center, with a view of the Main and the riverboats that moved along its course, a short walk from the trains that ran underground and the best shopping in the city that stood above them.

She took the train to Oberursel, a midsize town on the northern edge of Frankfurt, and from there a taxi to Klinik Hohe Mark. St. Mark's Clinic: home for the mentally unwell and, for the past three years, Kristof Berger's permanent residence.

The institution was a sprawling estate of functional buildings spread across acres of what would have been greenery if the weather had been warmer. She had called ahead for visiting hours, and when she stepped from the taxi, church bells in a cobblestoned town square somewhere in the distance confirmed that it was time.

Kristof sat in a warm, sun-drenched room where pastel yellow curtains framed the windows and softened the winter light. He stared with tilted head into nothingness, his hands in his lap and his feet together. At the opposite end of the room, the sounds of daytime television filled the silence, and although there were other patients in the room, Munroe did not notice them, so focused was she on Kristof.

He was different from the old photos in the reports, and as she saw the blankness of his face, her immediate thought was of how shameful it was that such a beautiful person had gone to waste. She wondered now, for the first time thinking beyond collecting on the contract, what had brought him to such a state.

Munroe wore a blond wig and brown contact lenses. They were the only items that bore resemblance to Emily Burbank, but she hoped they were enough to jog memories—if Kristof still had them. She sat in the chair next to him, and with her hand on his arm she said his name. He gave no response.

Unsure if he had registered her presence, she knelt down in front of him, leaning in so that her face was near his line of sight. She placed one hand gently under his chin and drew it up so that he looked at her. His eyes focused, and she smiled. He lifted his head on his own, and she withdrew her hand, remaining in front of him on the floor.

Munroe's voice was hushed and low. *"Ich will begreifen was passiert ist, damit ich Dir helfen kann.* Where did it happen, Kristof? What do you remember?"

He sighed and closed his eyes. His head drifted to the side, and his face returned to the emptiness he'd worn when she first saw him.

She stayed with him for nearly four hours. She spoke softly, explained her desire to locate Emily, and watched his face for clues that would allow her inside his mind. There were moments when he stirred from his torpor and looked her way. Once he smiled, but in all the time they were together, he didn't speak.

The afternoon faded, and Monroe left the institution, arriving over an hour later in Langen, a town on the southern edge of Frankfurt. On the cobblestoned pavement outside the station that split the city in two, she studied the oversize map. Dusk was coming, and with the last of the sun the temperature would dip further. She turned up the collar of her coat. It would be quick, a pass by the house to get a feel for what she would encounter when she returned to pay a visit to Kristof's mother.

A three-minute walk from the station, Frau Berger's house stood on a quiet and tidy street. Hers was a two-story home, small and narrow, with red clay roof tiles like the houses around it, though unlike the others it was in disrepair. The dark green paint on the shutters was cracked and peeling, and plaster from parts of the outside wall had crumbled, leaving the blocks underneath it exposed. The eaves were lopsided, drooping precariously at the back corner. Munroe's eyes were drawn to the windowsills, where on each one stood plants that flourished, and she saw that the six feet between the front door and the sidewalk was neatly lined and hedged with what would be a beautiful garden in the spring. In the fading light of the evening, the house looked forlorn and lonely.

Munroe returned to the station and paced for warmth against the cold while waiting for the train that would take her back into Frankfurt. At the far end of the platform, Frau Berger's house was visible, and on the third trip to the end Munroe spotted lights in the house and noted the time.

The following day she returned to visit Kristof and found him in the same chair wearing the same expression. When she approached, he lifted his head and smiled. She sat next to him, placed her hand on his arm, said nothing, and allowed the hours to pass in silence.

And then Kristof spoke, his voice thick and sticky, the words uneven. "We went where the money was buried," he said. "We ran together, and she was gone, where the money was."

Munroe waited, let the silence swallow them, and then in a whisper said, "Can you tell me where?"

"She was gone," he said. "She was gone, and it was red, and we never saw the place of the money."

Twice more he spoke, not answering her questions but repeating the same words. Munroe stayed with him for another hour and then left for Langen. On the train she reviewed the transcripts of Kristof's previous conversations. They were there, identical words: *where the money was buried.* She closed her eyes. The warmth and the rhythm of the train and the clack of the wheels lulled her to the edge of sleep. There was meaning in his words—something.

She found a florist on Langen's Hauptstrasse and purchased one of the more expensive items in the shop. It would, she hoped, be a welcome addition to the collection Frau Berger displayed on her windowsills and as such provide an opening into the woman's home. Munroe returned to the station and waited in the cold on the platform until shortly after dusk, when the lights in the house went on.

At Munroe's knock Frau Berger opened the door and wiped a hand on a spotless apron. Munroe took a step forward. *"Guten Abend, Frau Berger, ich bin die Mikaela*—I'm a friend of Kristof," she said. "I've been abroad and only recently learned what happened. I'm so sorry." She held out the living floral arrangement. "I wanted to bring you something."

There was a moment of uneasy silence, and then Frau Berger took the arrangement. "Thank you," she said quietly, standing in the doorway, moving neither to close the door nor to invite Munroe to stay.

Munroe stepped back a pace. "I'm sorry to have disturbed you," she said, and then turned to go.

"Wait . . ." The woman's voice was soft, distant. "Won't you come in for a few minutes? Perhaps drink something warm?"

Munroe paused, scratched her neck as if deciding, and then nodded and followed the woman into the house. Frau Berger showed her to a small sitting room in the front and then retreated farther into the downstairs area.

While Munroe sat, she surveyed the room and hallway. The Burbank report was accurate in describing the poor condition of the house, but it neglected the invisible obvious. The interior was worn yet spotlessly clean and well cared for. Curtains, sun-bleached and threadbare, were crisp and fresh, the windows were without a smudge, and there was no trace of dust on any of the old pieces that decorated the modest room. The sofa had been recently plumped. A small glass showcase displayed an antique collection of miniature ceramic pieces, and adorning the walls were photographs of Kristof from his earliest years. The woman was meticulous, proud, self-sufficient. The offer of money would have insulted her.

The fragrance of fresh coffee announced Frau Berger's return.

The conversation was light. Talk was of the weather and the differences between home and abroad. Munroe asked questions about Kristof as a child, and the woman spoke of him in the descriptive and colorful way that only an adoring mother could.

"It must have been a very big shock to you," Munroe said, "for Kristof to withdraw the way he did. Do you suppose something happened to him in Africa?"

"I don't know," the mother replied. She grew quiet. "I believe so. He would wake in the night screaming. That's why he originally went to see the doctors, you know, to calm the nightmares."

"I didn't know that," Munroe said. "Nobody says why he is away, only that it happened after he made a trip to Africa. They say things happened to him there that changed him."

A tear formed in the mother's eye. "I don't know," she said. "It's possible. He never spoke to me of it." She drew the back of a finger under her eyes. Munroe handed her a tissue. "There were some men who came to visit me, who offered me money if I would tell them where Kristof went. They were looking for a girl, maybe his girlfriend."

"Did they find the girl?" Munroe asked.

"I don't know," she replied. "I didn't want their money, and I sent them away. But there was nothing I could tell them anyhow. I don't know about any girl." Frau Berger's tears rolled steadily. "Sometimes I wonder," the woman said, "if I knew what happened, would it make it easier for me to bear it?"

Munroe moved from her seat to the edge of the sofa where Frau Berger sat. She placed her hand on the woman's shoulder. "Perhaps it would," she said. "I also want to know what happened. I want to help Kristof." Munroe was silent for a moment and then asked, "Are there no clues in the items Kristof brought back with him from Africa?"

The woman shook her head. "He brought nothing back. Not even clothes. Everything he had, I put into an envelope. They were from a secret belt, a pocket that goes under the pants. It was all he had."

"May I look?" Munroe asked.

Frau Berger nodded and rose. She motioned for Munroe to follow, then led her up the narrow staircase and to a room on the right. Unlike the rest of the house, the room was dusty, its air stale. Items were strewn across the floor and the bed was barely made, as if his mother had chosen to leave it exactly the way Kristof had on the day he left home for good. Perhaps in some hidden recess of the woman's mind she believed that he would return to it.

From a drawer inside a small wardrobe, Frau Berger pulled out a manila envelope and handed it to Munroe. "Everything he had with him is in here."

The two women sat, Frau Berger on the edge of the bed and Munroe cross-legged on the floor, where she spread out the contents of the envelope in front of her: a passport, two airplane tickets, a yellow vaccination card, two pills remaining from some form of medication, and a couple pieces of paper on which the ink had bled to indecipherability.

Munroe stared at the items, astounded by the wealth of viable information. At this rate the job would be over in a month.

She picked up the airplane tickets. The first was an unused South African Airways ticket from Johannesburg to Frankfurt with the same date and codes for the flight Emily was supposed to have taken. The second was undoubtedly the one Kristof had returned to Europe on, an Air France flight from Libreville to Paris. The ticket had been issued by a local travel agent in Gabon, of that Munroe was sure. From the IATA information, she could track down the originating travel agency if necessary.

The yellow vaccination record brought a smile. The doctor's stamps and signatures were all obvious forgeries. The entire stamp-filled booklet had no doubt been purchased somewhere along the journey in order to facilitate border crossings, a fake so similar to those that she used to carry.

She took his passport and flipped through the pages. The little book was nearly full. Most of the countries he had passed through had required an entire page for the issuing visa alone, not counting entry and exit stamps. Munroe lost herself in the pages tracing his journey from South Africa to Kenya and back again, following the trail of exit and entry stamps until they led to Namibia. She went slowly, flipping front to back through the pages, sometimes losing a thread in the muddle and then picking it back up again a few pages later.

She became aware of the time when Frau Berger excused herself and returned downstairs.

Following the trail from Namibia was difficult. There were no exit stamps. The nearest chronological entry stamp was into Angola, and from there she traced the trail to Gabon and then to Equatorial Guinea. There was an unused visa for Cameroon.

Munroe closed her eyes and ran her fingers over the postage-size stamps that had been affixed to the passport on the Cameroonian visa. He had not used it. He had gone into Gabon, gone into Equatorial Guinea, and returned to Gabon, but not Cameroon. Why? The information screamed in the silence. It was there, somewhere.

She removed a small digital camera from around her neck and took photographs of every passport page, both tickets, and for good measure she also got photos of the medication wrapping and of the illegible pieces of paper. She took one of the pills out of the wrapping and dropped it into a small Ziploc bag. Frau Berger might notice, but by then she would be gone with everything she needed.

Munroe returned the items to the envelope and then placed the envelope in the drawer that Frau Berger had taken it from. She closed Kristof's door loudly, hoping it would give notice that she was on her way down. From the kitchen came the smell of bread baking, and the woman greeted her at the bottom of the stairs.

"Frau Berger, I must be getting home," Munroe said. The woman's hands rested on the banister rail, and Munroe placed one of her own hands on them. "I don't know if there are answers or not," she said, "but I promise you that I am going to do everything I can to discover what happened to Kristof in Africa, and perhaps with that information you can find some peace."

The woman smiled. Her eyes were red, and Munroe knew that while she had been busy upstairs scouring the items for information, Frau Berger had been downstairs trying unsuccessfully to hold back the tears.

THE NEXT MORNING Munroe had photo enlargements made of the passport pages, and while she waited for their development, purchased a large map of Africa. Before returning to the hotel, she located a lab to analyze the tablet she'd taken.

Back in the hotel room, Munroe shoved furniture away from the wall in front of the bed, and there she taped the map and beside it the enlargements. Using the trail from the passport and filling in the blanks with Burbank's reports, she marked Emily's path across Africa.

She traced the steps methodically, double-checking as she went. Just as it had the previous evening, the trail brought her from Gabon through Oyem to the Mongomo crossing in Equatorial Guinea and back to Oyem. The trail ended with an exit stamp out of Libreville. But there was one glaring omission: There was no exit stamp from Equatorial Guinea.

Munroe circled the Oyem/Mongomo crossing in red and then stopped. *Mongomo.* She shook her head.

It couldn't be *that* easy.

She went back through the transcripts of Kristof Berger's conversation with the investigators. She ignored the English translations and read directly from the German. *Where the money was buried.*

Could it be so simple?

She stabbed her pen into the dot that marked the city and then lay back on the bed with her arms behind her head. She stared at the map. *Mongomo.*

She checked her watch. In two hours Houston would begin to wake, and she would be forced to make the obligatory phone call to Burbank's office to notify him of her next step. She picked up the phone and dialed Breeden's number.

The voice on the other end was groggy, Breeden's usual breathlessness noticeably absent.

"I've picked up a few leads," Munroe said, "and I'll be moving soon. I need you to do something for me."

"Sure."

"Going back about five or six years, I gave you an envelope and asked you to keep it for me. How quickly can you get it?"

"Sometime this morning."

"I need it sent to me overnight."

"Consider it done," Breeden replied. "Contact me if there's anything else—you know I'm here if you need me."

"Thanks," Munroe said. "I'll be in touch."

Munroe returned to the lab, and when she located the technician with whom she'd originally spoken, he handed back the photograph of the wrapping and the sample she'd given him and, in exchange for payment, a two-page printout. "In layperson's terms," he said as he handed it to her, "it's mefloquine hydrochloride. This particular tablet is sold under the trade name Lariam—it's an antimalarial typically used to treat against *Plasmodium falciparum* and also sometimes used as a prophylactic."

It sounded right; after Emily's bout with malaria, she'd been taking prophylactics. Lariam was what they'd used back then in chloroquine-resistant falciparum-endemic areas, and if there was ever a place that fit that description, the coastal region of West Central Africa was it. Lariam. The drug wasn't prescribed as much these days—the side effects could be brutal: homicidal tendencies, hallucinations, and psychotic episodes, among others. The worst of the effects were supposedly rare, but the odds didn't matter much when it was you or your loved one who was transformed into a raving psychotic. It would be a plausible explanation for Kristof's behavior, except that all indicators pointed to his breakdown's occurring long after he would have stopped taking the drug.

At the hotel Munroe put in the call to Burbank's office, and instead of being passed to his executive assistant as expected, was transferred directly to Richard Burbank. "Michael," he said in a half-chopped way that left the impression that someone else had been cut off as he switched lines to take the call, "I hadn't expected to hear from you so soon. Is it good news?"

"It's a little early to say," she replied. "I've done all that I can here in Europe, and I'm leaving for Africa in a couple of days—as per our agreement, I'm informing you of my plans."

"Where specifically are you headed?" he asked.

"I'm starting with Cameroon and Gabon," she said, "and I'll narrow the search from there."

"Cameroon. Gabon." His voice had a razor quality to it. "As far as we know, Emily never even got out of Namibia. Why aren't you heading to Namibia?"

Munroe's mouth tightened into a forced smile as if she were face-to-face with her client, and she waited before replying. "Mr. Burbank," she said, "you hired me to do this job because so far nobody else has been able to do it. I'm reporting to you on my progress because my contract requires me to. Beyond that, either you allow me to do my job without micromanaging me or find someone else to locate your daughter."

"You're right," he said. "I apologize. Obviously I'm anxious about this whole thing. When do you expect to leave?"

"I'm booked to fly out in two days."

"I want Miles Bradford to accompany you," he said. The request did not surprise her. That he made it so early into the assignment did.

"I'll wait for him in Douala," Munroe replied. "He's going to need visas. There's not enough time for him to get them and meet up with me here before my flight out."

"Cancel the flight. He'll be in Frankfurt in less than a week. You said Gabon and Cameroon—he'll have the visas. The two of you fly to Africa together."

Munroe shut her eyes, gripped the phone, and waited half a beat. "If it must be done that way, so be it. It's your expense account, Mr. Burbank, and it's your time." She replaced the phone receiver and swore under her breath.

She tossed a few belongings into a backpack and slipped the Do Not Disturb sign on the door. On her way out of the hotel, she paid for the next five days and left instructions for packages and messages to be held until she returned. It was Burbank's time and Burbank's dollar. He could bankroll a snowboarding trip in the Alps while she waited for babysitter Miles fucking Bradford to arrive.

From Frankfurt's Hauptbahnhof she took the next express train bound for Zurich.

IT WAS AN early afternoon four days later when Munroe returned to Frankfurt. The FedEx envelope from Kate was waiting, as was a fax from Burbank's office with Miles Bradford's flight arrival information.

In her room Munroe sat on the edge of the bed with the envelope in her hands. She tapped it against her knuckles, stared at it, and then, unable to bring herself to open it, tossed it on the bed and went to the window to watch the river and the boats and the happy couples strolling along its manicured banks.

Against this picturesque display, she deliberated rescinding the contract. Doing so would mean failure, but failure was always an eventuality. The nonstop success would hit a bump sooner or later, and if there was going to be a washout, this would be a good time to have it happen.

Returning to the past was inevitable. Somehow in the last nine years she'd managed to stay upright on a tightrope stretched between brilliance and insanity, the blackness of the abyss always with her, leaving her sometimes wondering if letting go might in the end be easiest of all.

Work had kept her sane, kept the line taut. It wasn't fear that held her back from Burbank's assignment or where it would lead, nor was it the contents of the envelope, symbols of the past that they were. It was uncertainty: If the line should snap, on which side of the abyss would she land? She'd planned to return when she no longer cared.

Munroe walked to the bed, picked up the envelope, and ripped away the plastic ribbon of sealant. Maybe she'd always care, maybe there was never going to be a good time, maybe she'd be running forever. Carpe diem. She emptied the contents onto the bed and ran her fingers over three pieces of history: a Cameroonian residency card, a vaccination card, and a forged Spanish passport.

CHAPTER 5

Of the eight people Richard Burbank had provided personnel files on, Munroe had to agree that Miles Bradford was best suited for the job—especially when it came to the mechanics of it all. His file, thick with details of a job history that had taken him through countries as diverse and hazardous as those she'd worked, was sparse when it came to personal information. There was little provided of use in building a composite of who the man was. This she knew: Miles was in his mid-thirties and former Special Forces. He now handled high-stakes private security.

"Mercenary" was the only word she had for a man like him, a former soldier who hired out his skills. And like the Cameroonian documents stuffed into her backpack, the word brought with it much unwanted baggage.

Munroe arrived at Frankfurt's airport before Bradford's flight touched down. Blending with others who waited, she stood opposite a large plate-glass wall that separated the waiting area from the luggage collection. She spotted Bradford as soon as he entered the hall. Short-cropped hair betrayed a tinge of red, his eyes were murky green, and he was average height with above-average looks. His overcoat outlined a well-built physique, and he moved with the relaxed assurance of a man who knew where he was going and was in no hurry to get there.

A small wheeled overnight bag trailed behind him, and he didn't stop at the luggage carousel.

Munroe left the area before he could spot her; he knew who he was looking for as well as she did. He would contact her at the hotel, and she would be away when the call came. He would wait for her—he had no choice—and that was how it should be.

She returned his call in the late afternoon, offering a plastic apology and arranging to meet him for dinner at Gargantua in the Westend, where she'd made reservations.

She wasn't being deliberately cruel in setting the first meeting there, but she was deliberately testing him. If he came by taxi, he would find it easily enough. But if he set out on foot, taking the local transportation as she would have been wont to do, it would prove to be an exasperating task. Restaurant Gargantua, with all its five stars, was situated minutes from the city's famed Palmengarten and the English-style Grüneberg Park, quietly tucked away within a house in a tree-lined residential neighborhood of prewar flats.

Munroe was seated and waiting at the appointed time, and when Bradford arrived a few minutes late, she stood to shake his hand. She wore a close-fitting black dress and four-inch heels that gave her a two-inch height advantage. Wrapped around her neck was a delicate beaded scarf that hung down against her bare back. It was an outfit that caused heads to turn, an image men desired to display on their arm as a trophy and then take home to conquer again in bed. She was as opposite from the photos and the information in her file as could possibly be managed, and it was intended as a willful statement.

His handshake was firm and confident. Not once did his eyes leave her face to wander down the length of her body. "Miles Bradford," he said, and as she sat, he seated himself opposite with the same calm, relaxed air with which he'd strolled through the baggage area. "It's an honor to finally meet you."

She placed her chin on folded hands and echoed his words, "To *finally* meet me . . ."

"I've been an admirer of yours for years," he said. "I was a security consultant for Radiance when you were working Macedonia and then later for Terra Corp right after you'd wrapped up in Uzbekistan—both brilliant pieces of work, I might add."

"Thank you," she said, and picked up her water glass, swirling it before taking a sip. "Information and security." She paused. "You must be at the top of your game if the same companies are hiring the both of us." And then, "I hope you had no trouble finding this place—it's somewhat tucked away."

"Not too much," he said. "I had to ask directions once or twice, but I was lucky to bump into people who spoke English." He glanced around the low-lit L-shaped room. "It looks like the reward will be worth the effort."

He had come on foot as she'd hoped. She suppressed a smile. "So," she said, "how long have you been working for Burbank?"

"Technically I don't. I've done a few things with him off and on over the years, but I work for myself—contracts."

"That's what I thought. He referred to you as 'his people,' made it sound like you were one of his employees."

"His people, huh?" Miles smiled an easy smile of straight white teeth and settled back into his chair. "He'd certainly like to think so. We go way back, him and me, but no, I'm my own boss, and like most businessmen, I go where the money is."

"And I assume there was money in the search for Emily?"

"Richard paid me well, as I'm sure he's paying you well. But I went to Namibia for Richard, for Emily—for all of us, really. She was a good kid. I've known her since she was nine or ten."

"I'm sorry," Munroe said. "I didn't realize."

A grin crossed his face. "Well, I'm sure Richard failed to put that into my file." The waiter brought the wine menu, and Bradford said, "Shall we order a bottle?"

"I don't drink when I'm working, but feel free."

He handed the menu back. "In that case I'll have what you're having. What've you got?"

"Water," she said, and then, after Bradford had requested a bottle of Selters, "Look, Miles, you seem straightforward and likable enough, but to be honest, I don't want you here. I work alone. I've never been babysat, and the only reason you're sitting in front of me is because Burbank offered me a hell of a lot of money to put up with the inconvenience. Things being as they are, I want to get a few of the ground rules straight."

"Fair enough."

"This is my investigation. I run the show, I call the shots. You're along for the ride—whether it's to pass on information to Burbank or cover my ass, I'm not sure. You do what you have to do, but don't get in my way, and don't question my judgment. Most of all, don't screw things up. If I want your opinion, I'll ask for it. If you have a problem with any of that, I need to know now."

"No problem at all," he said. His words came calmly, and the tone was nonchalant. He flicked the napkin over his lap and reached for the bread basket. "But since we're talking about ground rules, I have a few of my own so that I can do what I've been hired to do."

"Go ahead."

"I'm being paid to watch your back and keep you alive," he said. "Richard's got peace of mind, not to mention money, riding on you, and I'm his insurance policy. I know for certain that you're capable of taking care of yourself, but this was Richard's call, not mine. If it were my assignment, I wouldn't want me here either, so I understand your position. But like I said, it was his call, so don't take it out on me by making my job harder. You do what you have to do, I'll stay out of your way and keep my thoughts and opinions to myself. But I do need to know where you are every minute of every day and night, who you're talking to, and who you're paying off, and for what. If you can uphold your end of the bargain, I can uphold mine. Deal?"

"I'm not happy about it, but I can live with it."

"Good," he replied with a nod, and then, "Richard has told me next to nothing on where we go from here. What's the plan?"

"We start with Cameroon," she said. "Our flight leaves tomorrow morning for Douala. I'll update you as things unfold, but for now be sure you get eight sets of passport photos taken before we leave. I need them in my possession before we're on the plane."

The conversation had already been interrupted several times by the attentive waitstaff, and it took a longer pause with the arrival of the main course. The discussion strayed from small talk to the similar aspects of their work to small talk again, and it was over coffee when

Munroe reached for the folder by the foot of her chair and pulled out the file of her life's history that Burbank had given her. She slid it across the table. "You've probably gone over this already," she said. "But if not, it's only fair that you have it—I have yours."

Bradford put down his cup, reached for the file, and slid it back to her. "I assembled that file, Michael," he said. "I don't need it."

Munroe leaned back and allowed silence to engulf them. Bradford said nothing, offered no explanation or justification; he simply sat and returned her gaze with a placid expression. It was a rare reaction. Most of humanity, when trapped in an uneasy silence, would say something, anything, in order to free themselves from the discomfort of quiet.

"If you're the one responsible for that," Munroe said finally, pointing to the folder, "you certainly left out a lot of key information."

"Yes, I did." His voice was low and smooth, and he leaned forward and rested his forearms on the table. "Some information I couldn't get, but the rest didn't seem pertinent."

Munroe kept quiet, and when once again he didn't take the bait of silence, she angled toward him so that her face was close to his and in a whisper said cynically, "It's interesting that you'd find psychiatric evaluations to be so much less pertinent than a history of broken bones."

"I would have included them if they were accurate," he said. "But you and I both know that they aren't."

"You're not only a hired gun, you're also a psychologist? That's very impressive."

He smiled and leaned back against the chair. "Am I wrong?"

"I don't know. You're the expert." And then she mirrored his shift in seating position. "So," she said, and she smiled back and waited half a beat, "what's your theory on the scars? Apparently you don't believe that I'm suicidal or prone to cutting."

"Would it matter if I did?" he asked.

"Actually, yes, thank you for asking, it matters a lot. It determines what types of reciprocal behavior I can expect from you when we find ourselves under stress."

"Then no," he said, "I don't believe it—it contradicts everything I know about you. If you were planning to end your life you'd do it in a chuteless BASE jump off Angel Falls."

Munroe drew a slow, deep breath and then held up her right hand and spread her fingers. "Fewer than these," she said. "That's how many people grasp what you've just said." And then, after another moment of silence, "The funny thing is, everything I told them was true." She shook her head. "What a fucking mind job. You reach out for help and get labeled delusional." She pulled back a collection of beaded bracelets from the base of her left wrist and turned it over for him to see. "The scar's real, as are all the others, but they weren't self-inflicted." She turned her right wrist over, blemish-free, and placed it next to the left. "When I do a job, I do it properly."

"There's a lot I don't know about you, Michael," he said. "I don't know exactly what you told your doctors, and it's pretty evident from the file that I haven't been able to fill in the blanks of your teenage years. I do know that when you arrived in the United States, you didn't adjust very well and were later expelled from high school."

Munroe nodded and motioned for him to continue.

"In that same year, you were barred from several eskrima training facilities and kicked out of nearly every martial arts class you attended. Getting expelled from school I could understand, but the knife fighting and martial arts made me curious—especially the places you were going—tough guys aren't easily threatened, and if you go too far, they'll just as soon beat the crap out of you. It took me a while, but I managed to track down your first balisong instructor—he remembered you well and not at all fondly. He said you'd come close to killing him a couple of times, says you easily could have, and he still doesn't understand what stopped you. The stories from the others weren't much different." Bradford paused for a sip of coffee. "That ability and the spark of crazy that terrifies the hard-assed, it came from somewhere, Michael, and I have no doubt that's where the scars came from as well."

"You're a very perceptive man," she said. "Maybe I'll keep you around for a while—perhaps you can appreciate the mastery born from the will to survive."

THE FLIGHT OUT of Frankfurt connected in Paris and touched down in Douala at seven-thirty in the evening. Munroe stepped from the cool, dry interior of the plane to the open-air concrete halls of the terminal, and warm moisture washed over her as if she'd opened the door to a steam room.

In a shifting line that converged and separated, the passengers moved through the halls toward passport control. Dampness settled on Munroe's skin, weighing down her hair and fogging up the glasses of a tourist who walked beside her. And then, as if the heat had entwined itself around their bodies and in doing so encumbered their limbs, the speed of the pack slowed to a softer pace. By the time the first of the travelers arrived at health control, wet patches had spread under the arms and on the backs of their shirts, and some showed visible signs of exertion.

Munroe asked Bradford for his passport, and he gave it to her. At health control she handed over her yellow card and both of their passports with the pink-red border of a ten-euro bill peeking from between the pages. To the woman on the other side of the small kiosk, she said, "We seem to have misplaced one of our vaccination cards." The woman flipped slowly through both passports, and when at last she was finished and came to Munroe's yellow book, she studied the information and finally said, "Your vaccinations are expired."

The woman handed back the vaccination booklet, and Munroe placed another ten-euro bill between the pages and handed it back again. "I never noticed."

On the other side of the counter, the woman wrote something and then handed back both passports, two new yellow vaccination booklets filled with doctors' stamps and signatures, and two pieces of hand-cut paper stamped with the purple ink of her official stamp, signifying that each traveler was healthy and fully vaccinated. The euros had disappeared. "Go to passport control," she said.

Munroe walked slowly, breathing deeply, and took in the odor of mold and decay and smiled. It was the fragrance of year after year of rain and humidity that had permeated the walls and paint and become as much a part of the building as the steel rods that supported the structure and the bodies of the immigration personnel that exuded the acrid aroma of old sweat and unwashed clothing worn day after day.

It took a twenty-euro bill for Munroe to get through immigration on the expired Cameroonian residence card. At customs the official methodically went through their luggage and, finding nothing of value, nothing contraband, and nothing that might guarantee the night's drinking money, shoved the contents back into the bags and allowed them to pass.

Outside the building, under the dim fluorescent lights of the terminal, taxi drivers called out and porters jostled and chaos reigned.

The hotel was Parfait Garden, an aging multistoried structure off the sidewalk of Boulevard de la Liberté. The building had fewer amenities than the newer and higher-starred hotels in the city, but it had managed to maintain its aura of dignity, and Munroe had chosen it for the memories. It stood less than a kilometer down the road from the roundabout that branched toward Buea, and as she stepped from the taxi, she glanced in the direction that once was home.

Home. Whatever "home" was supposed to mean.

So close and still so far away, nothing there and no reason to return. Her mother had since repatriated to the United States, and Dad had married a Cameroonian and moved northwest to Garoua. She had not seen or spoken to either of them since leaving Africa; perhaps when the job was over, she would make the trip to the country's desert north and find the man who had been her father for thirteen years.

The staff at the front desk was polite and courteous despite Bradford's requirement of seeing and approving both rooms prior to check-in. Worse was that he insisted Munroe accompany him, the first of no doubt many inconveniences that having a babysitter-slash-bodyguard would bring. They bypassed the hotel's only elevator and climbed the wide carpeted stairway that wound through the center of the building. The musty scent of the venerable permeated the air.

Adjacent rooms next to the stairwell on the third floor met with Bradford's approval, and once he had left her alone, Munroe dumped her duffel bag and backpack at the foot of the bed, turned off the air conditioner, and opened the windows. Warmth and humidity filled the room. True acclimatization would take a week or more, and the air-conditioning would only slow down the process; until her body adjusted, the climate would siphon off her strength, leaving her sluggish and tired—better to get it over with as quickly as possible. From her backpack she retrieved double-sided tape and tacked the day curtains in place around the windows. It wasn't quite mosquito netting but would do the job until she could pick up the real thing.

She lay on the bed with her hands behind her head and stared at the ceiling. Whatever she thought she would feel upon returning, such contentment was a surprise. It was five weeks until Christmas, and this was the closest to home for the holidays she'd been in at least a decade.

MUNROE WAS UP with the sun, and for over an hour the sound of lively traffic and busy sidewalks had filtered through the open windows, calling her to meet them. She'd given Bradford her word that at least this once she would wait for him before leaving the room, and she was dressed and lying on the bed deep in thought when he knocked.

They took breakfast in the hotel's small dining room. The mood between them was light and the conversation friendly, and when they had finished and were waiting for the waiter to bring a second round of coffee, Munroe stood. "I'll find out where he's gone off to," she said.

The waiter had been on his way back from the kitchen when she stopped him. She placed a capsule of powder in the palm of his hand and followed it with a twenty-euro note. "My friend has been very difficult about taking his medication," she said. "If you put this in his coffee, the money is yours. If you get it in the wrong drink, you'll pay."

It was several minutes after the coffee that Miles began to show visible signs of somnolence. Monroe reached over and placed her wrist to his forehead. "Everything all right?" she asked. "You don't look very well."

"Not so good," he said. His words were slightly slurred. "I feel so tired."

"It might be the climate and the jet lag," she said. "It does that to you. It can take a while to get used to it. Let's get you back to your room."

By the time the elevator had taken them to their floor, Bradford was slumped over her shoulder. With some difficulty she got him into his bed, removed his shoes, and made sure the air-conditioning worked properly. Knowing he would wake thirsty, she set out a bottle of drinking water and tucked the light blanket around him.

It was a crappy deal. She would have preferred another way, but there were things to be done that belonged to no one else. "Sleep well," she whispered. She left his key in the room and, using a skeleton set, locked the door behind her.

She checked her watch; she'd be lucky to get back before dark.

The streets of Douala were narrow and full of loud and chaotic life. Bicycles laden with goods stacked five feet into the air fought for road space with Peugeot cars converted to share taxis and packed with twice as many people as they were built to carry. Traffic surged in disarray, vehicles jostled for position, their horns being applied as frequently as the brakes. Pedestrians crowded the sidewalks. Colonial buildings sat side by side with modern structures, and green fronds peeked above walls that separated homes from the cacophony of the streets.

First stop was the Société Générale de Banques au Cameroun and an account left abandoned when she had fled the country so many years ago. Munroe expected that it would have been closed due to inactivity, the money vanishing into the ether, or at the least be inaccessible. Rather, it was all there and had even accrued a modest sum of interest. She folded the bank statement and then at the FOREX window changed five hundred euros into Central African francs. It would be enough small change to last a while; most of the hotels and airlines accepted and sometimes preferred euros to the local currency.

Outside, Munroe hailed several taxis and sent each yellow car on its way until she got a newer vehicle, its engine integrity less questionable, the seats still solid and without the grime and reshaping of those that had borne too many passengers; with the driver she negotiated a return rate to Kribi, that sleepy party town three hours south of Douala.

Known for its pristine beaches, Kribi was quiet and relatively empty for most of the year but swelled beyond capacity during holiday periods. It was in Kribi that the past would converge with the present. She needed documents, and the man who could get them would be found there—she had spent several hours on the phone last night making sure of it.

Out of Douala the traffic congestion eased to the occasional overladen minibus. The road to Kribi traced its path inland and then parallel to the ocean, with farms of short palm trees used for producing palm oil bordering each side, their monotony broken by an occasional building

or the intermittent sight of young boys herding goats, pushing the animals along the road's dirt shoulders. The highway's two lanes provided
enough room for oncoming vehicles to pass without forcing one off the
tarmac. A steady breeze blew in off the ocean, and Munroe spent most
of the trip alternating between reviewing her notes and staring lazily out
the window, watching memories fly by with the scenery.

Unlike yesterday, today brought pangs of guilt and an overwhelm-
ing sense of sadness. There were tremors in the back of her mind, and
the voices began to stir, the first she had heard from them since accepting the Burbank assignment.

Perhaps the decision to return to Kribi had been a mistake.

CHApteR 6

Boniface Akambe was a large man. Not only in his height and girth but in that he wore fine clothing, drove a new four-wheel-drive Land Cruiser, and owned several successful businesses. He was also a good-looking man with soft skin and a desirable-size gap between his top front teeth. Akambe had twelve children borne by three wives, two of whom lived in Douala while the third, the youngest, kept house in Kribi. His situation had improved since Munroe had seen him last. He'd been younger then—they all had been—and he'd had only one wife, though if he'd had his way, Munroe would have soon become the second.

It was Akambe's family name and political connections that bought him protection and helped the businesses that fed his large lifestyle, but it was a lesser-known enterprise that had compelled Munroe to make this trip.

Kribi was exactly as she remembered—a small and lazy town with only a few main streets connecting the parts of the whole and far too many hotels for its size. Several new buildings had been added, but otherwise little had changed, and it took only a few minutes for the taxi driver to find the place Munroe had described.

The office was nondescript, on the ground floor of a three-story structure with peeling paint on the outside walls and water condensation dripping in a steady flow from an air-conditioning box that protruded over the sidewalk. Inside the office it was cool and fragranced by the lingering smell of mildew, and in several places the linoleum on the floor turned up its corners. A receptionist sat on a wooden chair behind a metal desk worn of its paint and showing makeshift repairs done over the years. In front of her was a manual typewriter and to the right of it an arrangement of manila folders, haphazardly stacked.

In the nine years that Munroe had been away from Africa, not once had the Fang language rolled off her tongue, but it came now in a familiar burst. "*Hakum ayen Akambe,*" she said. "Please notify him that I am here." She didn't need to provide more information, that she spoke in Fang was her calling card. With a look of surprise, the woman stood and went for a door on the opposite wall.

And then from behind came the rumble of Akambe's voice.

"Es-sss-sa," he said, drawing her name into three syllables. He exited the door of his office, arms wide in welcome and a huge grin spread across his face. "Essa," he said again. He clasped his hands together and then placed them on her shoulders and, holding her at arm's length, said, "It could only have been you. How have you been? How many years now?"

"It's been a long time," she said, returning the smile and relishing the warmth. "A very long time."

"Come, take coffee with me," he said, and then barked a few phrases to the woman who had returned to the desk. He stepped aside so that Munroe could pass into his office. In contrast to that of the front room, the furniture here was new, the flooring and paint clean, and his wooden office desk so large it nearly filled the back wall. Akambe sat in the oversize chair behind the desk and Munroe on the sofa that rested perpendicular to it.

"Essa," he said again after the coffee had been served. "Where have you been hiding yourself all of this time?"

"I've been across the ocean, studying and working."

"Ah," he said, and he leaned back and placed his hands on his wide midsection. "You went to your people. Quite the trouble it made when you left. Francisco spent a small fortune trying to find you. He finally stopped when he knew for sure that you were alive and had left the country."

A stab of guilt and the hollow ache that followed brought on a chorus of voices, chanting and calling her name, fighting for attention. She held eye contact with Akambe and, when the internal din had ebbed, said softly, "Have you heard from him?"

"I see him when he is in town, every few months."

"He hasn't left Africa, then?"

"He remains."

She winced and took another sip of the sweet coffee. "How is he?"

Akambe stirred another spoon of sugar into the creamy brown liquid and said nothing for a while, then looked up. "He's different. He works harder and plays harder, spends more time with women, drinking, behaving less like you and more like me." He gave a hearty laugh and continued. "And then he leaves for periods of solitude. He built himself a place near Ureca on the island." He paused, adding another spoon of sugar. "Time ages a person's soul," he said. "And they leave him alone as long as he supplies them now and then." Akambe was quiet for a moment. "You should make a point to see him, Essa. He deserves at least that."

She shrugged and put down her cup. "I will if I have the time. As it is, I am here for work and am pressed. I need your skill. Do you still make papers?"

"Sometimes yes, sometimes no." His head tilted right and left as he spoke. "What do you need?"

She handed him passport photos of herself and of Bradford. "I need two sets of residency cards for each of these."

"That I can do," he said.

"For both Cameroon and Equatorial Guinea."

"Ah," he replied, drumming his fingers on his desk. "Equatorial Guinea will take longer. And cost more."

"Preferably diplomatic status," she said, placing the rest of the photos on the desk and then laying a wad of cash on top of them. "If it's not enough, I'll pay the remainder when I return."

He flipped through the bills. "It's enough," he said. "Where are you staying? I'll have your papers delivered in five days."

"Hotel Parfait Garden," she said, and she stood to go.

Akambe raised his hand for her to pause and, full of importance, said, "Essa, I am looking for a wife."

She smiled at the predictability and then attempted a straight face.

"Boniface, maybe one day I'll take you up on your offer, but not today."
In the taxi she allowed herself an audible chuckle. Wife number four.

From Akambe's office the driver took her south of Kribi and turned
onto the narrow dirt road that went past the beach house. A thick hedge
ran the length of the property, blocking the view from the road, and the
driver stopped beside the metal gate that was the single visible entry
point. Munroe stepped onto the gravel driveway and stood, staring at the
barrier that divided what once was from life as it was now. Voices from
the past rose in unison, and she pushed back the screams into silence,
fought the urge to ring the gate bell, and instead returned to the car.
They drove north to Douala.

By the time Munroe reached the hotel, it was dark. She purchased
a bottle of water, headed for Bradford's room, and let herself in. Dim
street light filtered through the curtains, and Bradford's breathing was
steady and rhythmic against the hum of the air conditioner. She poured
water into a glass, knelt beside the bed, and leaned forward to lift his
head.

She touched the back of his neck, and his hand snapped around her
wrist, a movement swift and exact. He pulled her close until her face was
inches from his and in a whisper said, "You ever do that to me again
and I swear I'll radio tag you." She smiled and relaxed into him, and he
let go. She slipped a hand under his head, raised him up, and put the
glass to his lips; he drank greedily. When he had finished, he lay back
on the pillow with his eyes open a sliver and said, "Why the hell did you
do it?"

"I had some things I needed to do. Alone."

"Next time just ask. I'll give you space."

"Okay," she said, "I'll ask."

She stood and turned toward the door. "I'll see you in the morning,"
she whispered, and with the click of the latch, waves of internal tumult
boiled over.

    . . . Cry for sorrow of heart and howl for vexation of spirit . . .

With deliberate footsteps she walked across the hall, opened the
door to her room, and, for Bradford's ears, made the effort of both closing and locking it.

    . . . leave your name for a curse unto my chosen . . .

There would be no sleep tonight, not after Kribi, not after the gate and the beach house.

. . . the Lord GOD shall slay thee . . .

Munroe followed the staircase upward until she could go no farther and from there located the door that led to the rooftop.

. . . and call his servants by another name . . .

The air was cool with the relief of night, and in the darkness there was solace. She found a spot, dry and open to the sky, and lay back, face to the pattern of stars, familiar as they had been once before, as they had been on *that* night.

In the silence the voices in her head chanted and rose in crescendo: *The way of the wicked is death.*

She didn't fight them, didn't try to shut them off—there was no point. Tonight they were strong; tonight they would take her, and she would allow her mind loose to follow where they led, inevitably to where they had begun: the night she'd killed Pieter Willem.

That night the camp had been temporary, the structures quickly thrown together. The spot was well concealed and had access to the water and to the boats hidden in the mangrove swamps not far from the tributary that would carry them to the Muni River. There were six in their group, and the thatched-roof shelters that acted as home were spaced unevenly in the small clearing. The plan had been to remain until the delivery and then move back to Francisco's house in Kribi while they waited for the next shipment to come in.

Voices had carried in the stillness, and she'd crept closer to listen. Francisco and Pieter were arguing. Dusk was settling, and the pitch-black would follow in less than an hour. She could smell a storm coming and felt the change in the air. When the rain started, it would be impossible to overhear, and so she crab-walked until she could lean up against the shaky walls that held Francisco's shelter together.

Life had been good until two and a half years earlier, when Jean Noel and his mercenary buddy Pieter Willem had been added to the team. Jean wasn't bad; he saw her for what she was, a barely fifteen-year-old kid stuck out in the jungle, way out of her league but a necessary component to getting the job done. He was kind to her in his own way. When he wasn't working, he taught her how to make rope, tie knots, set traps, poison darts, and hunt noiselessly in the dark. He also showed her how to take care of a gun and how to use it. It was Pieter who taught her to kill.

A small man of hardened muscle, Pieter was charming and a master of words that endeared him to the listener. It was his eyes that she couldn't trust; from the day he'd arrived in Kribi, she had avoided him.

With Francisco's approval Pieter had taken it upon himself to train her to fight—"to defend herself" were the words he had used when presenting the idea. Even if Pieter had returned to South Africa, he still would have been too close. Yet she was forced into his presence for hours every day. She couldn't refuse. Francisco had given the order, and she worked for Francisco—more, she revered him. Eleven years her senior, Francisco was the older brother she'd lost when she was barely old enough to understand why.

Pieter's training had started as he promised—as training. Away from the rest of the camp, he set about teaching her to fight. The location of the camps changed, and sometimes so did the country as the crew moved nomadically with the pickups and deliveries, but her being in Pieter's presence remained constant. She didn't know where he'd learned his technique or what exactly he taught; he claimed to be a master in several martial arts, and she wouldn't have known one way or the other. She knew only that no matter how much she learned, she would return to her shelter bruised, bloody, and aching, and nobody at the camp would say anything about it.

Those were the good times.

As her skills progressed and she learned to fight back, Pieter would keep at her until she was spent and unable to move. Every day it ended the same, with her flat on her back, held down with a knife to her throat as he raped her, whispering taunts into her ear while his sweat dripped into her face.

He threatened to hunt down her family and kill them if she left camp—she had no doubt he would make good on his promise, and no matter what she felt about her family, death and torture by a sadistic madman was not what they deserved. They had no idea where she was, and even if they had, there was nothing they could do. The only person who would care if Pieter slit her throat would be Francisco, and physically he could never best Pieter—none of them could.

Then Pieter brought the knives into the training session. Each time the sparring began, she wasn't sure if she would live through the fight. Pieter deliberately cut her and regularly threatened to kill her. She fought to win, she fought to make him bleed, to end it, for the hell to be over. When her knife would connect with his flesh and the red liquid of life would smear across the blade, a shock of euphoria would go through her, always followed by the pain of his knife slicing another part of her body, and still it would end the same.

The better an opponent she became, the more Pieter tormented her. In an attempt to escape him, she refused to fight and then announced to Francisco—within earshot of Pieter—that she was trained and didn't need more. Pieter came to her that night and gagged her. He pinned her down on the ground and slit one of her wrists, mocking her as she struggled against him. After she had lost considerable blood, he pulled her out of the dirt and bound her wrist to stanch the bleeding. He stroked her face gently, kissed her, and told her that if she ever defied him again, he would slit both her wrists and dump her in the Atlantic for the sharks.

He left her alone for a few days, and she knew it was to provide time for her to think about what he'd said and allow recovery from the loss of blood.

Then she had tried to manipulate him off the team by begging Francisco to send him away. Unable to tell the real reason, she hoped he might indulge her, and when he didn't, she weighed the risk of the truth and chose life.

Then the sparring sessions were no longer enough to satisfy. Pieter began to trap her around camp. She never knew from which structure, tree, or rock he would appear; he seemed to take pleasure in devising ways to startle her. There was no place of solace or peace, and she lived on an emotional razor's edge.

Staying away from Pieter consumed her waking thoughts, and she found safety by sticking with other people. If Francisco was there, she stayed by his side, and if he was away, she sought out Jean Noel. She could sense Pieter hovering, and if he caught her eye while she was under the protection of company, he bore her a sweet sadistic smile. When she escaped during the day, Pieter would come at night, and so she took to sleeping away from camp in hidden places. The better she became at avoiding him, the more he seemed to take pleasure in hunting her down; the harder she fought, the more he came back.

With his viselike grip around her throat, he would draw the flat of his blade across her cheek and goad her with what he was capable of. He would pull her face toward him so that her eyes could not avoid him, and he would laugh.

"You will never be as strong or as fast as I am, Essa" was his taunt. "You cannot escape me."

She had no idea how old he was or how long he had been fighting for money, nor if the sadism came with the job. He told stories of coup attempts, of murder, of violence. That he was a killer she had no doubt, but she held everything else suspect.

Relief came from making runs to Kribi or Douala for supplies, or while on a delivery. They traveled to Kribi by boat, using Francisco's trawler and leaving the faster cigarette boats behind. On a delivery, during the two or three days it would take to motor or trek through the jungle on remote, soggy footpaths, she would be left alone to do her job, and when it was over, the torment would start up worse than before.

Knowing that escape was impossible, she subsisted on thoughts of revenge, and hearing Francisco and Pieter argue had given her hope. If there was a disagreement, Pieter might leave.

And with that thought her throat constricted, cut off the air, and she struggled to breathe.

It would not be beyond Pieter to force her to go with him. Her hands began to shake, and her mind raced. She was worthless to Pieter. If it was convenient, he would just as easily dump her overboard as rape her. But she was worth a tremendous amount to Francisco, and spite would be reason enough for Pieter to haul her out of the camp. The argument turned to shouts.

And then Pieter stormed out of Francisco's structure and headed for the mangrove swamp that led to the boats. Darkness was coming, and the wind blew stronger, thunder drew nearer; the rain wasn't far away.

She hadn't thought; she'd merely acted. She traced her way back to her bed and the stashed tranquilizer gun that no one else had use for and that Jean Noel had let her keep. She knew the routes as well, if not better, than Pieter, and she circled behind him, walking barefoot through the sludge, following from afar, alert, cautious not only of Pieter but of the elements. The last thing she needed now was to run into a mamba or any other poisonous creature that infested the lowlands. She would need to have a perfect shot, couldn't risk getting close; he was faster and stronger, and if she missed, she was dead.

His back to her, he untied the mooring of his boat. If he planned to leave in this weather, he would be preoccupied with getting out as quickly as possible, and so she risked shortening the distance. She crept closer until she could clearly see him. Aimed. Fired.

The discharge, like nearing thunder, shattered the stillness of the jungle.

The dart hit Pieter between his shoulder blades. He stumbled and fell to his knees. When she was certain it had begun to take effect, she moved closer, fired the second for good measure, and then stood over him, one foot on either side of his body. His eyes rolled up in their sockets. She drew a knife and paused; the words of the Old Testament screamed, *Thou shalt not kill.*

She pulled his head back, knelt on his chest, and slit his throat. The blood gushed from his veins in spurts like a broken fountain staining her. She watched him bleed and felt nothing, then let his head drop to the ground, stood over him, and whispered, *"The race is not to the swift, nor battle to the strong, nor yet favor to men of skill; time and chance happens to them all."*

She couldn't leave him on the path; better to drag him into the jungle and let the animals have his body. She went to his boat and checked the fuel supplies. It was enough to get to Douala if she emptied every extra storage container. She brought the engine to life and guided the boat upstream. With Pieter Willem gone, nobody would look for it—she needed to sort out the options.

The rain began to come. It started in slow, large drops of water, and the downpour intensified until the torrent was powerful enough to sting. By the time she crept back to the camp, darkness had long enshrouded the jungle, and she dripped water. There was not a sign of blood on her;

the rain had washed away the evidence. She shed her wet clothes, and climbed through the mosquito netting to her bed, where she curled in the fetal position and wept with racking sobs.

WHEN MUNROE FINALLY stood and left the rooftop, the first taste of sunlight had ushered the sky into hues of violet, and the bustle on the city streets shouted that the day had already begun. The internal voices were only whispers now; they'd bled themselves dry through the night.

How many passages were tumbling inside her head? She'd lost count. She had her father to thank—or curse—for every one of the verses that bubbled into consciousness. *Father.*

There had once been awe, inspiration, maybe love, always the desire for his approval, although it came in small conditional doses. On the rare occasions that he was around, his sole interest seemed to lie in the Book, and so she'd studied it, memorized it, and, like a monkey for an organ grinder, recited it to gain attention and praise. Mother wasn't much better, alcoholic that she'd become.

Life in Africa was sluggish, her mother had once said, moving like a languid fan stirring hot, stale air in circles; time lost meaning. The scarcity of amenities, convenience, and infrastructure added to the asperity of life.

For all the pieces of history Munroe was short on, one thing she knew: Her middle-aged parents hadn't expected another child when they'd taken the call as missionaries to Cameroon, and if there was ever a mistake, she had been it.

And so she'd grown up untamed, the local children as playmates, her playground the dirt roads that wound through the small hillside town. She ran with the others, ragtag and barefoot, kicking deflated soccer balls toward imaginary goals and jumping out of the way of the occasional car or share taxi. She hauled water from the creek with her friends and learned to pound cassava and cook in large aluminum pots on open fires behind their homes. She knew the native plants that passed for vegetables and sometimes sold fruit at the local market. She spoke their language and understood their customs.

Unlike the others, her house had air-conditioning, refrigeration, a maid, and a cook. Her father had a full-time driver, and there was a gardener who kept the aggressive foliage from reclaiming the property. All this until Munroe was thirteen, and her parents, in the ultimate act of pretending to care, sent her to Douala to be educated at the American School. It was a personalized version of boarding school, where meals and nights were spent with friends of the family. And there, at first behind her parents' backs and later as blatantly as possible, she began to run wild; biblical passages were all she possessed of home, hollow words that translated into abandonment by parents more interested in saving the lost than their own flesh and blood.

Munroe let out a sigh as she passed Bradford's room. His door was open, and although she didn't see him, she knew that he was aware of her having been gone for the night. Chances were he'd spent the same sleepless hours guarding the landing that led to the roof. She didn't bother returning to her room with subtlety; she merely opened the door and headed for the shower.

CHAPTER 7

They shared an uneasy truce, Bradford mostly silent as he accompanied Munroe about town. It may have been his way of giving space, although he was more likely nursing a grudge. If there was going to be payback, Munroe was confident it would come only after the hunt for Emily had ended, and so, over a late lunch, attempting to make nice and bring back some of the rapport they'd previously shared, she handed him an air ticket to Malabo.

"It's where we go next," she said, "Bioko Island, Equatorial Guinea."

Bradford took the booklet and flipped through the pages.

"Ever been there?" she asked.

He placed the ticket on the table and with a half smile said, "Nope. But it's where Titan has its oil wells."

Munroe said nothing and then, after a moment of silence, "It's odd that none of the reports mentioned that."

"Is it a problem?"

"I don't know." She ran her fingers through her hair and then folded her hands and placed her chin on them. "It does seem a freakish coincidence."

His eyes moved from the paper on the table up to hers. "What do you mean?"

"I suspect that Emily disappeared along the Equatorial Guinean–Gabonese border."

Bradford took in a deep breath and let it out slowly. He sat back in his chair, silent for a moment, and then leaned in toward her. "I know the rules, and I'm not questioning your judgment, but I have questions."

She nodded.

He was quiet again, head down, and then he looked up. "I was there, Michael, I was part of the team. I've seen the reports, I've spoken to people who saw her before she disappeared. How do you make the leap from Namibia to Equatorial Guinea?"

"I have information that others didn't have—a copy of Kristof Berger's passport, for one. I also grew up in this area, spent a number of years in Equatorial Guinea, Gabon, Congo, and the DRC, which was Zaire back then, so I know the history and legends in a way most don't."

"Why am I not surprised?" he said.

"How familiar are you with local history and politics?"

"Richard told me about Cameroon and Gabon, so I've done some research. Not a lot, but some. He didn't mention Equatorial Guinea."

"As an American, you don't need a visa to get into Equatorial Guinea, so I didn't bring it up. It's a strange and paranoid little country—anyone from around here who has lived there will tell you the same thing. Have you ever read Frederick Forsyth's book *The Dogs of War*?"

"Heard of it, never read it. Should I have included it in my research?"

She smiled wryly. "It's fiction, Miles, unless you believe the rumors. It's about a group of mercenaries who get hired to take over a small country when big business realizes it's cheaper than paying for mineral rights."

He nodded his appreciation of the idea and ran his finger around the rim of his glass.

"Forsyth was in Malabo when he wrote the book. No guess as to where he got the idea. Naturally, the book is banned in EG, although that makes no sense. It's the rest of the world that poses the threat." She picked up her glass and took a long drink, then continued. "A few years ago, a group of mercenaries nearly succeeded in turning the book into reality. They got busted purchasing arms in Zimbabwe."

"I remember," he said. "What a fiasco that was. Wasn't it Margaret Thatcher's son who pled guilty to financing the plot?"

"Exactly," she said. "Since then Equatorial Guinea has hired armed forces from Angola for protection, and last I heard, the Israelis are training the Moroccan presidential guard—which is no surprise, since they've been handling training in Cameroon for over a decade. Paranoid. But I digress."

"I understand about Kristof's passport," he said. "Visa stamps, right?"

"Correct."

"What does local history have to do with it?"

"Equatorial Guinea History 101," she said with a chuckle. "It takes some backtracking. Up for it?"

He nodded.

"In 1969, shortly after EG gained independence from Spain, President Macías Nguema claimed the country had been handed over with virtually no currency reserve. That was the start of, or trigger for, deteriorating governmental relations with the Western world and is where the nickname 'Auschwitz of Africa' comes from."

She paused.

"Go on," Bradford said.

"In 1979, the current president, Teodoro Obiang, led a nearly bloodless military coup against his uncle, and here's where local history diverges and the facts differ depending on who you ask: Before Nguema was tracked down and executed, he had taken what remained of the national reserves, supposedly around five million dollars, and buried it in a hut outside his house in his home village. By the time it was dug up, most of it had decomposed. He claimed he'd done it to protect it from thieves. I can't say it's entirely true, because the story changes slightly depending on who's telling it. And," she said with a shrug, "that story is brought to us by the same people who say that Obiang hacked Uncle Macías to death when he found him, while published history says Macías was executed about a month later by hired Moroccans. I tend to believe the latter."

"Why's that?"

"Because Macías Nguema made himself out to be a god and ruled by divine right. The locals believe that he drank the blood of his victims to imbibe their power. The stories of death, torture, and human-rights violations are well enough documented to put some credibility to the rumors. In any case, because of the superstitions surrounding him, I doubt that any of his own people would have done the actual killing— not even Obiang, whom, I might add, the state radio claims can kill with impunity because he is in daily communication with God."

Bradford was quiet for a moment. "So folklore and local history says Nguema buried the country's currency reserves before he died. And this ties in with Emily's disappearing here because . . . ?"

"This begs another question. How familiar are you with the transcripts of Kristof's conversations?"

"Not very."

"There was a phrase he repeated several times to the investigators and that he reiterated to me when I went to see him: 'We went where the money was buried.' It makes no sense taken on its own, but when put together with the country's history and the stamps in his passport . . ." She pointed her finger into the table. "It pinpoints here."

Bradford rubbed his palms over his eyes and let out a long breath. "I see where you're going with this," he said. "But how would Kristof have known the legend, and why would that be the one thing he says to both you and the investigators?"

"That I don't know."

He leaned back until the chair's front legs came off the floor, placed his hands behind his head, and stared up at the ceiling. After a moment he brought the chair down firmly. "So where *is* Nguema's village?"

"Nsangayong. On the eastern edge of the mainland, several miles from the Gabonese border."

"And you think that's where they disappeared?"

"I highly doubt it."

Miles narrowed his eyes and drew his lips tight. He placed the palms of his hands flat on the table, and Munroe wondered then if he might be ready to strangle her. He shook his head slightly, opened his mouth to say something, then shut it again. Finally he said, "If not where the money was buried, then where?"

"Where most people would have *assumed* that the money was buried. Nsangayong is a nondescript hamlet that doesn't even show up on a very good map. My money is on Mongomo, the current president's village, which is a whole lot bigger. It's only a few miles north of Nsangayong and where most people think Macías Nguema was from."

Bradford picked up his ticket and flipped through the stiff pages. "We're flying to Malabo—on the island. That's something of a detour."

She smiled. "Yes and no. The only way to the mainland from here is by sea or road—neither by any form of scheduled transport, so it's a tedious trip no matter how you look at it—and from Malabo we can catch a local flight. But besides that, everybody who's anybody in the country spends the bulk of their time in Malabo, and it's also where the government branches are located. I'd like to make the acquaintance of a few name-droppable people before wending our way to the backwoods of the mainland."

Bradford motioned to the waiter and ordered another drink. He turned to Munroe and nodded in appreciation. "So that's where the indicators point. Not bad for a week's worth of work."

"It helps to know the country and the history," she said, and then, "Miles, are you married?"

He laughed at first, but, realizing that she was serious, he stopped. "Divorced twice, but the second marriage only lasted eight months so it shouldn't count. Are you hitting on me?"

She smirked. "If I decide to hit on you, there will never be a doubt in your mind. In all seriousness, Miles, if you have anyone in your life who's important to you, call that person before we go." She leaned toward him in earnestness. "I know you've survived some pretty rough places, and being around the world as you have, it's easy to believe that one despot-run country is much like another. In most places you'd be right. But Equatorial Guinea is different. Maybe it's the years spent under communism, maybe it's because it's so small and so easily controlled, certainly some of it has to do with attempted coups, but I can't even begin to describe the level of suspicion and paranoia that runs through that country or the power to destroy that the president and his cronies have when you're within their borders.

"We'll be going in there asking questions of people who interpret questions as an insult and a challenge to their authority. If anything we do or say happens to raise the ire of the government, we will more than likely join a long list of 'disappeared.' You know as well as I do that our own government will be useless in helping us out. If you remember the Zimbabwe fiasco, then I'm sure you also know that there was already a ground crew inside Equatorial Guinea, and every person suspected of being a merc or in on the coup plot, whether guilty or not, is either wasting away in prison or has joined journalists and political opponents in front of the firing squad. It would be no different for us."

"Thanks for the heads-up," he said, and then, with a teasing grin, "It can't be all bad. Surely you have at least one good story."

Munroe flashed a smile. "A few hundred miles to the north, Nigeria produces some of the world's highest-grade sweet crude, and to the south is Gabon, another oil-producing country. At the time Cameroon was producing as well, and Equatorial Guinea, communist and dirt poor, managed to acquire short-range missiles." She waved her glass in a wide arc. "Needless to say, when the madman at the helm of that little country got his hands on his own private arsenal of warheads, the neighboring countries were not pleased. Such is the beauty of oil. The United States intervened by putting pressure on the sellers to get the explosives back. Naturally, the Equatoguinean president refused. So the sellers told him that the warheads were reaching their expiration date, and if they didn't get reset, they'd explode."

"So what'd they do when the bombs didn't go off?"

"Oh, the president was smart enough to return the missiles before the 'expiration date,' and that was pretty much end of that."

Miles laughed and chugged down the last of his drink. "You're not going to tell me that's real history."

She shrugged. "I heard it from one of the locals, but who knows?" She drummed the flat of her hands on the table and then stood to go. "You're not taking prophylactics, are you?"

He shook his head.

"Didn't think so. Ever had malaria?"

"Dengue fever, twice."

"Where we're headed, the malaria is particularly lethal." She handed him a small box. "You break a fever, take the pills. They'll keep you alive until we can get you medical treatment."

THERE WAS NO point in taking a taxi when walking would speed up the acclimatization, and so at Munroe's insistence the return to the hotel was on foot. They navigated the pedestrian traffic in silence and had gone nearly half the distance when they passed a storefront advertising phone service. Munroe paused and then, with Bradford following, entered the shop through a swinging half door that served more as a demarcation than anything else.

To Bradford she said, "I want privacy," and he stepped back to the street, leaning against the doorframe, arms crossed.

The interior was narrow, partitioned off from a clothing business that dominated the space. At the front was a counter and beyond the counter a hallway connecting four small pressboard cubicles.

Like the hundreds of similar businesses that dotted the city, the vendor filled the demand left by a national telephone company that took weeks if not months to process a request for phone service and required a deposit equivalent to the average person's yearly earnings for a line with international access.

Munroe chose the cubicle farthest from the front and from there called Kate Breeden. Ignoring an echo that bounced her voice back, she walked Breeden through the assignment to the present, laying out the line of intent for moving into Equatorial Guinea.

"Does Burbank know where you're headed?" Breeden asked.

"I spoke to him before leaving Europe. He knows I'm in Cameroon. He sent a babysitter, so I'm sure he's up to date. When I've got something definite, I'll give him a call, but until then a conversation would waste both of our time."

The primary purpose of the call was a contact arrangement: As long as Munroe was in Equatorial Guinea, she would communicate on a weekly basis. A skipped contact and Breeden should assume that something had gone wrong—it would be the only way for her to know. Breeden held Munroe's will and final instructions; she knew what to do.

The conversation had taken six minutes, and the woman who ran the service charged for nine. Munroe placed payment for seven on the counter and held up her wrist. "I timed it."

"Didn't you know," the woman replied, "time is different in the United States?"

"Every minute in the United States has sixty seconds," Munroe said, "just like it does here in Cameroon." And then, switching to the woman's tribal tongue, "You have your money."

Back on the street, Bradford said, "How many languages do you speak?"

"It's in my file," she replied dryly.

"Yes, I know," he said with a smile. "As an estimate."

"Twenty-two."

He let out a low whistle. "Is that any kind of world record?"

"Another forty and I might start getting close," she said. "Sometimes dialects count, sometimes they don't."

"How do you do it? I mean, outside of Arabic, the one other language that I do speak, I struggle with the bits and pieces. How do you manage so many?"

She shrugged. "I don't know. Language has been with me as far back as I can remember. A blessed curse or a poisoned gift—if you know what I mean."

"No, not really."

She turned toward him. "There was never a time I didn't understand whatever was spoken around me. By six I spoke English, my nanny's tribal tongue Mokpwe, Ibo of our Nigerian-born driver, Fang of the cook and gardener, and French, the language of the country. Then I started picking up dialects, and the locals began to view me with suspicion. They said I was a child witch because I knew things I shouldn't have known—they were afraid of the juju."

"Juju?"

"Witchcraft, power—superstition is very strong in the culture. I was young, I didn't really think much of it—like I said, language had always been with me—and I spent so much time mixing with the locals that it all made sense. But when I was a teenager, I moved to Douala and a wider social circle. Within a couple of months, I'd added Greek and Arabic to the mix, and by then I realized I was different."

"I'm surprised you didn't end up working for the NSA or the CIA or one of the other alphabet-soup organizations."

"I noticed that was absent in my file as well."

"What was?"

"The recruitment attempts and job offers."

"I take it you turned them down."

She gave a sarcastic laugh. "They don't pay as well."

"Hey," he said, "where's your sense of patriotism?"

She grew quiet and turned the question around in her head and then rolled it out in a whisper. "Patriotism?" She looked at him. "How many years were you in the armed forces, Miles?"

"Felt like half a lifetime."

She nodded. "You and every person who serves merits thanks and commendation, and you most certainly have it." She was silent for a moment. "I can appreciate patriotism, but that's about as far as it goes. I'm not like most people," she said. "I have no devotion or affinity to any particular country—for that I assume I'd have to experience a sense of belonging." She looked at him and searched his eyes for an indication that he understood, then added, "Patriots defend their homeland, Miles. Where is my home?"

"What do you mean? You're an American."

"Am I?" she asked. "What makes me an American? That I carry an American passport?"

"Well, partly that. It's also where your family is from."

"But is it where I'm from?" She sighed. "I was born here in Cameroon. Spent nearly eighteen years living here or around the borders, but I'm not Cameroonian. I understand the Turkish language and culture even better than I understand the American culture. But I'm not Turkish. I carry passports from three countries, have lived in thirteen, and speak twenty-two languages. To which country," she asked, "should I be patriotic? To which do I belong?"

"Which one do you identify with the most?"

She stared at him. "None of them." And then, regretting that she had said so much, changed the subject. "You didn't make any calls when we were at the phone vendor."

"Don't read too much into it," he said. "The people in my life know that what I do can be dangerous. I made my peace before I took the assignment."

"Did you realize what you were getting yourself into when you took it?"

The corners of his mouth turned slightly upward.

CHAPTER 8

The package from Boniface Akambe arrived at the hotel five days later by way of a knock on Munroe's door and a small brown envelope hand-delivered by Akambe's eldest son. While the teenager sat silent on the bedside chair, Munroe placed her original against the forgeries, brushed her fingertips along their faces, and then angled them against the light. Satisfied, she tipped the young courier and sent him on his way.

And then, alone, on the edge of the bed, elbows to knees, she tapped the packet against her knuckles. The cards were invitations that beckoned a return to the past. She tightened her fist around the envelope. Fuck it. It was one step closer to Emily Burbank and five million dollars, and maybe a clean break from the madness in her head.

She shoved off the bed and headed across the hall. Bradford opened the door before she knocked, and she moved past him into the room. "Malabo awaits us," she said. She sat on the bed, and next to the notebook that Bradford had lately carried everywhere, laid out four cards. "Your residency permits for Cameroon and Equatorial Guinea."

Bradford moved the book away and then tossed it into his backpack. He flipped the cheap laminate of a Guinean residency to and fro. "It seems so homemade."

"Probably is," she said, "just like the real ones." She paused. "Look,

Miles, I know you're no stranger to dangerous places, and again, I really don't want to insult your intelligence. Humor me."

Still looking at the cards, he said, "I march to your orders."

"You may not need the Cameroonian pieces. In Equatorial Guinea you'll be asked to show documents regularly, and police and military often confiscate them for ransom. Better these than your passport—whatever you do, don't let them have your passport. The residencies list you as a diplomat, so if it comes down to it, they should keep you from being hauled into a police station."

Bradford returned the cards to the bed and with a playful smile said, "And if they demand to see my passport or I'm hauled off anyway?"

"Well," she said, and blew out an exaggerated sigh, "since your job is to stick by my side, I doubt you'll end up in a situation that I can't talk you out of." She smiled. "But if you still manage to get yourself thrown in jail, then you can figure out how to get your own self out."

"Well, thank you," he said, and winked at her.

She stood. "It's too bad you've been hired to be a pain in the ass, Miles. Under other circumstances I think I'd rather like you."

"That doesn't count as flirting, does it?"

"No," she said. She walked to the door and turned to look at him before closing it behind her. Maybe under other circumstances.

THE FLIGHT WAS scheduled to depart in thirty minutes, and even by African standards the check-in procedure was moving slowly. Bradford glanced at his watch, the same stealthy flick of the wrist he'd been making for the last hour. Munroe placed a hand on his. "We'll be fine," she said.

At the front of the line, two women haggled with airline personnel over weight and piece allowances. Next to them a cardboard box, taped and tied with twine, leaked a sticky mess over the concrete floor, and the translucent walls of a zippered bag hinted of an assortment of vegetables and clucking chickens.

Bradford pulled the notebook from his backpack and scribbled across a page, the same rapid, illegible scrawl he'd been putting down since they'd arrived in Cameroon. Munroe angled herself to look over his arm. He winked and then deliberately turned to shield the page. Another line and half a minute later, he shut the book and shoved it back into his pack.

The local flight lifted off from Douala two hours late, with no apology from the airline or expectations of such from the passengers, only relief when the ventilation system kicked in, dissipating the odors of garlic and bush meat and bodies packed too closely together.

From the air, Malabo was a white-and-red swath that notched a piece of the coastline, a breach in the carpet of deep green that otherwise bordered the sea and rose into the mountains, and the fifteen-minute flight seemed a mockery in the face of the three-hour ordeal that had come before.

On the ground, evidence of change was everywhere. Hangars and new buildings carried signs of life and industry in place of overgrown vegetation and burned-out aircraft that had previously stood sentinel over a deserted runway.

Their passports were stamped without question. Women customs officers searched methodically through their belongings while armed military personnel stood watch in uniforms less tattered than Munroe remembered, and with weaponry more sophisticated.

Outside, while taxi operators clamored for attention, Munroe's focus was jolted by a man who stood in her peripheral vision.

He was near the terminal doors, one foot propped against the wall, a neglected cigarette in his fingers and on the ground the used remains of nearly a pack. When she made eye contact, he averted his gaze. She settled into the taxi, turned again toward the building, but he was gone.

The taxi picked up speed, and heat blew through the open windows. It was a two-kilometer stretch into the capital. Streetlights lined the median of well-paved tarmac, and along the road on either side were warehouses and container yards, businesses and buildings, all new and nicely maintained.

It was impressive change for the little country, which ten years prior had a tin-topped terminal connected to the city by a swampy, potholed road that ran through encroaching jungle and detoured over a marshy creekbed because the one-lane bridge had fallen apart.

The driver took them to the Bahia, the best hotel the city had to offer: three stories, clean and cool, and situated at the end of a small peninsula overlooking a panoramic view of the ocean. Inside the lobby the desk clerk was absent, and at the far left wall the bartender slept with his head on the bar. The quiet was broken by the hum of an air conditioner.

Munroe called out, and after a moment a woman shuffled in from a room off to the side, sleepy-eyed and with a look of annoyance. From under the front counter, she pulled out a transaction book, flipped indifferently through the pages to the day's date, and with deliberate tedium wrote into the book their names and passport information. After taking the money for two rooms, she informed them that the hotel had only one room vacant and that the second could be acquired that evening.

The room was clean and spartan, the bathroom bare, without even the customary bar of wafer-thin soap, but unlike lesser hotels here there was a roll of toilet paper and, besting the rest of the city, running water supplied by giant tanks that sat on the roof.

Munroe watched from the bedroom door as Bradford walked the length of the hallway noting ingress and egress and scoping the surrounding area from the windows. "If the second room is on another floor," he said, "we need to share space."

She shrugged and pushed off from the doorway. "We can discuss it," she said, "if it happens."

The restaurant was closed until evening, so they left the hotel in search of a meal and found the city quiet, streets and sidewalks empty as if the entire population had gone to sleep or simply disappeared in the middle of the day. A steady breeze blew in off the ocean, mixing with diesel fumes and mildew and the stench of garbage left rotting in the sun.

Malabo was a mixture of once-beautiful Spanish architecture, with its porticoes and colonnades that had somehow endured nearly half a century of abuse and neglect, and a jarring contrast of newer cinder-block buildings—assorted shapes and angles slapped together in any space wide enough to fit them.

At four, restaurants and grocery stores reopened, and the city's small matrix of one-way streets—originally constructed to accommodate horses and carriages, now paved and potholed—returned to a state of gridlock, unable to bear the burden of vehicles brought on by the rapid influx of money.

The face of the city changed with the setting of the sun. Streets that ran along the oceanfront hosted a series of hole-in-the-wall bars unnoticeable during the day but that, like those in a navy town, came alive for the evening. They filled with foreigners from the oil industry, and where the foreign men went, the local women followed, fawning over them, drinking with them, and, more often than would be readily admitted, accompanying them home for the night.

Away from the artery of the city, where the money flowed less freely, where the streets were dark without electricity and the population dense and overcrowded, the faces were different but the scene the same. Life and vitality and laughter came with the darkness. Cheap Cameroonian beer ran plentiful, while meals were prepared over outdoor fires and small children played in the empty streets.

There, at an open-air bar, barely discernible but for the crowd around it, Munroe and Bradford sat on rough-hewn wooden chairs around a makeshift table that had been covered in a red-and-white plastic laminate. Munroe leaned her head back and closed her eyes, breathing in the essence of the city.

They had come to this part of town only because Bradford couldn't dissuade her from it and she would have gone without him. He was alert, measuring the threat, judging the crowd; it was evident in the tightness that ran along his neck.

Eyes still closed, she said, "Miles, you can relax."

"I'm not paid to relax," he said.

She smiled, ignored him, and allowed surrounding conversations to swallow her. A few moments later, a discussion at the periphery brought Munroe upright, and she angled slightly to observe.

On a bench just at the edge of her line of sight, two men were joined by a third—the same man so focused on her at the airport. Like the two on the bench, he was young, probably early twenties, and like the others, he was dressed in casual slacks. Hanging off his belt were two cell phones.

Threads of the conversation lifted on the breeze. The men spoke in Fang of many things, including her and her companion, but the details wafted away. When the men had each drunk several beers, Munroe turned to Bradford and suggested another part of town.

They walked in the direction of the ocean through streets dark and devoid of cars. Along the sidewalks, on steps, and in doorways, people clustered, their laughter and conversation streaked by light and bathed in music that filtered from open windows.

The chatter that followed in Munroe and Bradford's wake told of humor in finding foreigners in this part of town. They were occasionally called out to, and several times children ran up asking for sweets.

Non-police street crime, like everything else in Equatorial Guinea, was rapidly increasing. Even so, compared to any city of its size in the surrounding countries, Malabo was relatively safe. Munroe felt and heard no threat, though her reassurances did little to set Bradford at ease. His posture said that he was prepared for an attack from any of the dark shadows they passed.

Unlike Bradford, she was not concerned about street thugs.

They found another watering hole, this one frequented by as many foreigners as locals and run by a Chinese matron and her daughter. Several minutes after they were seated, the young men from the previous bar arrived. They were now two instead of three, and when they sat at a half-empty table, the hostess treated them deferentially.

Munroe watched Bradford's body language and knew that he, too, was aware of having been followed. He turned to her, and she nodded a silent acknowledgment of what he didn't say. They sat and drank, and when she'd had enough of observing and being observed, they returned to the hotel and retrieved the key to the second room.

Bradford stopped her at the threshold of her door. "When did you first pick them up?"

She opened the door, held it for him to enter, and said, "One at the airport, two at the first bar."

"Do you know who they are?"

She pulled off her shoes and tossed them against the bed. "No idea."

He stared toward the window. "I don't like it."

"Of course not," she said. "You're not paid to like it."

He gave a humorless smirk, paused, and said, "Did you make out much of what they were saying?"

"Not enough to be of value." She stripped off her sweat-dried shirt and draped it over the back of a chair. The sports bra underneath was equally drenched, but that would wait until Bradford was gone.

He was silent, and she followed his eyes to her arms and abdomen, where slivers of white reflected the neon light of the room.

"Forty-two of them," she said. "If you must know."

"I'm sorry," he said. He raised his eyes to meet her stare. "I'm not usually surprised like that. I thought . . ." His voice trailed to silence.

"Your file isn't as complete as you imagined it was," she said. And then she grinned.

He scratched the back of his head. "The men following us . . ."

She nodded. "They're dressed well. They aren't military or police, which is a relief. What's puzzling, maybe troubling, is that, waiting as the first man was, they had to be expecting our arrival—or else we've been mistaken for someone else."

"What about being set up for a hit?"

She sat on the edge of the bed and looked up at him. "Seriously? I think that if they intended to relieve us of our meager worldly possessions, they would have made the attempt when we were conveniently on the wrong side of town."

She paused and then stood. "If I pick up even a wisp of information, Miles, I'll be sure to let you know." With that, she opened her door and motioned her head toward it.

THE MINISTRY OF Foreign Affairs was an aging colonial structure that had been gutted and renovated and somehow through the process had come out looking tacky through improvements. The building was shaped like a lowercase *n*, the bottom floor tiled and open for people and vehicles to pass through to an overgrown courtyard. On the left and up a flight of stairs, they found the office of the minister. It was eight in the morning.

The minister's secretary sat at a metal desk that was bare but for a half-sharpened pencil, a ballpoint pen missing its cap, and a well-worn notebook. From her they learned that appointments were made on a daily basis—first come, first served—and provided that the minister was in town, he might or might not take the time to see those who waited for him. She was able to confirm that as of yesterday he was in town, but she had no idea if he would be at the office today or tomorrow, or for that matter any day at all. She motioned to a cracked vinyl sofa and suggested that they sit and see.

Munroe sat, stretched out, and leaned back with closed eyes. Without the distraction of sight, she heard things otherwise missed: conversations in the background, whispers in the hallways, and the continuous scratch of Bradford's pen on paper.

She would wait today, tomorrow, as long as it took, within reason. She held no illusions as to how much information the ministry would provide even if they had it available; information was not the foremost purpose of the appointment. After Malabo the search would shift to parts of the country where few unaccompanied foreigners went. Meeting the minister would lay the groundwork to dispel suspicion of their movements and to provide the means to name-drop if necessary.

Over the course of the morning, several more appointment hopefuls joined the room. The hum of nearby air-conditioning units filled the silence, although in the foyer, where they waited, there was only heat and humidity, which the elevated ceilings did little to alleviate. By midmorning their shirts were heavy with perspiration. By early afternoon the minister had not shown up, and the secretary rose to leave, suggesting to those waiting that they try again at three or four.

Outside the building, mingling with a group of men loitering in the shade, was one of the men who had followed them last night. When they passed, he trailed behind. He was an amateur at best; his shadow nearly blended with theirs as he kept pace. They nicknamed him Shadow Two, caught a cab back to the hotel, and at three returned to the ministry, where they spent the afternoon as they had the morning: on the vinyl sofa, in the heat, waiting for an audience.

It was shortly after four when Munroe sat up from her half-prone position. "He's on his way in," she whispered.

The bustle started at the bottom of the wide stairwell and increased in volume as the minister, followed by a small entourage, breezed through the hallway leading to the foyer. He was on the phone, ignoring the few who followed, and in the waiting area he stopped, nodded, and then retreated to his office, where he remained for an hour before leaving again, apparently finished for the day. When he and his retinue had gone, the secretary picked up a purse from behind the desk and to the small waiting crowd said, "Try again tomorrow." And then she left the building.

The crowd filtered out, and Munroe stood and stretched, breaking up the kinks in her neck. She turned to Bradford. "Let's go get dinner."

He tucked his pen into the notebook and put it away. "How would you rate today?" he asked. "A total wash?"

"Not in the least," she said, twisting sideways until her spine popped. "The discussions in the waiting area were fascinating." She waited a beat and then laughed when his face clouded over. "Waiting is a part of life here, Miles. There's no point in trying to rush it. In the meantime I listen, observe, and learn. We're in no hurry."

They walked in the direction of the hotel, and when they rounded the block toward the coast, caught sight of Shadow One, the man from the airport.

As they neared the coastal avenue that functioned as the city's main artery, the sidewalks were crowded and there was an unusual level of police activity. Whistles shrilled through the distance, and makeshift barricades blocked vehicles from entering the street.

Preferring to avoid contact with the local police if at all possible, Munroe flagged a taxi. The driver shook his head at her request and rattled off an explanation before driving away.

"The president is passing through," Munroe said to Bradford. "The city is basically shut down—roads to the airport, the port, anything across the main street as well. Could be an hour, ten hours, two days, or who knows until it clears, so we walk. If anyone talks to us or asks us for our papers, don't say a word. Do you have your Guinean residency handy?"

Bradford nodded.

"Okay," she said, waited a beat, and then, "Let's go."

On each of the corners that connected the street to the coastal avenue, police officers clustered into groups of three and four, their demeanor shifting from attentive to festive and back again. Very few carried firearms or had access to a vehicle, their sole power appearing to lie in whistles and citation booklets. Munroe and Bradford passed, and the officers, more focused on traffic than on pedestrians, paid little attention to them. They had reached the other side and were nearly beyond the road leading down into the port when an officer blew his whistle.

"Ignore him," Munroe said under her breath. "Don't even turn around."

The whistle blew again, and they kept walking. It was only after the officer yelled in their direction, commanding the two *blancos* to stop, that Munroe slowed and threw Bradford a warning glance.

chapter 9

Two officers walked toward them with brisk strides, navy blue uniforms frayed at the hems, ill-fitting and spotted with stains. The older of the two wore a piece of industrial cord as a belt and, in addition to the whistle, carried a black baton-shaped stick slipped through a makeshift loop on his pants. He didn't stop until he had invaded nearly all of Bradford's personal space, and then he said loudly, "You must obey the law, you must obey!" and demanded to see Bradford's papers.

"He speaks no Spanish," Munroe said, and the officer, inches from her face and smelling of cheap beer, commanded that she interpret.

He examined Bradford's residency card and after a few moments handed it back and demanded to see Munroe's. He looked it over and then gave a grunt and waved it in her face. "Your residency is invalid," he said as if in triumph. "You have only two names. You are here illegally."

Munroe stared at the ground, bit down hard on her lip, and, when the urge to laugh had passed, looked into his eyes and with a voice full of humility said, "I apologize for having only two names. Sadly for me, I was only given two names at birth. It's not unusual where I come from."

The officer's face darkened, and he placed a hand on his baton. "It doesn't matter how things are done in your country. You are in the

Republic of Equatorial Guinea, and you will respect the way of our land and our laws. You have only two names. Your residency is invalid."

"I understand what you are saying," she said, "but I was only given two names, and the representative who signed my permit understood this."

The officer scowled and said again, "You are here illegally. The law provides peace to the republic, and foreigners must also abide by it." With slow and deliberate movements, he placed the card in his chest pocket. "Present yourself at the police station tomorrow morning. Until that time I will retain your document." Then, with the younger officer following, he walked stiffly to the cordoned-off avenue.

Bradford watched them go and in a whisper said to Munroe, "What was that all about?"

She hooked her arm in his, drew him around in the direction of the hotel, and started walking. "That," she said, "was an example of why this country is what it is. No matter how much the well-intended try to intervene or how much oil is pumped out of the ground, some things are unchangeable or made worse by the presence of money. When nepotism is de rigueur, today's goatherd becomes tomorrow's despot, and a shiny new whistle and a used uniform are all it takes to create a new tyrant."

She looked over her shoulder toward the officer who stood again on a corner with three others dressed in blue. "The laws are arbitrary. It's fine to drink and drive, but you'll be cited for having a dirty vehicle. It's illegal for you to offer a bribe but permissible for them to accept one. According to him I've broken a law by having only two names." She sighed in quiet amusement. "As for us, the only thing to do is flow with it and do our best to stay out of trouble."

"Are you going to try to get it back?"

"The residency card? Nah. If I want it back, I'll need to spend the better part of tomorrow and possibly the rest of the week at the police station attempting to figure out who has it and what hoops I have to jump through for it—not to mention shelling out a small fortune." She gave his arm a playful squeeze. "I had the cards made so that I wouldn't have to deal with that in the first place."

They stayed in the hotel that evening, Munroe preferring to avoid another encounter with the police while the city was cordoned off. Instead of roaming the streets and socializing with the locals, they dined on the hotel's patio, where each of the umbrella-capped tables hosted its own assortment of oil-related patronage.

When the waiter came to clear the table, Munroe stopped him and nodded toward the far end of the dining area, where two of the Shadows nursed imported Spanish beer and occasionally passed a furtive glance in their direction. "Do you know them?" she asked.

He followed the direction of the nod and then, looking back at the table, said, "Perhaps it would be better not to know them."

She requested three of what they drank, and when the waiter returned with the beer, she took the cans and stood to leave the table. As she did, Bradford stopped her with a hand on her forearm.

"Where're you going?" he said.

The warmth of his fingers wrapped around her skin, and Munroe's vision blurred to gray. She waited a heartbeat and took a breath, then leaned down toward him, looked him full in the face, and said softly, "I'll tell you this once, Miles, because I like you. Touch me that way again and I swear I'll break every one of your fingers."

He removed his hand. "I'm sorry," he said. "Bad habit."

"To answer your question," she whispered, "I want to know who they are and what they want." And then she straightened and walked across the patio to where the Shadows sat.

She stood in front of the men with a smile of demure innocence. In Spanish she said, "I've seen you around town," and then, placing the beer on the table, "Can I join you for a drink?"

There was a moment of silence. Without waiting for an answer, she pulled out a chair, and with a teasing glance in the direction of the one who'd been so focused on her at the airport, she sat. She leaned toward him with girlish coyness and stuck out her hand. "I'm Michael."

After a second's hesitation, he took her hand and returned the smile. "Nicolas."

His hands were small and thick, and the grip was solid. He wore a heavy gold ring and on his wrist a Fendi watch. Across the table his companion sat with arms crossed, and in Fang he whispered a warning. Nicolas said nothing and instead turned to Munroe and motioned toward his companion. "My cousin Teodoro." She flirted in Teodoro's direction, offered her hand, and said sweetly, "Are you scared of me?"

Both men laughed. It was a nervous laugh, but it was the opening she needed. She pushed a beer at each of them, then popped the top of her own and raised it in a mock toast.

They drank, and she engaged them with harmless questions about life in the city. In turn they asked about Bradford.

"Is he your boyfriend?"

She gave a playful smile. "No, he's not."

"Your husband?"

A pout. "Not that either."

"Are you married?"

Raised eyebrows and wide eyes. "Are you looking for a wife?"

Laughter.

Munroe ordered a second round of drinks. Behind her, Bradford sat, leaned back in the chair with his arms draped loosely across his stomach, legs stretched out under the table. His eyes were half closed, and though to anyone who might have noticed he appeared pleasantly relaxed, to Munroe he screamed attentiveness. She ignored him.

For the fourth round of drinks, Munroe switched to distilled alcohol, knowing that the boys were used to chasing beer with the harder stuff. During village celebrations, half-filled glasses would be refilled with the nearest bottle, lending to mixtures of vodka, whiskey, wine, and more—she would bring it on.

A few more rounds and Munroe shifted the conversation from the mundane to their homes and families. Children? Yes. Wives? Only Nicolas. Teodoro could still not afford to buy one—pay the dowry rather—but he had girlfriends and children. Brothers and sisters? Many. Famous parents? A chuckle. Maybe one day.

"You speak Fang," she said. "Are you from the mainland?"

"Yes. From a large village, an important village."

She smiled in adoration. "The most important village in the country?"

Laughter. "Of course."

Shock. "But nobody's village could be more important than the president's village."

"That is our home!"

Pay dirt.

The questions continued, friendly and noninvasive: the landscape, the animals, the tribal customs, each innocent detail building on top of the last as she constructed a composite picture of the Mongomo area, of the roads, military presence, and security on the mainland, knowing what to expect and what had changed. After the boys had put away their eighth round, her questions shifted to why they'd been following her, and at that, Nicolas stood and excused himself and Teodoro followed suit.

The conversation was over.

Munroe watched them stroll across the patio, their walk not quite as coordinated as it had been when they'd come in, and once they passed through the doors leading out to the front of the hotel, her posture tightened and the look on her face changed. The charade was done, the information gleaned far beyond what she would have hoped to gain, all but the most critical piece. She returned to the table, where Bradford still sat stretched out with half-shut eyes. "With both of them drunk and gone," she said, "Shadow Three will soon be in the vicinity. I'm heading to bed."

He tilted his head back to look at her. "Sit with me? I have a question."

She pulled a chair from the table. He was silent for a moment, his eyes studying her, and she sat quietly, watching in return. Finally he spoke. "Why do you do it?"

He gave a breathy chuckle, ran his fingers through his hair, and leaned forward. His expression straightened. "Why debase yourself, put on that doe-eyed doll act, the performance? I don't get it. You're one of the most brilliant people I know. To watch you stoop to that level, it's so . . . I don't know . . . insulting . . . painful."

"If I'm making an ass out of myself, I'm the one who's the fool—why should it bother you?"

He shrugged.

Munroe sat forward in her chair, mirroring his position. "Listen, Miles, there are a lot of things in my life I'm not proud of, but tonight certainly wasn't among them. I do whatever it takes to get the information I need to be able to do my job, and the doe-eyed doll act, as you

.put it, was what those guys would respond to. It's why I'm paid what I'm paid to do what I do—the information I need is out there, and I will *always* find a way to get it. Tonight was child's play."

She stood to go and then placed her hands on his shoulders, bent down, and whispered in his ear, "I know just as well as you do why it bothers you, Miles." And she walked away.

LIFE IN THE tiny capital started before dawn in preparation for the coming of the water. It was accumulated in the mountains during the night and then released to flow through the pipes of the city. By seven or eight, the stream trickled into droplets and the faucets ran dry, and whatever water remained, collected in buckets and containers, would have to last until the next release. Those living in more elevated areas would be fortunate to collect enough water to bathe, wash dishes, and flush toilets. For a country with one of the highest rainfalls in the world, water in the capital city was a scarce commodity.

At eight, Munroe and Bradford hailed a taxi for the five-minute trip to the ministry. The blockades that had shut down the city the day before were gone, and the narrow roads were already teeming with life.

They were not the first to arrive in the foyer of the minister's office; an elderly woman, no doubt recently arrived from a village, sat at one end of the sofa. She wore a bright floral-patterned dress that had obviously been kept and cared for over many years. Her shoes were from another era, laced-up leather, worn and resoled, clean and polished. Her hands, gnarled from decades of hard work, lay folded in her lap.

The woman hailed from the mainland, a survivor, one of the few left from the missing generation, those who somehow managed to survive the genocide of Macías Nguema and his decade of terror. Through the waiting of the morning, she graced Munroe with stories rich in history and legend.

It was nearly noon when the minister arrived. He was without his entourage, and as he passed through the foyer, he nodded at Munroe and Bradford. A short while later, the secretary directed the two of them toward the closed door of his office, and the elderly woman remained on the sofa, silent, giving no protest that her turn to speak to the great man had been overlooked.

When the minister received them, he remained seated behind a large wooden desk. His handshake was as soft as his hands, and he wore a tailored Italian suit. He spoke in English, his voice dry and raspy. He gestured for them to sit in the chairs facing his desk—plush and antique, upholstered in well-worn deep red velvet.

Having dispensed with the pleasantries and ample humility and praise for the Republic of Equatorial Guinea, Munroe handed him a photo of Emily Burbank followed by a sheet of paper with Emily's physical data. "We are looking for a friend of ours," she said. "She has been missing for a while, and we have reason to believe that she is or was in Río Muni, possibly in the Mongomo area. Knowing the reliability of your government and the care with which you treat foreign visitors, we had hoped that Your Excellence would know something of our friend, perhaps having received word about her. We are checking with you first before traveling ourselves."

He took the photo, looked it over intently, and followed with an air of disinterest. Then, while he gazed indifferently at it, he said, "How long ago did she enter the country?"

"We're not certain of the exact date," Munroe replied. "About four years ago."

"It's a long time," he said. "So many things can happen in four years. I wasn't the head of this ministry four years ago."

"I understand."

"And her purpose for entry? Which company was she working for, or perhaps a church?"

"She was here as a tourist," Munroe replied. "At least that is what we understand."

"Do you mind if I keep this?" he said, and then, without waiting for a reply, tucked the photo and the sheet of paper into his breast pocket. He eased back in his chair. "Nothing comes readily to mind, and I make no promises, but I can have my people look into it and then get back to you. I would suggest you return tomorrow morning. I will be in the office by nine."

They left the foyer for the stairs, and on the ground floor was the minister's H2, black and shiny, parked under the center of the building. Munroe stopped in front of it and stared at her reflection in a window.

"What do you want to bet that vehicle is the only one of its kind in the country?"

"Should it matter?" Bradford asked.

Munroe shrugged. "Not to me or you. I'm sure it will to the owner when it comes time for new parts, but who I'd think it would matter to most is the woman on the vinyl sofa upstairs waiting to speak to the great man who before the discovery of oil was just as poor as she is." She turned from the Hummer and walked toward the street. "And he has no driver," she said.

"I suppose that means something?"

"Yes," she said, almost as if to herself. She stopped and turned for a second look, then stared at the ground for a moment. Finally she said, "People of importance are rarely without an entourage or at least a driver. The president came into town yesterday, which means that most of the sycophantic ministers are not even showing up for work today." She was quiet. "He came alone." Another pause. "You know, it's possible he came to the ministry for nothing more than to see us."

THE DOWNPOUR STARTED in the early evening and continued on through the night, a heavy pelting of water that thundered against rooftops and drowned out the sound of all else. By morning the city streets were shallow rivers rushing toward the ocean. Pedestrian traffic was light; when the water's onslaught against shoes and clothing came as much from the ground as it did from the air, only the most desperate ventured into it. And like the population of the city who watched the rain from doorsteps and windows and under porticoes, Munroe stared out the balcony window, debating against returning to the Ministry of Foreign Affairs and knowing that she would go anyway.

By the time they arrived and assumed the position on the sofa that they'd filled for the past two days, they were drenched. The foyer was empty, even the secretary absent. "He won't show up," Munroe said. "When it rains like this, everything shuts down for a de facto holiday. Between the rain—which is over half the year—and all the official holidays, it's surprising any work gets done at all."

Bradford flicked water off his neck. "If you'd told me that at the hotel, I would have worn my bathing suit instead."

"*That* I'd've liked to see."

Without a second's pause, he pulled off his shirt and, wrapping it around his fists, wrung it out. The water joined a puddle by his feet, where a stream of droplets from his pants had already collected. "How long do you plan to keep doing this?" he asked.

Munroe smiled at his torso. "The waiting?"

"Yeah."

"With three weeks until Christmas and then everything shutting down through mid-January, we'll have to get what we can in the next week. If we don't have it by then, we head to the mainland." She paused for a second and then pointed to his legs. "What about wringing out your pants?"

He winked, pulled the damp shirt back over his head, and said, "I don't think so." And then, "What do the people who live here do for entertainment?"

"You've seen the bars—work, drink, and food, that's all there is— and the women—if you're up for a good dose of HIV."

By afternoon the rain had eased slightly. Shortly before the close of the business day, the minister arrived. He was alone, as he had been the day before. From the foyer he invited them directly into his office. He was brusque, formal, and lacking the undertone of friendliness he'd borne toward them the day prior. "I have no new information for you," he said. "But it is possible that Don Felipe, Malabo chief of police, does." On a piece of lined paper, he wrote in a quick scrawl. "A brief letter of introduction," he said. "Take it to him and see what he can do for you."

"Forgive me for asking," Munroe said. "But if our friend was last seen in Río Muni, is it likely that the police on Bioko Island have information?"

"You would have to find that out for yourself. I do know that Don Felipe is also head of the presidential security detail and a confidant of the president. It's possible he has learned things that I am unaware of." He handed Munroe the paper and then stood and took them to the door.

In a pattern that had become more than familiar, they were followed from the ministry to the hotel and again from the hotel to the restaurant. During dinner, on more than one occasion, Munroe caught the eye of one of the Shadows, and in acknowledgment they would smile or nod in return. She saw that they no longer drank alcohol and in response to this had soft drinks and desserts sent to their table.

The next morning she and Bradford located the office of the chief of police in the city's single-story station, an overpacked structure with scuffed and mud-splattered walls. The windows were empty rectangles fenced by open wood-slat shutters, and from them the sound of striking typewriter keys filtered to the outside.

The anteroom to the police chief's office was taken up completely by three desks and an ancient sofa, and the small space that remained was occupied by people waiting to speak with the man. Munroe left the letter of introduction with an aide and returned to the building's bare front entrance. She leaned against an empty space that served as a window and, prepared to wait the better part of the day, watched the passing traffic.

Within minutes a plainclothes officer approached. "I work for Don Felipe," he said. "He is on his way to the station now." He opened a door that connected to the building entrance. "Please wait," he said, and then he left them.

Like the anteroom, the office was filled nearly wall to wall with furniture, the pieces having been pushed so closely together that Munroe's and Bradford's knees touched when they sat. Cut through the wall above a plywood-barricaded, glass-filled window was a boxed air-conditioning unit that almost managed to cool the room but did nothing to erase the stale smell of must that permeated the building.

Don Felipe entered the room accompanied by two young men wearing civilian clothes and holstered sidearms. He carried with him the letter that Munroe had left. He shook their hands, took a seat across from them, and then, almost as an afterthought, offered them coffee. He spoke in brusque, commanding Spanish.

"Silvestre Mba has asked that I help you," he said. "Tell me more about this girl that you are looking for."

Munroe handed Don Felipe another photograph of Emily Burbank, along with a sheet of paper identical to the one she'd given the minister, and, in words similar to those she'd previously used, explained the desire to find Emily.

Don Felipe took the photograph and, as the minister of foreign affairs had done, studied it intently, then handed it to the young man who stood silently to his right. "In the Republic of Equatorial Guinea," he said to Munroe, "we have an illustrious record of wholesome relationships with our guests. We treat all foreigners fairly and properly, and if something ill should befall a man or woman who is in our great country, it is because that person has failed to live by the law. In fact, our president, representative of God to our people, is known as a good friend and a supporter of human rights by your country. There are many things you Americans can learn from us."

Don Felipe lit a cigarette. He leaned back in his chair, one leg crossed over the other. He drew a deep breath and then exhaled the smoke into the room. Taking a second draw, he reached forward and placed the cigarette in the ashtray. "I know of this girl you are looking for," he said. His eyes remained fixed on Munroe. She sat expressionless, holding eye contact, and silence ensued. To the man who stood on his right, Don Felipe spoke in Fang, ordering the retrieval of a document.

When the aide left the room, the silence continued, broken only by his return. He carried with him a small envelope, which he handed to his boss. "I believe," Don Felipe said to Munroe, "that this document brings you to the end of your journey," and he placed it on the coffee table and slid it to her.

Inside was a single piece of paper, which Munroe looked over and then returned to the envelope. Don Felipe ground his cigarette into the ashtray. "The law is supreme in the Republic of Equatorial Guinea," he said. "No person is immune to it. Now that you have the information you came for, I recommend you return to your country."

Munroe nodded. "Thank you for your kindness and your warm welcome," she said, and then, "As I'm sure you are aware, the trip from my country to yours is very long and tiring. I have heard wonderful things about the beaches of Bata and of the animal habitat EQUOFAC. Before returning home, we will vacation for a few days."

Don Felipe rested in the chair. He was silent for a moment, his eyes focused on Munroe. Finally he stood and shook her hand, "All respectful visitors are welcome in our land." He walked with her toward the door and opened it. "It's unfortunate," he said. "Some have entered who are unwelcome—dangerous people from the neighboring countries. My men and I do the best we can to keep the peace. If you choose to stay, that is your decision, but please know we cannot guarantee your protection against such unwelcome elements."

"I thank you for your graciousness and concern," she said. "Your people are blessed to have a protector such as yourself." She turned, and with Bradford ushered out next to her, the door closed.

It would have been less than a ten-minute walk back to the hotel had Munroe opted to go on foot. Instead she flagged a taxi. Bradford raised his eyes in question as she did so, but she offered no explanation. She remained silent for the ride, her head kicked back against the seat, staring up at the roof of the car, and Bradford, too, said nothing.

At the hotel she headed toward her room and would have shut the door without a word if Bradford hadn't placed a hand against it. "Michael, I really want to understand what just happened." She paused and then held the door open for him.

He sat on the chair by her bed, and she walked to the glass door that led to the balcony and stared out the glass. "I didn't catch even half of what went on in there," he said. "What did he give you?"

She was still staring out at nothing. "Emily's death certificate."

Silence filled the room, and after a moment Munroe turned toward Bradford. His shoulders were slumped forward, and his head was in his hands. He ran his fingers through his hair and then straightened. "So she's really dead?" His face was tight and expressionless. "I never supposed that when we got the news it would come so unceremoniously."

Munroe turned again toward the balcony. "That paper is worthless. Trust me, if there was even a remote possibility that the document had value, I'd be out of here in a heartbeat—job over, mission accomplished—collecting a fat bonus for providing hard evidence of what happened to Emily." She turned to Bradford. "No, the search just got a little more dangerous and a lot more complicated."

"I'm not questioning your judgment," he said. "If you believe there's still a chance she's alive, I'll grasp at that straw, but I really have no idea where you're going with this."

Munroe walked to the bed, sat down, and opened the envelope. "We'll start with this," she said, "although there are so many things wrong with it, it's hard to know *where* to begin." She bit on her lip and squinted at the document. "For starters, there's the paper itself." She held it up so he could see the designs printed around the border and the details of the heading. "See the number at the top? It's five-thousand-CFA paper— government paper. It has to be purchased from the Ministry of Finance."

His face was completely blank.

"Anytime people want an official document, they have to buy one of these and then take it to whatever government branch has the information they need. If you want goods processed through the port, the approvals are put on government tax paper. You want a birth certificate? Government tax paper. You want a license for your vehicle? Government tax paper." She handed it to him. "Someone had to pay for this at the Ministry of Finance and bring it to the police station. I doubt that the clerk who typed it out and is making fifty dollars a month was the one to do it."

"So what you're saying is that whoever requests an official document has to supply the tax paper in order to get it?"

"Exactly," she said. "And that brings us to the next glaring inaccuracy: A death certificate in this country is meaningless. Nobody has them or has use of them. When there's a death in a village, there's no autopsy or police report—certainly no 'cause of death' to be determined. There's a village ceremony, a burial if the person is lucky, and that's the end of it. You ask the government for a death certificate and the big question is going to be, what for?"

"But we've got one."

She nodded. "I'll get to that in a minute. This document is just a lot of misspelled wordiness that certifies that the person named died in the Republic of Equatorial Guinea." She pointed at the paper. "No details whatsoever. It doesn't even say where it happened or what nationality she was. For all the flaws of this country's government, let's not forget the ten years they spent under communism. They're real big on redundant paperwork and following procedures by whatever the day's formula may be. At the least we should expect an indication of whether she died on the mainland or the island."

"Look, Michael," he said, "I want to believe you more than you can possibly know, but why would they even have that document? Wouldn't it be so much easier for them to simply say that they have no idea what we're talking about?"

"I can think of several possible answers to that question," she said, "but here's what I think holds the most water: This piece of paper doesn't even prove that Emily was in the country. They got Emily's name from us—copied it off the bio we gave Mba at the ministry. What this piece of paper means is that someone who was educated abroad, who knows what a death certificate means to people like us, doesn't want us snooping around the mainland and hopes that this is enough to convince us to go home."

Munroe took the death certificate and sealed it inside the Ziploc bag that held her passport and that she kept in a security belt worn underneath her pants, around her waist.

"Miles, things are going to get dangerous from this point. We were issued a threat, and if we're not careful, someone's going to make good on it. Maybe you should call Burbank, see if he'll let you out of the assignment."

"I stay," he said. "So what's next?"

"We need to get out of the city as soon as possible, preferably in the direction of the mainland." She looked at her watch. "We've got time before the GEASA office closes."

Like most places of business in the city, the airline headquarters was located on the first floor of a three-story building. The office was small, dark, damp, and empty but for a desk on either side of the room. There were two people in the office, one a secretary or clerk, the other someone of importance who took their money and wrote out the ticket information by hand. The transaction was completed within fifteen minutes—they would be on the first flight leaving in the morning.

On the way out of the office, Munroe handed Miles his ticket. "Flying to Bata is a bit like playing Russian roulette," she said. "Literally. The machines are old Russian planes that get no maintenance. They're stuffed beyond capacity and flown until they go down—usually into the ocean. Hopefully tomorrow won't be the day."

Munroe stopped midstep and searched up and down the street through the pedestrians and a steady stream of vehicle traffic. Bradford followed her eyes.

"Did the Shadows follow us here?" he asked.

"I was certain of it," she said.

"So was I."

"Think they could've gotten good enough to avoid our spotting them?"

"I doubt it," he said.

"So do I."

Munroe and Bradford walked the return trip to the hotel hoping to spot a Shadow and find relief in the normalcy of being tailed, but instead they found that they were alone.

Over dinner they said little to each other, and for the first time since arriving in the city Munroe heard the wisps of threat. It came not in words but in the silences, in things unspoken and in the background banter among the hotel employees that was no longer there.

The waiter, previously friendly and good-humored, was tonight solemn and taciturn. He brought their drinks, and Munroe had them sent back, requesting unopened cans, and then in unspoken agreement neither she nor Bradford ordered anything to eat. Rather, they sat in silence nursing Coke out of the can, pretending to be amused by a rowdy party of drunken expats two tables down. And when they had sat long enough so as to keep up appearances, they left the patio to return to their rooms to wait for light and get out of the city.

They had decided that it would be best if they both slept in the same room. Bradford returned to his to retrieve some of the bedding as well as his belongings, and while she waited for him, Munroe kicked off her shoes. When she tossed them against the bed, the first signs of dizziness hit. She doubled over to steady herself, braced herself against the bed, and felt darkness closing in. She opened her mouth to yell for Bradford, but no sound came. She crumpled to the floor, and the last thought to go through her mind was to wonder how the hell it had happened.

CHAPTER 10

West coast of Bioko Island, Equatorial Guinea

Awareness came slowly through a haze of confusion, and Munroe struggled toward lucidity, attempting to attach meaning to the stimuli hammering at her senses. First came the dank smell of oxidized metal and then the cold of steel through clothing. It was dark, and the air had a salty dampness to it. She lay on her side, gagged and hands secured behind her back. Her feet were bare and, as far as she could tell, bound to something heavy. Cigarette smoke hung in the air, and voices spoke hushed and rapidly in a language that had no meaning.

Where the hell was Bradford?

There was movement—the erratic regularity of a small boat rocking on the open ocean. From behind came the low whine of an engine that indicated slow forward speed. There was starlight, and a lamp on the prow highlighted the shadows of four men. The boat was no more than fifteen feet long and, but for a small cabin on the bow, open-aired. She could smell rain in the distance, knew they could smell it, too.

Three feet away one of the men lolled against the gunwale. Near his face was the soft glow of orange that brightened as he inhaled. On his belt he had a knife and, holstered close to it, a sidearm.

The mental fog continued to lift, and confusion segued to anger. The patio with Bradford, the hotel room, darkness. The images merged and collided. Internal pressure built steadily, was rising from her gut into her chest, a hammer percussing as a war drum whose beat would end when blood was spilled. Her vision blurred to gray, and she wrestled it back. Thought before action, knowledge before battle.

Her eyes followed the guard as he smoked, and she twisted so that her hands could reach her ankles. Wrapped around her feet was a chain that ran through a section of metal pipe. A weight. An anchor. Hauled off to be dumped like garbage. No questions, no accusations, no torture, and no chance for explanation or pleading—brought to the water to disappear, to be wiped off the face of the earth.

The fucking bastards.

The internal drumbeat pounded harder, faster, and the urge to strike became unbearable.

Breathe. Think.

In the distance the sky was tinged by the glow of natural gas burn-off. She turned to the stars and, as she had on so many occasions in the past, found the map written in the equatorial night sky. The flare worked as a marker to gauge the distance. They were close to the coast. Close enough to swim if she could survive the treacherous currents. How far out were they? A quarter of a mile? It had to be less.

The man at the gunwale straightened and turned. She froze. He came closer and reached his hand out, snapping his fingers in front of her face, and when he received no response, he kicked her in the ribs. She groaned. He turned his back, and the light on the prow framed his profile. In spite of his weapons, he wore civilian clothes. He dropped the cigarette and faced her again, squatted and fumbled with the buttons of her shirt.

The percussion rose higher, louder, drowning out the sounds of the boat. One movement, swift and soundless, a serpent's strike, was all that it would take to reach for the knife, slit his throat, and dump his body in the ocean. She tested the strength of the nylon that held her wrists. The guard's commander barked an order, and the man stopped, stood, threw a second kick to her gut, then lit another cigarette and walked back to join the others.

Take him, take them all. Pilot the boat to the shore and then . . . and then what? Return to Malabo with no place to hide while attempting to smuggle herself off this prison of an island? Breathe. Think. Time. Time was necessary in order to gain information, to understand, to strategize.

Munroe glanced at the glow on the horizon. The oil companies used helicopters to airlift their sick employees to Cameroon. It was an option. She gritted her teeth, yanked her right thumb out of its socket, squeezed the hand free of the restraint, and then relocated the thumb with a silent, painful snap. She looped the nylon around both wrists to hold her arms in position and then tested the chains on her feet and found them loose. Careful so as not to let the metal grate on itself, she pulled her ankles out and, confident it would not be a problem to get free of the anchor, replaced them.

Luba. She could take the boat to Luba and refuel there.

And then the moment of opportunity was gone. From behind, the engine cut and the boat coasted, rising and falling with the rhythm of the water. Hands pulled her up by the scruff of the neck and then, positioned under her arms, dragged her to the hip-high gunwale and propped her up.

Another burst of rapid discussion in that indecipherable language. The hands slackened momentarily, and the dead weight of her body slumped forward. The hands picked her back up, and then there was silence. Through half-opened eyes, she saw the commander reach for his weapon, and in that instant she understood the argument.

He raised the gun, and she pushed with her legs, propelling herself backward, falling headfirst over the edge, into the ocean. Water churned around her with an audible hiss. Bullets. Heat like a knife blade caught her left arm below the shoulder. The anchor tightened, and the weight at her feet flipped her right side up and plunged her downward. Unable to loosen the chains, she kicked. With her hands she pried until her right foot came out. The plunge stopped ten yards below the boat, and still the anchor held tight around her left ankle. Her lungs ached for air, and in panic she clawed at the chain. No time. Think. She forced her fingers between her foot and the chain, bought an inch, and then was free. She kicked off from the ocean floor and swam toward the light, removing the gag as she went.

She broke water under the prow of the boat, only her face breaching the surface. She held her body protectively beneath its bulk as it rocked with the motion of the water, drank in the air one greedy gulp after another, then filled her lungs and sank. Under the boat she wrapped the gag around the wound in her arm and tied it as tightly as she could in an attempt to ward off the call to the deep-sea predators. She surfaced again, took another breath, and dove, this time putting as much distance as she could between herself and the boat.

The men paced about the sides, searching for movement on the water. They drew the light around the gunwales, firing shots occasionally. Their voices were angry, accusatory, and Munroe knew they could never report the incident. She was, as far as they were concerned, very dead.

She turned onto her back, gazed at the stars, righted herself, and pushed east.

The surface currents were fast-flowing, and it was nearly two hours before she felt the smooth-rough edges of worn lava rock beneath her feet, another ten minutes to stumble over the jet-black, odd-size boulders that made up the stretch of coast. Away from the waterline, she dropped to her knees and then collapsed, chest heaving, taking in air, arms and legs limp as rubber. In the far-off distance, barely more than a pinhead of light in the blackness, a boat buoyed on the water. Munroe dragged herself to where the boulders touched the jungle, a niche of shelter from both the air and the sea. There would be no hiding from the rain that would soon arrive, but that didn't matter.

Alone in the blackness, with the ocean to the front and the jungle at her back, she heard the sound of her own laughter splitting the silence.

It was the west side of the island. No matter where she had washed up, the road could not be more than a mile or two inland, but a mile or two of raw jungle. Without a path it would mean breaking a trail barefoot. Better to wait until dawn.

She felt for her belt. It was still there, tucked safely under her pants. It increased the options somewhat; the credit cards were worthless, but there were fifty thousand CFA and two hundred water-soaked euros to barter with.

She dozed occasionally and was glad for the first rays of sun that crept between the mountains, providing enough light for her to begin moving about. Finding potable water before the heat intensified was imperative in order to avoid dehydration. She had drunk during the night when the rain had filled the porous holes in the rocks, but that water was gone now. Not far away, the shadows of tall, lean palms jutted out over the water. Under the fronds they were thick with coconuts. She flexed her wounded arm, and ribbons of heat traced up and down it.

The bullet was lodged in muscle, and the arm was weak. The thirty-foot climb was possible, but not worth the risk.

She followed the coastline south until the boulders gave way to gritty sand, and there she found groups of coconut palms with recently fallen fruit at their base. She chose a green one with tinges of brown on the ends and, using rocks to cut through the fibrous husk, reached the seed and cracked it carefully to preserve the liquid. She drank and proceeded to the others until her thirst had been quenched, then filled herself on the rubbery meat of the young nuts.

She continued along the coastline, frequently scanning the water's horizon for boats. The soles of her feet blistered and bled from the sharp edges of the rock. When the heat of the sun became too strong, she sought shelter in the shade and slept until the late afternoon brought relief and she could set out again.

Another mile south and a faint trail led away from the coast into the green. She followed it, and after nearly a mile the undergrowth changed from thick jungle foliage to short, squat trees in uneven rows fighting for light between the giants, their stubby trunks spotted by fat pods ripe with bitter cocoa seeds. The footpath ended at a solid line of tarmac.

It was the Luba road, a two-lane highway that originated in Malabo and ran three-quarters of the island along the coast until it stopped at the second-largest city on the island—the city of its namesake—a deep-water port with a population of three thousand. It was the only road that ran along the west coast, and myriad small interior villages were joined to it by their own narrow dirt paths.

Across the road a swath of land had been cleared, and raw cement blocks stacked on top of each other formed a half-constructed home with iron-red rebar reaching to the open sky and thick carpets of green mildew creeping up from the base of it. Other than the sounds of birds and the buzzing of insects, the stretch was completely silent. Cars would pass along eventually, perhaps even as many as three or four an hour. All that was necessary was to sit and wait.

Munroe pulled the CFA from her belt and shoved it in her pocket—she might need it to pay for space in a share taxi if nothing better materialized. She sat against the trunk of a large tree, far enough away from the road to remain hidden, close enough to spot approaching vehicles. In the shade of the foliage, the air was wet with a mud-scented humidity and the soil rich and spongy and teeming with life.

There was perhaps another two hours before dusk, when the armed soldiers who set up checkpoints every few miles along the road would be out in force, drunk and trigger-happy, and only the bravest or the craziest of drivers would attempt to travel along it. Until then the range of vehicles passing would be anything from small share taxis with their springs busted from the weight they bore to the overworked trucks of the European construction crews on never-ending development projects. With any luck one of the trademark shiny air-conditioned Land Cruisers of the oil-company executives would pass. It was the safest bet when it came to getting around: blend in with their crowd to become instantly invisible.

In the silence, Munroe plowed a stick through the dirt, etching the ground absentmindedly while working through the options and the previous day's events. As in a football coach's game plan, circles and lines appeared in no apparent order—rapid strokes, jagged lines—and like the circles slashed into the ground, her thoughts ran around pell-mell but always returned to their place of origin: Emily Burbank.

One second. Six inches. The mental tape replayed itself, an endless recording: the gun moving up through the dark toward her face and then the plunge backward into the water. One second before the bullet. She gritted her teeth and drove the stick faster, harder. Dumped in the ocean because she hadn't taken the hint to leave the country. Emily Burbank.

Until last night the assignment had been business. Now it was personal: Someone had ordered her dead and had nearly succeeded in putting a bullet in her brain. Another circle, another strand of thought. If she followed the interdicted trail to Emily Burbank, the answers would come hunting, seeking her out. And when the answers presented themselves, she would take retribution, even if it turned out to be against the president of the goddamned country.

Bradford. Where the hell was he? Why wasn't he in the boat? He'd been with her the entire time they'd been in the city. He was booked to fly to the mainland just as she was. Had he already been tossed overboard?

She rubbed her hands over her eyes and pressed her fingers against the bridge of her nose. What a fucking liability he'd become. Instead of one missing person, the job now included two.

No.

Bradford was capable of taking care of himself. If they'd been hauled off in the boat together, there was nothing that could be done about it, and if he hadn't been—she stabbed the stick into the ground and it snapped in two—he sure as hell had better be looking for her right now.

She picked up another stick and dug it through the soil, gouging one rut after another. Emily Burbank. Mongomo.

Malabo was the only city on the island where reliable and not-so-reliable transport across the water could be had. Malabo: an enticing prison, the city so easily locked down, the airport, the port, the hotels, banks, and city exits carefully watched. There were the oil companies and their compounds—to get onto one of those meant a chance, however slight, of being airlifted off the island to Cameroon. Too many ifs, so much dependent on bureaucracy and the decisions of others. No. Not the oil companies. Not Malabo.

If the mainland was unreachable through the capital, then perhaps through Luba.

Time. Information. She rested her head back against the trunk of the tree. A conversation with someone who better understood the local political climate was now a necessity—and access to money, supplies, and modern communications equipment. Above loomed the green of the jungle, and there was only stillness.

Munroe examined the wounds on her feet. The skin was stripped away from portions of her heels, and dime-size blisters had formed and burst under the balls of her toes. Another couple of weeks and she'd have several millimeters' worth of nature's shoe leather to pad around on, but until then walking was going to be rough. She needed shoes, and they could be found a dozen or so miles to the north. The temptation was certainly there, but returning to Malabo was out of the question. Not for shoes, not for Bradford.

She sat and waited, and over time bright red spots formed on her uncovered neck, forearms, and feet, the telltale signs that near-microscopic insects were feasting on her blood. In the bush one could only sweat and itch and wait, and the numbing quiet of the emptiness explained why doing nothing was such a favorite pastime of the locals.

She would have checked her watch if she'd still had one.

The rumble of a large vehicle carried through the silence. Munroe crawled closer to the edge of the road and, seeing the flat nose and wide body of a construction truck approaching, stood and walked several feet onto the tarmac. The vehicle had green license plates, a variation reserved for companies with special status, and in the cab were the shadows of two.

The truck slowed and then stopped, sending a cloud of dust rolling behind it. The passenger window rolled down.

"Hello there!" Munroe called out. "Are you headed to Luba?"

The door on the passenger side opened, and a man stepped down. He wore faded jeans and a worn T-shirt, and his face and forearms were tanned to the point of being nearly brown. His work boots were dusty and spotted with cement, and Munroe couldn't help but wish they were on her feet.

"We go Luba," he replied, the words broken and thickly accented. He gestured with his head. "You come?"

Italians.

Munroe nodded and climbed up to the air-conditioned space between them, the blast of cold a welcome relief against her sun-dried skin.

The driver stared at her feet, her disheveled clothes, and the spots on her arms. "What happen to you?"

The vehicle lurched forward in a cloud of cement dust. The passenger handed her a liter bottle of water.

"*Mi sono perso*," she replied, and drank without stopping until the bottle was empty. "Separated from my friends and very, very lost."

With the first words in their language, the gravity of her situation was apparently quickly forgotten. Both men broke into wide smiles. "*Ma tu parli Italiano?*"

She smiled back. "I speak some, enough to get by." There was something deeply affecting about language. If expected, it meant nothing. But

if it came by surprise as a gesture of friendship, it was an instant opening, a form of flattery guaranteed to attain the objective for its master,
and Munroe used it accordingly.

The driver was Luca, a fifty-two-year-old native of Bari who had been
a construction foreman in Equatorial Guinea on and off for nearly eight
years. Salvatore sat in the passenger seat, younger, but not by much.

He searched behind the seat and brought out a first-aid kit. Between
bumps and jolts along the road, Munroe patched up her feet, and when
the men asked about the stained cloth tied around her arm, she shrugged.
"A scratch," she said, and changed the conversation through questions
of her own. They entertained her with stories of life in Equatorial Guinea
and about their families back home, whom they saw only a few months
out of the year.

The pay they earned for working on the island more than made up
for the difficult conditions, and the malaria didn't bother them as much
as the tumbu flies whose larvae bored under the skin and used the host
to feed and incubate.

They approached a bend in the road. Luca slowed the truck and
turned to Munroe. "Do you have papers?"

Two passports and one of the residency cards. But she wouldn't risk
losing the passports, and under the circumstances a residency card could
prove problematic. "I had nothing on me when I was separated from my
friends," she said.

Luca brought the vehicle to a stop on a narrow dirt shoulder that
encroached into the wall of green. He rubbed his forehead and then
motioned with his hand down the road. "We are coming to a checkpoint.
They will want to see your papers. They won't let you through without
them."

Munroe calculated the options, read them in Luca's face, and, as
if rehearsing lines for a well-scripted plot, said, "If the papers are a
problem, I'll find a way to continue on by foot." She paused and then
attempted to stand and move past Salvatore in the passenger seat. "I
don't want to cause problems for you. Thank you for your help and for
the wonderful conversation."

Luca held out his hand and stopped her. She knew he would. "It's not safe for you on foot." He tugged on his grubby cap and lifted it, scratching his head. "We have beer with us to offer—they won't look in the back."

He replaced the cap, climbed out of the cab, and motioned for her to follow. The rear portion of the truck was open and carried equipment and supplies. "Stay under the tarp until we come to get you," he said. "There is another checkpoint beyond this one before reaching Luba, possibly two—you never know." He made sure she was secure, and from under the tarp Munroe heard the door slam and felt the engine rumble to life.

Once past the checkpoint, she shifted so that she could see out from beneath the ceiling of blue plastic and breathe the fresh air.

THE TRUCK SHUDDERED to a stop on one of Luba's few paved roads. Puzzled, Munroe retreated farther under the tarp. Luca and Salvatore spoke rapidly in a muted conversation that she strained to overhear but could not make out. After several minutes the cab door slammed, and for the third time the vehicle lurched forward.

When the truck fell silent for the last time, it was in a barren compound outside the city. Neither Luca nor Salvatore came as they had promised, and after waiting what felt to be a half hour or more, Munroe worked through alternative scenarios. She would sleep now while she could and slip away when the deep of night settled.

It was footsteps that woke her. She reached for her knives and only after her hands came up empty did she remember where she was; it was an instinctive reflex she had not made in nearly seven years. She flipped to her stomach and prepared to move. The footsteps came closer, and Salvatore called out softly.

Munroe answered in a whisper and then slipped out from the tarp. She sat on the edge of the truck bed, feet dangling over the side, and Salvatore climbed up next to her. He had been delayed, he said, because there was military around town demanding to see papers. Since she was without hers, they thought it best to wait before coming. Salvatore handed her a pair of shoes and then some socks. "I don't know if these will fit," he said. "But you can't go walking around with your feet like that." The shoes explained the stop in town. They were canvas stitched directly to flat rubber soles, imported from Nigeria or Cameroon, and they were at that moment the most beautiful pair she had ever seen.

Munroe placed them on her feet. They were a little loose but would work. She handed him a five-thousand-CFA note. He smiled and refused it. "The hostels in town are full," he said. "They are always full. If you can't find your friends tonight, you can stay here on the truck. But the workers will start unloading early in the morning."

She pointed to the shoes. "Are you sure I can't pay for these—or for the ride?"

"No, no," he said. "You're not the first traveler to find yourself in a difficult position in this lunatic country. We help when we can."

Munroe waited until Salvatore was out of sight and then slid off the flatbed and slunk into the shadows. She kept off the streets and wound in the direction of the shoreline.

The pervasive smell of wood smoke and fish gnawed at her until she gave it notice, and once aware of it she worked her way back toward the source. It came from a clearing south of the town where small homes had been constructed out of homemade cinder blocks and topped with corrugated metal. Women tended a cooking fire outside the back of the largest structure. Around them men and children sat on upturned crates and straight-backed wooden chairs, talking, eating, and laughing. Ducks waddled and roosted nearby, and chickens scratched near the fire, picking up small morsels that had been dropped. A kerosene lantern hung from a tree not far from the group and another from the door of one of the structures. Other than the fire, the lamps provided the only source of light.

Bubi was the language spoken by those native to the island, a soft singsong of words strung together in a manner distinctly different from the harsher Fang that dominated the mainland and the capital. Munroe had heard it spoken occasionally, but not often enough to converse, and so she opted for Spanish to call out an evening greeting.

The adults responded with smiles and conversation, the children with bashful stares. She played the part of the quintessential traveler, and they answered her questions, chatting about the city and describing the best places for swimming. They invited her to eat, and she offered a few thousand CFA, which they refused and she insisted upon their taking by placing the money in the palm of one of the young children. In addition to the fish, there were plantains cut into strips and deep-fried in palm oil, plus forest snails in an oily tomato paste.

She made small talk with the young men and asked about boats capable of handling a trip to the mainland. They shook their heads and then discussed the question among themselves in their own tongue while she listened intently. Such boats were in Luba occasionally, they said, but not now. They offered to take her to the shore in the morning and introduce her to men who owned boats, and she countered with additional CFA for a spot under one of their roofs. Her bed was the concrete floor with a jacket bundled beneath her head for a pillow. Sleep came easily, everything about the evening having been comfortingly familiar.

The next morning Munroe stood on the shoreline under a half-moon and stars in front of a row of boats resting on the sand, a miniature armada ready for deployment. Their condition was as the young men had described, wooden fishing vessels old with dry rot. The smallest of them were pirogues, some with outboard engines and others without. A few of the boats had sails, and the largest, a wooden boat ten feet long, had a near-new outboard motor. She paced around it and ran her hands along the hull. It had the space to carry enough fuel to travel the distance, but it didn't have the integrity to make the trip over the open water.

In silence she walked away from the others and stood beyond the edge of the breaking water. She picked up pebbles and threw them out into the waves in rapid succession, attempting to quell a building rage. Trapped on the island, a prisoner, time lost for nothing. It would mean having to risk the return to Malabo after all and, from there, finding a way to the mainland. The airport was out of the question. So was the main port. She stared up at the patterns of light in the black sky and willed a solution into existence.

There was another way. Boniface Akambe had said *he* could be found near Ureca. She'd wanted to see him, yes, but not under these conditions. But then limited options meant working with what was available. She negotiated a ride to the south of the island on a skiff.

She would travel to Ureca. Best known for the sea turtles that returned to its shore each year to nest, it was an isolated village where conservation groups had made headway against poaching by paying the locals to guard the beaches during nesting season. The village was accessible only by sea or via a thirteen-hour trek through the jungles between the Grand Caldera of Luba and Mount Biao.

Somewhere in that direction she would find Francisco Beyard.

The sun's first rays had already begun to peek over the mountain by the time the boat's owner returned from town. He brought with him extra fuel, drinking water, and a piece of cloth that would work as a tarp. Two young boys with him loaded an assortment of supplies that had nothing to do with the trip. They would be bartered and sold in Ureca, providing the entrepreneurial boatman with extra money.

The trip passed in relative silence. They hugged the coastline, following it around the widest part of the island. The occasional small village broke the monotony of green that advanced to the border of unending blue. Under the tarp Munroe dozed fitfully, in turn lulled to sleep by the steady rock of the boat and the cloud-covered sky and awakened by apprehension at meeting Beyard.

Scripts of possible introductions worked through her mind. The promise of money would possibly appeal to him. If not that, then what? Appeal to the memories of a friendship destroyed when she disappeared without so much as a word? If he would not take her off the island, the alternative was a grueling hike back to Luba and a return trip to the capital to face the possibility of a permanent resting place at the infamous Black Beach Prison.

Francisco Beyard was a risk worth taking.

EVIDENCE THAT THEY had arrived at Ureca came from signs of humanity along the shore and the landmark rock that jutted upright out of the empty beach twenty feet into the air like an isolated obelisk. The boatman brought the boat as close to the beach as possible, tilted the engine upward, and together he and Munroe—gritting through the pain in her arm—pushed it thirty feet through shallow waves until it rested solidly on dry land. The sand was soft and deep brown, unlike the stretches of porous boulders and black rock that lined the western shore.

Young boys shirtless and shoeless played nearby and ran to greet them as the boat came to rest. The boatman barked orders to them and passed out trinkets. They took up his bundles and led the two of them inland.

The trail to Ureca climbed steadily upward through a quarter mile of lush greenery still wet with recent rain. The village was a tidy collection of houses, neatly demarcated and separated by narrow dirt pathways that had never been used by a motorized vehicle. Unlike the cinder-block houses in the villages to the north, most of the homes in Ureca were wattle and daub, their roofs covered with thick thatchwork.

The boys brought Munroe to the home of the village elder, chattering as they went inside. They soon came scuttling out, followed by an aged woman. She wore a worn T-shirt, and wrapped around her waist was a colorful cloth, a matching band around her hair. Her weathered face was adorned with cutting scars. She greeted Munroe and motioned her inside.

Munroe was offered a seat opposite a man who was certainly much younger than he looked. He sat regally on a wooden chair, his hand atop a polished stick. Munroe was treated graciously, and when she had accepted coffee and they had begun to drink, he asked why she had come and he requested the documents that permitted her to travel to the village.

She handed him her residency card and explained that although she did not have a paper from the Ministry of the Interior, she was part of a diplomatic mission with several requirements, not the least of which was to visit Ureca. Because of its uniqueness, she explained, it was one of the most important villages on the island, and as the village elder he was one of the most important men. He nodded in agreement and asked no more about the papers. As indirectly as possible, she asked questions that would lead her to Beyard's location.

The elder was thoughtful and slow to speak. He provided information judiciously, and his reticence gave Munroe reassurance that Beyard's reach had extended into the elder's pocket.

He was not far away.

Full of dignified humility, she apologized for coming without a gift for such an important representative and explained that part of her responsibility on this mission was to meet with a man who would provide transport. Because she had traveled in haste, she had come empty-handed, but this man would aid her in bringing back a gift.

The elder was silent for a moment, and Munroe refrained from speaking, knowing that he weighed potential reward against the potential loss of reward should he displease his paymaster. Finally he spoke.

"I cannot say for sure what is or what isn't," he said. "My eyes and ears are not as young as they once were. But there are whispers that at Point Delores young men occasionally find work."

"It is obvious," she said, "that you are a very wise man and that your people are fortunate to be blessed with a leader such as yourself." He nodded again, and with his permission she took her leave.

She found the boatman with his wares spread about him, surrounded by the women of the village. Voices were raised and spoke in rapid succession as they bartered. Munroe understood traces of the conversations, words coming to her in flashes of illumination. Another few days and she would be conversing, another week and she'd be fluent.

When the racket settled and the crowd thinned, she called to the boatman. Just one more small trip and his end of the bargain would be complete. Point Delores, she had learned, was a nesting area a few miles farther along the coast.

They beached the boat as they had earlier in the day, and from the sands Munroe searched for signs of humanity. A small pirogue sat above the waterline and, not far from it, a path recognizable only by an occasional footprint and foliage that had been disturbed. She knelt and touched the earth. It was wet, heavy with water. The footprints had been recently formed. The path led inland for less than half a mile and ended at a small clearing that encircled three buildings.

The largest of the buildings was a block house similar in style to those on the north of the island; the others were wattle and daub. On the roof, together with the corrugated metal, were several solar panels, and electrical wires leading from one of the smaller structures intimated at a generator. A screened-in porch fronted the central building, and to the side of the porch two young men sat dozing in the shade.

They did not move when she approached. She knelt beside them and in their own tongue said softly, "Excuse me."

Her aim had been to avoid startling them, but from the looks of

fright they bore, she had failed miserably. In Spanish she said, "I came
to find the Merchant." And when in their faces she found affirmation of
the property's owner, she added, "Is he at home?"

The shorter of the two shook his head and then said, "He returns in
the evening."

"Good." She smiled. "I will wait for him inside."

Munroe paid the boatman the last of her money and instructed him
with words to repeat if questioned about her purpose for visiting this
part of the island.

In the silence she turned toward the house and opened the screen
door. She let herself in through the front door, and the young men
watched with obvious indifference. Memories played like time-lapse
photography.

Another life.

She entered directly into the living room, an open space that belied
the small size of the house. It was sparse and empty, the walls plastered
and painted white, the furniture consisting of a rough-hewn sofa and
two chairs. The floor was concrete painted over with brown floor paint,
and it was all spotlessly clean, somehow suggesting the sterile environ-
ment of a well-kept clinic. The shutters were closed and the air hot and
stale. She tried the fan. There was no electricity.

From the living room there were doors off a small hallway, and she
could see through the open door to the kitchen. She lay down on the
sofa, ignoring the temptation to look around. She had invaded his house,
but some things were still sacred. In the stillness and quiet, her eyes grew
heavy, and she was pulled downward into sleep.

IN THE FOGGY distance of consciousness, Munroe heard shouting. Aware
that time had passed but not how much, she struggled to wake and pull
herself out of the sticky haze of sleep. A web of heat and exhaustion
enveloped her and dragged her back down.

The deep roar of a generator split the silence and drowned out the
human voices. The lights in the room blinked on and off and then put
out a steady wattage. A breeze cut through the stale air in the room
as the fans began to oscillate. The temperature had changed, dusk had

come. The mosquitoes would be out in force, held at bay by the netting that covered the windows.

Footsteps on the porch were followed by another barrage of shouting. The voice was familiar. She was awake now, and uncomfortable. She shifted on the sofa. The front door slammed open and shut. He stormed into the room and then, making eye contact, stopped in midstep, almost tripping over himself.

CHAPTER 11

Beyard righted himself, then stared at her for a moment. "Hello, Essa," he said finally, the words rolling off his tongue in a rich, thick mixture of accents. The initial shock that had registered on his face faded, and all that replaced it was nonchalance.

He walked toward the kitchen without another look and said, "Can I get you something to drink?"

"Yes, please," she called out after him. "Water will be fine."

Cupboard doors banged. "I must say"—his voice was raised but muted by the distance—"when my boys told me I had a visitor, you were the last person I expected." He walked back into the living room. "I'm surprised to see you here. Not just here, you know, although yes, it is even more unexpected, but to see you at all . . ." He paused and motioned around the room. "In the same room with me, or even in this country." He handed her the glass. "It's tepid. The idiots who work for me let the generator run out of fuel."

She raised her glass toward him and took a drink.

They both sat in silence, he facing her, his forearms on his knees, she with her legs stretched over the edge of the chair. He rolled his glass between his palms. She watched him, studied him. He was more muscular, his hair no longer sun-bleached blond, his tan not as deep, but he was still weather-beaten, his chiseled features emphasized by the lines that only extended outdoor exposure could bring. His eyes were still strikingly blue.

He was the first to break the silence. "How did you find me?"

"I was in Kribi a few days ago and spoke with Boniface. He mentioned you'd set up shop in this general direction. I knew what I was looking for."

He leaned back and with a half smile said, "Atavistic in the end," and then, after a long pause, "So you asked about me?"

"Yes, I did." She waited, unsure of which direction to take the conversation, and then said, "How's business?"

His face still wore the half smile, and as he watched her, she knew that his mind had kicked into analysis mode. "You didn't travel halfway around the world from wherever it is you came from to ask me about business, just as you didn't meet with Akambe to find out where I was."

"No," she replied, meeting his gaze and then shifting to look around the room. "I'm making small talk. Other business brought me to Boniface, and I asked about you because I wanted to know how you were. I hadn't intended to drop in at your hideaway."

"But here you are."

"Yes," she said slowly, "here I am. Unfortunately, it's that same 'other business' that has brought me here. I need a ride off the island, and I'm willing to pay you well for it. I'd also like to hire your expertise."

He said nothing, and his eyes wandered to the grimy piece of cloth still wrapped around her arm. Then he stood. "Have you eaten?" he asked.

She cocked her head to the side to look up at him and remained seated and silent.

"Whatever it is you want," he said, bending toward her and lowering his voice to almost a whisper, "can be better discussed on a full stomach. Come."

She followed him into the austere kitchen, and he lit the burner under a pot that sat on the stove. Against one wall was a tiled counter that ended in a metal sink. Handmade cupboards had been built into the far-right wall. The stove and refrigerator sat side by side on the left wall, fitting together only because they were both so small. The stove was divided in two, half of it running off propane and the other half on electricity. A screened window over the counter looked out into the yard.

Against the coming darkness, he closed the shutters from the inside, the slanted wooden slats allowing air to continue to circulate.

A small table and two handmade chairs stood against the remaining wall. Like the living room, the kitchen was sparse and clean. He pulled a place setting out of the cupboard. "Don't ask what it is," he said as he served her from the simmering pot, "it won't kill you."

Forest rat, monkey meat, it made no difference—whatever it was, she'd had worse. He sat across from her and watched as she ate, and when she finished, he took the plate from the table and placed it in the sink. "How long since you've eaten?" he asked.

"I don't know," she said. "Dinner sometime yesterday."

He nodded toward her arm. "What happened?"

"Drugged, beaten, and shot. I would have been dumped into the ocean except I jumped first—I'm supposed to be dead."

He propped himself against the sink, arms crossed at his chest, legs crossed at the ankles, staring at her in silence with the slightest semblance of a smile. He shook his head almost imperceptibly and then went to the refrigerator and pulled out two bottles of beer. He handed one to her, knelt beside her, and took her left arm in his hands. He lifted the bloodstained material away from the wound and pressed lightly around the edge of it, and she winced. He put his hand to her forehead. "You're burning," he said.

"I know."

"The bullet needs to be removed. I've got a bottle of Black Label somewhere in the house. You might want it." She gave him back the unopened beer.

He returned to the kitchen with the whiskey and pulled a shot glass from the cupboard, then handed both to her. "How long has it been since I saw you last?" he asked. "Ten years?"

"Nine."

"Nine years. It's a long time. You look good, by the way."

"So do you."

He set a pot of water on the stove and then left the kitchen again, returning a few minutes later with a small metal kit that brought with it another wave of memories. He dropped a few items into the boiling water.

After several minutes he withdrew from the pot a pointed precision blade that looked like a scalpel. "It's been a long time," he said, and he laid it on a cloth on the table in front of her, together with several other items. "Do you trust me?"

She dumped a shot of the whiskey into her mouth and swallowed. "I always have, Francisco."

He removed the wrapping from her arm. "Misplaced trust can be a dangerous thing."

She downed a second shot and then a third. "Was that a warning?"

He shrugged. "A lot of time has gone by, Essa. You've changed. I've changed."

The bullet had hit when she was still upside down and had entered underneath the arm and traveled in the direction of the elbow. The alcohol took the edge off as Beyard sliced into the muscle but didn't do much when he removed the bullet. She wanted to scream, wanted to hit him, resisted both. Beyard extracted the bullet from its resting spot and held it up to the light, examining it before placing it on the towel before her. "A souvenir, perhaps," he said. She downed another shot as he irrigated the wound with hydrogen peroxide.

"You're lucky, you know." He pushed a needle into her, threading the first stitch through the open wound.

She clenched her teeth. "How's that?"

"That you found me here." His face held a look of concentration, and another bolt of pain went up her neck. "I'm not here that often. Tonight I dropped off a load of supplies and planned to head out for the next month—wasn't even planning to stay the night. What would you have done if you hadn't found me?"

"Dunno," she said, and her voice shook as he pushed in the needle for another stitch. "Probably wait as long as I could, use a mirror to do what you're doing now, eat through your supplies, write an IOU, and then do the long-walk thing back to Malabo."

Beyard laughed an involuntary laugh, and she flinched as his hand moved. "I guess at the core you haven't changed much."

"Have you?"

His face grew serious, and he drew the last stitch. "As long as there's no infection, you should be fine," he said. "You might have to baby it for a while, I had to cut pretty deep."

By the time he finished, she'd downed nearly three-quarters of the•bottle. Drunk and exhausted, she made no protestation when he undressed her and put her in his bed. He left the room, and she collapsed into a grateful fog of forgetfulness.

When she woke, it was dark, and even with her eyes closed the bed floated in soft circles. She was aware of time having passed; in spite of the dark, it had to be at least afternoon. On a low-lying table on the other side of the mosquito netting, she found four half-liter water bottles. She took one and drank from it, dampening the fuzzy dryness that coated her mouth and then, in spite of the spinning room, pulled herself up out of bed. She fumbled in an attempt to open the shutters and let in some light, realized that a blanket had been nailed up over them, and couldn't remember if it had been there last night.

But for her panties, she was naked. She searched for her clothes and instead found a freshly laundered pair of Francisco's pants draped over a chair with her security belt lying on top of them and a shirt hanging off a nail on the wall behind them. Off to the right of the chair was the bathroom, a bare rectangular room with a concrete floor that slanted toward the northwest corner and ended in a metal drain cover. To the right of the drain was an eighty-liter bucket filled with water. Using a scoop, she bathed with the cold water, taking care to avoid the wound on her arm.

She found Francisco in the kitchen. He was silent as he busied himself, and when he saw her in the doorway shielding her eyes from the day's brightness, he stopped and closed the shutters. "Good afternoon," he said. "I was just getting ready to check in on you."

"Thank you for the clothes," she said. "And for your bed." She took a seat at the small table and put her head in her hands.

"How's your arm?" He set a mug of coffee and two white pills in front of her, took her arm and rolled up the sleeve, examining the makeshift bandaging.

"It doesn't hurt as bad as my head."

He pressed lightly on the wound and then lowered the sleeve and placed her arm back on the table. "Paracetamol is the best I can do," he said. "I'll change the bandages when you feel better."

"Thanks," she said, and swallowed the pills with a sip of the black coffee.

He transferred the food onto a plate and set it on the table. "If you're hungry," he said, and then he left the kitchen. Food was the last thing she wanted, but it was necessary. She toyed with the fork as she listened to him knocking about in the bedroom, and she'd managed to finish about half the plate when he returned to the kitchen.

Beyard pulled the second chair out from the table, turned it around, and sat down, resting his arms on the back of it. "I didn't sleep much last night," he said. He jabbed an index finger toward his forehead and twisted it. "Too many questions and a lot of memories."

Munroe started to speak, and he held up his hand, "There will be time, I hope, to answer the questions and lay the memories to rest. Last night you said you wanted to pay me to take you off the island. I want to hear more about this—regardless of what my answer may have been, perhaps I now have little choice. I need to know, Vanessa: Who wants you dead and does whoever it is know you are here?"

She was quiet for a moment, and finally she said, "I don't know."

He sat in silence, watching her, and she knew he would not speak until she had answered fully.

"I have ideas," she said. "I know why and have a vague notion of who gave the order. I wasn't followed here, but of course in spite of my precautions there is the possibility that when the boatman returns home, he will talk, and talk will travel, and eventually it will get back to Malabo."

"And this . . . what did you say? Notion. This notion of yours?"

"I've been hired to locate a girl who went missing four years ago, and so far the information I have points to the Mongomo crossing into Gabon. There were two of us. My assignment was to find the girl, my partner's assignment was to keep me out of trouble—not that it did much good. I have no idea what's happened to him." She stopped and took another slow sip of coffee. "We were followed from the airport and watched closely when we went about town."

"You were in Malabo asking questions?"

"Yes."

"Brilliant." There was no attempt to hide the sarcasm.

"It gets better," she said. He raised his eyebrows. With an effort she reached around and pulled the belt from under her pants. Her body was stiff and painful. She opened the Ziploc bag, removed Emily's death certificate, and handed it to him. He took it and, while his eyes scanned the paper, said, "You say she disappeared in Mongomo?"

"I believe it was in that area. I can't be certain until I've gone there to prove it one way or the other."

"And you got this paper in Malabo?"

"Yes, from the chief of police. He called in one of his people and had this delivered to me, then afterward suggested I return home."

"A veiled threat."

"Not so veiled."

Beyard stared at the paper and read it through a second time. His brows were furrowed. "What's in this for you?"

"A lot of money," she said.

Beyard sat back from the table. "It's not the way they do things here. Hauling you into the police station for questioning, yes. Torture, yes. Death from beating and starvation at the Black Beach Prison, yes. But to put you in a boat and dump you into the ocean, I've never heard of it. Who were the men that did this?"

"I'm not sure. They wore civilian clothing and spoke a language I haven't heard before."

"The presidential guard?"

"I speak Arabic."

"Angolans?"

"Perhaps. They were packing Makarovs, not that it narrows the playing field by much."

He stared again at the death certificate, then placed it in the bag and handed it back to her. "And you say they had this waiting for you?"

"More or less, yes."

Deep lines remained creased across his forehead.

"I am certain that what happened to me was a result of searching for this girl."

"So stop searching," he said. "It would be the easiest way to stay alive."

"I can't do that."

"Why not?"

A damn good question: Why not? She looked straight at him and simply said, "I just can't."

He let out a quick snort. "Maybe there will be time later to argue semantics." He stood. "When word reaches the capital, they'll be headed this way, and it won't take them long to begin looking for me. My ship is a kilometer or so up the coast. We'll leave at dusk." He turned and stared at her and then squatted so that his eyes were level with hers. "If it had been anyone else, Vanessa, I would have turned them over to the authorities myself and stayed to watch the execution. I lost you once. I have too many unanswered questions to let it happen again—at least so soon."

"I'm prepared to pay you well."

He shook his head slowly and gave her that same half smile. "And how do you propose to do that, when it is because you have no money and nothing of value to barter that you come to me?"

"I had planned to come see you when the job was over, Francisco. Not to ask for your help but simply to see you. This," she said, pointing to herself and then to the room around her, "was, as you say, a last resort. It's true I'm stranded at the moment, but it doesn't mean I'm without resources—they're just not here on the island." She paused and then asked, "Do you have a satphone?"

"I have one on my ship."

"How much do you want, Francisco? Name your price."

"I want nothing," he said. "I'll do what I can for you, Essa, because it's you, and only that."

She had begun to stand and then stopped.

Beyard was no altruist. He was a cutthroat, and there was always payback; he wanted something and would demand it eventually. "When this is over," she said, "you'll have the option of living your dream and leaving the continent."

"Perhaps," he said, and then, "Go sleep off the hangover. You'll need your strength come evening."

She returned to the bedroom, because compliance with Beyard's requests would be the easiest way to get what she wanted, but she didn't sleep, didn't even make the attempt. Her head was still fuzzy, and though it was difficult to focus on processing the pieces of information that made up the puzzle of the past week, her mind replayed endless loops of conversations and events and cogitated over Miles Bradford and what had happened to him.

Francisco came while it was still light. He carried a backpack and handed her a smaller one. "Can you carry it?" he asked.

"What's in it?"

"Just a few things I don't want the bastards to get their hands on when they loot the place."

The trek to the ship took them away from the coast via a faint path that wound steeply upward. Heading into the lush volcanic jungle, the trail skirted whatever habitations dotted the coastline and snaked around behind them. Francisco broke the path ahead, and the outline of his body, the smell of the wet earth, the pack on her back, and the sucking sound of footsteps in the silence were all a flashback in living color that brought with it the long-unfamiliar sensation of home.

The path curved down to the coast almost as quickly as it ascended, and near the waterline Beyard uncovered a hidden dinghy. They shoved the small boat forward and climbed inside. The trawler sat in deep water off the coast, and they boarded from a ladder off the side. By the time Beyard hoisted the dinghy and brought it over the deck, the sun had set and darkness covered the water.

The ship was larger than his last. As with his previous vessel, Munroe knew that the rusted and nondescript exterior was a well-disguised shell for a state-of-the-art home on the water. Beyard led her from the deck to the living quarters below.

"What do you think?" he asked.

"Impressive."

"It's a former Ukrainian fishing trawler, originally built for a crew of fifteen. Doesn't look anything like what it used to."

"I can imagine," she said. She walked from room to room, peering inside each one. They were small and compact, every space taken advantage of, and some had signs of having been recently occupied. "Where's your team?"

"Around."

"On the ship?"

He shook his head. "We will rendezvous. With all the oil-related movement going on in Equatorial Guinea, it's been more difficult to work. But there are ways. And other businesses."

"You don't worry about leaving your ship unattended while you're ashore?"

"I don't often do it," he said. "I usually take a fast boat to the island and leave the trawler with my crew, but no, I don't worry. We're in the middle of nowhere—who's going to mess with it? The local fishermen know to leave well enough alone, and if someone who knew what he was doing did find their way onboard . . . well, you know how it goes—I've got it covered." He stopped and opened a door to a small cabin, reached in, and turned on the light. "This one's yours."

"Where will you be?" she asked.

"Down the hall or up in the pilothouse." He jabbed his thumb in both directions. "The phone is also in the pilothouse. I'll take you there once you're settled."

She stepped inside the cabin to look around, and the door shut behind her. Only when she reached to reopen it did she realize that there was no handle and no way to get out.

MILES BRADFORD STOPPED and turned in a slow, dazed circle, taking in the chaos of the living room, where books and glass shards littered the floor. The coffee table was overturned. There was a crack in the mirror over the mantel and a hole next to the entertainment center where he'd put his fist through the drywall. He stared at his hand and wiped at blood that trickled from two of his knuckles.

The situation felt better now that he'd destroyed something.

There were no words for this. So much work down the goddamn drain. He'd played out any number of scenarios in his head along the way to finding Emily, but losing track of Munroe wasn't one of them. He'd seethed during the entire trip back to the United States, rage pressing against cracks in his resolve, looking for an escape valve, until it finally exploded in the seclusion of his home. Bradford kicked again at the sofa, then stopped and shook out his arms and shoulders. Enough.

He glanced again at the surrounding mess, sighed, pulled out his cell phone, and dialed. It had been a long while since he'd last had to call in the housekeeper to clean up after an outburst. She in turn would telephone her husband, and together they would put the place back in order, patch up the wall, and by the time he returned tonight, only the smell of fresh paint would be left as testament to the lapse in exercised calm. Bradford stepped over a lamp and checked his watch.

An hour to catch the flight to Houston.

BRADFORD STROLLED THROUGH the hushed corridors of Titan's headquarters. The corporate staff either ignored him or pretended not to see him, and a nod at Burbank's assistants was enough to gain access to the boss's office.

Bradford opened the door and, seeing Burbank, stopped midstep. Titan's driving force sat hunched over the desk at the opposite end of the room, fists tight and body curled, obviously unaware of Bradford's having entered. In the awkwardness of the moment, Bradford half turned to leave, then paused and remained transfixed, watching the silent emotional struggle until the moment turned painfully long.

He rapped softly on the doorframe, and when Burbank raised his head and gave a wan smile, Bradford said, "Hey," and stepped into the room.

Burbank straightened, stood, and walked across the distance, his face shifting from stricken to calm as he went. He clasped Bradford's hand warmly and with his voice cracking said, "Miles, what the hell happened?"

Bradford shrugged, and his shoulders slumped as if the air had been let out of him. Burbank stood motionless, and neither man spoke, as though they shared an unbearable burden that would only grow heavier with words.

Finally Burbank nodded in the direction of the sofa and said, "Come, let's sit down." He poured a drink from the wet bar, handed it to Bradford, then sat opposite him with his elbows on his knees. "I haven't slept since I got your call," he said. "Seriously, what the hell happened? What more have you found out about Emily? What about Michael?"

Bradford gulped down the contents of the glass, put it on the table, and with deliberation said, "Honestly, Richard, I don't fucking know."

"What do you mean you don't know? How could you not know?"

"One minute we're following a logical trail to the mainland, next minute—poof, Michael's gone and I'm persona non grata."

The two men sat in silence for several more minutes before Burbank spoke. "Miles, I apologize. I've been so focused on this thing with Emily. I just . . . Listen, are you okay?"

Bradford nodded and stared at the glass on the table. "Yeah, I'm fine. We were close, so goddamn fucking close." His eyes shifted to Burbank. "The answers are there, Richard. I can feel it."

Burbank drew a long, deep breath and shifted back in his seat. "You really think there's hope?"

"More than we've had since the beginning."

"That's the difference between us," Burbank said. "For four years I've been tormented by not knowing, and now that I finally have some sense of closure, I can grieve and let it go. But you, you push for more."

Bradford sighed. "I've already explained it, Richard. Even if Michael was wrong about the death certificate, you're the closest you've ever been to getting answers. Real answers. Real closure. Not this 'never really knowing for sure' thing. I was right about bringing Michael in, and I'm right about this."

"You'd return to Malabo?"

Bradford straightened so that he sat upright. "No, the mainland. We were headed to Bata when Michael disappeared."

"This being persona non grata, it won't be a problem?"

"There are ways around it."

Burbank took a deep breath. "Miles, I'm conflicted. If you think there's hope of finding answers, then of course I want them, but not at the expense of losing another person. If Emily did disappear in Equatorial Guinea, and now Michael . . ."

"That's the other thing," Bradford said. "I'll be tracking down Michael first."

"Her body?"

"The woman."

"But you said she's dead."

"It's what I was told, yes."

Burbank said nothing, and Bradford continued. "That woman has got insane survival instincts. If she's alive, and I'm certain she is, she's going to be pissed off and heading for the mainland. I need to be there."

"Assuming she's alive—which, no offense, after everything you've told me, I find difficult to believe—there's no way to know what she'll do. You're wasting your time, my friend," Burbank said, and then stopped. "That is, unless you know something I don't and you're holding out on me."

Bradford shook his head. "Research and gut instinct."

Burbank stared toward the plate-glass windows. "I don't know, Miles, it's a stretch. It's really a stretch—another futile pursuit, except this time I risk losing a good man for nothing."

"With or without you, I'm going back. I'd rather have your support."

Burbank's focus returned to Bradford. "If you're determined to go, then of course you have my backing, but I'd rather you not. I have the closure I need, so there's no reason left, certainly no reason for you to put your life at risk."

"Come on, Richard, you can't be serious."

"I am serious. I'm emotionally exhausted. I've been riding this roller coaster long enough. You want to go, you go—I'll have my office sort out the details." Burbank's face grew vacant, and his gaze returned to the plate-glass windows. "And be honest, we both know there's a chance you won't be coming home."

Bradford said nothing, and Burbank sighed the deep exhale of defeat.

"Before you go," he said, "get what you've seen and heard down in writing. The details you've uncovered—Michael's disappearance, the government officials and the death certificate—everything you've told me and anything else you remember. Consider it your parting gift should you never return."

Bradford nodded, and Burbank picked up the phone and, after a brief conversation with his lawyer, returned it to the cradle. "He's got time. You can see him on your way out." And then, after a pause, "So what happens next?"

"I find Michael."

"You're so sure she's alive?"

"Enough to bank on it," Bradford said.

"And you can find her?"

Bradford gave a soft smile. "Yeah. That I can do."

CHAPTER 12

3.10° N latitude, 9.00° E longitude
West coast of Cameroon

From within the pilothouse, Francisco Beyard stared out over the trawler's foredeck, arms crossed, motionless, except for his eyes, which scanned the steel gray of the ocean. He leaned over the console, punched coordinates into the ship's navigation system, and felt the vibrational shudder of course correction down to the core of his soul.

Nine years and she'd come back into his life as suddenly as she'd left it.

Nine fucking years since he'd traced her to the murky water of Douala's port.

There had been no warning, no indication. Just there. Or not. No good-byes, no thanks-for-all-the-memories, no fuck-all-of-you-and-your-despicable-existence. Just a vanishing, leaving him in agony while he spent two months of nausea and sleepless nights putting the pieces of the puzzle together; maddening days following a nonexistent trail; coming at last to the dead end of the freighter and the weathered deck-hand with his stories of knife fights and linguistic skill and of the boy, Michael, who could only have been Essa.

He had stood helpless and transfixed, watching the *Santo Domingo* shrink into the distance, the final tie to her severed. And there, with

Valencia, Spain, whispered into the wind, the trail ended with no way to follow it further.

He had paced the docks, convincing himself that he didn't care, reminding himself that he'd been doing just fine before she'd entered his life.

And it was the truth, though so much more the lie.

Like four generations before him, he was Cameroonian, a white African with no other passport, no other nationality, and no white man's country to return to when times got rough. This was home, his land, and since he was thirteen he'd had only one goal: to leave it. To amass a fortune with which he could build a good life outside Africa, somewhere in the world, anywhere, where hard work was rewarded and couldn't be wiped out in a flicker by the favorites and family relations of whatever sham democracy happened to be in power.

From pre–World War I France, his paternal grandparents and great-grandparents had come and built a life on the continent, all of it come to ruin in the heartbeat it took to raise the ire of the local government. Over. Finished. Generations of hard work obliterated pretty much overnight because his progenitors had picked the wrong continent. They should have chosen the New World, where those willing to tame the wilderness kept what they carved out.

His mother's family hadn't fared better in Equatorial Guinea. They'd come to Bioko Island in the late 1800s and had owned cocoa plantations until, six months after Independence, the bloodshed began. The educated and foreigners of all colors were the first targeted, and his mother's family fled to Douala, attempting to start over with nothing while they watched their homeland, once one of the wealthiest countries in Africa, deteriorate into a killing field.

By his late twenties, by anyone's standards, Beyard was ahead of the game. But the taps of currency had really begun to flow when he found Vanessa Munroe. It had been no accident. Gossip surrounding the unusual girl filtered through Douala's expatriate community, and he had arranged the meet through the Papadopoulos brothers, using their beach home in Kribi.

Under the pretext of running an errand, Vanessa's boyfriend, Andreas Papadopoulos, had left them in the quiet of the garden. Tall, gangly, and, with the exception of striking gray eyes, awkward-looking, she was not what Beyard had expected. In the quiet she studied him and then turned away, resting her forearms on the back of a wooden bench.

Standing so that his arms rested next to hers, he said, "Rumor has it you speak Fang."

She nodded. "And several of the other local languages as well."

"I need an interpreter for the evening," he said. "If you can manage that, there are five hundred francs in it for you."

Without facing him she said, "Five hundred francs is a lot of money if you want someone who speaks Fang. Ten thousand CFA would get you the same thing from a waiter at La Balise."

He smiled. "True, but you don't look like you speak Fang. More important, I need someone I can trust."

She turned and brought her eyes to his, eyes that threatened to penetrate and read thoughts. "And you can trust me?"

"I don't know," he said after a moment's pause. "Can I?"

The hint of a smile settled at the corners of her mouth. "It'll cost you five hundred francs to find out."

THE RENDEZVOUS WAS on the patio of a building at the edge of town that functioned as a hotel of sorts during the high seasons. The night was alive with the mingled sounds of laughter and the rhythms of soukous playing over a nearby radio. The smell of roasting meats and smoke from wood-burning cooking fires wafted through the air.

The only requirement Beyard had of her was that she listen to everything said around them. In the foyer while passing to the patio, she pulled him aside and warned of being held at gunpoint should they make the transaction.

The meeting was filled with veiled threats and bad French that soon turned to shouting. They left the hotel without completing the sale and hadn't yet pulled out of the potholed dirt parking lot before he offered her a full-time job.

In response she stared at him and then shifted to rest her head on the window. Gazing out the glass, silent, arms crossed, she said, "I know who you are and what you do and what working for you would mean."

"Sleep on it," he replied. "Tomorrow we can talk."

The next morning he invited Andreas to breakfast and, in questioning deeper into Vanessa's missionary background, was surprised to realize that the teenagers' relationship went far beyond the innocent puppy love the Papadopoulos parents assumed it to be.

"She's your age?" Beyard asked.

Andreas looked up in a shock of silence. "Younger."

"Sixteen? Seventeen?"

"Fourteen."

Beyard let out a low whistle. "Her parents? Do they know?"

"They know. She throws it in their faces. Sometimes I think she's using me just to get at them—not that I mind, you know." He smiled, almost bashfully. "She took me to her home this Christmas to meet them, and I swear the freakiest, loudest sex of my life was with her parents six inches from my head on the other side of the wall. Trust me, they know."

"So they don't care?"

"Oh, sure they care. What are they going to do about it?"

"Take her home? Send her to live with relatives? Cut off her money?"

"She refuses to return home, she already lives with friends of the family, and even if they did cut off her money, she'd find a way to get by." Andreas shrugged. "In the end her father indulges her. Emotional blackmail, I guess."

Beyard repeated the job offer over lunch. If she would agree to work for him, he would cover her living expenses, pay for whatever distance-learning education she chose, and give her a percentage of each job he collected on. She didn't answer, said she'd think about it, told him to come back the next day, and when he did, he learned that she'd left Kribi.

It took several days to locate her in Douala, and when he did that, she gave no apology and said simply that she would take the job but wanted a larger percentage. When he balked, she shrugged, turned to go, and he yielded.

He moved her to his beach home, gave her the run of the house, and rarely saw her when work was slow. But when on the job, she stuck by his side, a silent partner with the power of observation and linguistic skills worth many times the percentage he'd conceded.

It was in the hours after, the pressure off and the money safely away, that they talked and drank into the night. He taught her to play chess, she intrigued him with observations on the cultures they lived among, he introduced her to fine wine and classical music, and she recited local legends and argued theology with him, their conversations often turning philosophical.

It was almost a year later that he learned she had set him up, that months prior to being introduced, she had researched him—located information he didn't even know existed—analyzed him, understood what drove him, what made him tick, and then used Andreas, not to get to her parents but to get to him. Knowing that the brothers would talk, she'd planted ideas and stories, framing the context in order to pique his curiosity. She knew he would come looking, and when he did, she baited him with the one ability he lacked and couldn't resist. In the end she'd gotten exactly what she wanted: emancipation and money.

He'd laughed; in some perverse way it had pleased him to know that he, the consummate strategist, had been played. But that night he began to see her differently, as an equal. It was then that he realized she was no longer the gangly teenager he had brought into his house. Her body and her face had changed from those of an awkward girl into those of a beautiful woman, and with this realization came the desire to possess her. No, those were the afterthoughts. What he really wanted was to fuck her, and after that he wanted to own her, both body and mind.

She had fallen asleep on the couch, long legs trailing out from the thin blanket in which she'd wrapped herself, and he'd knelt in front of her and watched her sleep. He was so close he could feel her breath on his cheek—she could have been his—and he'd reached out a hand to touch her and then pulled it back. It was a conscious decision, a strategic decision. It had nothing to do with any notion of goodness or morality; he lived life by his own rules, getting what he wanted as ethically or as ruthlessly as necessary, because it made no difference. He was who he was without pretense or excuse, and his life amalgamated barbarianism and culture. Until now he had never denied one desire for the sake of another. And if he had known then the pain this change of view would bring, he would never have laughed.

In time, having his base in Kribi began to be a problem. In its own right, his property was secluded and, as was critical, had access to both sea and land. But it wasn't enough. He needed a location with less scrutiny, and that was what drew him to Equatorial Guinea. Río Muni, the mainland portion of the country, was just south of Cameroon's border and Bioko Island a short trip, depending on which boats they used. The location was propitious in that it was almost equidistant between Libreville and Douala, and as Equatorial Guinea was dirt poor, with no navy or coast guard to speak of, there was virtually no risk of bumping into authorities while transporting goods from one location to the next. It seemed to be a form of poetic justice that the country responsible for his familial poverty would soon be responsible for his rise to wealth.

He added extra men to his team and brought in mercenaries for protection. He used work as an escape from the euphoric ache that drove him to distraction when Vanessa was in his presence, grateful that Pieter Willem had her away for so many hours of the day. In spite of her repeated requests that Francisco remove Willem from the team, he never did.

Beyard's reputation grew, and so did the rumors surrounding the woman who accompanied him. He didn't understand the whispers and the extent of the superstition, because she never mentioned them. It was only after she was gone that he realized it was more than his heart that was so deeply entwined with her, that his success was steeped in legends, that the people he dealt with were terrified of the juju she commanded. And suddenly the juju was gone.

He had stood that day on the docks of the port staring out over the ocean, watching the *Santo Domingo* until it disappeared over the horizon. And then, hating her, he'd returned to Kribi to start over with what was left. He'd rebuilt, figured it out, just as he always had. And now she was back.

MUNROE RAN HER hand over the door where the missing handle should have been. Her fingers traced the doorframe and tested the strength of the door itself, noting metal through the woodlike veneer. She placed her ear against it, listening for the sound of Beyard in the hallway, and, hearing nothing, knocked lightly and said, "Francisco, can you open, please?"

Silence.

The hinges were on the outside.

She pulled the residency card from her belt and slid it between the door and the frame at the latch.

Nothing.

Her fingers moved to the walls, testing as she went.

Metal.

The cabin had a small bunk on each wall, a table that folded out between them, and cupboard space above the beds. There was no port-hole and no bathroom.

This was a cell. A prison.

A sea of gray washed over her, and she fought it back. She'd expected payback, but not in this way and not so soon.

Munroe dropped the backpack on a bed and then, after staring at it a moment, emptied the contents. Slowly, in shock, she sat beside them. They were her personal belongings, an assortment from the items she'd left abandoned when departing Cameroon: a hairbrush, a notebook, and a few articles of clothing.

She picked up the hairbrush and ran her fingers along the bristles, held on to the thick brush head with one hand, the handle with the other, and, gripping tightly, pulled hard. The pieces separated, and a four-inch blade slid out from under the bristles. It was a memento of her time fighting off Pieter Willem, one of many crude weapons she'd constructed in an attempt to never be defenseless. She shoved the pieces back together and tossed the brush onto the pile. No matter what Beyard's intentions, she would never use a blade on him that had been intended for Willem.

A shudder ran through the ship. The engines had been given life, and they were now moving through the water to an unknown some-where. In the silence the walls of the room weaved claustrophobically closer, and Munroe turned off the light and lay back on one of the beds. She took in a deep breath and followed it with a second and then a third, working backward into a state of calm and clarity.

Unless Beyard planned to let her starve, he would return. She had two days before Breeden expected contact. Two days with no watch and no way to gauge the time; waiting was all she could do.

The movement of the ship and the vibration from the engines remained constant, and it was two hours, three at the most, before she felt the differentiating tremor of footsteps down the hall. She tucked the hairbrush into her pants at the hip and returned to lying on her back with her arms behind her head. She did not get up when the door opened.

Beyard stood in the doorway, a silhouette against the light in the hall.

"Don't tell me this room was reserved for me," she said.

"You're not the first guest, if that's what you mean."

"What do you want, Francisco?"

"I don't know yet," he said. "And until I do, I want to be sure you aren't going anywhere. In the meantime I've kept my promise, I've taken you off the island."

She watched him, studied his posture, and analyzed his intonation. "Where would I go? We're on open water."

She sat up. His body tensed.

"I'm not scared of you, Francisco, and I have no reason to run away."

"You've done it before," he said, his voice soft, melancholic. "I have no guarantee you won't take one of the small boats in the night."

"True," she said, and she stood. Unable to see his eyes, shrouded in shadow as they were, she gauged how fast she could move by the minute reactions of his body. "But why would I want to do that when you've already said that you would help me? I not only need to get to the mainland, I need your knowledge, your expertise, once I'm there."

"I have no interest in providing my expertise."

She took a step toward him. "I was willing to pay you well, but obviously money no longer interests you." Another step forward, casual and slow.

Her hands were an exaggerated supplement to her words. "I need to travel to Mongomo, and I would like you to come with me. Tell me what does interest you—name it and I can find a way to get it for you." Nearly close enough to reach him.

"I spent two months searching for you," he said. "I had no idea what happened to you, didn't know if you were dead or taken for ransom or just plain lost." His voice trailed off, and then he jerked his head up, eyes dark and angry. "Two months, Vanessa. Do you have any idea what kind of hell that was?"

She reached out to softly touch his forearm, and in the same second that the warmth of her hand touched his skin and his face shifted to follow the movement of her fingers, she slammed a fist into his jaw. The force of the impact sent him reeling backward, and she moved with him, landing a second blow and then a third, forcing him against the wall.

He held his jaw and shook his head, eyes wide. Blood trickled from the corner of his mouth and painted his fingers. Before he could react, she stood in front of him and pulled the hairbrush apart, holding the blade inches from his face. "I could have killed you," she said. "Never forget that." She snapped the pieces back together and dropped the brush on the floor.

And then she softened her stance, lowered her voice. "I meant what I said, Francisco. I've got to get to Mongomo, and I don't know anyone who knows that backwater hellhole better than I do, except for you. Now that I've found you, I'm not going anywhere."

Silence filled the hallway.

Slowly Beyard slid down the wall to the floor, one knee bent, the other leg stretched across the corridor, his shoulders slumped, a hand over his eyes, and he wept in silent shudders. Munroe stood over him in shocked horror, and it was then that she understood.

She slid down beside him and put her head on his shoulder, and the past came flooding back, the memories of so many events and the clues she had missed while she was consumed with avoiding Willem.

"Francisco," she said, "I am so sorry. I had no idea."

He put his arm over her shoulders and pulled her to him, held her so tightly she would be bruised in the morning. The heat of his breath reached her hair and neck, and the remnants of tears touched her skin. She relaxed into him. Time passed, and the display of emotion faded. Control returned, and Beyard said, "Why did you do it? Why did you disappear like that?"

"I had to escape who I was becoming," she said, her voice barely a whisper.

"You could have told me, could have said good-bye, let me know you were okay."

"I'm not saying what I did was right, but you know as well as I do that if I'd told you I was leaving, you would have begged me to stay."

"Every night you came to me in my dreams," he said. "My greatest fear was that Pieter had come back for you to spite me. Every night I was reminded of the times you'd asked me to send him away and I'd refused." Beyard's voice caught and he breathed deeply, then continued. "When I learned that you'd left Africa, I hated you. I hated you for the sickness in my gut that followed me through every waking moment. And strangely, I was also happy, because I knew you were alive and that you had made the decision yourself, that it wasn't Pieter who'd done it."

"Willem is dead," Munroe said. "That night when the two of you fought, I followed him to the boats. I slit his throat and fed him to the jungle."

Beyard let her go, then pushed her back and turned her so that she faced him. His expression shifted from the open mouth of shock to a disbelieving smile.

"Why would you do that?" he said finally.

"Because he was a sadistic psychopath and by killing him I not only avenged myself for daily torture and rape, but I saved his future victims from the same or worse. It was his boat that I took back to Cameroon—I scuttled it just south of Douala. It's probably still there." She paused. "I had to leave, Francisco, or become the monster that he was."

Beyard grew quiet for a moment while the full impact of what she'd said filled the silence of the corridor, and then he pulled her close again and held her tightly. "I didn't know, Essa, I swear it. Looking back, it should have been so obvious, but I didn't see it."

"I know," she said. "And I hid it from you because I knew that if you were aware, you would have tried to protect me and gotten killed in the process."

"He told me he enjoyed sparring with you because you forced him to stay sharp. He said you were as gifted with a knife as you were with languages."

"Or as cursed," she said.

"Do you still carry them?"

"The knives? No. It's too easy to kill when a knife is in my hands." She looked at her palms, felt the permanent macula of blood, and clenched her fists. "I still train to keep my reflexes sharp, but even training knives are dangerous in the wrong hands. When I fight, even in practice, I'm overpowered by the urge to survive, to kill and win. Willem is not the only one dead by my hands."

"Last night I saw the scars on your body."

"They're from Willem. All but two or three."

Beyard said nothing, just held her tighter and then whispered back, "Promise me that when this is over, when it's time for you to go again, that you will let me know where you are and of your decisions."

"Perhaps," she said.

THAT NIGHT SHE slept on a settee that doubled for half of the seats at the small galley table. Beyard had offered her any cabin she wanted, including his own, and she had declined. In the morning after breakfast, he brought her to the pilothouse, showed her their coordinates, and answered her questions about the ship's navigational equipment. When she was satisfied, he pointed her to the satellite phone and left.

It was two o'clock in the morning in Dallas, and the champagne in Breeden's voice was flat until she heard Munroe speak.

"Michael! Where are you? We heard from Miles that you were dead, that you'd drowned and your body had washed up on shore."

Munroe opened her mouth and choked. Then, gathering focus, said, "Miles Bradford is alive? You spoke with him?"

"Yes and no. I mean, yes, he is alive. I haven't spoken with him personally. I got a call from Richard Burbank about two days ago. He's taken Bradford off the case."

"You can tell Burbank that the news of my death is greatly exaggerated and that I'll be continuing the assignment as contracted."

"To what intent? He says there's a death certificate."

Munroe rubbed a hand over her eyes. "Yes, that's true up to a point."

"So it's true, then? Emily is dead?"

"The certificate is worthless, except to prove that someone doesn't want me searching for Emily. There's more to the story, and I'm building the puzzle."

"As far as Burbank is concerned, the case has been closed."

"That's his call. If he wants to wrap it up, he owes me an additional two-point-five million. I'm going on with it whether he pays further expenses or not. Someone tried to kill me, and I'm not stopping until I get to the bottom of it."

"I'll contact him first thing in the morning. Do you have a number where I can get back to you? Where are you? Do you need help? Are you all right?"

"I'm fine," Munroe said. "I'm borrowing a phone, and I'm staying tucked away until I can sort out my options, but I'll give you a call back in a few days."

"Do you need anything? Is there anything I can do?"

"Just make sure Burbank gets the message, and if he closes the assignment, make sure I get paid. I'll be in touch."

Munroe resisted the urge to slam the phone into the cradle. Miles Bradford: alive and back in the United States. Vanessa Michael Munroe: drowned, washed up on shore. Richard Burbank: closing the assignment because of an alleged death certificate. What the hell? Miles Bradford had a lot of explaining to do, and if he had anything to do with her night out on the water, she'd be going after him next.

She dialed again.

"Logan, it's Michael."

There was the sound of the phone being fumbled and then glass shattering and then Logan's voice. "Holy shit, Michael! Kate told me you were dead. I've downed countless fifths in your memory. What the hell happened?"

"It's a long story that I can't get into right now, but I'm going to need your help. How soon can you work on a supply list?"

"I can start on it tomorrow. How big is it?"

"I'm not sure yet. I've got to discuss the job with a consultant, and I'll get back to you. In the meantime contact Kate and tell her you have an order number coming up so she can get you the money. I've already spoken to her. She knows I'm alive and keeping the assignment open."

"No problem," he said, and then, "Listen, I know you can take care of yourself, but I'm worried about you. What's this shit about you washing up on shore?"

"I'm not exactly sure," she said, drawing each word out slowly. "But I will find out. I have a few things to sort through, and then I'll get back with you—hopefully during your normal waking hours."

"I was up," he said, "drinking to your memory."

"Thanks, Logan. Save it for the real thing."

MUNROE FOUND BEYARD in the ship's hold. Originally designed for icing and storing fish, it had been gutted and converted to dry storage and docking space for the fast boats. A long-hulled cigarette boat sat on a wheeled rack locked in place by bolts in the floor, and next to it was an empty rack, and above them two more. Beyard worked his way around several dozen wooden crates that sat on pallets on the opposite side of the hold.

She cleared her throat to announce her presence. "Where's the shipment headed?" she asked.

He didn't look up. "I don't care, really," he said, and bent down to tighten a winch. "Sierra Leone, Liberia, Nigeria—makes no difference."

"It does to the people who end up at the other end of them."

He found her eyes and gave her a wry smile. "Maybe we can discuss it over a bottle of cabernet and a game of chess."

She held eye contact and cursed inwardly. How had she ever failed to miss that he was so goddamn charming? Her foot found the bottom rung of the railing, and she rested it there, leaning her forearms on the top rail. "When's the drop?" she asked.

"Tomorrow night. We rendezvous with my team this afternoon to pick up what they're bringing in, and then we head north for a handoff at sea. It's a straightforward job with no slogging it through the bush. After that I'll take you wherever you want to go." He stopped and looked at her for a moment, then said quietly, almost as if begging, "Essa, I would really like it if you'd be by my side for the handoff."

"Just like old times?"

"Just like old times," he said.

"Who are we dealing with?"

"Nigerians."

"Sure, I might even be useful." And then, "Do you have some time free? I'd like to get your advice on a few things."

"I'll be in the pilothouse in half an hour. Meet me there."

WHEN SHE KNOCKED on the door, he was bent over a series of charts that lay spread across a table braced against the wall. He slid the charts aside to make space for her, and the smile on his face said that he was genuinely happy to see her.

She sat on the edge of the table, dangling a leg over the side, and said, "How long is the list of people in this country with the power to have me dumped into the Atlantic?"

Beyard let out a low breath and leaned back in his chair. "It's hard to say, really, without knowing who the men were that carried it out. If we assume that they were Angolans, then it would have to be someone within the presidential family, someone connected enough not to risk a similar fate if the president was displeased about it. If they were merely rank-and-file military, the main issue, I suppose, is who *you* are, who you're connected to. If you don't have any important connections, the list of who could do it grows exponentially longer."

Munroe stared out the windows. The ship was surrounded by various shades of blue that stretched to the horizon, connecting in the far distance with the barely visible mountainous peaks of Bioko Island. She ran her fingers along the back of her neck. So many pieces of the puzzle and but for the central figure of Emily Burbank, none of them connected.

"What do you know about Titan Exploration?" she asked.

"Besides the inconvenience they've been to me, what's to know?" He shrugged. "They've been around for the past four or five years, started as a small presence off the coast of Río Muni, and once they struck oil, the operation grew and has continued to grow ever since. They just finished bringing another offshore well online last month. A tanker shows up about once a week, fills, and goes."

"The girl I'm trying to find is the daughter of Titan's founder."

Beyard sat quietly and tapped his pen against the table. "What was she doing in Mongomo? Why not Bata, why not Mbini?"

"I don't think her travels here had anything to do with Titan. It seems to be coincidence."

"Well, if she was connected to the captain of one of the oil firms and something happened to her here, I can see why someone in this country might not want you looking for her."

"That doesn't explain why I was followed upon arrival."

"True."

"And," Munroe continued, "if someone in the government is covering up her disappearance, did that person even know who she was when whatever happened, happened?"

"Do you have a photo of her?" he asked.

"Not on me, but I can get one off the Internet if you have access."

He pulled out a laptop and connected the modem through the phone. "It's painfully slow."

Munroe retrieved a page with Emily's high-school photo, downloaded it, filled the screen with her face, and then turned it toward Beyard.

He sat quietly, staring at the picture. "I've seen her," he said.

Munroe shook her head. "You're messing with me, right?"

"No, I'm serious. It was just over three years ago at the Bar Central in Bata. Her hair was different, but it's the same girl—same eyes, same nose. She was with a group of local men. Maybe there was another woman, I don't remember. She was pregnant. At the time it struck me as odd. I couldn't remember ever having seen a pregnant foreigner in Equatorial Guinea, and if I had, perhaps it was a Spaniard, but never a blond girl as white as she was. I must've been staring, because she turned to look at me. I smiled at her, and she smiled back."

Munroe pursed her lips. "You're certain it's the same girl?"

"It's been three years, Essa, I'm not going to stake my life on it. You know as well as I do how few foreigners are on the mainland, and how fewer still are women. They stand out."

One more puzzle piece.

"You said that after the handoff you'd take me where I wanted to go. Is Bata an option?"

"I can't take the trawler to the port, but I can get you there."

"And afterward will you go with me on to Mongomo if that's where the search takes me?"

Beyard sighed. "If there's no way to stop you from going, then yes, I'll go. I'd like to see you stay alive. Someone's got to watch your back. It might as well be me."

She smiled. "Thank you," she whispered. "Now I need to know how much it's going to cost me."

He was quiet for a moment, and then his eyes shifted from the windows directly to hers. "What I want in exchange," he said, "is your promise that when this is over, you won't simply walk off. I want to know where you are and how to contact you."

She felt invisible shackles snaking around her wrists and ankles, took a deep breath, and said, "If that's what it takes, I promise."

CHAPTER 13

2.40° N latitude, 9.30° E longitude
West coast of Cameroon

It was midafternoon when Munroe first heard the sounds of activity around the ship. From the wheelhouse she had a view of the entire deck. Alongside the trawler were three smaller boats, each loaded to capacity. Five of the crew had already boarded the trawler, and one stayed on the water to guide the deck cranes as they were manipulated over the boats to lift them out. None of the faces were familiar.

One at a time, the cigs were brought over the cargo bay and lowered directly onto the wheeled storage racks that waited below. A smaller crane located inside the ship unloaded the cargo from the boats, which were then wheeled into place and locked down. Halfway through the loading, Munroe left the pilothouse for the hold to get a better view. In less than half an hour, all three boats and their cargo had disappeared from the ocean and into the belly of the ship, and it wasn't until the lockdown was complete and the crew headed for the stairwell that they noticed her watching them.

The echoes that had reverberated off the walls fell silent.

Beyard wiped his wet hands on the back of his pants. "My apologies, gentlemen," he said. "Let me introduce you to our guest. This is Essa Munroe."

Their words came fast, a jumble of accents and languages overlapping one another. Beyard held up his hands, and there was quiet.

"It appears," he said to Munroe, "that your reputation precedes you." He winked at her. "For some inexplicable reason, you are something of a legend in these parts. I'm sure these gentlemen will enjoy the opportunity to discover whether the tales they've heard are true."

Beyard introduced his team, and one by one she shook their hands. They hailed from four countries—Romania, the United States, South Africa, and in addition to Beyard there were two others from Cameroon. English was the lingua franca, although some spoke it less than others, and French filled in the gaps.

Over a midday meal, Beyard regaled his crew with stories of times gone by, exaggerating with poetic license events that needed no exaggeration. Munroe enjoyed the humor and the retelling of happenings she had blocked out for nearly a decade. Beyard spoke animatedly and caught her eye on more than one occasion. When he did, her face flushed.

After the meal the mood of the crew changed from festive to somber. They would be traveling north through the night, and preparations would need to be made before the handoff. The galley emptied, and the ship fell ghostly silent.

There was nothing but time—that and the rocking of the ship. Munroe walked the vessel, familiarizing herself with every space, and then, restless and with nothing more to do, she searched out Beyard's team. The only member of the crew who appeared to be left on board was in the pilothouse. George Wheal was Beyard's second-in-command on the ground and first mate at sea. An African-American ex-SEAL, at six foot six he towered over the rest of the crew.

She stuck her head beyond the door and knocked on it. "Can I keep you company?"

"Sure, come on in." Wheal's voice had a booming quality that reminded her of Boniface Akambe.

She sat in the chair next to him, both of them watching the water as the trawler churned up the coastline. Munroe was first to break the silence. "So what got you into this fine mess of a job?"

Wheal swiveled his chair, peaked his forefingers, and peered over the tops of them. "When you're trained to blow things up, there aren't a lot of options in civilian life. Francisco needed a guy who could make things go boom, and I needed a job. Voilà, here I am."

She studied his face and his chocolate skin, then turned toward the ocean and smiled. "The locals treat you differently from the others, don't they?"

Wheal chuckled and rubbed a hand over his head where his hair would have been if he'd had any. "Yeah, until they know better, they treat me like I'm Beyard's houseboy. Or, if we happen to be going through the bush, a porter. It helps being a big guy," he said with a laugh that filled the room. "It gets you some respect at least."

She nodded knowingly. "Works both ways, doesn't it? You mention Africa back home and all that comes to mind is animal documentaries and Masai running around with spears."

Wheal smiled. "Yeah, it works both ways."

They sat in silence until Wheal rose to fiddle with the knobs on the console. "Is it true what they say about you?" he asked. "That you speak to the locals as a god and they see you as divine?"

Munroe laughed and then said, "No, it's not true."

"So someone just made that shit up?"

"Not exactly. They believe I'm a powerful witch and are terrified of the juju." She shrugged. "I speak the languages, know the cultures, and understand the nuances behind what they do—legends grew from that. You can't really blame them, considering the level of superstition. Hell, there's still even the occasional human sacrifice."

"You and Beyard," Wheal said. "You used to be tight, huh?"

"Yeah, we were." She tucked her legs up in the chair. "Has he told you much?"

"He only talks about you when he's drunk, but I've been with him for seven years, long enough to make some sense out of his ramblings. I'd be lying if I said I didn't find your presence here troubling."

"Do you find me threatening?"

He flashed a toothy grin. "Not even if *all* the stories I've heard are true."

She rolled her eyes. "Which they probably aren't." And then, meeting his gaze, she stared at him for a moment and said, "So what is it?"

He shrugged and turned away. "I'm only looking out for him. Looking out for myself. We've got a decent thing going here. Don't mess it up."

"You think I will?"

"I know you will," he said. "Francisco doesn't do this because he likes it. He does it because he's a fucking brilliant strategist and it comes naturally to him." He glanced at her. "With you around, his mind's not going to be on the next job, it's going to be on you. For me that's a problem."

She stood to go. "I can appreciate your perspective. If the roles were reversed, I might look at it the same way." Her hand was on the door. "You're a good man, Wheal. For what it's worth, I'm glad Francisco found you."

THE CLOCK ON the dining-room wall showed that it was after midnight. Even with the steady rocking of the ship and the hum of the engines, Munroe hadn't been able to fall asleep. Too many memories clashing with puzzle pieces that didn't fit. She poured a cup of coffee and then on impulse poured a second for whoever was in the pilothouse.

She knocked on the door, and when Beyard answered, she hesitated, debated, and then let herself in. She handed him the mug. "Couldn't sleep," she said. "Figured whoever was up here would want the company."

He took it from her, placed it on a narrow ledge, and squeezed her empty hand. "I'm glad you're here," he said. "I was just thinking about you."

"What about?"

The silence was filled by sounds from the radarscope, its monochrome band keeping time, a metronome of sorts. Beyard gave a glance at the console, stood, and then took her mug from her hand and placed it on the ledge next to his. With one hand around her waist, he drew her close and traced the curve of her neck with his fingers. He brushed his lips against hers. "Just thinking about you," he whispered. He moved his lips closer, his hands behind her neck, his fingers through her hair. He smelled of salt and the ocean and all things familiar. Her eyes followed his as they traced the outline of her body. And then he kissed her lightly, hesitated, and pulled her again to his mouth. The kisses were deep, passionate. His hands ran over her shoulder blades, to her neck, and down her spine.

She didn't resist and didn't reciprocate. After what he'd said in the hallway, she understood where this came from and hadn't yet sorted through the options of what to do with it and how to use it. Francisco reached for the buttons of her shirt, then he stopped and backed away. He stroked her face. "I have wanted to do that for eleven years," he said, drawing her close and holding her to his chest. "I could be consumed by you. It would be so easy." Then he let go and turned away to face the windows and the navigation console. With his back to her he said, "Stay with me through the night?"

She took a seat behind him, and they sat in silence for some time, she staring at the back of his neck and he facing the prow.

"Tell me about your life," he said.

"Anything in particular?"

"Have you been happy?"

"I haven't been unhappy."

"It's not the same thing," he said. "What about marriage? Have you found your match?"

Such a simple question, so many complex ways to answer. She said only, "No, I haven't."

He turned to look at her briefly and then faced front again. "It's difficult, isn't it? For people like us, to find someone who understands and can live with who we really are, without judgment, without trying to make us conform to their own preconceived notions of life."

He was quiet again, and the time passed between them.

"I left the continent, Essa," he said, "after I tracked you down and knew more or less where you'd gone and that you were alive. You never told me of the legends that followed you. By the time I figured that part out, we'd had several disastrous deliveries. Then Jean left. I had put together enough of a fortune to pull out, so I did. I packed up and left, tried to start over in France, and when that didn't work, I went to Spain. I was back in Africa within two years."

He turned to look at her.

"It wasn't the business that failed. I made money in Europe, set up new contacts that I still use. Could have gone on indefinitely." He pounded a fist into his chest. "It's inside. I couldn't live their life, couldn't adjust." He got up to check the navigation console and then sat down again. "So here I am, back where I started, back in my element where I thrive—hate it but thrive. No matter how despicable it may be to you, at least I am there to look at myself in the mirror each morning, which is better than the alternative."

She stood and, putting her hands on his shoulders, worked out the tension in his muscles. "We all have our demons, Francisco. Some are harder to fight than others."

He reached a hand up and placed it on hers, then gently pulled her in front of him. "What are your demons, Essa?"

Her smile was sad, and she shook her head. "The aloneness. The invisible walls. Always the outsider looking in. Different. Unusual. I despise their world and the superficiality of it all and yet still want to be a part of it. I wonder sometimes how much simpler a life of naïveté and unawareness would be." She moved away and returned to the seat behind him. "I have on occasion found people I could trust with who I really am, and when that happens, I walk away."

He turned to look at her, clearly puzzled.

She shrugged. "It's safer that way—for them, for me. It's far easier to bear personal pain than the responsibility of someone else's. I feel safe around people as tough as I am, but they don't come along that often." She smiled wanly. "So I walk away."

She stayed with him until shortly before dawn and then stood to go.

"Will you sleep?" he asked.

"If I can."

"Take my cabin, please. You'll rest better there and"—he held up his hand—"I swear on my own life that I won't lock you inside."

"All right," she said, and left.

His cabin was larger than the others. Instead of dual bunks sand-wiched tightly together, his had a double bed and its own bathroom. The cabin was well lived in, a home whose occupant never left for long, yet it still managed to have an aura of sterility, testament to Beyard's fas-tidious nature. Built into one of the walls was a floor-to-ceiling bookcase filled with volumes ranging from the intellectual to the mundane and, in a recess that appeared to be built specially for it, a marble chess-board. Munroe glanced at the board, at a game in play, and lifted one of the pawns. A tacky gum had been stuck to the bottom of each piece to keep them from spilling across the board with the rolling of the ship. She analyzed the game and then showered and for the second time slept in the clothes she was wearing, falling asleep on top of his bedspread. Sometime later, somewhere on the border of awareness, she heard him come into the cabin, felt him lie next to her on the bed, and then sleep came again.

By next nightfall they had moved into the waters off Nigeria's coast, their position precoordinated and pinpointed by GPS. The lights on the trawler were out, the engines quiet, and there was enough heavy artillery on hand to supply a small conflict. On top of the pilothouse, Lupo, the Romanian, lay hidden with a silenced sniper rifle, and the rest of the crew were stationed around the ship wearing Kevlar and cradling sub-machine guns. Clouds thick with rain blocked out what light the moon and stars would have provided, and at ten minutes after two a single light flashed on the horizon, followed several minutes later by the sound of engines across the water.

Beyard stood on the prow. He faced the approaching ship, and Munroe stood behind him at a distance; it was her position, the observant, silent shadow. He was an outline, tall, shoulders squared, a shape blending with the night, a man in control and secure in his surroundings. She knew that his mind ran strategy, a giant chessboard to be played in real life. To watch him and stand in awe of him was familiar from the past, but the emotion running beneath the admiration took her by surprise. In Beyard's confidence was a power, a force that lesser men could never hope to imitate, and she was drawn to that power.

From over the darkened waves, the other ship loomed, not as large as the trawler but sleeker and no doubt faster. Munroe watched as a Zodiac bearing five men closed the distance between the two ships. She waited until she could gauge the extent to which they were armed, then, as the first began to climb the ladder, retreated into the shadows. Three of the Zodiac's five boarded, and Beyard strode toward them.

Their leader was a short, heavy figure in battle fatigues. His men stood silent where they'd stepped onto the deck, and he moved forward, greeting Beyard with a strong handshake that implied a shared camaraderie. He handed Beyard a briefcase, and the banter between the two was easy and familiar. The commander's English was perfect, absent any indication of pidgin, and crisp with enunciation that contrasted sharply with Beyard's bastardized English.

The wind stifled the sounds of their conversation, and so Munroe turned her focus to the trawler's crew, confirming their positions in relation to one another. She moved around a railing near the side of the ship, and it was then that she heard the low, nearly inaudible whine of an electric engine. She glanced at Beyard, who was nodding in approval over the open briefcase, then up toward Lupo, invisible on the pilothouse roof.

The sound of the engine cut. Munroe turned toward the ladder, saw that the commander's men were no longer there, and in that instant a burst of gunfire shattered the night.

She dropped, palms to the deck, and the first rush of adrenaline coursed through her veins. She waited. Listened. And then inched toward the side of the ship, peered over, and confirmed a second Zodiac, empty. She swore under her breath. The commander and his men were familiar with the trawler and its layout; she'd seen that in their interaction with Beyard. This wasn't a handoff at sea but a goddamn hijacking—the pilothouse and the hold with its cache of weapons, those would be their targets.

On deck, Beyard was gone, as was the commander, and the ship had turned driftwood silent. Munroe took a deep breath, mentally placed the crew, then knelt and took off her boots. The cold of the ship's metal spread from her toes to the marrow of her bones. There would be no halfway tonight, no truce. If the trawler were to be taken, she and the crew would be executed, and should they succeed in defending it, the enemy must die. It was the cold-blooded reality of treachery: One way or the other, the ocean would claim her dead. Munroe stood, bare feet fueling the savage ecstasy of the hunt to come.

Another burst of gunfire erupted aft, followed by the muted clap of the sniper. Munroe hugged the wall and moved toward the foredeck, where Wheal had been. There was another hiss from the sniper, followed by a padded thud, then an exchange of gunfire.

Silence.

Munroe slid around the corner. Wheal, crouched low, signaled in her direction, motioned fore, then held up three fingers. She nodded and gestured for a knife. He slid one to her, and Munroe took it, retreating the way she'd come. With the blade between her teeth, she slipped over the side of the trawler.

The Zodiacs had been left empty. Stupidity or overconfidence, Munroe wasn't sure, but their failure to guard egress would cost them. She sliced at the fabric of the first Zodiac, eyeing the silhouette of the enemy ship less than three hundred meters away. The Zodiac collapsed under the knife, took on water, and sank while the ghost rising out of the waves stood sentinel, no doubt waiting for a signal to close the distance. Munroe slit the material on the second boat, scurried up the ladder, and slithered onto the deck, cautious not only of the intruders but of moving into the kill zone of one of the crew.

A fusillade of bullets from one of the submachine guns ricocheted off the stairwell that led to the pilothouse. There was return fire, silence, and then another thud on the deck. Hidden as he was with a night-vision scope, Lupo had a temporary advantage. Against how many, though? That was the question.

Munroe moved amidships to a hatch that would feed away from the deck with its high probability of getting caught in the crossfire, then to the hold, the only direction in which Beyard could have disappeared. She dropped down into the dank belly of the ship, and the black swallowed her. Disoriented by the lack of light, Munroe's fingers traced the railing, and, sightless, she moved forward, one cautious step at a time.

Awareness of a presence came finally, not from the front as she expected but from behind, an expulsion of breath so soft it raised the hair along her arms. In a fluid movement, she slipped over the top of the railing and held herself in place while a whiff of body odor and soap, cigarettes and cooking oil, passed by. There was no way to gauge his height or even the strike distance, rendering the surprise of a knife useless. But there were legends and superstitions. Here in the dark, they were a weapon.

Unable to pinpoint her location in relation to the items in the hold or ascertain the length of the drop, Munroe hung to the bottom rail, turned to face the opposite wall, pitched her voice an octave higher, and in accented pidgin English hissed, "Who dares disturb my sleep?"

Hesitant footfalls mixed with the chambered echoes of her voice, and so she said again, this time more forcefully, "Who dares disturb my sleep?"

The presence swore, mumbling under his breath just clearly enough that she could discern his language. In Ibo she repeated the phrase once more. She traced his reaction by the elevated breathing. Soft and singsong and slightly louder, she said, "Leave me."

He did not turn but faltered, and she persisted, reaching out into the dark until she snagged his bootlace. *"Mek you no woreemee,"* she wailed. *"Or I go kee you."*

His breathing became frantic. She could follow him now, knew the direction he faced, gauged the height of his head, knew that she must strike, and as she slid over the railing, the man bolted back the way he'd come. Munroe followed only far enough to guarantee that he'd gone through the hatch. With any luck, Lupo would have him as soon as he hit the deck.

Munroe returned to the railing where it joined the stairs. Whatever others were in the hold—and she was certain that at the least this was where the commander remained—they had heard the voices, and she would draw on that to flush them out. Following the stairs to the floor of the hold and moving cautiously through the dark, she cycled through Hausa, Ibo, and Yoruba, calling and taunting, gradually becoming aware of more than one presence through the footsteps and shuffling.

Halfway across the floor, she bumped into one of the enemy, startling him more than she startled herself. He yelped, swung wildly, but before he could fire his weapon, she'd plunged the knife into his throat, cursing inwardly at the speed, at the instinct, at one more death she would never be able to wash clean. She dropped his body softly, setting his arms and legs spread-eagled.

Passing the keel of one of the cigarette boats, she picked up a whisper from Beyard, perfectly spoken to blend with the chamber's echo of ghostly wails. She belly-crawled in his direction.

"There were five," he whispered.

"We need starlight," she said. "Can you get the top open?"

"Take me three minutes."

She moved from under the boat to the front of the hold, and there

she waited until the first ambient rays of the cloud-covered moon began
to seep in. Shrill and harsh, she yelled, "See your dead! I have taken
him! Leave now and live!"

The response was a rapid report of assault weapons, which came in
sporadic bursts, punctuated by yells and curses, all filling the cavernous
hold with an ear-shattering din. And then from the rim of the opening
gap came the repeated hiss of the sniper. The hold fell silent.

At last the commander's voice reached out from the darkness. "Even
I have heard the legends," he said. "We will leave."

Munroe followed the sound of his voice and, silent through the shadows, came behind him, put the knife to his throat, and removed his
weapons. The commander's call to his men was followed by the sound of
their rifles falling, and from within the hold two stepped into the center.

All lights off, Beyard turned the trawler northwest, putting a slow distance from the enemy ship, and then the commander and the four men who
remained were left to swim while the dead were dumped overboard. With
so much blood, chance dictated that sharks would finish the fight. The
briefcase—now emptied—in which the lure of payment had been delivered was also dumped, and the crew swept the ship for tracking devices
and explosives. As a precaution they would rotate the guard until dawn.

IT WAS FOUR in the morning when Munroe knocked on Beyard's door.
He called out an answer, and when she opened the door, he stood by the
bed, a thick towel around his waist, his hair and body still wet. She froze
silent for a moment and, realizing that she stared, blushed. His physique
had improved with age—either that or she had never appreciated it the
way she should have. What was he now—thirty-seven, thirty-eight? "I
need to make another call to the United States," she said.

"If you give me a minute," he said, "I'll go up with you. Augustin is
in the wheelhouse, I'll take over for him until you're finished." He patted
the bed, an invitation for her to sit, and returned to the bathroom. When
he came back, he was dressed, and he sat beside her.

"It was nice having you with us," he said.

She nodded. Smiled.

"Would you come back if I asked?"

"Knowing that I've built a good life for myself beyond this," she said, "would you ask it?"

"I don't know."

She ran a palm across his clean-shaven face. "What if I asked you to come with me, to be part of my life?" It was a rhetorical question meant to challenge, not to invite, but he ignored the undertone, took her palm, and kissed it.

"If I could, I would spend every waking moment of every day as a part of your life," he said. "But there's nothing out there for me, Essa. I already know that."

He leaned over and kissed her forehead, then stood. She took the hand he offered and followed him to the pilothouse, where she put in a call to Logan.

LOGAN SOUNDED RELIEVED when she said hello. "I'm glad to hear your voice," he said. "It means you're still alive, still safe."

"You worry too much," she said. "I'm in good hands." She glanced at Beyard, whose back was to her.

"Do you have the supply list?" he asked.

"Actually, no. That's why I'm calling. I might not need it—things may be more straightforward than I'd thought. But don't go anywhere, I'll check back in a few days."

"Michael, before you go—I got a call from Miles Bradford last night. I think you need to talk to him."

"Say again?"

Logan drew in a breath. "It will take too long for me to explain it all, and it's convoluted. I just think you need to call him."

"I suppose that means he knows I'm alive?"

"He knows it now because of me. Before that it was just speculation on his part. Apparently he's tried to talk to Kate and she won't give him the time of day."

"Fine, give me the number." She jotted it down as he spoke. "Thanks, Logan, I'll be in touch."

She stared at the paper and then dialed. When Bradford picked up, she said, "It's Michael. You wanted to talk with me."

A second of silence on the other end, and then Bradford's voice: "Are you okay?"

"I am now." And then, "This call is costing me five bucks a minute. Make it fast, make it good, and make it worth my time. What the hell is going on, and what's this bullshit about my body washing up on shore?"

"Until I spoke with Logan last night," he said, "I had only believed you were alive, wasn't sure, couldn't know. It's a relief to have it confirmed, to hear your voice." His tone was full of genuine sincerity. "I've been trying to get in contact with Kate Breeden," he said. "She won't take my calls."

"So I've heard."

"Listen, Michael, there are several things I think you should know. First, it was the U.S. embassy that informed me you had drowned and washed up on shore. Second, the local officials never produced a body, and when I got too demanding about it, I was informed that my stay in the country was over and I was put under guard until the next flight out. I'd had reservations about your disappearance from the beginning: I knew I'd been drugged and thought it was you who did it. When I went to your room to confront you, there were signs of foul play. I searched the hotel and the area around it and nearly had my skull cracked by a police officer when I got into a fight with some of the hotel staff, who wouldn't or couldn't give me straightforward answers about whether or not you'd left.

"I've had more than one conversation with Richard about the situation, laid out the scenario of Emily's being in Equatorial Guinea as you'd given it to me. He has latched onto the issue of the death certificate and refuses to acknowledge the strangeness of it. Says he's tired and that this is closure for him."

Munroe was quiet and then said, "I have an eyewitness who's placed Emily alive on the Equatorial Guinean mainland within the past three years."

Silence.

"You there?" she asked.

"Yeah." His voice was tight, strained. "I'm just thinking about what you said, the possibility of what it means. What are you planning to do?"

"I spoke with Kate several days ago. She told me Burbank pulled the plug on the assignment. My contract gives me a year to locate Emily, and if he rescinds, I'm guaranteed a shitload of money, which I will happily take. But I'm not leaving. Someone tried to kill me, Miles, and you know as well as I do that it's because of my search for Emily. I have no idea why it was me and not you or both of us, but I *will* find out. I'm going to Bata with or without Burbank's blessing, and I'll keep going until I find her or find my killer, whichever comes first."

"I want to go with you," he said.

Munroe laughed. It was a harsh laugh, sarcastic and unfeeling. "You weren't much help to me the first time around. I can't think of any reason I'd need you the second time."

"You don't get it, do you?" His voice was hard. "Emily is like a niece to me. I took Richard's assignment for her, not for him. You don't give a damn about her. *You* took this assignment for the money, and now it's about revenge. I want in because I care about her."

"Forget it, Miles," she said. "I don't need a liability on my hands, and I have all the help I need." She hung up without giving him a chance to respond.

She pulled a sheet of paper out of the fax machine and drew a diagram, an outline of tenuous facts surrounded by big, fucking, glaring holes. And in the middle, attached to nothing, she added another: By morning the U.S. embassy was already aware of her death. Chances were they'd been notified before she'd even been taken onto the boat. She sat in front of the paper staring, willing the answer into focus.

Nothing. She needed more pieces.

It was Beyard's hands on her shoulders that returned her to the present. "We can take it to my cabin," he said, "go over the details there." She nodded and folded the diagram, and he picked up a two-way radio, calling Augustin back to the pilothouse. In another hour the sun would begin to rise.

"THE EMBASSY HAD already been informed of my death by morning," Munroe said.

She lay on Beyard's bed, her hands behind her head, studying patterns on the ceiling. He was next to her, lying on his side, quietly watching her. "It would be useful to know who informed them, what branch of government, who in that branch," she said. "I need to get the embassy's phone number. I'm sure it's on a consular sheet somewhere on the Internet."

He traced her profile. "We'll get it," he said, "But first you need to sleep." She began to sit up in protest and he put a finger to her lips. "You know as well as I do that clarity and focus will come with sleep and food. We have time. We won't be in Kribi until sometime in the afternoon tomorrow."

She lay back down and in that moment of acquiescence understood that Beyard was dangerous.

He continued to run his finger along her body, tracing it down her throat and over her chest. His gaze followed his hand, and so he avoided her eyes. "On one of those calls," he said, "you used the name Michael. It's the same name the deckhand from the *Santo Domingo* gave me."

His hand rested on her stomach, and she took it and brought it to her lips. "It's a moniker I've taken for the work that I do."

"You've never told me what it is that you do."

"It's a topic for another time," she said. She turned to look at him and then rolled over and straddled his pelvis, pinning his hands with hers. She leaned over him and touched his lips with hers. He breathed a sigh and then without warning jerked his hands free, grabbed her by the waist, and put her back down on the bed. "Don't toy with me, Essa," he said.

He was strong. Powerful.

"Why do you assume I'm toying?" she asked. "I want your body as badly as you want mine."

He smiled. His eyes were sad; his mouth was cruel. "You couldn't possibly."

He stroked her hair, still avoiding her eyes. "When you were here with me, I resisted what I wanted most, and when you were gone, I spent years trying to forget what it was that I wanted." He brushed his hand lightly over her neck and down her chest. "And here you are again. In front of me, beside me, mine for the taking. I'm not sure whether I love you or whether I hate you and want to destroy you."

"Does it matter?" she asked.

She knelt on the bed and removed her shirt, took his hands and brought them to her breasts, and then bent and kissed him, touching her mouth lightly against his, teasing him with her tongue. He searched out her eyes. "This is a game of control for you," he whispered.

She grazed down his neck, and his breathing quickened.

"If it is," she said, "what does the strategist in you tell you that it means?"

He stared at her for a second and then wrapped his arms around her, brought her to him, and filled his mouth with her, and when he did, a heat gripped her throat and shot through her body.

It was one thing to allow a man access to her body, another thing entirely to allow a man access to her soul.

CHAPTER 14

2.00° N latitude, 9.55° E longitude
West coast of Equatorial Guinea

The sea was an endless sheet of steel gray reflected off the cloud-covered sky and the trawler a small black blemish on the horizon. It was nearing sunset, that period of day when the sky would change into brilliant hues and the ocean would undulate with color. Munroe leaned into the wind and the ocean spray, closed her eyes, and allowed her thoughts to flow in random patterns, willing synapses to connect and make sense of patchwork pieces of information that continued to bring more questions than answers—and found nothing.

The cigarette boat cut across the water with considerable speed, closing the distance on the city of Bata, which was now at some invisible point over the horizon. Three hours earlier the trawler had weighed anchor off the southern coast of Cameroon, and, with the exception of George Wheal, who had agreed to remain with the ship until Beyard returned, the crew had dispersed to the mainland. In the pilothouse Munroe, Beyard, and Wheal had sat poring over hand-drawn maps that Beyard had assembled throughout the years and debated over supplies and transportation for the few possible routes through Bata and into Mongomo.

The project was Beyard's now. Munroe had never officially given it to him; he'd taken it, dissected it, and then meticulously planned it, a master strategist setting out pieces to one more living chess game.

It was a throwback to another life, another world, and as it was then, there would be no discussion now about doing the job her way. Beyard was no lackey; conceding command was the price she would pay for his participation.

And then Bata was there, its red-and-white visage faintly visible on the horizon. They continued south a few miles past the city, just beyond the reach of the port, to one of Beyard's properties, where they would exchange the boat for a land vehicle.

THE WOOD OF the dock was worn smooth and weather-beaten, held fast by solid pier beams driven deep. It ran from the back of a well-manicured property over the sands of the beach, fifty feet out into the water, and tied to it was a small fishing boat, the wood still raw and new. Beyard guided the cig to the opposite side of the pier and with a confident hop moved from the boat with the mooring ropes.

The house stood on two acres, a single story that seemed to spread out and melt into the lush landscape. From the back door, a woman walked toward them. Her skin was soft brown, her features smooth and perfect, and behind her a small child followed, barely walking and clinging to the shapely dress that skimmed her ankles. Her smile was genuine, and she greeted Beyard with a familiar hug. In all the planning of the afternoon, Beyard had failed to mention a woman or her child, and when she greeted Munroe with the casualness of an equal, Munroe pushed away hostility and forced a mask of pleasantry.

The woman smiled when Beyard spoke, and the electricity that flashed between them betrayed a history far beyond the platonic. Beyard knelt to the eye level of the child and tickled his rounded tummy, then pulled the youngster to his arms and tossed him in the air. Peals of laughter filled the property, though Munroe heard nothing but the rush of blood pounding in her ears and stood paralyzed with an ersatz smile plastered to her face.

Beyard put the child down and turned to Munroe. His mouth was moving, and she forced the sound to register. "This is Antonia," he was saying. "She, her husband, and their three children live here—it's their house and their land unless I happen to be in town." He nodded beyond the house. "There's a guesthouse on the far end of the property. That's where we'll stay the night."

The guesthouse was furnished with necessities and not much else. The building consisted of two rooms: a bedroom with a small bathroom annexed to it and a larger room that functioned as a living room on one end, a kitchen on the other, divided by a four-place table. There was no air-conditioning, but the ceilings were high and a steady breeze tempered the humidity.

By the time they had showered, darkness had settled, and Antonia, not one of the servants, brought food from the main house. From the bedroom Munroe heard her enter, and from behind the closed door she traced portions of the muted conversation. There were spaced silences. Lingering. And then the front door closed, and both Beyard and the woman were gone, and Munroe realized that she'd been holding her breath and felt a stab of self-loathing because of it.

The emotion she felt was a violation of the cardinal rule of survival; it skewed reason, clouded logic, had to be eradicated. Munroe took a deep breath and exhaled. She needed control, and to regain it required internal shutdown. Another intake of air, and she closed her eyes and then against her better judgment fought it, argued against it, and finally postponed it. Beyard was a rare equal, a man with skill and motive to destroy both her and the assignment. The danger was an intoxicating lure, difficult to abandon.

It was twenty minutes before Beyard returned. Over dinner they conversed—Munroe knew it with her eyes—Beyard's moving mouth, a shrug, a flirt, the sound of her own voice traveling through her head and Beyard's charming smile in response. It continued through the meal, external harmony enshrouding internal turmoil. Shutdown was inevitable. But it could wait.

They were awake before daybreak, that time of darkness when the jungle came to life with ascending simian and avian orchestras that shut out the predatory calls of the night. The air was damp with a light mist, and when the sun rose, it brought a thickening to the humid heat.

Beyard's transportation was a nondescript Peugeot, originally beige or possibly white, now permanently rust-colored. Unlike everything else he owned, whereby aged appearances disguised state-of-the-art equipment, the Peugeot was decrepit. In response to Munroe's reluctance to use it, Beyard insisted. "It's better for us this way," he said. "My other vehicles are known. With this one we are provided a certain sense of anonymity, and in any case we're not going far—in about five kilometers the roads become paved."

"We're not taking this thing to Mongomo?"

"No," he said. "We'll use the Land Rover for that, possibly one of the Bedford trucks."

"Do you have easy access to one?"

"Shouldn't be too much of a problem," he said. "When I'm not using them, they're leased out to the Malaysians and Chinese—I have a company that handles logistics from the logging cut sites to the port. It's a legitimate cover for the trucks and gives me the opportunity to pay my dues in terms of hefty contributions to the local fraternity of nepotists. During the rains I'll use them if we have to haul through the bush, so it won't be out of place."

Munroe nodded and then said, "If I want to leave a few things behind, do you have a secure spot?"

"I do," he replied, then led her back to the guesthouse bathroom and with a skilled set of hands removed a section of the doorframe and pulled out from the wall a narrow sealed container that held several thousand euros. "Should still be some space in there," he said, and handed it to her.

She pried the lid loose. "How secure is this property?"

"No military will enter, if that's what you mean."

She removed the Equatoguinean residency card from the security belt and placed the belt with her passports, credit cards, and Emily's death certificate into the container. "What guarantee do you have?"

"Antonia is the oldest and favorite niece of one of the president's wives, and Antonia's husband is connected to the president through the military. Between the two of them, the property is safe."

She sealed the lid. "That's good for them, but it doesn't protect your valuables." She nodded toward the container in her hands.

He smiled and took the container, slid it back into the wall, and replaced the boarding. "You have to know everything? All my secrets?"

Munroe shrugged. "Whether you tell me now or not doesn't really matter. When I want information, I get it. I'll find out one way or the other."

"All right then," he said. "Antonia and I, we go way back—I'm the father of her eldest son. He's eight, so you can do the math." While he spoke, Beyard walked toward the front of the house, and Munroe followed. "About four years ago, when our relationship was shot to hell and there appeared to be no future for us, she married her current husband— she's wife number three. He lives in the capital, and she sees him once or twice a month."

Beyard opened the door of the Peugeot for Munroe and fiddled with the handle in order to get it to remain closed. He slid into the driver's seat and slammed his own door several times before cranking the engine. "I bought this place for her," he continued. "Put it in her name. It's her insurance policy and will buy her freedom if that's what she chooses— you know how it goes here—and now that the oil companies have their compounds nearby, it's a valuable little piece of real estate."

Munroe knew well. When an Equatorial Guinean woman married, she became bound to the husband and his family, often becoming a form of property. Divorce, although technically possible, placed an impossible burden on the woman: By law the husband kept the children from the marriage and the woman was required to pay back the dowry or else be imprisoned, and imprisonment in the country's decaying mixed-gender jails was little better than a death sentence.

The vehicle sputtered forward. "I think you would agree," Beyard said, "that my confidence is well placed and the property is safe."

Munroe looked at him sideways and crossed her arms. "Yes, I would agree." She paused and turned toward him. "It may have been nine years, but you haven't changed much. There's always a price. You're using her."

He looked at Munroe, taking his eyes off the dirt track that passed for a road. "I've never denied it," he said. "The fact is, she doesn't care."

"And her husband, does he care? Surely he knows your history, knows you use this property, knows you're sometimes here when he's gone—he can't be happy about that. He probably wouldn't mind if you disappeared."

"Nah," Beyard replied. "I'm the one who introduced the two of them, and he's one of my best friends." He shrugged. "Things are what they are, Essa. My relationship with Antonia ended four years ago and, I might add, through no fault of hers. I'm the one who's fucked in the head. We have a son together, and regardless of what things are now, I want her to be happy. Whether I'm using her or not, she still comes out ahead, and so does the boy." He turned to look at her. "Satisfied?"

"I suppose." And then, after several moments of silence, "Does your son know you're his father? Do you see him often?"

"Yes, and not very. When he turned seven, I took him to Paris. He stays with friends of Antonia's family and goes to one of the best schools in the city. And yes," he said in answer to Munroe's unasked question, "at my expense. I fly him home twice a year. I'm determined that he will have two worlds to choose from when he grows older, and I've made arrangements that should anything happen to me, he will be taken care of." And after he'd been silent for a moment, "You of all people are in no position to be judgmental about using or not using someone, when you are at this very moment using me to get what you want."

"I've offered to hire you. That you won't take the money is not my concern."

Beyard smiled. It was a smile of knowing, of understanding. "Essa, perhaps in your other life, among other people, such words would have meaning—but not between us. You and I both know that games of semantics are meaningless when we have a deeper understanding of human nature. And you *are* using me. You know what I want more than money, and you give it to me like a drug, in small doses, feeding me until it becomes an addiction. Don't make the mistake of thinking that I don't know it. Just as Antonia does with me, I have given you permission to use me. You and I, Vanessa, we are very much alike."

FROM BEYARD's PROPERTY the road was nothing more than a deeply rutted dirt track that cut through encroaching foliage, and as the vehicle crawled along it, a branch occasionally brushed through one of the open windows. A couple of kilometers from the property, the track connected to a wider dirt road, which later converged with tarmac, and where the orange-red dirt ended, they crossed the first checkpoint.

Several strands of barbed wire were strung across the road, and two makeshift wooden sawhorses blocked the lanes and worked to keep the nearly nonexistent vehicle traffic from passing. There was one weapon shared among five men, and to the side of the road an assortment of logs and stones circled a ground cooking fire over which an aluminum pot boiled. Beyard bantered with the commander of the group and then, five beers lighter, the Peugeot was on its way across the tarmac heading up the only segment of the coastal highway that was paved and into Bata, the largest and primary city of Equatorial Guinea's mainland.

With a population of seventy thousand, Bata was the second most populous city in the country, but in land area was larger than the capital. Unlike Malabo, which was dense, overcrowded, its narrow city streets congested, Bata was long and spread out, the streets wide and relatively empty and most of them paved. The buildings that fronted the ocean were two- and three-storied, constructed in the style of Mediterranean and Spanish villas. Farther back from the shore, the buildings were mostly one-storied squares of cement-block houses built for functionality without regard to aesthetics, albeit widely spaced and neatly set along the street edges.

Several kilometers south of the city lay the port, where the natural resources of the country were shipped out at an astounding rate, and below the port were the foreign compounds, where oil companies housed their employees in little pieces of America transplanted to West Central Africa. Several kilometers to the north was the single strip of tarmac that served as the largest airport of the Equatoguinean mainland and that operated only during daylight hours when visibility was good—a strip long and wide enough to accommodate a 737 and nothing larger. Leading out of the city to the east was the highway that ran through the north-central heart of the country, previously red clay that transmogrified into an impassable swampy muck during the seasonal rains, now tarmac paid for by oil.

The Peugeot shuddered and sputtered before finally coming to rest in front of Bar Central. The establishment was one of the city's most popular restaurants, doubling as a watering hole, and it was, Munroe hoped, the first step to picking up Emily Burbank's trail.

Like Malabo, Bata was a city without entertainment, a place where a trip to an air-conditioned grocery store was a day's highlight, and in the absence of everything else, the restaurants and bars were the de facto social gathering points. Those who ran them felt the pulse of the city, knew the rumors, heard the gossip, and were keenly aware of the faces as they came and went. And like most of the restaurants in the country, Bar Central was owned and operated by expatriates, in this case brothers originally from Lebanon. The eldest of them now stood behind the bar at the cash register, and when he noticed Beyard, he offered a generous mustachioed grin, raising his hand in a semi-salute. A few moments later, he joined the two of them at their table, shook Beyard's hand, and embraced him in a brotherly hug. He and Beyard joshed back and forth for a moment before the man pulled up a chair.

His name was Salim. His black hair was peppered with gray, and his eyes were a dark hazel. Although he couldn't have been older than forty-five, deep stress lines across his face put him closer to sixty. Beyard introduced Munroe, and when he did, Munroe took Salim's hand and said, *"Assalamou alaykoum."*

Salim smiled widely—*"Wa alaykoum assalam"*—and then to Beyard, "I like this girl. Where did you find her?"

The conversation continued in small talk until Munroe slid a printout of Emily's Internet photo across the table to Salim. *"Nabhatou an hadihi al bint."*

Beyard intervened. "We would very much like to know if you've seen the girl," he said. "But if anyone asks, we only came for breakfast."

Salim pushed back from the table and said, almost as if in surprise, "Francisco, my friend. That you have to ask? For you, anything." And, turning to Munroe, "Yes, I've seen the girl." He ran a finger around the back of his ear and tilted his head to the side. "Last time maybe six months ago."

"She comes here often?" Munroe asked.

"I wouldn't say often. Maybe once or twice a year."

"She comes alone?"

"Alone? No, never. Always with people. And her husband, he comes more often."

Munroe was silent for a moment. "She's married?"

Salim gave a shrug and a half smile. "Married? Well, I don't know that a dowry has passed or documents have been signed, but that she's with him, yes, I am very sure about that. He has the last name of Nchama, that I also know."

"Mongomo clan," Beyard said.

"She lives here in Bata?" Munroe asked.

"Again, I don't know," Salim answered. "But I think no."

Munroe tucked the printout into her shirt pocket. "If you don't mind me asking, is there anything in particular about this girl that caused you to remember her—anything specific at all?"

Salim shrugged and was silent. His finger wandered again behind his ear, and finally he gave a slight smile and said, "I know my clientele; after a while you get used to the way things are, patterns. For the most part, like remains with like. The Spaniards, they socialize with the Spaniards, the French with the French. It is not often you see one of the men of this country with a non-like woman over whom he claims ownership."

"Did she appear happy, unhappy, fat, thin, well dressed, poor?"

Salim sat back for a moment. "The last time I saw her, she was thin, almost frail, and her hair, it was much longer than this picture and wound tight around her head. She was dressed modestly but expensively, somewhat like the wealthy women of the local men—a particular style not African yet not Western. She did not appear so much sad or unhappy as just . . . well, perhaps vacant."

"What about the times you've seen her in the past?" Munroe said. "How would you describe her then?"

"Truthfully," Salim said, giving a slight laugh, "I can't say that I have ever studied her. I've seen her maybe four or five times over the past few years, but I've never paid much attention."

"I appreciate it," Munroe said, and then, "If you remember anything more, would you contact Francisco?"

Salim nodded, and then said to Beyard, "You should know you are not the only ones showing pictures around the city."

Munroe, who had been in the middle of taking a bite of pastry, stopped, replacing it on her plate. "There are others passing around photos of this girl?"

"A photo of *you*," he said. "You've nothing to worry about from me. I expect no trouble, and if I'm asked, I can positively say I did not think you resembled the photograph." He gave another chuckle. "Perhaps it would be better for your sake not to be seen around the city for a few days."

"What did he look like—the person with the photo?"

"There were two of them. One military but without a uniform and the other a younger man, maybe in his twenties, possibly from the Mongomo clan. He was well dressed." Salim stood. "One moment," he said, and then walked to the bar counter and pulled a piece of paper from beside the cash register.

"They gave me this number to call in case I should see you." He handed the paper to Beyard, and Munroe slipped it from him and into a pocket.

"Did they leave the photograph?" Munroe asked, and then to Beyard, "The particular photo being used would tell us a lot about who is looking."

"They left nothing except the number," Salim said. "But the photo was not of such good quality that you are easily recognized."

Outside in the car, Munroe turned to Beyard. "If it was just me, I'd attempt to gather a bit more information before heading out of town, but it's not just my neck, and you know the city better than I do. You have an opinion?"

"I think you should take a nap in the backseat, where you'll be out of sight," he said. "There are two more places where I have trustworthy acquaintances. Let me see what I can find out."

The news from the two other restaurants was similar: Yes, they knew or had seen Emily Burbank, not often, maybe once a year. The manager of La Ferme was certain that Emily did not live in Bata and believed Mongomo was her home. Both confirmed that there had been two men the day before yesterday looking for a white woman, but neither knew why.

In the backseat of the car, Munroe shifted to avoid as many of the protruding springs as possible, crossed her arms over her face, and closed her eyes. Random thoughts rushed, collided, and merged. It was no longer one puzzle; it was two—possibly three. She pulled in air, and with each deep breath, worked backward into a state of clearheaded focus, placing the new pieces of information against what she already had. There was a fit somewhere, the answer just beyond reach, tantalizing strings of thought that floated across the recesses of her mind and then vanished.

And then a connected synapse: The minister of foreign affairs and the Malabo chief of police—when they'd been presented with the photo of Emily Burbank, the odd look on each of their faces could only have been disguised recognition. Emily was familiar to them in a personal way. A large piece of the puzzle slipped into place. Emily Burbank was the constant, the segment of data that made sense.

If today's news was accurate, then as of six months ago Emily Burbank was alive and out in the open among the population of Bata. There was no secret of it, she was neither hiding nor being hidden. But neither had she, in the past four years, contacted her family—surely she must know they were looking for her. The texture of the developing trail was there, materializing, touchable, waiting to be found and followed. If Munroe could get to Mongomo, Emily was within reach.

Beyond Emily the events shattered into scattered, jagged pieces. Munroe and Bradford had been followed around Malabo from the time they'd arrived. She'd ended up on the boat, while Bradford was escorted out of the country. The men on the boat would have assumed she was dead and, even if for no other reason than to avoid admitting the fuckup, would have reported her as such.

To be searching for her here, now, someone in the local military had to know that she was alive and that this was where she was headed. Munroe could not shake the lesser and more treacherous possibility— that the men passing around her photo had been informed of her whereabouts by someone closer, someone who knew her movements, who would have been able to arrange to have her followed from the moment she'd set foot in Equatorial Guinea.

The men with the photo had been in Bata two days ago. Where had she been two days ago? Somewhere off the coast of Nigeria. How many of the people who knew she was alive were aware she was heading to this city?

Logan. She hadn't mentioned where she was or where she was going.

Kate. Kate knew just about every step she was taking—but Bata? No, that part had been left out.

Francisco. He'd had no idea she was in Equatorial Guinea before she'd shown up at his house and could never have arranged to have her followed. Unless . . . unless he'd learned of her imminent arrival from Boniface Akambe. The dots were there, perhaps the connection.

Bradford. *Shit.* She'd told Bradford about Bata, and he had been there with her in Malabo nice and cozy in his bed right about the time she'd been trapped by an anchor on the ocean floor. He'd known all their movements in advance. And when she'd turned up undead and undrowned, he'd insisted on returning to Africa, coming with her to Bata.

Three puzzles, each with similar coloring, identical pieces, and interlocking shapes. To Beyard she said, "We should probably get out of town."

She remained in the back while he maneuvered through the city, and when most of the buildings were behind them, she climbed into the front. Beyard reached out his hand and swept a strand of hair off her face. "This thing you do for a living—your job that you still haven't told me about. You're a strategist?"

"Not like you," she said, and then she laughed. "Actually, quite a bit like you. I go into developing countries and gather information—usually abstract and obscure—and turn it into something that a corporation can use to make business decisions."

"So finding missing people, this is not what you do for a living?"

"No," she said, twisting on the seat until she was turned toward him. "What if we found a partnership that suits both of us?" she said. "Something legal that doesn't involve getting shot at. You'd be very good at what I do—we could work together."

"Let me think about it."

They rode in silence until, rounding a slight bend, they came upon a checkpoint less than a hundred feet ahead, one that hadn't been there earlier, a group of men closer in appearance to the well-trained and heavily equipped presidential guard than the motley band they'd encountered in the morning.

There were eight soldiers and three vehicles, each soldier armed with an automatic weapon. Flares and portable road blades sealed off the tarmac. The vehicles, an SUV and two pickups, were black, and the windows on each tinted. From the interior of the SUV, shadows of additional men played against the windows, and the vehicle was parked so that the windshield was not visible from the road.

Beyard slowed the car, his eyes hard, lips drawn tight. "I've got a carton of cigarettes in the back. If that fails, then cash. We assume the worst, which is that they're looking for you. We act on the best—that they're out for a joyride. On the floor underneath the seat is a cap. Put it on."

At a crawl the Peugeot closed the distance. Beyard's face was expressionless, and his eyes moved rapidly from the men to the vehicles and the road ahead, and Munroe knew that, like hers, his mind had moved into a state of hyperalertness, interpreting the data and scanning the future against possible scenarios.

Two of the soldiers stepped onto the road and ordered the vehicle off the edge of it. Munroe fished under the seat for the cap and said, "Do you have any tools? Pocketknife? Carpet cutter? Anything?"

"Check the glove compartment. I might have a screwdriver."

She found the cap. It was grimy and covered in dust, and she slipped it on. Many of the locals had difficulty distinguishing the features of one foreigner from the next, even more so if working with photographs. The cap would help distort appearances. Ten meters to the checkpoint.

Munroe kept her body upright and her eyes straight ahead while her fingers moved through the contents of the glove compartment and turned up a penlight, which she shoved into a pocket.

Beyard brought the vehicle off the road, sandwiching it between the tarmac and thick foliage. He shut off the engine, and Munroe reached across his lap, took the keys out of the ignition, flipped the ignition key off the ring, handed it to him, and kept the remainder of the keys in her fist.

Three soldiers approached the car, two with their weapons aimed at the occupants while the third demanded the vehicle's paperwork. Beyard passed the documents through the open window, and when the man turned to walk with them in the direction of one of the vehicles, Munroe caught his profile and recognized him as the one who had kicked her on the boat. While the paperwork made the rounds, Beyard stepped out of the car. He kept his hands visible, pointed to the trunk, and then lifted two fingers to his mouth. "I left my cigarettes," he said.

The soldier nodded toward the rear of the car and followed Beyard with the weapon. Beyard pulled out the carton and returned to the driver's seat, where he made a show of breaking out a pack. "They've now got another vehicle stationed behind us just where the road bends," he said. "Two men, same equipment."

"At least one of these guys was on the boat with me that night," she said. "I don't recognize any of the others."

"If you see authority, point it out to me," he said.

"Might be in the SUV. I see shadows."

A bush taxi approached the checkpoint from the direction they'd come. The vehicle held six occupants, and the roof was hidden under the bundles piled high on top of it. Two soldiers standing on the opposite side of the road approached the taxi, peered through the windows, and then, without asking for papers or vehicle documents, moved the road blades aside and waved it through.

Beyard flipped a cigarette out of the pack and fiddled with it. "If you saw what I saw," he said, "we have a problem."

"I saw it," she said. "I've got a residency card on me that I need to get rid of. I don't want to give them documented proof that I'm the person they're looking for."

Beyard pulled a lighter from the ashtray, lit his cigarette, handed the lighter to her, and then stepped out of the vehicle with several packs of Marlboros in his hands. He leaned his back against the car door, placed the packs on the hood, and said to the soldier nearest to him, "Care for a smoke?" The man remained still, neither moving nor acknowledging Beyard's question, and in response to the lack of reaction Beyard began a monologue, his voice loud enough to be heard by the soldiers nearest to him: the weather, the food in the city—everything and anything, it didn't matter, he simply talked.

Munroe set the residency card on the floor in front of her and lit a corner of it. It was a slow burn, the plastic wrapping itself around in curls while it let off noxious fumes. The flame had burned a third of the way through the card, taking with it the photo and most of the personal information when the mood outside the vehicle shifted. Munroe stomped on the flame and shoved the remainder of the card into the seat cushion.

The soldier who had originally taken the vehicle's documents returned without them. In a language familiar from the night she'd been shot, he barked a command to the two standing beside the vehicle, and they ordered Munroe out. Beyard pulled a long draw on the cigarette and blew smoke into the air. Not good. Beyard was a nonsmoker, and that he was going through the motions of a habit he found particularly disgusting was an old signal, a warning. Comply.

Three soldiers crossed the road and joined the three already there. One of them ordered Munroe and Beyard onto the ground and one at a time kicked their legs apart, pulled their hands back, and cuffed their wrists. Under gunpoint she and Beyard were forced into the back of one of the trucks. They were shoved onto their stomachs, and while they lay on the bed of the truck, the soldiers sat along the rim, weapons held toward the captives. The vehicle lurched forward.

After a few moments of driving, they left the road. Munroe could feel it in the jolts of the truck, hear it in the way the sound of the vehicle's engine carried through the chassis, smell it in the way mud and living things permeated the air. She struggled to keep her head from slamming against the floor. They were working a small track now. The lighting changed, and she caught glimpses of green. Deeper into the bush.

She couldn't see Beyard—her head was turned opposite—but she could feel him. He had moved closer, a gesture no doubt meant to reassure, but there was nothing reassuring about the situation. Black, muddy boots were only inches from her face and just above them a touch of dull metal, the man's weapon pointed at her head.

The truck stopped without warning. The soldiers emptied the vehicle, and Munroe was pulled up from behind and dragged backward out of the truck. Her head hit the tailgate on the way out, and she fell to her knees. A throbbing penetrated her skull, followed by a telltale trickle down the side of her face and the acrid smell of blood. Her vision blurred gray, and internally the percussion of war began to beat out. At eye level was the belt of one of the captors. Sidearm. Ammunition. Knife. The urge to strike welled, instinct began to flow, and then in an instant the fury collapsed into itself, a fire without a source of fuel. And she was immobilized.

A split second of fear brought on by the sight of Beyard had swept her back. Fear. It was probable that in working out her own escape, Beyard would be killed. Instead of every sense shifting into overdrive toward self-preservation, she was fucking worried about Beyard. It was new, this sensation of fear. She'd never had to cultivate the demons and primal instincts lurking underneath the surface. Control them yes, ward them off yes, but never to call on them. It was a god-awful time for feral instinct to go domestic.

She was forced to her feet. Not far from the vehicle lay a narrow trail that led into the bush. The soldier standing closest stuck his weapon into her ribs and nodded in the direction she should go, and when she didn't move, he pushed her. The color of the trees phased from emerald to drab olive, and the internal percussion was a very faint tap against her chest. The undergrowth was dense and the trail difficult to find, and when she slowed, looking for direction, the weapon behind her connected with her back. The inner hammer pounded. She smiled a smile of death and clenched the fist that still held the keys. With her thumb she repositioned them so that they protruded between the slits of her fingers.

It was impossible to tell how many of the men followed behind, or if Beyard was following the same trail or had been forced onto his own private death march. She could make no movement, no plan until she knew where he was and how many men walked between them. She risked another jab to the ribs and called out, the bleat of a Peters's duiker, one of the small antelope that inhabited the underbrush. A few moments later, it was returned. Beyard was back there somewhere following the same path.

The trail ended abruptly at the edge of a small gully. Fifteen feet of mud and gnarled and twisted root systems separated the top, where she stood, from the bottom, where a murky, rust-red river cut through the landscape. During the rains the river would be pregnant and swollen with water, but now it was only a remnant of itself. Between the trail and the river's edge, there were a few feet of space, nothing more. The soldier yanked at her wrists and pushed her to her knees, his weapon pressed into her neck. She faced the river, her back to the trail, and his belt was at eye level, his weapon only inches from her cheek. In the stillness the sound of footsteps came from behind and with them the call of the duiker.

Beyard was placed as far away from her as the foliage would allow. His hands were secured behind his back, and she was sure that, like her, he was on his knees with a soldier positioned next to him, weapon angled toward his head. And then there was relative silence.

There were more men approaching. They were near, still moving down the trail; how many was impossible to tell, although instinct told her they could be no more than six.

An execution would take place, and the men guarding them now would do nothing without the orders that were getting closer by the second. Munroe closed her eyes to focus. She could possibly get out alive. If she had to worry about Beyard, there was no telling, and every heartbeat of hesitation was a hastening to her own demise. Things were what they were; it was now or never.

She moved her right thumb out of its socket and slid off the cuff, popped the thumb back, and tightened the keys in her hand. She shifted her weight forward, pulled taut, and then looked up at the soldier. When he turned toward her, she smiled sweetly and in Portuguese said, "Will you kill me now?" He said nothing and turned his face so that he stared out across the water, but she had spotted what she wanted. His eyes had dilated in registered recognition. He was Angolan.

She continued, "I cannot die without speaking of the treasure." Her voice was soft and lilting, each word uttered slowly and precisely. "You will find it buried underneath the mound on the beach five kilometers south, where the mouth of the river meets the ocean." With each word she lowered her voice until at the end the lie trailed to only a whisper. It was involuntary—the man could not help himself; with each word his head moved nearer to hear what she said.

She struck like a mamba. Deadly. Silent. Fast. Without a sound the keys tore through the man's neck, replacing his trachea with a gaping hole. The force knocked him to the ground, and air and blood bubbled from his throat. His fingers struggled to find his weapon, which lay just beyond reach, and Munroe kicked it with her foot. There could be no gunshot, only stealth and silence. She moved on top of him, grabbed his head, and twisted for the snap. She rolled to her belly, held on to his body with one hand and the weapon with the other, and slid down into the gully, catching her footing on the root system protruding through the mud banks. She grabbed the knife from his belt, took the sidearm and shoved it in at the small of her back, slung the assault weapon over her shoulder, and then let go of the body. It slid down the embankment, landing facedown in the muck of the river, lending a deeper red to the water. It had taken five seconds, long enough for Beyard to die ten times, but there'd been no sound of gunfire, no noise from the distance where he'd knelt. Munroe rose to the edge, ready to take the soldier that guarded him, and was greeted by Beyard's boots as he slid after her into the gully, dragging a body with him.

Her hands worked quickly, searching the body of Beyard's guard for a key to the handcuffs. "How the hell did you manage that?" she asked. She found nothing.

"You think I survived this long by letting other people fight my battles?" He breathed out a cruel whisper of a laugh. "Thanks for the distraction." He gave a forced smile and then dropped the body into the gully and hissed, "Move."

She leaned into the bank and crab-walked, a half swing, half jump, throwing her weight forward and balancing against whatever she managed to hold on to. Speed was all that mattered. Beyard was close behind, and like her he had an assault weapon slung across his back as he worked the bank, hanging on to whatever he could to keep upright and avoid sliding to the bottom. Sounds of confusion filtered across the gully, and Munroe and Beyard scrambled up into the foliage. They'd managed to get about forty meters from the spot of execution. On their stomachs they began the slow crawl forward. Silence was now their best friend. The empty cuff dangled off Munroe's hand, and it made her nervous. In spite of precautions, the cuffs made noise when any two parts of metal connected. Faint. But noise nonetheless, and any noise would attract gunfire.

Elbows to the spongy ground, they moved deeper into the bush. Munroe had a guess as to where they were, but only a guess, and when she was certain there was no way to be seen from the banks, she rolled to the side and motioned for Beyard to lead. The unmistakable hiss of a Gaboon viper sounded not far from her head. She remained motionless and after what seemed an eternity cautiously rolled back. The snake's venom could kill in fifteen minutes, and civilization was a hell of a lot farther than that.

A staccato of gunfire sounded from the way they'd come, and then silence. They crawled forward a foot at a time, listening and then moving again. If the soldiers had followed them into the gully, they had not found the area where they'd entered the bush; all sounds of pursuit had moved in other directions. Another round of gunfire disturbed the canopy, farther away than the previous burst and far enough in the distance that no voices could be heard.

They moved from their stomachs to a crouch and, as they covered distance and the silence deepened, to a full walk. And then thirst and time became the enemies.

It would have been different during the rains, when red clay mud would ooze through their clothes, into their hair, across their faces, and would sting when it mixed with sweat and dripped into their eyes and the taste of it filled their mouths. It would have coated their skin and worked as camouflage and kept the biting insects at bay. And the rain that transmogrified the clay into mud would have been plentiful and easily quenched their thirst. But the rains had begun to dissipate weeks ago.

At some point in the hours of the nocturnal morning, when the silence was deepest, when the calls of the night jungle had stilled, and before the predawn awakening, they made it back to the guesthouse. They'd utilized the dirt road for the last kilometer, hanging tight to the edge in case they needed to disappear into the foliage. They had maneuvered past one checkpoint, the typical ragtag group of warriors, several of them drunk and passed out, the others half dozing. Beyond that, no sign of military.

Their thirst was nearly unbearable, and by the light of a near-full moon they maneuvered skillfully through the kitchen to water. They drank in rapid gulps, water dribbling down their faces streaking the grime and dirt, a strange form of war paint, and when Munroe could drink no more, she searched for a paper clip, wire, anything she could use to open the handcuff lock or work as a shim. She found nothing. Those were items so familiar in the West, that other world.

Beyard left for the bedroom and then returned, cuffs off, and placed a key in her palm. She released the lock. "Thanks," she said, and in one drawn-out movement slapped the mud-crusted cuffs around his wrists and pulled the pistol out of the small of her back.

She leveled it at his head.

chapter 15

Beyard's eyes found hers, and even in the dark it was evident that his face registered shock.

"What the hell do you think you're doing?"

His words came in a garbled, half-choked whisper that held no control or calm.

"I don't want to kill you," Munroe said, "but I'll blow your fucking head right off if I have to." She kicked a chair toward him. "Sit."

He did as he was told, and it was clear that he did it out of confusion and an attempt to understand rather than because of any genuine fear. She pulled the penlight from her pocket, aimed it at his right eye, and stood in front of him just beyond his reach. "I consider you a personal and strategic threat," she said. "I'm tired, hungry, and mad as hell, so don't try my patience. I want answers, and I want the truth, even if you think it'll piss me off. I haven't got time to waste, and lies, distortions, and half-truths will only cause this to end with you dead and me gone."

Beyard squinted at the light and shifted away from it. "I've never lied to you," he said.

"There have been omissions," she said. "Do you take me for an idiot?"

She waited for a moment, allowed silence to fill the room, and studied his eyes and the shifting tension of his face for the invisible cues that would betray his deception. "When was the last time you spoke with Boniface?"

The corners of Beyard's mouth twitched slightly, and he turned his head to the side. He took a shallow breath, and in the split second it took for him to bring his eyes straight at her, her suspicions were confirmed.

"If this is about Akambe," Beyard said, "I'm speechless."

"Answer the fucking question."

"About two weeks ago."

"He told you that I was heading to Malabo."

Bravado shifted to discomfort. There was a pregnant pause. "Yes."

"He gave you pictures, didn't he? You sent people to follow me, to watch my movements."

A deep inhalation and then, "Yes."

"And you had me drugged and taken out to the boat to be killed."

"No."

The tightness in his face and inflection in his voice said truth; she raised the weapon as if to fire and said, "You're lying."

"Vanessa, I swear it," he said. "I had nothing to do with what happened to you on the boat. When I spoke with Boniface, he told me he'd worked papers for you and that you were moving in the direction of Malabo. At first I felt only anger—I wanted to hurt you. And then I was curious, wanted to know what you were like, why you were here, what you were doing. I was afraid to see you personally, didn't know how I would react. So I had you followed."

Munroe shook her head slowly. "'Misplaced trust can be a dangerous thing,'" she said. "Those words meant something, though I didn't know it at the time. All this while, at any point, you could have told me—given me the information I needed to make the connection—and you didn't. And now twice in the past week I've been taken at gunpoint by the same group of men, and you're the only connection between those events," she said. "They never asked to see my ID, never even got a good look at me. Explain that."

"I'm as puzzled and confused by it as you are," he said. "What? You think I planned that? Pretend I'm about to get my own head blown off right beside you? What a fucking stratagem that would have been.

It wasn't just you almost killed out there today. At this point I want answers almost as badly as you do."

"What about Malabo?" she said. "Your bumbling idiots disappeared right before I was dragged off."

"It was coincidence," he said. "I swear, I had nothing to do with that. No matter how angry I was with you—to kill you? No, Vanessa, I could not do that." He paused and looked at her with a sly smile. "I've known what you are capable of. If I hated you that much, I would have done the job myself, made sure it was done properly—not hired some half-assed group of fuckups to do it for me." He paused, and when Munroe said nothing, he continued. "When I heard that you had purchased tickets for Bata, I told my guys to pack up shop and to notify me when you'd left town. It was only the next day, when you weren't on that plane, that I knew something had happened—what exactly was anybody's guess. Among the possibilities was that you'd gone to the GEASA office as a ruse and that your true destination was somewhere else."

Munroe stepped closer and, standing directly in front of him, pressed the muzzle of the gun under his chin and forced his head back. She moved behind him, tracing the weapon against his neck as she went. His eyes followed, although his head did not move. She continued until the muzzle was at the base of his skull and she stood an arm's length behind him.

"Emily Burbank," she said. "How much of the information that you've fed me is accurate?"

"I have never lied to you," he said. "What would be the point in that?"

"You did see her three years ago in Bata?"

"Yes."

"The information given to us by Salim and supposedly said by the other two friends of yours—was it genuine?"

"All true as far as I know. I had an idea that they might have seen the girl. That's why we went there."

At the tail end of the explanation, Munroe heard the inaudible, words that shouldn't be. She took a deep breath and for a brief second tilted her head toward the ceiling. "Francisco," she said, her voice soft and singsong, "I can smell the omission, taste it, touch it. What are you not telling me?"

He was silent.

"I need to get moving, so say what you're going to say. Or don't." She punched his head forward with the gun. "Whether you live or die—your choice."

He sighed. It was a deep breath, and in the exhale came the sound of defeat by the inevitable, finality, as if by whatever he was to say next he executed his own death and was willing to accept it as it was. "When I saw the girl in Bata three years ago," he said, "I recognized the men she was with. I know who they are and where to find them."

In a silent scream, Munroe clenched her teeth and kicked the back of the chair, nearly knocking him out of it. "You fucking almost got us killed," she hissed. "For nothing! Goddamn it, Francisco, you knew! What the hell could the point of today possibly have been? You fucking knew!"

"I wanted to be sure the information I had was up-to-date."

The explanation wasn't right, it didn't fit. Even with her judgment clouded by fury, she knew it.

"That's bullshit!" she said. Then she took a deep breath and, monotone, in a near whisper, said, "I'd love to kiss you right now, stroke your hair and tell you how sorry I am to have to do this." She moved one carefully placed foot at a time until she was once again standing in front of him. "You've meant more to me than any other person I know," she said, and raised the gun to his forehead. "Good-bye, Francisco."

His voice cracked, and in a half scream he yelled, "Wait!" And then, just above a whisper, "Goddamn it, Vanessa, what the hell do I have to do to prove to you that I'm telling the truth?"

"You haven't told me all," she said. "Killing you is a matter of self-preservation, Francisco. A necessary evil. No offense. I'm sure you'd do the same if the roles were reversed."

He let out a long breath and then lowered his eyes. "How long is the assignment going to last?" he asked. "Two weeks, maybe three. Get in, get out, easy, simple. Well, maybe not as easy now, but I didn't have a gauge on that this morning. When the assignment is over, what happens to you? You go back to your world, and I stay in mine. I have you only for as long as this project continues." His eyes met hers, challenging.

"Given that scenario, why don't you give me a reason not to go into Bata?"

However pathetic, it was the truth she'd needed to snap events into focus. She moved the light out of his eyes and shut it off. "That is the most lame-assed crap excuse I've heard in my life." She flipped the safety and with a shove returned the gun to the small of her back. "What the hell were you thinking? You of all people should know better than to make tactical decisions based on emotion." She took his wrists and released the cuffs. "Consider this payback for locking me in the cell on the ship."

He sat still on the chair and stared at her, rubbing his wrists where the handcuffs had been. "Even a grand master makes a mistake now and then," he said. He looked up. "I don't know whether to kiss you or smack you."

She crossed her arms and stared. "I swear, Francisco, if I find that you've double-crossed me, you're a dead man. I will hunt you down, and there is nothing you or any one of your men could do to keep me from fulfilling that vow."

"I'll admit I haven't been completely straight," he said. "I should have told you about tracking you in Malabo, and I shouldn't have withheld information about the girl, but beyond that I've done nothing to sabotage your work. I don't give a shit about your assignment or this girl that you're trying to find, but I do want you alive, and I'd like you with me for as long as possible. Is that good enough for you?"

"For now."

"And you might as well know that I haven't been able to get in contact with one of my guys since the night you were shot. He's possibly one of the two passing your photo around Bata, although I swear I have nothing to do with that." Beyard continued to rub his wrists. "Were you really going to kill me?"

"I don't know. At the least I would have left you here and taken the boat to Cameroon."

She moved across the house toward the bathroom, and he followed. Her fingers ran along the doorframe until she found a grip. Beyard stood behind and remained silent while she separated the segment from the wall, pulled the container from its hiding place, and slid the belt out.

"How would you take the boat?" he asked. "You don't have the key."

She strapped the belt around her waist and tucked it under her pants. "I wouldn't need one any more than you would," she said. "But even so, I could get it if I wanted." She looked off in the distance toward the main house. "It's in there."

"Antonia doesn't know where it is."

"She knows which rooms you frequent the most, and thanks to you"—Munroe knocked on the wood in her hands and then shoved the frame back into place—"I know where to look."

Beyard opened his mouth to say something, and stopped. He nodded in the direction of the main house. "Let's go."

IN THEIR ABSENCE the cig had been refueled, and it carried enough additional fuel in storage to make the trip twice. The noise of the engine shattered the silence, and Beyard guided the boat away from its mooring. When they were on open water, he placed a small box in Munroe's hand. "Truce," he said. "A gesture of goodwill—without it I'm lost from my ship, and I'm giving it to you because I trust you and hope that you trust me. When you activate it, we'll get our coordinates and George will know we're on our way in."

To the east the color of the sky had shifted from star-studded black to deepest blue. By the time they coasted alongside the trawler, the sun had fully climbed into its arc across the sky. On the deck Wheal nodded at Munroe and grasped Beyard's hand with both of his. "Didn't expect you back so soon," he said.

Beyard reached for a hose that lay curled against a wall a few feet away. "We ran into a few problems," he said, and cranked the tap, hosing himself off, shoes, clothes, and all, the force of the water carrying with it the mud and gunk of the previous twenty hours. Dripping wet, he handed the hose to Munroe, and to Wheal he said, "We'll be up in the wheelhouse in ten minutes. Will you meet us there?"

Still grimy but minus the mud and in clean clothes, they gathered in the pilothouse. For Wheal's benefit, Beyard summarized the events that had brought them back to the ship. He spoke in English and even with his lack of fluency was descriptive in the telling of it, although his version neatly left out all mention of the guesthouse from the moment the pistol had been placed to his head.

When he was finished, they sat in silence. There was no need to say what they all were thinking. The minutes passed slowly and were emphasized by the regular ticks of the radarscope that filled the quiet. Beyard bit on the edge of his thumb, Wheal tapped a pen against the table, and Munroe sat with her head kicked back and her legs stretched out.

Wheal was the first to speak. "I want to know what happens next." He turned to Munroe. "You know that if you go back in, you're playing against terrible odds—it's a high-risk venture, the stakes being your life and"—he paused and nodded at Beyard—"more important as far as I'm concerned, Francisco's, if he decides to go with you. Is what you're after worth that much?"

Munroe tapped her fingers against the table, a steady Morse rhythm, and then nodded almost imperceptibly in answer to Wheal's question. "Yes and no," she said. "I'm willing to put my life up against it, I'm not willing to put up Francisco's—or anyone else's, for that matter. It's a decision he has to make for himself, but I've got to go back in regardless."

Wheal rested his forearms on the table. "Listen," he said. "We're all a little nuts to be in this business, a little fucked in the head, a little short on fear. I don't give a rat's ass that you've got a death wish, but what you're setting out to do is suicidal, and that's where I draw the line. Not because of you. Go fucking die, I don't care." Wheal nodded again toward Beyard. "My job is to keep him out of trouble, and you"—he pointed at Munroe—"are trouble."

"Oh, how sweet," she said with the high pitch of patronization. "You're playing daddy. Does Francisco get grounded if he breaks curfew?"

Predictably, Wheal eased back from the table, straightened, and crossed his arms. Outwardly, Munroe's face was placid; inside, she was amused. He had an eight-inch, hundred-pound advantage, and his was the posture of an alpha male adept at intimidation. She'd taken on guys his size before, and what she lacked in bulk and strength she more than made up for in speed and agility. In another time and another place, the challenge would have been more than welcome. She would've continued to provoke him until he exploded, then, and like lightning, would have gone up over the table, and the pain from the ensuing fight would have been cathartic—but not here.

"I can't give you what you want," she said. "The status quo has already been disrupted, and even if I walk away, nobody, especially not you or me, has the power to put things back the way they were. I don't want to see what you have here ruined any more than you do, but it's out of your hands now, you know that."

"If I'm going to lose my friend, I'd like to know it's fucking worth it."

"I have no answers for you, George. It's possible we'll wind up a couple of decomposing bodies in a ditch. It would be tragic and, considering statistical probability, long overdue. Yes, I could walk away and guarantee myself a few more days, but for what? So this can haunt me for the rest of my life? No thanks. Whether I want it or not, I'm locked in. I'd also like to get my hands on the bastard who wants me dead. And there's the issue of Emily Burbank: If she really is alive, I need to find her, out of principle and to fulfill a promise I made to a mother in Europe." She turned to Beyard. "I appreciate what you've done for me, and I really don't expect you to accompany me, but I *am* going back, and when I start setting things in motion, it would be helpful to know what you're planning to do."

Beyard, who had been silent throughout the exchange, with his arms crossed and his chin on his chest, raised his eyes and said, "Do you even have to ask?"

Wheal leaned forward into Beyard's line of sight. "This thing is worth your life?"

Beyard let out a snort. "You know me better than that."

"Then why the hell go?"

Beyard sat back and wrapped an arm over the chair. "I have my reasons."

Wheal stood and placed his hands on the table, leaning down so that his head was almost level with Beyard's. "This is fucked up, Francisco, you know it's fucked up. You're risking everything we've had. Seven years of friendship." Wheal snapped his fingers. "Seven years of partnership. For what?"

When Beyard said nothing, Wheal walked toward the door. "The two of you can sort it out. This is insane, and I want no part of it."

When Wheal had left the room, Beyard said, "I've crossed the Rubicon."

"You can still change your mind."

Beyard rested his elbows on the table and placed his chin against his folded hands. "No," he said. "Regardless of how events play out, there's no going back."

Munroe put her feet on the table and tilted back in the chair. "All right then," she said. "We're going in again, and this time we do it my way."

The look of concerned sadness that had been on Beyard's face opened into a smile of amusement, but he said nothing. Munroe ignored what the smile implied. War was a boys' club that she'd infiltrated long ago, and he, like so many others before him, would figure it out eventually. "We'll need supplies that you don't have," she continued, "so I'll need to make a few calls. If you've got connections and friends in the government, this would be a good time to call in some favors, find out what they know, and see if we can't learn something."

"Do you still have the number that you got from Salim? What we get when the phone is answered could be enlightening."

"It's pulp in one of my pockets."

It took Beyard an hour to make the rounds by phone, during which time Munroe assembled a supply list that she e-mailed to Logan, and then, unable to reach Logan by phone, she and Beyard retreated to the galley, where they put together a meal from an odd assortment of frozen and canned goods. It was the first they'd eaten in over a day, and between shoveled-in bites they discussed what little Beyard had learned.

The events that had transpired off the coast of Bioko Island and by the edge of the Boara River had apparently never happened. No word or rumor floated through the capital, and if the orders had come through official channels, they had escaped each of the people Beyard relied on for information. The U.S. embassy in Malabo provided few additional clues. Notification of Munroe's death had come from a fisherman who'd described in graphic detail a body found along the shoreline and who'd produced a residency card he claimed had come from it.

Munroe brought a piece of paper to the table and began to sketch.

"We're working through an information blind," she said. "What are the givens?"

"We know that this girl was alive a few months ago," he said. "That she lives in Mongomo, that she's married to or is the mistress of Timoteo Otoro Nchama, vice minister of mines and energy, and that someone in the Equatoguinean government is willing to kill to prevent you from getting to her."

Munroe kept her eyes on the paper and rapidly diagrammed. "The big question to which we have no answer is why. We also don't know who."

"Have you considered the possibility that this girl does not want to be found? That it is she who is pulling the strings to keep you away?"

Munroe stopped writing, looked at him, and one corner of her mouth turned up, twisting her lips into a half grin. "I've considered a lot of possibilities," she said. "But not that one."

"It's worth a thought."

"Yes it is," she said, and returned to the paper. "We can assume that wherever Emily is, she's being watched—protected or threatened. We can assume that, like in Bata, at each of the country's gateways someone is watching for me, and that no matter how many times I attempt to enter, I will be tracked. I don't know how and I don't know why, but since it's me that the trouble follows, I won't be going in again."

"What the hell, Essa? Two hours ago you nearly started a fight with George because you insisted you were going back."

"Oh, I'm going," she said. "But not as me."

Munroe stopped writing and turned the paper around so Beyard could follow. "There's one group of foreigners who can come and go as they please. They have the president's blessing, nobody hassles them, nobody looks, nobody wants to know: Israeli military." She tapped the pen onto the paper and continued to diagram. "So under the cover of an envoy out of Cameroon, we enter from the northeastern gateway and beeline south to Mongomo."

Beyard stared at the paper, his lips drawn tight, and shook his head slightly. "I'm not sure if you're completely mad or a fucking genius."

"I guess we'll soon find out," she said, and returned to the paper once again. "Since this is the dry season and the roads are passable, best-case scenario we can be in and out in two days. Worst-case..."

Munroe paused and sighed. "There are a few critical unknowns making it difficult to define worst-case. It should be a clean in and out, there and gone before anyone is even aware of our presence. Should be . . ." And her voice trailed off.

"Mongomo will be our point of greatest vulnerability. It's what concerns me most," she continued. "There are any number of reasons that looping back the way we enter might not be possible, and the way I see it—and you have more experience in this than I do—we have two alternative return routes out of the country. Potentially fastest and most problematic is east into Gabon—a roughly five-kilometer run to the border. Second is working the tracks through the center of the country to the coast—more dangerous because of time spent inside the country and the variables that could turn up along the way, but once we get to the coast a much cleaner getaway."

"Both are viable," Beyard said. "If we have trouble in Mongomo, we have to rule out Bata as a gateway—we'll be expected there. Mbini would work. It's slightly farther south, off the beaten path, and I have contacts there." He leaned back and after a moment said, "Last word has it the Israeli presence is extremely small and limited to specific areas. There are no female forces in the country, and should we encounter genuine troops, our cover will be blown."

"All true," she said. "Which is why two days from now I will be heading to the training base outside of Yaoundé to get a feel for what the Israeli operations are like in Cameroon, get onto the base if I can—make a dry run of it. I'll be gone for a couple of weeks."

"It sounds like an unnecessary risk," he said. "Cameroon may not be Equatorial Guinea, but it's not far from it. You get caught and you've not only blown your original objective, you'll lose the next ten or fifteen years of your life rotting in some hole of a prison."

"I know," she said. "But I also know what I'm doing. I won't get caught."

"Considering the way things have gone so far, you sound extremely confident."

Munroe stopped and stared at him and then without further explanation said, "Gathering information is what I do for a living. I won't get caught." She returned to the paper. "Your job: We'll need transportation with plates and papers for Cameroon, Equatorial Guinea, and Gabon. If we locate Emily and she wants to come with us, we need to be prepared to extract her and as many as three children. The two of us will also need Israeli military passports."

"Two vehicles?"

Munroe nodded.

"It's all doable," he said. "And I'm certain Boniface can handle the vehicle papers and plates, even the papers for Emily and a few kids. I'm not so sure about the military passports. He'll have to go through Nigeria for those, and even still, Israeli military passports are pretty rare—especially if we need two of them. Imitations would work. The border guards certainly have not seen enough of them to know one from the other."

"Imitations are fine," she said, and she continued to sketch, "although it's not the border guards I'm concerned about. The vehicles will have to be fitted to smuggle weapons and equipment."

"None of this should be a problem," he said. "But we're looking at a serious amount of cash, and it's my understanding you haven't got much money with you."

"Once we get into Douala, I can front you sixty thousand dollars. The rest will take a few days—I'll need to have it wired over. We're going to need weaponry," she said.

"Except for the MP5s we keep onboard, I'm limited to Russian or East European, sometimes Chinese."

"We need to keep it as authentic as possible."

"I'll figure something out."

"Ammunition?"

"Have plenty."

"Lupo was using a Vintorez when he was playing sniper on the pilothouse roof. What are the chances I can have it?"

"Everything is negotiable," he said. "If the price is right, I'm sure we can arrange something."

By the time Munroe got Logan on the phone, he'd already started work on the supply list. "Some of these items are going to be hard to come by," he said. "Might take a couple of weeks to track them down."

"Two to three weeks should work, but there's a catch this time—I need you to deliver most of it to me in person."

"You're shitting me."

"I kid you not. There are a few things I need sent ahead to the FedEx office in Douala: the pilot uniforms and the Hebrew-English learning system. For everything else get yourself a visa and prepare to fly to Douala. Funding goes standard through Kate. Having you courier this stuff in is the only way I can guarantee that it gets into the country. I figure you'll know how to pack it to avoid hassles going through airline security, but if not, let me know and I'll walk you through it. Can you clear your schedule?"

Logan's response was a barely audible grunt, and she could hear the keyboard clacking in the background.

"E-mail me your flight itinerary as soon as you have it. You're looking for the earliest return possible, preferably in and out on the same day, even if it means different airlines."

Another grunt.

"If for any reason funding is going to hold things up, use my retainer; it should cover everything. And, Logan, last thing: I've got two days," she said. "After that I can't guarantee when or how often I can call, so does that give us enough time to confirm everything for the time frame we're working?"

"It should."

"Then I'll be back with you in two days. And, Logan?"

"Yeah?"

"Thanks."

TWO DAYS. NOT because it was what she wanted, but because it was necessary. Remaining on the ship would put space between the phases; the downtime was critical in allowing the bits and pieces of information accumulated over the past weeks to filter to the bottom of the mental pool, to shift from one game plan into the next. Downtime was typically difficult to deal with; in the stillness, internal pressure would steadily build, urging toward action and the rush of adrenaline—but, regardless, the stillness was critical.

The silence this time was different. When supplies had been packed, the weapons disassembled, meticulously cleaned and put back together, and there was nothing more to do to kill time, the hours passed over the chessboard and in philosophical discussion with Francisco, a throwback to another time, the world forgotten, and Munroe was at peace.

Two days later she stood against the railing and watched the trawler's deck crane lower one of the cigarette boats to the water. It was dawn, and the ocean was calm and the air empty except for the noise made by the machinery. Munroe turned from the railing and reentered the pilothouse. She'd been trying since five to reach Logan and would continue to call at fifteen-minute intervals until he picked up. She checked the clock. It was late evening in Dallas; she should already have been able to reach him. On the sixth attempt, he answered. "I've been trying to get you for over an hour," she said.

"Battery died. I've been hunting down the supply list, haven't had time to recharge."

"How are we?"

"We'll have what you need within the next ten days," he said. "The FedEx package is already on its way. They said three days, but we all know that means at least a week. The uniforms were the hardest to come by, but I've got a guy working on those, and I've been guaranteed delivery within a week. I dipped into the retainer. There's been some kind of delay with the funding, and I've been too busy to figure it out."

"Don't bother with it," Munroe said. "I need to call Kate anyway, and I'll make sure it's settled. Do you have your itinerary?"

"That's the other thing. Apparently Miles Bradford is heading your way, and Kate suggested he bring the items, save me the hassle. And truthfully, Michael, if he can, I would appreciate it, because I've got a shitload of work stacked up for me."

Munroe was silent for a moment and then said, "If you don't hear anything else from me on it by tomorrow, then arrange to get the items to Miles. Ten days, right?"

"Yeah, ten days."

The news about the supplies was good. Miles Bradford was a problem.

"We don't have a lot of choice," Breeden explained in answer to Munroe's query. "Between your insistence on continuing the assignment and Miles's determination to return to Africa, Richard Burbank changed his mind about rescinding. He wants Miles with you, and since you're under contract, there's not much we can do about it. The good news, though, is that since the contract is still open, Richard covers expenses, and considering the bill that Logan just sent me, that's not a small thing."

"That's only a third of it," Munroe said. "I need you to wire twice that in cash. I'll e-mail you the bank information."

"I'll get it to you as soon as I can. The accounting department at Titan is giving me the runaround—they want itemization before releasing for expenses, and I've been trying to get in touch with Richard to get it sorted out. Apparently he's out of town."

"You know how it goes," Munroe said. "We won't know what the money is for until it's already spent. And half the time it's for greasing palms and oiling the machinery of bureaucracy. If you can't get ahold of Burbank by tomorrow, just do what we've done before. Put whatever label you want on it, whatever it takes to be sure I get the money and that Logan gets the funding he needs. He had to dip into the retainer."

"I'll take care of it today."

Munroe replaced the phone, stood still for a moment, and then, with clenched teeth, slammed the palm of her hand into the wall and kicked the chair closest to her. Beyard, who'd been standing on the other side of the room, said, "Whatever the problem, surely it is not the wall and the chair that are to blame."

"Better the furniture than a person." She sighed and sat in the chair, looking up at Beyard. "We have a problem," she said. "Or a wrinkle, or whatever the fuck we want to call him."

"Him?"

"Miles Bradford, my partner from Malabo. I'm sure you know who I'm talking about. He's flying to Douala in about two weeks' time, and either I kill him as a matter of prevention or he's coming with us to Mongomo."

Beyard sat in the chair opposite and after a moment of silence said, "Essa, there's something you're not telling me. This man who was your partner, he is already familiar with the scenario, and if my sources were accurate, you have worked well together. Logically, he would be an asset to this assignment."

"There are two things, Francisco." She drew herself up so that she looked him directly in the face. "First, I don't know if I can trust him. That he was left while I was hauled off to be murdered and dumped overboard doesn't sit easy with me, but I can work with it. What angers me most can't be explained by logic." She paused. "I simply don't want him here." She motioned toward the navigational controls. "I don't want to share this with him, don't want to share *you* with him. This . . . this is a part of me that is sacred, my own. I don't want it tarnished by an intruder who already knows everything else about me that there is to know. This is mine."

Beyard nodded and then stood. "In your words: 'You of all people should know better than to make tactical decisions based on emotion.' I don't want an intruder any more than you do," he said. "But the plan comes first. If he's a risk to the enterprise, we can remove him, but I think we would want to be very cautious in that regard." He held his hand to her. She reached for it, and he pulled her to her feet.

They took the cig north to Douala, docking at the southernmost edge of the port. The docks were crowded with people and with metal containers stacked three or four high, each filled with items that waited to clear a customs procedure fraught with requests for bribes and dubious processing fees. Muscular bodies glistening with sweat unloaded goods while trucks long ago retired from work in the Northern Hemisphere stood nearby with engines idling, belching smoke. The smell of burned diesel fuel mingled with the odor of decay and the aroma of salt and fish coming off the ocean.

Beyard's driver met them, and they unloaded the boat. Money had changed hands, papers had been signed, and there would be no questions asked as they drove into the city with a small arsenal behind the backseat. The first destination was the Société Générale de Banques au Cameroun, and when the money had been withdrawn and transferred to other accounts, they navigated the streets to a modern two-bedroom flat that stood in the heart of the city.

The apartment was one of four on the ground, with three walk-up levels above, and the building stood next to two others that were identical, all in a quiet compound surrounded by a high cement wall that had been whitewashed and glass-topped and gleamed bright under the sun.

It was there that they would rendezvous once all the pieces had been put into place.

AT FIVE-THIRTY THE next morning, Beyard dropped Munroe off at the bus station. She had originally planned to leave alone, to disappear into the dark of the early morning, but Beyard wouldn't hear of it. He'd insisted on taking her to the bus station, and if he'd had his way, he would have waited until she'd boarded the five forty-five bus for Yaoundé. Munroe knew it wasn't so much a protective gesture as that he didn't want to let her go. She kissed him, then pulled away. "If I'm not back in ten days, it's because something's happened," she said. "I'm not leaving you." And then, when the red of his vehicle's taillights had finally pulled out of the depot and vanished down the street, Munroe caught a cab and returned to the city center.

Alone.

After nearly four weeks of continual companionship, solitude brought with it the feeling of nakedness soon replaced by the exhilaration of freedom. On Avenue de Gaulle she located a reputable barber and waited on the doorstep until the place opened for business. It was time to revert. And then time to shop and, after that, a four-hour trip to the capital.

chapter 16

Yaoundé, Cameroon

It was shortly after five that afternoon when the bus pulled into the city's depot. The area was hard-packed dirt surrounded by low-lying buildings, and teeming with passengers and their boxes and bags, vendors with their wares, and pickpockets and thieves.

Munroe stepped from the bus and slung a heavy backpack over her shoulder. She wore a short-sleeved button-down shirt, untucked, faded jeans, and heavy, flat-soled boots, which hadn't been easy to find. Her hair was military short. A wide elastic bandage wrapped her meager chest, the same improvisation utilized the night she'd boarded the *Santo Domingo*, and she wore strong masculine cologne. But for these she'd made no extra effort. The clothes and hair were subtle cues, enough to distract the eye and make a first impression, and while the subconscious effect of cologne was never to be underestimated, unless she needed to age past nineteen it had always been attitude and behavior that truly confused the mind.

She took a cab to the Hilton Yaoundé, the best the city had to offer. The hotel was eleven stories of white concrete, and like a giant monolith it dwarfed most of the buildings that lined the streets in either direction. Yaoundé, although the capital, was smaller and less developed than its sister on the coast. But it was where the country's president lived and thus where the elite guard was stationed, and so it was there that she would find the Israeli forces that trained them. She wanted to be in their presence, learn their language and their manner of behavior, and if possible observe how they interacted with the men they trained.

Perhaps, if she'd been desperate, she would have taken the route of sneaking around, smuggling herself onto the compound, and acting like a spy, as Francisco no doubt expected she was doing. But there was no need for that. There were better ways, faster and with less personal risk.

Munroe showered and slept for a few hours and then, as the evening deepened, transferred to the hotel's bar and casino. There were only three types of venues where she expected to find what she was looking for: foreign cultural centers and embassies, international schools, and what little nightlife the city had to offer. The Hilton was as good a place as any to begin looking.

It took two days of cultivating potential information sources before the first genuine lead materialized. After nights that lasted until nearly dawn and mornings that began shortly after, it was at La Biniou, taking a meal far too late for lunch and still too early for dinner, that segments of language, recognizable but without meaning, filtered across the dining area. The voices belonged to three teenagers, and it was evident that within the small group there were a sister and brother, and if body language was any indicator, the third was friend to one and surreptitious lover to the other.

Munroe observed the three and was drawn to the sister. She was sixteen, seventeen at most, had curly dark hair, dark eyes, a beautiful smile, and a playful personality. She was the younger sibling, there with her girlfriend no doubt, and oblivious to the smoldering lust between the two across the table. She would make an excellent mark.

If all other things were equal, Munroe would prefer a female. While men had to be bribed or threatened or their suspicions overcome while they were befriended to get them to spill their secrets over drink, women naturally loved to talk. And while it was no secret that a man would say most anything when desperate to get between a woman's legs, that was not the way Munroe worked. Women, on the other hand, responded to attention, and while in the persona of a male she could bypass whatever insecurities the female form brought on and gain direct access to a woman's mind. The problem was that things were very seldom equal.

Munroe tapped her fingers lightly against the table and watched the trio over the top of a traveler's guidebook. The girl would be the easiest way to the parents and, from them, to the rest of the community.

She stood, walked to the table with the guidebook in hand, and in broken French and then fluent English introduced herself as Michael and asked for clarification on several of the book's entries. She conversed with the brother and between words made eye contact with his sister and passed her a flirtatious smile or two. The brother was helpful, but it was the sister who invited Munroe to sit and join them, and at the end of forty-five minutes Munroe had also been invited to dinner at their house the following evening. In another place, another climate, the invitation might have seemed audacious, but not in the world of the Cameroonian expatriate, where the community was small and far away from home.

The girl's name was Zemira Eskin, and with that piece of information as well as the phone number and directions she'd been given, Munroe headed to the British cultural center. It took less than half an hour of chitchat to discover that she'd been invited to the home of Colonel Lavi Eskin, commander of the Israeli forces in Cameroon.

The news brought Munroe's plans in Yaoundé to a full stop. There was no point in digging further; contact with too many in the community would only backfire. She had no choice but to wait, and in the solitude Francisco filled her mind. He was disruption from the focus needed for tomorrow, broken strands of thought in the web of information her mind attempted to spin.

Unable to concentrate, Munroe called the United States and after several attempts got through to Kate Breeden. The conversation was brief. Munroe received confirmation that the money had been wired to the account in Douala and reassured Kate that she was indeed alive and well and had no plans to reenter Equatorial Guinea, at least not until after Bradford arrived.

And then Munroe called Francisco. Hearing his voice dropped her into a cocoon of warmth where it was dark and familiar and safe. The conversation lasted only long enough to pass on the transfer details, but what she wanted more than anything was to remain on the line, to drag out the information if only to continue to hear his voice. What she wanted was to return to Douala, to him.

Munroe replaced the phone in its cradle and hung her head in her hands. This frame of mind was dangerous; it was how mistakes were made; it was why business and emotion were necessarily disparate; it was why she should have shut down that night outside of Bata. She could still do it—needed to do it—but didn't want to. In the silence, voices filled her head, but they were not the demons from within—they were Francisco.

It was nearly seven the following evening when Munroe stood at the gate in front of the house that Zemira had directed her to. The neighborhood consisted of large compounds, their upper stories and clay-tiled rooftops peeking beyond the eight- and ten-foot walls that surrounded them. Like most cities on the continent, Yaoundé had no street addresses or house numbers. There would never be mail service to the door—not even DHL or FedEx could manage that. Directions were composed of road names and landmarks, distance and neighborhoods, gate colors and house descriptions. And what Munroe faced now fit with what she had been given.

Armed guards opened a walk-through portion of the gate and called ahead before allowing her onto the property. Zemira welcomed her at the door, and Munroe greeted her with a kiss on each cheek, each lasting only inappropriately long enough for the teenage imagination to flourish, and she then presented a bouquet of flowers. "For your mother," Munroe said.

"Ima," Zemira called over her shoulder. "Come meet Michael."

Zemira's mother was a petite woman who looked young enough to be her sister and left no doubt as to the origin of her daughter's good looks. She introduced herself, took the bouquet with a gracious smile, and asked a few polite questions before returning to whatever part of the house she had come from.

It was when they were seated at the table that Munroe met the compelling focus behind the trip to Yaoundé. Colonel Eskin entered the room, and seeing Munroe, he reached for her hand, and she stood to shake his. His lips smiled, his eyes said, *If you touch my daughter, I'll castrate you,* and the rest of the table heard, "Welcome." He was five foot eleven, with a full head of salt-and-pepper hair and what Munroe later realized was a delightfully dry sense of humor. By all appearances he was a husband and a father at home for dinner with his family, and if he was used to giving orders and having them obeyed, it was obviously not under this roof.

"So, Michael," he said, placing a helping of food on his plate, "Zemira tells me you are new to Yaoundé. How long have you been in Cameroon?"

"This time only a couple of weeks, but I was born here."

The mother passed a bowl in the direction of her daughter. "How interesting. Were your parents military? Diplomats?"

"Missionaries," Munroe replied, and shrugged. "It's been interesting coming back. It's amazing how little changes over time, at least according to what I remember."

Then the colonel: "How long do you plan to stay?"

"Only another week, unfortunately, but I'll return eventually." The truth, however obfuscated, was always the best story, least likely to be questioned and easiest to modify.

Under the table Zemira brushed lightly against Munroe's hand, and Munroe winked at her. So began the tightrope walk of the evening. Munroe had no background research to pull from, no idea of the man and his history or interests or passions, and so she was forced to listen for clues in the talk around the table. And then as each piece became a clearer part of the composite, she shifted into the character that would endear the mother, earn the father's approval, and keep Zemira just slightly off balance. Munroe's mind worked in a state of hyperawareness, of ratiocination and calculation that translated into exact responses, and by the time the evening was over and the colonel had offered his driver for the trip back to the hotel, Munroe was mentally and physically exhausted. The results had been better than she'd hoped: lunch tomorrow at the colonel's office to view his collection of model military aircraft.

At the hotel sleep came easy and lasted long. It was the healthy exhaustion of an assignment, exhaustion that brought focus to the present, which silenced the internal voices and kept her mind free of Francisco.

The next day's lunch turned into a partial tour of the facilities, and while the colonel played guide, he recounted abstract snippets and stories of daily life in the training of the elite forces. By the time Munroe returned to the hotel, she had seen and heard all she'd needed.

There was nothing holding her in Yaoundé, no reason to stay. Good-byes weren't obligatory, but neither was there any point to being an ass and skipping town, and so she called Zemira, invited her to dinner, and was sure to have her home early enough to keep the colonel happy. Then, unwilling to wait for the morning bus, Munroe hired a taxi, paid a round-trip fare for a one-way ride, and left Yaoundé. The insanity of driving the roads at night was a risk. A calculable risk. Francisco beckoned.

It was after midnight when she arrived in Douala. She'd told Francisco that she would be back in ten days, and she had wrapped it up in six. She stood now on the doorstep of the apartment, key in hand, and knocked first before inserting it. The door opened from the inside, and Francisco stood facing her, bare-chested and barefoot, face blank, simply staring. Except for a table lamp that illuminated a side of the living-room sofa, the flat was dark, and it was obvious he'd been up reading.

"Are you going to let me in?" Munroe asked.

Francisco stepped aside to let her pass. She entered and dropped the backpack on the floor. He closed the door and turned toward her, the shock on his face replaced by neutrality.

"If this is a problem," she said, pointing first to her head and then to her body, "I have other clothes and a wig." In response he pulled her close, held her head to his shoulder, and wrapped his hand around the back of her neck. "I missed you," he said.

"I know," she whispered. "Me, too." And then, "Trouble sleeping?"

He nodded, brought her mouth to his, and when she kissed him back, he pushed her away and held her at arm's length. He unbuttoned the shirt, pulling it down over her shoulders.

"I'm still the same person," she said, but saw on his face that the words were unnecessary. He loosened the bandage that secured her chest, allowing the elastic to unfurl and drop, and forced her against the door. All the reserve, all the control was gone. She wrapped her legs around his waist and kissed him back just as forcefully. He grasped for her face, for her mouth, and somehow, after knocking first against the hallway door and then against the wall, brought her to the bedroom but never made it to the bed.

Afterward as they lay on the floor, tangled in sheets that had been torn from the bed, pillows scattered beyond them, he said to her, "We could find a compromise, perhaps take the trawler to an island, someplace where we could live and forget the world."

She smiled, rolled over, and then straddled him. She had no words for this: to care, to want, to fear, to hurt in the knowledge that for his sake and hers there would necessarily be a good-bye. She leaned forward, placed a kiss on his forehead, his chin, his mouth, and then, saying nothing, lay beside him, head on his shoulder.

The next morning Munroe knew it was late before she'd opened her eyes, and when she did, Francisco was beside her, staring. She smiled and whispered, "How long have you been watching me sleep?"

"An eternity and a heartbeat," he said, and then traced his fingers along her forehead and down her jawline. "Promise me that you'll never walk away without warning. I can bear it if you promise me just that."

"I promise," she whispered.

No pain of captivity came with the words, and she smiled and closed her eyes.

IT WAS FOUR days later at Douala's international airport that Munroe stood in a pilot's uniform on the tarmac near the Jetway, waiting for the Air France flight to taxi to the terminal. The A340 had landed minutes earlier and was now a mark in the distance, growing larger by the second. Not far from where she stood, baggage handlers and ground crew prepared for the disembarkation, and they paid little attention to her or to the white van that passed as an ambulance idling nearby. Such was the simplicity of uniforms: No one looked, especially in a place like this where an extra ten euros were all the identification a person needed.

Bradford was bringing with him two trunks courtesy of Logan. They would be filled primarily with junk that would pass for what a typical traveler would pack, and if Munroe was lucky and Logan had been kind, some of it would be in her size and style. Buried among the superfluous would be communications equipment, uniforms, video equipment, GPS systems, and a mobile satellite phone high-tech and expensive enough to catch a signal from the remoteness of the equatorial jungle. The trunks would have been specifically tagged, and Munroe had taken great pains to be sure that Beyard knew what he was looking for.

Once the matériel was inside the country, they would be fully equipped for the run to Mongomo, and these were items that they couldn't afford to have pass through Cameroonian customs, not even a cursory check by a bribed official. The ambulance would make sure the goods were safely escorted into the country, and Bradford's unconscious body would help complete the picture.

The A340 turned toward the gate. Munroe waited to see if the machine would position for the passengers to disembark at the Jetway or, as was typical, via a mobile staircase. The plane continued to the terminal, and the Jetway began to scroll, so she headed up the stairs. According to plan, the trunks would be loaded into the ambulance by the time she returned with Bradford.

Munroe stripped off the pilot bars that had done their job through a perfunctory security check, tucked them into a pocket, and stood waiting beside the door hatch with a wheelchair. She greeted passengers as they disembarked, and if the airline personnel felt she was out of place, they said nothing. Munroe spotted Bradford before he stepped off the plane, and his eyes went from hers to the wheelchair and back again, the look on his face saying, *I can't believe you're doing this.*

She stepped beside him and said, "If you would, Mr. Bradford, it's for your own well-being."

He sat, and before Munroe began to wheel him away, she handed him a small bottle of orange juice. "We're taking you out in an ambulance," she whispered over his shoulder. "So be a good little boy and take your medicine."

"I'll go along with the ruse, but there's no way I'm taking this," he said.

"You'll do it or I use a hypodermic." She smiled, not at him but for the benefit of those who might be watching. "You fucked up in coming back, Miles. Deal with it. You want to be here, you play it my way." She took the bottle of orange juice from him, unscrewed the cap, and handed it back. "Drink up."

His expression was a mixture of anger and helplessness. After watching him tilt the contents of the bottle into his mouth, Munroe grinned and wheeled him down the Jetway.

CHAPTER 17

Douala, Cameroon

It was warm, but not in a suffocating way. Mosquito netting hung from the ceiling, draped in a kind of shroud. Miles Bradford blinked and then took a deep breath. He was on a narrow bed, still clothed, although his shoes were no longer on his feet. A row of small windows lined the left wall, and filtered light came through them, casting odd shadows about the room. His head hurt and he was hungry, and recollections of the last words he'd heard from Munroe tumbled around in his mind. He hadn't expected to be greeted with a hero's welcome, but a friendly "Hi and welcome back" wasn't asking much. Sure, he'd gone against her wishes in returning to Cameroon, but it hadn't called for this level of hostility. He should have expected it, though. The woman really didn't play well with others.

In other circumstances he would already have been at the windows, already gotten a bearing on the surroundings and known what the chances for getting out were, might have even knocked a few heads in, Munroe's included. But this was different. He didn't want to escape, he wanted her trust, wanted to be there when she went back to Equatorial Guinea to search for Emily—had to be there. He lay still for a moment and then, when he reached through the netting for the glass of water standing on the low table by the side of the bed, saw that he wasn't alone in the room.

In a chair to the right, a few feet away from the bed, sat a man with features slightly distorted by the folds of netting that separated them, and although the man's head didn't move, his eyes followed when Bradford shifted to reach for the glass. Without breaking eye contact, Bradford brought the glass to his mouth. The man had a strong, toned body, was a little taller than he, perhaps older. He had no visible weapons, and the way he was sitting indicated no ill intent or threat.

Bradford drank the water in several long-drawn-out swallows, and when he had finished, the man leaned forward, rested his elbows on his knees, and said, "Good morning."

Morning. How long had he been under?

Bradford nodded in reply and held the glass lightly, ready to utilize it as a weapon if he had to. This was Munroe's game; he would see where she was taking it.

The man asked, "Do you know who I am?" Bradford remained silent, and the man said, "You are Miles Bradford, American, private security, mercenary, assist to Vanessa Munroe in this assignment of hers, am I correct?" The voice was rich with accent, and although the words were neutral, the tone had an edge and brought with it something else—a warning, perhaps.

Bradford nodded again.

"I am Francisco Beyard: gun runner, drug runner, businessman, and strategist. It falls on my shoulders to decide your fate. Welcome to my world."

And then it made sense. Munroe's missing years and the way she'd regrouped back on the Equatoguinean mainland as quickly as she had without money or supplies. These were old connections, and this man was a figure from her unknown past—"Vanessa's" unknown past. Bradford drew himself up to lean back against the wall and said, "Am I here as a guest or a prisoner?"

Francisco Beyard shrugged. "I would hardly call you a prisoner. Escape from this room, from this house, would be fairly simple, and were you to vanish into the streets of Douala, it would make my job so much easier. You have brought the supplies Vanessa needed, and so you are free to go anytime. But you don't want to leave, you are determined to return to Equatorial Guinea with us, and that is why you and I are here in this room having this . . ." He paused. "This conversation."

"I'd like to talk to Michael if she's around."

"I'm afraid that's not possible. You see, Mr. Bradford . . ."

"Miles."

Beyard nodded. "You see, Miles, I care nothing about this project of yours or this girl you hope to find. My interest in this venture—my only interest—is protecting Vanessa. As I understand it, you were the one responsible for bringing her into the assignment. You were the one with her in Malabo when she was taken from the hotel and for some reason you were left untouched. Now you insist on returning to Africa to accompany her, though your help is unneeded and unwanted. This does not bode well for you. I'm sure you understand my position."

"I had nothing to do with what happened to Michael," Bradford said. "I'm just as confused about the chain of events as I assume you are or she is."

"But you are extremely eager—even demanding—to accompany Vanessa back into the country. Why is that?"

"It's my job."

Beyard shook his head slightly. "It was no longer your job at one point, and yet you persisted."

"Look," Bradford said, irritation breaking through in his voice, "I've known Emily and her family since she was a child. I've been through hell with both of her parents while they tried to locate her—her mother eventually killed herself over this. After four years of searching, we finally have a tangible trail to follow. I'm not going to let it go. I have a personal interest in bringing Emily home."

"And you don't feel that Vanessa is capable of doing this?"

Bradford began to say something and then stopped. No matter what he said, he would back himself into a corner.

"What you've just told me," Beyard continued, "Vanessa has also told me." He paused and stared at Bradford, rubbing his thumb against his chin. "But this is not the primary reason you have returned. You know it, so do I, so does she. In order to assess with certainty what threat you constitute to Vanessa—and by implication to myself—or to the assignment, I need to understand what compels you to return, the things that run deeper that you are not telling."

"It is what it is," Bradford said. "I don't have anything more to tell."

Beyard stood. "As I suspected. And so I've made arrangements for you to fly back to Houston—your flight leaves tomorrow morning. You will be sedated, and I will accompany you to the plane to be sure that you are on it. I suggest that you don't return or attempt to find us, and should you be so foolish as to try, I will personally see to it that you are stopped. This is my home, Miles, and I am well connected. Do not underestimate me." He turned to go. "There will be no more questions. I'm sure you're hungry. I'll have food sent to you."

Bradford closed his eyes and took a deep breath. It wasn't all bad. He could leave the house—it wouldn't be that difficult—keep tabs on them, follow them. Yeah, right. Maybe on another continent, in another country, but not this one. He didn't know the land or the language, didn't have time to acquire resources and assets. Munroe would be traveling into remote areas, would know he was there and eliminate the threat she found in him. No, if he wanted to be there when Emily was located, the only way was by gaining Munroe's trust. She had calculated this, was manipulating the situation and using this man, Beyard, as a buffer so that the only way to her was through him. There had been no bluff in Beyard's voice, no malice. He presented an opportunity that would soon be gone. Bradford debated until Beyard's hand was on the door and then said, "I loved her mother."

Beyard stopped, turned.

"What guarantee do I have," Bradford asked, "that this will be enough?"

"None," Beyard said, and returned to the chair where he'd been sitting. "But motive is a powerful thing, and I need to know what yours is. Ultimately Vanessa will make the call. I am . . . how should I say? I am the screening process."

"The truth is, I made a promise to her mother. The night before she killed herself, she made me swear I would bring Emily home."

"An oath is something I can understand," Beyard said. "Why was it made?"

"I loved her," Bradford said. "It really is that simple."

Beyard nodded. "And this man Richard Burbank, the father, the one you manipulated into hiring Vanessa, he was no doubt unaware?"

"Manipulated." Bradford gave a quick snort and shook his head slightly. How much could they actually know? "Yeah, I manipulated Richard into hiring Michael, and no, he didn't have a clue about the extent of the friendship that Elizabeth and I shared."

"So you are the one responsible for Vanessa twice having been nearly killed?"

"Oh, I'm sure she's been nearly killed many more times than that," Bradford said, and then quickly followed with, "I was responsible for getting her hired, but like I already said, I had nothing to do with what happened in Malabo or whatever the fuck else you're talking about. I certainly don't want to see her dead. I want her to find Emily."

Beyard said nothing and, with arms crossed and legs stretched out, stared at Bradford while silence filled the room.

Finally Bradford spoke again. "Richard introduced me to Elizabeth about a year after they'd been married. We've never been friends, Richard and I. Acquaintances, business associates, I guess you could say. We've worked together on and off over the years on assorted deals, and it was at some formal business event that I first met her. No matter what it looked like on the outside, they weren't happy. Richard is a controlling, demanding asshole, and it carried over into their marriage. Elizabeth turned to me for advice, and in time we became very close." Bradford's voice caught, and he paused for composure. "I would have done anything for her, you know? God, I loved her." He raised his eyes to meet Beyard's. "Yes, we were lovers.

"I was with her the day before she died—I'd gone to see her at the retreat where she'd been staying. I'd been making fairly regular visits just to check on her, but on that particular day she was different, stressed, nervous, had difficulty focusing. Richard had come to see her the day before to talk about her will. Apparently everything she had was to go to Emily, and with Emily having been missing for nearly a year, Richard wanted her to rewrite the will. For obvious reasons the conversation didn't go well. Elizabeth refused to believe that her daughter was dead. Richard seemed to think otherwise.

"She spent a lot of time talking about Richard, about him forcing her to make changes she didn't want to make. She made me promise that I would do everything I could to find Emily, that I would bring her home." Bradford looked directly at Beyard. "I did, and the next day Elizabeth was dead."

Beyard was silent for a moment and then finally said, "Why Vanessa?"

Bradford smiled. Almost laughed. "You're from her past. I guess you don't know much about her present. Michael deals in information, and as far as I know, she's the best there is at getting it. You give her a scenario, a country, whatever it is, and she'll find a way. Doesn't matter the language, the gender, cold, hot, war zone, military dictatorship, whatever—she gets it. I used some of the stuff she put together for a couple of the security jobs I worked. It was always accurate, always good." Bradford paused and brushed his fingers through his hair, sighed and stared toward the window. "I was running out of time. It had been four years since Emily'd disappeared, and I realized that unless we tried a different avenue, we'd keep turning up nothing. I'd been watching Michael for a couple of years, had assembled something of a portfolio on her." He stopped and looked at Beyard. "Before you start jumping to conclusions, my curiosity was purely professional—admiration, the way one artist admires the work of another. Anyway, I knew that Michael's assignment in Turkey was close to finished, so I brought what I had to Richard and asked him to give it one last shot, told him that if Michael couldn't track down Emily, nobody could, and that he could know for certain that she was dead, and he could have the closure he wanted." Bradford shrugged. "That's pretty much it, from the beginning, my side of the story. True to form, Michael began to deliver, and then we got to Malabo and the shit hit the fan, and I'm still trying to figure out what the hell happened."

Beyard put his hands on his knees and said, "Well, Miles, that's a very interesting story." He stood. "One last thing: I have been asked to collect a notebook. It's inside your bag there. I have seen it but prefer to allow you the courtesy of giving it to me rather than taking it from you."

"Is there any difference?" Bradford said, and swung his legs over the side of the bed. "Either way I have no choice."

"A matter of semantics."

Bradford nodded, dug the notebook out of his bag, and handed it to Beyard.

"Thank you," Beyard said, and opened the door. "You're free to leave, stay, wander, as you wish. Make yourself at home."

"I'd like to talk to Michael."

"She's not here at the moment." Beyard glanced at his watch. "Three hours, perhaps."

chapter 18

When Munroe returned to the apartment that afternoon, she found Miles and Francisco sitting at the kitchen table, empty bottles of beer between them, conversing like long-lost drinking buddies. Without intending it, she stared until the room grew silent, then rolled her eyes in disgust and walked to the bedroom. Whatever she'd expected upon returning to the flat, it wasn't to see the two of them interacting like old friends. Was it some fucking mercenary code of brotherhood they could sniff off each other?

She dropped the items from her arms onto the bed and returned to the kitchen. The boys were still talking but weren't as jovial as they had been, and when Munroe reached for a glass from one of the cupboards, Francisco caught her eye. She could see from the masked strain on his face that he was concerned about her reaction, and so, without acknowledging Bradford's presence, she walked to the table, leaned in front of Francisco, and kissed him.

He responded by pulling her closer, kissing her harder, and from the corner of her eye she saw Bradford shift, visibly uncomfortable with this display of affection. She suppressed a wicked smile and whispered into Francisco's ear. She might as well have lifted a leg and peed on him; she was marking territory, establishing dominance, letting Bradford know that regardless of what might have transpired between the two of them while she was out of the house, she was still the one running the show. Francisco reached for her hand and stood, and as he walked with her out of the room, he said to Bradford, "Make yourself at home." Munroe glanced over her shoulder, saw genuine pain in Bradford's eyes, and was satisfied.

In the bedroom Munroe knelt on the bed and wrapped an arm around Francisco's neck, pulled him close, ran her hands up his chest, and kissed him. He returned the warmth of her mouth and then took hold of her wrists, stepped back, and said, "Don't do it, Essa. I know this is manipulation, and it isn't necessary." And then he brought her hands to his lips. "Don't try to control me—you already own me, what more do you want?"

The counterplay, the shift in control dynamics, and the challenge that came with it brought on the giddy urge to laugh. Instead she wrapped her arms around his neck and put her cheek to his and with an ear-to-ear grin across her face whispered, "I'm sorry."

He sat on the bed, pulled her down with him, and said, "There's a lot we need to discuss," and with her head resting on his shoulder he repeated what Bradford had told him. When he finished, Munroe stood and walked across the room to the window and stared into the compound. "I wish I would have known these things before taking the assignment," she said.

"Does this validate your view of Miles as a threat?"

She turned toward Francisco. "If I understand it correctly, Miles wanted to find Emily, ran up against brick walls, and so manipulated Richard and used Richard's money to get me to find her?" She let out an involuntary chuckle. "It's brilliant, really." She turned back toward the window. "If what he told you was true, and you seem to believe it is, then no, Miles is not a threat, at least not directly and not that he himself is aware of." She shook her head slightly. "I've been set up to fail," she said. "Fucking bastard."

"Who?"

"Richard Burbank, the guy who hired me, the poor bleeding-heart father who's so desperate to find his daughter. Him." And then, seeing a look of puzzlement cross Francisco's face, she said, "Never mind. You don't have the information to understand where I'm coming from with this. Has Miles made any phone calls, accessed the Internet since he's been awake?"

"No. That I can guarantee."

"And what are your views on his coming with us?"

"I believe under most circumstances he would be an asset. He knows his shit—I'd take him on my team if he was accepting offers. Frankly, I'm tempted to make one. Additionally, he knows this girl personally, and when we find her, that can only be a good thing."

Munroe nodded. "Fine. What about the notebook? Do you have it?"

Beyard pulled the book from a drawer and handed it to her. Munroe opened and read. A smile formed at the corners of her mouth, and a few pages later she laughed. Who would've thought? The gun-toting tough guy was writing a romance novel, and from the looks of the notes it wasn't his first.

Munroe found Bradford on the living-room sofa, hunched over the coffee table eyeing the chessboard. She sat down beside him. "Do you play?"

"It's been a decade or more," he said. "And I was never very good. You?"

"I used to play often with Francisco—obviously, it's been a while." She nodded toward the board. "I rarely beat him, but this time I'm giving him a run for his money." She handed Bradford the notebook. "Have you been published?"

"Yeah," he said, and his cheeks flushed color. "Four books."

"I suppose we all have our little secrets," she said, and smiled a half grin. And then, in seriousness, "We're leaving at first light tomorrow. If you want in, you can have at it, but there are a few stipulations you'll have to agree to. One: You cannot under any circumstances contact anyone without my explicit approval—no calls or e-mails, period. Two: If you become a liability, we will leave you wherever we are and you'll have to work your own way out."

"I can live with those."

"And I'm no longer your job," she said. "Whatever the terms were in your arrangement with Richard, they've changed. I'm letting you come along because Emily knows you and it might come in handy when we find her. You're not coming to protect me or stick by my side, and you'll have to agree to follow my instructions whether they go along with what you think is your assignment or not. Will that be a problem?"

"I'll manage."

She nodded. "Then welcome back." She took a deep breath and said, "I wish you'd have told me about Richard from the beginning. It might have saved me from getting dumped into the ocean, and we might already have found Emily by now."

Bradford hesitated and then said, "Told you what about Richard?"

"That he wasn't the one behind this whole assignment—you were. Not to mention that you were fucking his wife."

Bradford drew a breath and his face grew hard, evidence she'd struck personal, pushed him far. Although she expected him to react, after a moment's pause he said only, "I don't get it, you think Richard is out to get you?"

"Did you tell Richard we were going to Malabo?"

"Yeah."

"What about Bata?"

His whisper was so low she could barely hear it. "Yes."

"I don't have all the dots connected yet," she said. "But it's looking like Richard has had his hand in this somehow. From the way Francisco tells it, you've been the main person concerned with finding Emily, regardless of how Richard represented himself to me. That's a strike against him. That Titan Exploration just happens to have its oil wells in the same country that Emily goes missing could be coincidence, but I don't think so—at the very least, Richard has governmental connections in Equatorial Guinea. That's strike two. Someone close to me has been feeding information to the bad guys—it's the only explanation I have for some of the events that have taken place. Strike three."

Bradford ran his hands through his hair and then stared up at the ceiling. His breathing was slow and deep, and finally he said, "But why?"

"I don't know, Miles. There are a lot of unknowns at this point. But if I had to make a guess, I'd say it was money."

Disbelief was written on Bradford's face. "Richard has more money than God."

"Maybe he does and maybe he doesn't. I'm living proof that what you see is not always what it is. You said Richard was trying to get Elizabeth to change her will. That says money. You're a smart man, Miles. Don't tell me you haven't thought of it yourself."

"You know, the thing with Elizabeth, I can understand that. He was a crappy husband, and maybe it was about money then—that happened before Titan hit oil, before his big break. But for all his faults, he is a good father, and he loves Emily, and he's suffered a lot through this. It may have been me pushing for it, but Richard has financed each step, never hesitated once. It was only this past year that he started to protest, and it was never about the money. It was because of the personal pain that came from not being able to let it go. Why would he want the one person who can find Emily killed? It makes no sense."

"Maybe someone else is using him. There are too many unknowns, but I'm willing to place a hefty bet that when we find Emily, a lot of the answers will be waiting with her." She stood. "And now I have to make a phone call that I wish I didn't have to make."

Munroe picked up the phone and dialed Burbank's office. As before, she was immediately transferred to his direct line, but this time she was left on hold for at least five minutes. When he picked up the phone, the exhaustion in his voice carried through the wires. "It's been a while, Michael. I've heard that things have been rough for you over there—I hope all is well."

"Things are fine, Mr. Burbank," she said. "As required, I'm calling to update you. As I'm sure you've heard through Miles, and though it may be difficult to believe, we have eyewitnesses who've placed your daughter alive on the mainland of Equatorial Guinea, the latest sighting now within the last six months."

"Yes," he said. "It was amazing news, still is. Getting word about the death certificate was devastating, though a relief in a way. It meant that we could lay her memory to rest. And then to follow that with the hope that she might possibly be alive, it all seemed like such a cruel joke. I've been on an emotional roller coaster since."

"I assure you the sources are genuine," she said.

"What's the next step?"

"Now that Miles is here, we're waiting on a few details to get sorted out. I'm estimating a week before we're ready to return to Río Muni— the Equatoguinean mainland."

"A week? That long?"

"About that, yes."

"Thank you, Michael," he said. "This is excellent news, although honestly, I'm terrified of falling prey to false hope. Please let me know as things progress."

"Of course."

THE CALL OVER, Munroe turned to Bradford and then to Beyard, who had just entered the room. "If we're lucky, we just bought ourselves a week."

CHAPTER 19

Turnoff to Ebebiyín, Cameroon

The road was dry, the atmosphere hazed by harmattan—fine Saharan dust blown from the north—which clouded the sky, cut visibility, and filled the horizon with the orange-tinged illusion of smog and pollution. Munroe checked the rearview mirror, caught the outline of Beyard's vehicle, and returned her focus to the pothole-pitted road ahead, stopped and shifted into four-wheel drive.

She worked the clutch and gas heading down, then up, a chunk of missing road that had most likely washed out during a previous downpour. Bradford stared out the passenger window with his arms crossed. It was more or less the same silent position he'd held since Douala and under the circumstances probably as close as he could get to turning his back to her. Whatever the mood, he was certainly entitled to it; she'd been treating him like crap since he'd returned to Cameroon, and though it would eventually be necessary to make nice, now wasn't the time.

They had left Douala before dawn, routing east to Yaoundé and then south, the quality of the road rapidly deteriorating the closer they drew to the border. Entering Equatorial Guinea from Cameroon was inconvenient at best. The countries were separated at the coast by the Ntem River, and where the water no longer delimited them, the countryside was thick with dense forest, through which village populations were able to traverse on foot, often unaware of the exact place one country ended and another began. There was only one vehicular transit point along the 120-mile stretch, and they were now driving down the road that led to it.

A gate barring the road and a small building standing next to it marked the entrance into Equatorial Guinea. Munroe slowed to a stop. By all appearances the checkpoint was deserted. When after a minute no official exited what should have been an office, she switched off the engine and stepped into the afternoon heat.

The one-room structure was empty, bare-board walls with a cement floor and holes for windows, and the only sound came from the insects that buzzed along the ceiling. Munroe stood in the doorway for a moment, then turned and walked toward the metal barricade. It was held in place to adjacent poles by three chains, which meant they would need to locate three officials, each with a separate key. The border didn't close until five, but with the post deserted, traffic nearly none, and it being midafternoon, the authorities were no doubt already finished for the day. It wasn't too much of a stretch to expect that at least one of them had already returned to his village, taking the key along for the evening.

Through the dust caked on Beyard's windshield, she could see him leaning on the steering wheel, eyes following her movements, and when she strode toward him, he stepped out of the vehicle. "Three locks," she said, "empty office." She stared in the direction of town. Somewhere along those streets, in some bar or hotel or restaurant, was an unknown face expecting her to arrive within the week, waiting to pass along the word and thus guarantee that she never made it to Mongomo.

If they'd come to the country under any other pretense or if they'd had more time, perhaps a wiser move would have been to turn back, head west, and then cut tracks across the unmarked border. Here they were set out like targets on a firing range, and if the artifice of an Israeli convoy was transparent, they'd know it soon enough.

Women and children approached the vehicles, some trying to get Bradford's attention through his window and others crowding around Beyard and Munroe, each offering items for sale. A boy of eight or nine balanced a dirty plastic basin filled with bananas on his head. Beyard examined a bunch and then pulled a handful of loose change from his pocket. He knelt down at the boy's eye level, handed over the cash, and flashed Munroe a dashing smile; the unriddling of the missing officials had begun.

It took thirty minutes before they were able to locate the first official with his key, another forty to find the second. It was two hours before the third was found, and when he was, he was drunk and unable to locate the key until Munroe, unwilling to offer bribes or wait out the length of time it would take to play the game, began to name-drop. With the appropriate level of threat provided, the missing key was swiftly produced, and the convoy moved into the town of Ebebiyín. By now even the most incompetent of lookouts would be more than aware of their presence. If there had been someone waiting—and Munroe was sure that there was—no threat or whisper of awareness to the convoy's intent had blown on the wind.

The village of several thousand was a gateway at the crossroads between Gabon, Cameroon, and Equatorial Guinea: a marketplace and hub of activity for miles to the west and south; a small grid of mostly unpaved roads and the whitewashed and red-stained buildings that fronted them; and like most rural towns on the continent, life here moved at a lethargic pace. It took less than ten minutes for the convoy to crawl through the sprawled, dusty streets, and when they were on the narrow but paved stretch that would take them to Mongomo and were far beyond the reach of townsfolk curiosity, Munroe turned the vehicle off the road.

Verdurous vines that thrived in the open light of the swath of tarmac created a wall of green on either side of the road, and so, in view of any vehicle that might pass, Munroe and Beyard moved quickly, switching out Cameroonian plates and papers for Equatoguinean, stashing the old ones behind door panels, and minutes later they headed back onto the road in vehicles registered in the name of the country's president. There were still eighty kilometers to Mongomo, and with the improved road conditions it would be possible to reach the city by early evening. But they would wait until tomorrow's dawn; it would be far better to approach the target house with a full period of daylight ahead, and staying in Mongomo overnight created too much exposure.

A half hour after dark, they went off-road, following a track that connected a small village to the Mongomo road. In the hour since Ebebiyín, they had covered forty kilometers, the empty stretch taking them past an occasional bush taxi, several abandoned and cannibalized cars, and expected roadblocks; nothing out of the ordinary that would signal awareness to their presence and the relative silence among the local military frequencies so far confirmed that all was in order.

Before reaching the designated village, the convoy detoured into the bush, where they would bide the night well hidden in the black of the forest. In the dark, Munroe felt for the vehicle's communications equipment, and when she had disconnected it, she placed the pieces into a duffel bag, slung the strap over her shoulder, and opened the door. She stepped into the night, and Bradford said, "Where are you going?"

She nodded to the rear. "Other vehicle," she said, and although she knew it was unnecessary, added, "Keep the lights off and, unless you want to get devoured by mosquitoes, the doors and windows shut. Don't run the air conditioner—the engine noise will attract attention. I'll be back at dawn." She shut the door before he had a chance to respond, knowing he'd hate her all the more for it.

Munroe slid into the backseat of the rear vehicle. Francisco was in the front, reclined, hands behind his head, and when she shut the door, he brought the back upright and climbed between the front seats to where she was. His foot hit the duffel bag. "What'd you bring?"

"Everything that transmits."

He slid next to her and maneuvered her onto his lap so that she faced him. "Still don't trust him?"

"Not enough to leave it with him overnight," she said.

His hands were already inside her shirt. She removed his uniform, and like two teenagers on a forbidden tryst, hormones transcending heat and discomfort, they left the interior of the vehicle as damp and humid as the air outside.

It was well past midnight before they finally returned to the front and reclined the seats in an attempt to sleep through what was left of the night. The mirrors of the lead vehicle reflected dim specks of canopy-filtered moonlight, and Francisco nodded in their direction. "You didn't need to bring the equipment," he whispered. "You know he's not the one trying to get you killed."

Munroe stared out the passenger window.

"I see the way he looks at you when your back is turned," Francisco

said. He paused and turned his head toward her. "You're a very perceptive woman, Essa. You can't help but know that he wants you alive as
badly as I do."

"I'd have thought it would bother you, and instead you advocate
for him."

He reached out and touched her cheek. "It does bother me. I want
him away from you, I want you to myself." He sighed. "But I don't own
you, and that's beyond my control." He turned and faced front again.
"All I'm saying is that I know the torment, and there's no need for you
to be deliberately cruel."

She closed her eyes. It was so much more than that. Until the
unknowns became clearer, it was difficult to discern how far Bradford
could be trusted, and keeping him off balance was the easiest way to
gauge him. Munroe put her feet up on the dashboard and drew a deep
breath. "I don't want to talk about him," she said. Didn't want to talk
about anything, really, because as unplanned as it was, history was about
to be repeated: A trio of two foreign men and a woman would be heading
into Mongomo, and no matter what they found when they reached the
city, the proverbial shit was going to hit the fan.

Though none of them would readily admit it, they all knew that
getting back out was going to be dicey. Tonight was the calm before the
storm.

Calm.

Munroe breathed again and felt the relaxation of assignment wash
over her.

They entered Mongomo in the early morning while the streets were
still in the beginning stages of bustle and activity. For a village on the
edge of civilization, one completely surrounded by the wide, sweeping grandeur of lush vegetation and without direct access to any center
of industry, Mongomo showed surprising modernity, testament to the
windfall of oil money finding its way to the extended families of the clan
that filled the presidential palace.

Shortly after eight they stopped in front of the city's police station,
and while Beyard waited with the vehicles and continued to scan the

local frequencies, Munroe and Bradford sought out the highest-ranking officer available. Once pleasantries had been dispensed, Bradford, acting as Munroe's superior, spoke emphatically, a foreign-sounding nonsense that Munroe, very much the younger male subordinate, interpreted as a request for assistance. The officer obliged by providing an aide to direct them to the house of Timoteo Otoro Nchama, vice minister of mines and energy.

The dwelling was a single story, spaced widely from its neighbors and set ten meters off a quiet unpaved street whose outlet narrowed into a verdant footpath that led toward rough cinder-block houses and, beyond them, the jungle forest. Munroe drove by the house once and then, leaving Beyard stationed at the street entrance in the second vehicle, returned the guide to his workplace, a tactical gesture that had nothing to do with kindness.

On the second sweep, Munroe made the full length of the street to the narrowed outlet before looping back to park in front of the house. The lack of vehicles fronting the house pointed to the minister's being away from home, and the ease of access to the property meant a smaller chance of being trapped should the encounter proceed in a less than favorable direction. It also meant being visible from the street, and by the pedestrians and neighbors who had already begun to take notice of their presence.

Munroe and Bradford walked the distance to the front door, and she stood to the side, out of sight. Bradford rapped a three-beat knock on the heavy wood, and in the silence they waited. There'd been shadows in the windows during the first pass, and Beyard had already confirmed that no one had left the house since. Another moment of silence, and at Munroe's nod Bradford knocked again.

His hand was coming down on a third try when the door opened and an older woman with a worn dress and flat shoes looked out at him with disinterested annoyance. From her appearance Munroe assumed maid or nanny, but it was difficult to tell, she could just as easily be mother or sister. The woman spoke no English, and as Bradford could not converse in any of the local languages, he handed her his business card and motioned for her to carry it inside.

A few minutes later, the woman returned and gestured for Bradford to follow. Munroe joined him, and though the woman showed initial surprise at Munroe's emergence, she led them both to the interior of the house with apparent acceptance and without comment. They had gone only a few steps when a petite blond woman entered the foyer at a brisk pace and, seeing Bradford, stopped short, gaped, and then burst into tears. The cherubic teenager from the high-school photo had been replaced by a woman aged beyond her years.

There was a second of uneasy quiet filled by sobs, and then Bradford said, "Heya, kid," and walked toward Emily and wrapped his arms around her shoulders. She buried her head in his chest, her shoulders quivering with each rapid inhale, and Bradford stroked her hair and in a half whisper said, "Hey, it's all going to be okay."

He looked toward Munroe with a distressed smile. From here they were winging it. Emily had disappeared four years ago, now she was found, and with the exception of Munroe having faced two attempted military executions, nothing more was certain.

Munroe felt a wave of disequilibrium; after everything that had come before, reaching the target now had been unsettlingly simple.

Emily straightened and sniffed, and through tearful laughter she said, "Come on in, let's sit down." Her words were strained, as if this were the first English she'd spoken for as long as she'd been missing. To the woman who had answered the door and now hovered in the shadows, she said, *"Nza ve belleng café."*

Munroe smiled in recognition of the Fang language and shifted so that the camera lens attached to her lapel faced Emily directly. It was the most straightforward and least intrusive way to document whatever would transpire, and there were two machines establishing a record of it: one was snuggled in her shirt pocket and the other was with Beyard, receiving the signal wirelessly.

Emily led them to the living room and sat on the oversize sofa. Bradford sat next to her, and she glanced at him repeatedly, each time a smile breaking through the etched lines of distress on her face. They were smiles of innocence, shock, nervousness, confusion, but most of all unadulterated happiness. Whatever Beyard's suspicions, this girl wanted to be found, no doubt about it, which begged the question, why in the four years that she'd been missing had she not contacted her family?

Emily turned to Munroe and hesitated. Bradford said, "Emily, this is

Michael." Munroe stuck out her hand, and Emily shook it, with another smile. "Your family has been trying to find you for the past four years," Bradford said, "and Michael is the one responsible for finally tracking you down."

Emily withdrew her hand, the smile fading as she tilted her head to the side, squinting as if processing what had just been said, and then she turned to Bradford and said, "What?"

Munroe said, "Emily, we're here to assist you if you want it. We've come prepared to get you out of the country. Is this something you're interested in?"

Emily nodded slowly. "It is," she said, "but I don't understand. Why now? I've been asking to go home since I got here."

Bradford glanced at Munroe, and she gave him a look back that could only be interpreted one way: Either Emily had gone batty or they had a major fucking problem. Probably the latter. Munroe's heart pounded, her mind drawing threads of thought into a partial tapestry, then she paused, knowing the answer to her next question before the words left her mouth. "Emily, who have you asked?"

Emily began to reply and stopped when the maid entered the room with a tray of cups. She set it on the coffee table, and Emily folded her hands in her lap and waited. The seconds passed, each one a painful breath, until at last the woman left the room.

"I don't trust her," Emily said. "I don't think she speaks English, but I don't know for sure. She's my husband's aunt, and she reports everything I do to him."

Munroe stepped to the couch and knelt in front of Emily so that their eyes were almost level. "We came to get you out of here, to bring you home if that's what you want. Is it what you want?"

Emily nodded.

"Then listen carefully," Munroe said. "I've been nearly killed twice trying to get to you, and chances are whoever tried before is going to try again if they find out we're here. The information we've been given and what you're telling us contradict, and if we don't get the facts sorted out soon, we might not make it out of the country alive—meaning that if you're not killed along with us, you'll be stuck here. Emily, we need to know who you've asked about returning home, who is keeping you here, and who is trying to kill me. Can you help us with this?"

"I asked my dad," Emily said. "It took me a long time, maybe a year, but I finally got through to him, and when I did, he was angry and refused to talk to me." Emily's words were starting to flow, her speech was less stilted, and the fluency—even the accent—was returning. "I was able to contact him only that once, and I've never been able to speak with my mom. I've also asked my husband so many times. I used to think that one day he'd let me go, but now he hits me if I bring it up, so I've stopped asking." A tear dropped from her cheek onto her lap, and she sniffed and ran her fingers under her eyes. "He says that by keeping me here he's doing me a favor, that without him I would be dead, and that I can never leave and I should be grateful." She lowered her eyes. "So I really don't understand why you've come now."

"Where is your husband right now? Malabo?"

"I think so."

"The people who tried to kill me are hired Angolan forces that normally take orders from the president. Does your husband have connections that would allow him to use them for other purposes?"

Emily shrugged. "I don't know," she said. "I don't know about his business or work. I know some of his family. He's the president's nephew, and his brothers are important."

"Is he the only one keeping you? Are there others?"

"I don't know," she said. "I think he's the main one." She looked to Bradford. "I have no money, and people in town, they all know me. If I leave, someone will see me and tell my husband. I tried. He found me before I got out of the country, kept me locked in the house for a few months until I promised I wouldn't leave again."

"We'll get you out," he said. "You have my word on that."

"I have two boys," Emily said. "One is two and a half and the other almost a year old—what about them?"

Bradford nodded. "We have passports for you and the children."

"I'll go pack," Emily said, and Munroe put a hand on hers to stop her. "We're going to leave the house with you in the clothes you're wearing. You'll want to tell your husband's aunt that we're going out to eat, and have her get the kids ready. She needs to believe you're coming back in a few hours."

Emily nodded and then called for the woman. When she had finished relaying the instructions and the woman had left the room, Munroe, puzzling over dots that had no apparent connections, said, "We don't have a lot of time and don't need every detail, but as best as you can, could you tell us why and how you ended up here? Start with Namibia."

Emily gave a forced smile and brushed a strand of hair out of her eyes. "There were three of us," she said. "Me, Kristof, and Mel. We'd been traveling together since Kenya, had backpacked most of the east and south, wanted to go up the west coast, wanted to see if we could get as far as Nigeria and then fly back. We didn't have a lot of time, because my mom wanted me to come home and Mel had some stuff he had to get to. We were in Windhoek and were trying to work out how to get to either Congo or Gabon, because Angola was too dangerous.

"We met this guy, his name was Hans something, and he and Kristof hit it off real well, because Kristof was German and Hans's family had come from Germany. He was a bush pilot, and he said he flew into Angola all the time, and when he found out we were trying to get north, he said he was flying to Luanda that afternoon and offered to let us come along. He said that in Luanda we could probably catch a boat or another flight into Gabon, and so we decided to do it. I called home and spoke with my dad to let him know what we were planning and that I'd contact him as soon as we got to Libreville."

Munroe caught Bradford's eye. His brows were furrowed, and confusion was clearly written across his face. Any contact by Emily after Namibia would have been critical to finding her, and this conversation with its direct geographic reading had never been mentioned. Munroe was tempted to stop Emily and ask for clarification, but she didn't.

"He said he was looking forward to me coming home," Emily said, "and he asked if, since I was going to Gabon, I planned to visit Equatorial Guinea. We hadn't been, because there wasn't much information on the country and it seemed more hassle than it was worth." She paused as if thinking through the last statement and then looked at Munroe again and said, "He told me it's where he had his exploration projects and about how wild and primitive it still was and those legends about the old president and how he buried the national treasury outside his village.

"We flew to Luanda, and I think it was that same night we caught a cargo ship to Gabon. We were in the capital for about three days and then decided to go overland into Cameroon. That's when I told the guys the stories from my dad about Equatorial Guinea, and they thought it would be cool to travel to a country so few people went to, so we decided to go through Equatorial Guinea to Cameroon. We got visas, and then, since I couldn't get either of my parents on the phone, I wrote my dad an e-mail and told him where we were headed."

"Why your dad?" Munroe interrupted. "Why not your mom?"

"Well, when I'd spoken to my dad when I was in Luanda, he told me my mom was visiting some of our friends at their ranch in Wyoming and wouldn't be back for a couple of weeks, so if I e-mailed, to e-mail him and not her."

Munroe glanced at Bradford for confirmation on the detail about Elizabeth's visit to Wyoming, and Bradford shook his head, and Emily, apparently oblivious to the exchange, continued.

"We were on the road to Mongomo from Oyem, outside the city, and at the checkpoint some of the military started harassing us. At the time it didn't seem that big a deal—we'd been through this type of thing before in other places. But then Mel started to freak out. A few days earlier, maybe a week, he'd started acting kind of strange, jabbering to himself, acting kind of paranoid sometimes. But then he'd be normal, and we'd tell him what he'd done, and we'd all have a good laugh. But this time was different—he went completely crazy. He was screaming, and then he attacked one of the soldiers, and then after that everything kind of jumbled together." Her voice went flat, and she stared into the middle of the room. "They killed him," she said. "Right there, with machetes, while Kristof and I watched. And then Kristof started to run, and I didn't know what to do, so I followed him. We were running for a long time, and I almost got away. I think Kristof got away. The last I saw him, he was running for the border, and then I got hit and passed out.

"When I woke up, I was in the city jail. I was covered with blood and bruises, and my arm was broken, and I think a rib or two was cracked. My leg hurt really bad, too, so I think it was also broken. I had lots of cuts, I think from the machetes." She reached down and lifted her dress above the knees, revealing thick scars on her legs, the recognizable product of deep gashes and no stitches. "I have more," she said, "on my stomach and back. I don't know how long I was there. I woke up a few times and would just pass out again. The next thing I remember, I was in a clean room and not in as much pain, and that's when I first met the man who's now my husband. He said he'd rescued me and that he knew who I was and he'd make sure I got home. He was really nice to me.

"But he never sent me home. He promised he would when I got stronger, but there were delays. It's really hard to know how much time passed, but I think maybe three or four months later he told me my life was in danger and the only way to be safe was to marry him. I tried to run away twice, and each time I got locked up. There were threats, and I got beaten a few times, and there were other things, too." Emily paused and swallowed, looking around the room, and Munroe could tell that she was fighting back tears.

"I think it was about a year after I got here that I got ahold of a phone with international access. I tried to call my mom, but the number had been disconnected." She turned to Bradford. "Do they still live in Houston?" Bradford gave a hesitant nod. "So then I called my dad's office. It was difficult getting through his secretaries, but I finally got him on the phone. It was very weird. I told him who I was and where I was and that I wanted to come home but that the people here wouldn't let me leave, and he told me never to call again. Maybe he thought it was a prank call—I don't know. I was never able to get in contact with him again, even though I tried. One time I got caught on the phone and my husband beat me worse than any other time and told me never to do something so foolish again, that I had been stupid and risked my life.

"Around then is when I realized I was pregnant, and since it seemed that leaving wasn't going to happen, the only thing I could really do was try to make my life better here, so that's when I agreed to marry Timoteo and stopped running away or trying to make calls. Things have been more or less okay since then."

THE TWO-WAY RADIO clipped to Munroe's belt chirped and jolted her from the conversation. Bradford gave her a nervous glance; Beyard would

attempt contact only if it was an emergency. Munroe unclipped the camera from her lapel and pulled the machine from her pocket, stuck the
machine in Bradford's hand. While she pinned the camera on his collar,
she whispered, "We're probably going to need this for more than just
proving she's alive. Get her to provide personal data for the camera,
today's date and place, date of birth, mother's and father's names—
basically a statement. It would be good if she could include some childhood memories that you and I wouldn't know about."

Bradford turned to Emily, his smile showing the stress of having
heard the two-way go off. Munroe left the room and then, certain she
was out of earshot, responded to the call.

"Get the front door open," was all Beyard said.

CHAPTER 20

Munroe strode to the front of the house. The foyer was quiet, and though she had no doubt that the household snitch was hovering nearby, she opened the door and Beyard slipped inside. His uniform was gone, replaced by jeans and a T-shirt thick enough to nearly hide the outline of the pouch that hung against his chest. His face was hard, pure business. He handed her two vacuum-packed sets of civilian clothes.

"State radio just announced putting down an attempted coup," he said. "Local military is looking for people in the Mongomo area wearing Israeli camouflage, and they've given descriptions that could easily be you and Miles or me. The paranoia around town has already started." He paused for a second, and when she said nothing, he stated the obvious. "There's no coup, Vanessa. They're looking for us. It won't take long for the men at the police station to connect the dots. We need to get out of here."

The drumbeat of war tapped out inside Munroe's chest. This couldn't have been the household informer—it was too fast, came too certain. Only three people knew of the plan to enter the country using Israeli military camo: Logan was in the United States, and the other two were in this house. She took a deep breath and pinched the bridge of her nose. This was the reason she always fucking worked alone. No tagalongs, no partners, no unnecessary components to screw things up.

"Get the satphone, the passports, and five thousand euros," Munroe said. "We leave those here with her. I'll get Miles."

Beyard wedged a piece of plastic under the front door, and Munroe tilted her head upward and took in a drink of air, fought back the rage, and then walked calmly to the living room. She'd been so close, so fucking close.

She entered the room, and Bradford looked up. Emily, who'd been talking about her childhood, stopped. Munroe said only, "Emily, I need to talk to Miles."

Out of the living room and where Emily could not overhear, Munroe whispered in Bradford's ear, explaining the situation in as few words as possible. His face twisted through a series of emotions, ending at what Munroe read as horrified shock. His hands had tightened into fists, and through clenched teeth he said, "I'm not leaving her."

"If we take them, it will slow us down and risk getting us all killed— it's better that she stays."

"I can't leave her," he said again.

"She's been kept alive and secure here all these years," Munroe said. "She's safer here than with us."

Bradford remained still and said nothing.

"Have it your way." Munroe knelt to unlace her boots. "Figure out how to get her out on your own. Francisco and I are leaving while we've still got a chance." She stripped off the uniform and removed a shirt from the pack Beyard had given her and pulled it over her head. "You do what you need to do."

Bradford ran his fingers through his hair and stared at the ceiling. He breathed as if he might hyperventilate, and Munroe knew he was running scenarios. He'd come, there was no doubt. Bradford knew as well as she did that even if the vehicles separated and he took Emily and the kids in the opposite direction while she and Beyard ran decoy, with the border crossings closed as they inevitably would be—if they weren't already—he wouldn't be able to get them out of the country on his own. Munroe handed him the second pack of clothes, and he took it. "Francisco's coming back with the passports, the money, and the satellite phone," she said. "We're not abandoning her, Miles."

Emily was still on the couch when they returned. Her hands were in her lap, and she clenched them, staring at the coffee cups on the table. When they walked into the room, her head jerked up. "We're not going, are we?" she said. "After all that, we're not going."

Bradford sat beside her and shook his head. "Em, plans have changed."

Munroe said, "The people who've tried to kill me are on their way here. We need to go, and if you come with us, there's a chance you and the children won't make it. We're going to leave you with money, passports, and a phone. If we make it out, we'll be back."

"I'm willing to take the risk," Emily said. "Please let us come with you."

"We can't do it, Emily."

"One way or the other," Bradford said, "we'll get you out of here. It might take a month, could even take a year, but I'm coming back for you, I promise."

Beyard entered the room with a small case and handed it to Munroe, who in turn handed it to Emily, who was now crying.

"I'm sorry," Munroe said, and then, to Bradford, "We're leaving in two minutes. Show her how to use the phone." She and Beyard walked out of the room, and Bradford joined them a minute later.

Beyard had already combined the matériel from both vehicles into one, and Munroe left the keys to the second under its front seat. They pulled away from the house, and Beyard drove slowly, eyes ahead to the activity that went on beyond the length of the street. The military was now out in force, detaining pedestrians unlucky enough not to have reached the safety of indoors. What few vehicles remained on the roads were being pulled over, the occupants forced out with their hands above their heads. The atmosphere crackled with paranoia and brewing violence.

Munroe was in the backseat, leaning to the side so that the headphone clamped to her ear was not visible from the windows. She watched Beyard's face in the rearview, his lips drawn tight and stress written in his eyes. There were only three routes out of the city, all of them cordoned off, and if it came to fighting their way through, they were severely outgunned.

Vehicle documents in the president's name and an impressive

performance by Beyard got them through the first cluster of assault-weapon-carrying soldiers. They were several minutes from the straight four-mile stretch that ran to the border, and if their luck held, they could get that far before the level of hostility ratcheted up a notch and the papers no longer worked. Munroe pressed through the frequencies; where there should have been commotion and activity, there was only static and silence, and then finally she caught voices.

She bent her head toward the floor and struggled to pick up the sounds of a conversation in Fang that ended as abruptly as it had begun. "The land borders have been cut off," she said to Beyard. "They don't say anything about the coast."

"We're not going to get through this way," he said, and Munroe felt the vehicle lurch and then surge. She braced her feet against the back of Bradford's seat while she held her hands cupped over her ears. Again the vehicle jolted. Beyard had looped to the end of a street that ran parallel to Emily's street and was taking a footpath out of the city. Foliage slapped against the windshield, and the suspension groaned. From the path they lurched into a streambed.

"Anything?" Beyard asked.

"Nothing," Munroe said, her fingers working the scanner controls while she continued to brace for stability.

"They know we're listening."

"How the hell . . . ?" Munroe's voice trailed off. Someone knew they were in Mongomo, knew about the camo, knew about the scanners—what the hell else? She dropped the headphones, switched off the machine, and glowered at the front seat. *Shit.*

The water's course flowed southwesterly, and they followed it, churning up the shallow bed for several miles until the creek routed north, and there they broke trail into the bush and headed in the direction of the interior. As far as could be determined, they had not been followed out of the city, so the atmosphere of violence had been traded for the deceptive stillness of the deep forest. They would travel southwest until they converged with the tracks that led to Evinayong, and in the heart of the country they would disappear long enough for the frenzy to die and the pursuers to assume they were no longer around. They had supplies to last several days, and utilizing the resources of the forest could stretch them to two weeks.

The goal was Mbini, a low-water port eighty kilometers south of Bata, nestled at the southern mouth of the nearly mile-wide Benito River and surrounded by pristine white beaches and rolling surf that elsewhere in the world would have given birth to a chain of five-star resorts. It was from Mbini that open longboats ferried passengers to and from Gabon and where a prearranged boat fueled and waiting would not appear out of place.

By nightfall they had put a hard thirty kilometers between themselves and the edge of civilization. They were camped under a tarp fringed by mosquito netting and strung from the roof of the vehicle. Munroe sat against the rear wheel with her arms wrapped around her knees, face coated with dirt, body aching, and right forearm bloody where it had been deeply scratched. Beyard had wandered into the dark, and Bradford sat against the front bumper with his legs stretched out, arms crossed, and head tilted toward the sky. Munroe was silent; she had nothing to say that wouldn't resemble spit venom. Events had spiraled out of control, and the information that had led to this had come from the inside. Logic said it had to be Miles or Francisco, but it didn't feel right, wasn't exact. Munroe dropped her head to her knees and let out a deep sigh.

"It wasn't me," Bradford said.

Munroe raised her head, and Bradford continued, "I can count. There aren't many people to pin the blame on, and I'm the one you hate the most and trust the least—that makes me the prime candidate, but it wasn't me, Michael."

"Concerned I'm going to leave you here?"

"I should be, but I'm not." He was calm, his voice low, and his head was still tilted up. "I'm concerned that by focusing on me you'll be misdirected. Figuring out where this is coming from has become a matter of self-preservation for me as well." He paused and then looked out into the darkness. "I know how you feel about Francisco. I hope you haven't let it cloud your judgment."

Munroe returned her head to her knees, and an exhausted smile played across her face. Respect for Bradford had just moved up a notch. "I don't hate you, Miles," she said, "and I trust you more than you think I do." And then she was aware of Francisco's presence. He moved like a cat through the bush, stealthy and quiet in their direction. In the dim light of the smoldering ground fire, she saw the cords along Bradford's neck tighten and knew that anger seethed beneath the surface. She knew that he, too, was aware of Beyard's presence. And then Beyard stepped into the light carrying with him a pair of forest rats. He sat at the edge of the tarp, back turned while he skinned and gutted. Munroe watched the flick of his wrist and the knife as it splayed meat and bone, understood the sting of betrayal and knew that, barring intervention, tonight someone would die.

She stood and opened the back door of the vehicle, reached under the seat and released two of the PB6P9s housed there. The suppressors were already in place, and Munroe snapped in magazines, her ears strained to create a visual picture of what went on behind her back, quiet out of habit, not concern. The two outside were consumed with distrust of each other and in their wariness would be oblivious to her actions until it was too late. And then she turned and leveled a gun at each man. Bradford looked up, lips tight and eyes hard. Beyard sighed, said, "Not this shit again," and continued working the knife.

Munroe said, "Scoot the knife this direction, if you please." Beyard did as she said, and she tossed a roll of duct tape at each of them. She nodded at Bradford. "His feet." And then to Beyard, "The same to you." When their feet had been secured, she had Beyard fasten Bradford's wrists, and then, with the weapon pressed to his spine, she used her free hand to tape his in place. When both men were secure, she had them shift so that their backs were to the vehicle, Bradford at one wheel, Beyard at the other.

The forest rats that Beyard had skinned lay on a rock next to the fire. Munroe placed them on sticks above the coals, then picked up Beyard's knife off the ground and felt the balance and weight of it in her palm. When the blade began to call out, screaming to be used, she shoved it into the ground at the feet of the men.

She sat cross-legged in front of them and nodded to Beyard. "So? Go ahead and say it."

He was silent for a moment and then turned to Bradford. "And to think I actually liked you. You're a motherfucking double-crossing traitor. You fucking sold us out—" Beyard's voice cut off, and he made a lunge for Bradford.

Munroe kicked his feet. "Hey!" She aimed the gun at his chest. "Cut it out."

Beyard stopped and struggled back to a sitting position.

"Miles, what about you?" she asked.

"It could only have been one of the three of us," he said, "and it wasn't me."

"Fucking hell it wasn't," Beyard said.

Munroe stood, picked up the knife, and walked to the fire. Pieces of the puzzle were coming together, and events that previously had no meaning had been given context. Behind her the men's voices got louder. They talked over each other, accusations flying, their verbal sparring a cacophonous backdrop to her reflections. She stabbed at the smoking meat. Why give a shit over being tracked and killed by the country's armed forces when the job would be taken care of tonight by two alpha males waiting to carve out each other's hearts? The racket from behind her reached a dangerous volume, and she turned and let off a round between the men, the bullet spitting up dirt. "Shut the fuck up," she said. "Both of you."

The two men were inclined toward each other. Beyard had a trickle of blood flowing down the side of his face where Bradford had managed to get in a head butt. They both stared at her now, mouths open but silent.

"You're going to have to call a truce," she said. "Because I refuse to wake up tomorrow with one or both of you dead, and if it means that I have to complete this journey with the two of you trussed up like goddamn guinea fowl, I swear to God I'll do it. Look at you." She pointed with the guns. "Think for a minute, damn it. You're both about to kill each other for the same fucking reason." She stopped and took a breath. "For all you know, it could be me."

"It's not you," Beyard said.

"Yeah. I know that. Thanks for the fucking vote of confidence. But the fact is, it's probably not one of you either."

"If not one of us, who?"

"Richard Burbank does come to mind."

Bradford said, "You told him it would be at least a week, and you certainly didn't give him details about the scanners or camo or anything else."

"Logan has those details," she said, and as the words left her mouth, her stomach churned, waves of exhaustion swept in, and she wanted to vomit. Logan was safety, he was sanity, a surrogate brother, the only home she had left. If he was the one selling her out, then it was game over. It wasn't a matter of outsmarting him or exacting revenge, which wouldn't be that goddamn difficult—if it was Logan, what was the fucking point?

Munroe looked at Beyard. "Did the radio say anything about the make of vehicles we were driving or how many? Any information at all that the three of us and only the three of us would know?"

He shook his head.

"Think about the possibilities in that." She sighed and sat down. "Look, we already know that Richard Burbank has his hands filthy in this. The information could be coming from Logan—for all we know, Burbank's got his phones tapped. So the two of you just fucking chill and let's work through this thing, okay?" She paused. "If I cut you loose, do I have your word that you'll play nice?"

The nods of agreement were lackluster and noncommittal, but there nonetheless. She reached for the knife, stood, went to the fire, turned the meat over the coals, and then walked to the vehicle and cut their hands free. She backed away with a weapon toward each of them and said, "Don't fucking move. You can sit there comfortably while we talk about what the hell is going on and decipher what information we have to work with. After that you can undo your legs."

Beyard rubbed his wrists and stared into the night. "If the information leak isn't coming from one of us," he said, "at this point it doesn't much matter where it's coming from."

"No, it doesn't," Munroe said. She sat and placed the weapons on the ground, pressed her fingers to her temples. Survival mattered. And with the three of them now incommunicado, the leak, wherever and whoever it was, could go fuck itself.

Her mind, exhausted as it was, shifted into analysis mode. Survival would depend on who in the country was acting on the information, what resources that person had at his disposal, and how long he could keep up the hunt.

With the farce of a coup having been used to flush them out, there were really only two possibilities: Either this thing went all the way up to the president or to someone close to the president—and it didn't take a genius to figure out who was pushing the president's buttons.

Munroe stood and to Beyard said, "Have you worked a theory yet?"

"Partially."

"Good."

She walked to the vehicle, trained a weapon at Beyard, who was closer, and said, "Don't move." And then with her free hand she reached into the back, pulled out the laptop and the drive that held the footage of Emily, loaded the drive, and brought the computer to Beyard. "We have to look in two directions; there are two sets of motives. There's Richard Burbank, and there's here. I've got Burbank's angle. I want you to watch this," she said. "I need you to analyze this from the Mongomo perspective."

The footage ran for nearly forty-five minutes, and when it was finished, Beyard returned to the spots where Emily spoke of being captured and of her treatment by the man she now called her husband. Beyard replayed the segment several times, then shut the laptop and handed it back. "If she's to be believed, Nchama's been trying to protect her."

"You're kidding," Bradford said. "The guy lies to her, beats her, locks her up, spies on her, and for all we know rapes her, and you're saying he's trying to protect her?"

Munroe closed her eyes and held out a finger to Bradford. "He may have been telling the truth, Miles, and for the rest, it's acceptable to the culture." She paused. "Please, if you don't mind, just stay quiet for a few minutes." And then to Beyard, "Go on."

"Nchama told her that her life was in danger, and all events that we've seen so far indicate that he believed this himself. I would venture that his trying to protect her is why you were dumped into the ocean— he believed you were a threat."

"Why would he think that?" Bradford asked.

Munroe held her hand to him as if to say, *Be quiet,* but Beyard answered anyway. "It's a logical assumption," he said. "Whether Nchama was deliberately informed of your arrival and then misinformed of your motives—and I suspect that Richard Burbank would be the one to have done it—or whether your presence and questions triggered his fear, either way you are there, asking questions about Emily. The result is the same. The threat from which he initially tried to protect her has returned, and it forces his hand."

"That would explain Malabo and Bata," Munroe said. "But the alleged coup? That's far more serious. Are we ruling out the president in this?"

Beyard shrugged. "Untangle the web, Essa. What do we know? Where is the foundation? What holds everything together? Where do the connectors lead?" He paused. "Return to Occam's razor. With as few assumptions as possible, what takes all circumstances into account and explains what we see? With what little we hold certain, does anything point to the president?"

Munroe stared at the ground. Her mind ran in circles. Events. Threads. She pushed out. Stretched. Returned. Where Emily had once been the common strand, there stood Richard Burbank. "No," she said. "At this juncture nothing points to the president."

Beyard nodded. "Then we return to Nchama, and we assume that the hunt for us will continue until we are either dead or gone from this place."

Munroe looked toward Beyard. "Based on the footage, based on events, Nchama cares about Emily, sure," she said. "He's trying to protect her, sure. But does he care so much that he's willing to put his own life on the line should the president realize there is no coup?"

They were all silent.

"For what does a man risk his own life?" Beyard asked.

Munroe said nothing. She stared again at the ground, tracing her fingers through the soil, taking them along the virtual paths that her mind traveled. Forward. Back. There again. Occam's razor. Simplicity.

She turned to Beyard. "A man risks his life to save it from the greater fear."

Richard Burbank.

They were quiet again, and the moments ticked by. Finally Bradford said, "This whole time, all your theorizing, it's all based on the supposition that Richard wants Emily to remain unfound or, worse, dead. After what Emily said, I'm not going to argue it, but seriously, why would he go through all the trouble and expense of hiring you to track her down

when if he'd just let it rest none of this would have happened in the first
place?"

"Because you pushed him into hiring me," Munroe said. "He was
appeasing you, keeping up the act of grieving father. For some reason
he believes it's important that you buy into his story. Maybe you know
something he's afraid of. Maybe he knows how close you were with Elizabeth, is worried that she told you something, I really don't know."

Munroe pressed her palms to her eyes and took a deep breath. "Okay,
backtrack," she said. "We know now that from the beginning Richard
Burbank knew that Emily was alive and, more important, where to find
her. I'm not the first person he's hired to track her down, and I'd venture
to say he's spent a hell of a lot more money during the first four years
than he did to hire me. The difference is that success in locating her
created an unexpected complication. Once we started getting close, Burbank had to act—that's why he closed down the project, why he didn't
want you coming back to Africa. You'd seen the death certificate, didn't
know that Emily was alive, and he could work with that, but by getting
in touch with me, by insisting on returning, you effectively signed your
own death warrant at Burbank's hand."

"But still, why? Why does he need Emily to be missing?" Bradford
hesitated. "Or dead?"

"It's money, Miles, it has to be. Haven't you ever wondered why Richard waited until Emily was almost eighteen before legally adopting her?
He was her stepfather for . . . what? Around ten years? If he really cared,
if it was to mean something, why not adopt her when she was young?
You're a smart man, Miles. Surely you must have considered this.

"You said Richard wanted Elizabeth to change her will, and that
indicates that there was either a prenup or some other legal mechanism
that prevented him from inheriting. Maybe Richard had hoped that Elizabeth would change her mind over time, and she didn't. By adopting
Emily when he did, Richard gave himself options—inheritance rights
through Emily. He probably thought that if it ever came down to it,
he could manipulate Emily in a way that he couldn't manipulate her
mother.

"This is a man who at the very least abandoned his stepdaughter in
the middle of Africa and has thwarted efforts to find her, and I wouldn't

be the tiniest bit surprised to find out that Elizabeth's death wasn't a suicide. It was very convenient for him, I think, to have Emily tucked away
here in the land that time forgot, everyone believing she was dead, though
she is still very much legally alive and able to inherit. Once Emily died,
which was probably in the plan, the fortune would transfer to him."

Bradford shook his head. "You can't possibly believe that Richard planned all this, got Emily into Equatorial Guinea and had her
kidnapped?"

"Burbank is an opportunist, Miles. I think he hoped something
would happen to Emily while she was in Africa, even gave her a little
shove in the right direction by suggesting Equatorial Guinea. And then
when something did go wrong, he pounced on it and made it work for
him. If none of this had happened, if Emily had gotten home safely, I
have no doubt that some other tragedy would have occurred—Elizabeth
first, then Emily."

"Have you ever been wrong?"

Munroe was quiet for a moment and then said, "Yeah. I've been
wrong." Another pause. "But not with this. Burbank is patient, he's
waiting it out; in another three years he can make Emily's a legal death
and take it all, so long as she never shows up to challenge the claim."
Munroe stopped, tilted her head up, and took in a steep drink of air. She
whispered, "Only now there's a glitch in the plan. You and I know where
she is." Munroe held eye contact with Beyard. "Until now Emily has
been safe, but unless we disappear and the information we have disappears with us . . .

"Fuck," Munroe said, and then, with the implication permeating the
air, she stood, turned her back on the two men, and stared out into the
night.

"So what do we do?" Beyard asked. "Go back and get her?"

In answer to that impossibility, Munroe said nothing, and Beyard
continued. "You thought you were doing the right thing by leaving her.
You were trying to protect her, couldn't have known all this at the time.
Neither did I."

"It makes no difference to her what my motives were," Munroe
said. "Dead is dead."

The silence was broken by Bradford. His eyes were closed, and he knocked the back of his head against the vehicle. "I. Am. So. Fucking. Stupid," he said. A head bang for every word. Munroe locked eyes with Beyard, and then they both turned to Bradford.

"I don't pretend that it makes sense," Bradford said. "I don't understand why Richard would need or care about the money, but Emily has a trust. When Elizabeth died, everything Emily inherited went into the trust until she could be located. There's a board that manages it, and they've been writing the checks for the searches. It's the trust that's paying you, not Richard." He turned to Munroe, and if she hadn't known better, she would have suspected tears. "I signed an affidavit," he said. "Richard said he'd back the project again if I'd sign an affidavit stating everything I knew, including the details of Emily's death certificate. I was so fucking blinded by wanting to find Emily that all I could think about was keeping on the job. I never suspected ulterior motives." Bradford looked at his watch. "The board is meeting in five days, and he's taking the affidavit to them."

"What does that mean?" Beyard asked.

Munroe said, "He's going to try to sell the board on the affidavit in lieu of the actual death certificate to get them to turn over her trust." To Bradford she said, "What do you think the chances are that the board accepts it?"

He shook his head. "I don't know, I just don't know. Based on their past decisions and what they've authorized in order to find her, I tend to doubt it."

Munroe sighed. "If they don't, then either we permanently disappear or Burbank is going to need physical evidence of Emily's death." She sat, wrapped her arms around her legs, and placed her chin on her knees. "Or," she said, "we can cut Burbank off at his feet and get proof of Emily's being alive in front of the board."

Bradford said, "But will Emily be safe until then?"

Munroe stared into the forest. "I don't fucking *know*, but what choice do we have? Until we can unravel the relationship between Burbank and Nchama—until we can nail Nchama's motives and his fears—figure out what role he plays in all of this and why, there are just so many goddamn fucking unknowns." She paused and again pressed her palms to her eyes. "Emily is the mother of his children. Nchama has kept her alive all these years—the footage truly points to his trying to protect her—so it makes sense that she should be okay for at least a few more days."

Munroe returned to staring toward the jungle and, as if thinking out loud, said, "I could use a goddamn phone right about now."

"What would you do if you had one?" Beyard asked.

"Call Burbank and pass along misinformation—give us a chance to sort through this shit. If he's convinced we won't make it out of here, it should also buy Emily more time."

"I've got a phone at one of the cut sites," Beyard said. "I've got a couple of trucks there, too."

To Bradford, Munroe said, "Excuse us for just one minute," and then she switched to French and said to Beyard, "If they find us anywhere near the cut site, there's a chance they'll link this to you. Your cover in this country will be permanently blown."

"If they find us there, then yes, that is a valid concern," he said, "although it is not the loss of cover that worries me. I think you overestimate the chances of our getting out of this mess. If having access to the phone will make a difference . . ." His voice trailed off. He stared into the darkness, and Munroe knew that he was running probabilities: risk against reward, life against death. "There's also the issue of time," he said. "If we keep going the way we are now, it'll take us a week to get to the coast. If we take the tracks to the site and switch out with a truck, we can use the roads and be at the coast within twenty-four hours." And then he smiled a sad half smile. "Maybe this forces me to again consider life beyond Africa."

"We'll move in the morning," she said. "We keep the destination to ourselves. Information to our friend is on a need-to-know basis—if anything goes wrong, it's down to you and me." Beyard nodded, and then in English to both of them Munroe said, "Are you guys good? No fighting? No blood?"

There was still reluctance in the agreement, but less than there had been earlier. Munroe reached the knife between their ankles and slit the tape, Bradford first and then Beyard; it would be a sleepless night.

Bradford looked at the dried blood and the swelling under Beyard's left eye. "Sorry about your face."

"Maybe one day I'll have the chance to return the favor," Beyard said. And then he laughed, stood, and stretched his legs. He stepped toward Munroe, crooked an arm around her neck, drew her near, and kissed her forehead. "Listen," he whispered, "you have got to fucking stop pointing guns at me and tying me up."

She gave him a wry smile. "He would've killed you tonight. He might still try."

She turned toward Bradford. "I accept responsibility for the decision to leave her behind. If I'd known then what I know now, I would have done it differently. . . . I am going to do everything in my power to put an end to this."

Bradford nodded. "I know."

They took the night in shifts, and but for a time or two when Munroe drifted off, she spent the hours wary of the latent animosity between the men, ready to intervene if necessary, and with headphones over her ears, hoping to pick up some piece of information off the silent scanners.

CHAPTER 21

Coastal region, Río Muni, Equatorial Guinea

It was midafternoon, and the sun hung low in the sky, adding threads of pink to the yellow-tinged horizon. The area was razed into a wide sweeping circle of orange-red dirt that had been pushed into wandering mounds by machinery and tree trunks. The ground was gutted by wide tire tracks, fat stumps were the last testament to arbor giants now fallen, and a border of lush green marked the periphery of the site. Munroe kicked at a clod of dried clay, stared out over the expanse of barren ground, then leaned against the vehicle door and watched Beyard in the near distance, where he stood by a loaded flatbed truck, conversing animatedly with the driver.

They had pushed since dawn to get this far, utilizing overgrown and unmarked tracks to speed the journey and in the process of getting the vehicle through had added another layer of mud and bruises to those acquired the day before.

The conversation over, Beyard turned back, and when he drew close, Munroe said, "They're making a hell of a mess out of this place."

He followed her eyes. "I've been around it for so long I've become immune."

They stood in silence and stared at the wasted landscape, and then he said, "It's going to get worse. Pretty much all of the country's commercially productive forest is under concession—if things keep going as they are, in five, six years it'll be completely exhausted. Oil reserves won't last either. What to do?" He shrugged. "Fucking spoilers." He climbed behind the wheel, and Munroe got into the front seat. "We're headed a half kilometer that way," he said, pointing, "We should definitely get there before dark."

They followed a rut-filled dirt road out of the site toward the west, and at an unmarked junction notable only as a break in the thick foliage Beyard turned north.

Munroe glanced at the backseat, where Bradford lay seemingly asleep with his arm draped over his head, and she shifted back to Beyard. "I suppose you haven't made out too badly through all this, spoilers and all."

He threw her a look and then returned his focus to the road. "I do what I do."

"So why the drugs, the munitions, the risks involved, when you do so well through legitimate business?"

"Because I'm good at it," he said. "And I get an adrenaline rush." He smiled. "And don't make the mistake of thinking this is legitimate. Legal, yes, but let's not kid ourselves that it's anything other than raping the country to feed the presidential coffers."

"Do you care?"

"I'm a realist, Vanessa. I don't care, but I don't lie to myself either."

THE SECOND CUT site differed little from the first, with the exception of a few attempts at constructed shelter and a makeshift tin shack that sat on the edge of chaos. Next to the tin was a six-wheeler with canvas raised over the back, and Beyard stopped beside it, got out of the vehicle, and banged his hand on the body of the truck.

The rear canvas parted, and a short, stocky man stood in the flap of the doorway. His face lit up into a smile, and he held out a hand, which Beyard took and used to clamber into the truck. Munroe waited in the silence, Bradford still stretched out on the backseat, and a few minutes later Beyard returned and said, "Go on in. Manuel has everything you need."

The interior of the truck was dark and dank and permeated with the smell of mildew and wood rot. Along each side was an unmade cot, and the floor was littered with used dishes and discarded remnants of food. At the front a small wooden table bolted to the floor held a smattering of electronics. Manuel turned to Munroe and said in Fang, "The boss tells me you speak my language."

Munroe nodded, and Manuel reached for a collapsible satellite dish. "I have to put this up top," he said, and then pointed to the phone. "The boss said you use whatever you want."

Munroe waited for the sounds overhead to still and the truck's engine to roll over, and when the phone powered on, she reached for it, closed her eyes, and breathed deeply. The next five minutes would change everything. She drew another long drink of air and followed it with a slow expulsion, working backward into the frame of mind, conjuring horror and fear and becoming the part. And then she dialed.

When she stepped from the truck into the dimming light of the evening, most of their supplies were on the ground and Beyard was on his back inside the vehicle with disassembled parts around him and twisting a bolt underneath the rear seat. "How did it go?" he asked. His voice was muted by the pieces between them, and Munroe stepped closer.

"Only time will tell."

"So now what?"

"Now we wait." She paused and looked around. "Where's Miles?"

Beyard threw a piece out on the ground, then knelt and peeled away the vehicle's ersatz floorboard. "He took a walk."

Munroe stepped into Beyard's line of sight. "What exactly does that mean?"

"You tell me. He had a filled duffel bag and said he'd be back in the morning. I offered him the two-way in case we had to pull out before then. He declined, said it would be better for all parties concerned if he didn't take it."

"Did you do an inventory count?"

Beyard nodded. "Two of the assault rifles, five hundred rounds, a few heavy pieces. And he took the sniper."

"Shit, Francisco, the Vintorez was mine." She paused, scratching the back of her head, and looked toward the trees in the near distance. And then she turned in a complete circle, taking in the periphery, and shook her head; a slow smile crept across her face. Bradford was on watch and determined to prove trustworthiness; he'd prepared to take out a military convoy if one showed up. "He's within four hundred meters," she said, and then, turning her back to the forest, nodded at the truck. "Is this home for the night?"

"Yes. We'll load now and head off first thing in the morning. Manuel will drive so we can stay out of sight." He stepped toward the vehicle in which they'd arrived, kicked a tire. "I'm going to dump this thing in the forest away from the site," he said. "I don't want any of this coming back on any of my people. I'll be back in a couple of hours."

"Shouldn't I come?"

"If you're up for the long walk back," he said. Then he smiled and hooked his finger into Munroe's collar and pulled her close. "Even layered in two days' worth of grime as you are, I find you irresistible." He paused and raised his eyes from her mouth to the forest behind her. "If I kiss you, do you think he'll take a potshot?"

She leaned into him and brushed her lips against his. "I'm sure he'll be tempted," she said. Then she grinned, stepped back, and opened the vehicle door. She slid into the front seat. Beyard followed and cranked the engine.

At FIVE IN the morning, Munroe was jolted out of a sleep she hadn't intended to fall into. The combined total of six hours of rest over three nights was taking a toll. The interior of the truck was sightlessly black, but from Beyard's breathing she knew he was awake. She lay on the cot with headphones on her ears, and in an attempt to clear the fuzz that filled her head, she swung her legs to the floor and rested her elbows on her knees. "Channels have opened up again," she whispered. "Seems they've taken the bait. They're sending most of their men back to wherever it was they came from and holding a large contingent around Mongomo."

"We should probably get moving," he said. "Try to get to the coast while our luck holds out."

"What about Miles?"

"He knows we're leaving. I wouldn't suggest waiting past dawn."

Munroe sighed and lay back down. If Bradford didn't arrive by first light, she would head out to look for him. The option of leaving him behind had ended when the puzzle snapped into focus and she'd begun to formulate a plan for retribution. She remained on the cot, dozing, until the sky changed from deepest black to navy blue and she knew the shift had come, not from stepping outside but from an internal clock that through long experience had been synchronized to nature.

Across the aisle, Beyard took a deep breath and sat up. "Are you awake?"

"Unfortunately."

"We need to get going."

Manuel slept in the open outside the truck, on a rolled-out mat, and while Beyard woke him and the two made preparations to depart, Munroe stared toward the forest and the brightening sky. "Give me half an hour," she said. "I want to see if I can find Miles. I really don't want to leave without him."

From the top of the truck, Bradford's voice said, "There's no need."

Munroe opened the cab door, used the floorboard to step up and look over, and, seeing Bradford, said, "Shit, Miles, how long have you been up there?"

He smiled and said nothing, sat up and then ambled down with an AKM in one hand and the duffel bag dragging behind him.

Before the sun crested the horizon, they moved out of the site along the only road that led to Mbini. Manuel was supplied with ample money for bribes, and if all else failed, they would fight their way through. Inside the canvas, Munroe sat on a cot with the headphones to her ears, Beyard lay on the other, and Bradford sat on the floor with an assault rifle across his lap. The heat and lack of air was stifling, and distance was measured by time, bumps, jolts, and continual gear shifting.

They had been moving for just under two hours when Munroe straightened and placed her fingertips to the headphones. "How far to the coast?" she asked.

"Forty-five minutes if we're lucky," Beyard said.

She stood and reached for a Kevlar vest. "It's going to be close. They've been tipped off, and there's a convoy moving down the coast out of Bata toward Mbini." She snapped magazines into pockets and tossed the remaining vest to Beyard. "Sorry, Miles, we only brought two—got them before we knew you were coming with us."

He nodded and patted the weapon on his lap. "Been through worse."

The truck began to slow, and Munroe stood on the front table and with Beyard's knife cut a hole in the canvas just above the metal frame. There was a checkpoint ahead, the soldiers a ragtag group of four. She signaled this to Beyard, and when the truck shuddered to a full stop, she positioned the weapon using the frame as a bipod and kept the unit leader in sight as he approached.

The conversation between the commander and Manuel began as light banter and shifted quickly in tone as the military man began to check the truck and Manuel offered pecuniary incentive to avoid it. Two of the commander's men walked toward the back, and Munroe gestured this to the others. Beyard and Bradford shifted position along the rear. The voices at the front were raised, news out of Mongomo no doubt playing into the equation.

Munroe curled her index finger and rested it on the trigger; taking out the road patrol wasn't ideal, but if that's what was required to get to the coast, so be it. Manuel passed a wad of cash out the window, and she paused. The commander stared at it, hesitated, and took it. He called to his men, and moments later the truck started up.

Munroe remained on the table and watched the road and the stretches of landscape where the rain forest had long since been exploited and the terrain partially reclaimed by secondary forest. She sniffed the air, could smell the salt, and knew they were getting close. They turned off the road before entering the city proper, looped south toward the beach along a well-used track, and stopped in a hard-packed clearing two hundred yards from the shore, where a small collection of houses stood abutting the ocean. Rust-red rooftops were visible above the foliage, and from beyond the houses came the rumble of the water. If the boat was ready, as it should be, five minutes was all that it would take to be gone from this place.

The truck stopped. Munroe threw the strap of a duffel bag over her shoulder and climbed into the sunlight. Beyard circled to the front of the truck. He spent a moment in hushed conversation with Manuel, and Munroe caught snippets of hurried instructions. Beyard handed the driver a thick pouch, and with a nod of assent Manuel slipped out of sight into the verdure.

With the driver gone, Beyard returned and placed the transponder and a key in Munroe's palm. "I need five minutes to swap out the plates," he said. He pointed to a footpath from the parking area to a house on the perimeter. "The extra fuel is inside. You'll know the boat as soon as you see it. Can you ready her?"

"Leave it," she said, and stood in his way, "It's not worth it."

"Essa, *my* life may be mine to gamble, but I won't risk the lives of my people. I need to buy them time, and we need the boat readied—I can't do both." He scooted behind her and planted a kiss on the nape of her neck. "Go."

She stood for a second's deliberation and then slapped the side of the truck. "Let's go," she said to Bradford.

He pulled what he could carry from the truck, and together they followed the path that Beyard had pointed out.

On the shore were several boats, one of them a paint-worn skiff differentiated from the others by the powerful outboard. Munroe dumped the bag into the boat and looked back toward the trail.

From the shore she could see the top of the truck's canvas and down the road the top of an antenna moving toward the truck. She stood on the boat's prow to get an extra three feet of height and caught a streak of black moving with the antenna.

Time slowed, her heart raced. She reached for the nearest weapon and, as her fist closed around it, took off running for the truck. Each forward stride up the sand was an excruciating time-lapse drop into eternity.

Around a bend the clearing came into view. The internal war drum pounded, and the world faded to gray. Beyond the truck were three black vehicles and, standing beside the truck, blocking Francisco, were nine men, heavily armed. Francisco stood with his fingers laced behind his head, and to the right of him was the same commander who had nearly shot Munroe that night on the boat. His sidearm was pointed at Francisco's head.

Francisco turned toward Munroe. Their eyes locked. He smiled. And in the half second it took her to raise the rifle to her shoulder and take aim, the commander fired.

Pressure tore through Munroe's head, claws ripping her skull open from the inside out. The air was empty of all oxygen. She couldn't breathe, and through eyes not her own she watched in slow motion as Francisco dropped to his knees and fell face-first into the dust.

And then the world went black.

Every muscle, every fiber shrieked the command to get to him. She lunged. Strong arms held her back. A hand was over her mouth. Someone was screaming, the agony of a person burned alive, surreal and horrible, the howls, all of them coming from inside her head. And then there was silence followed by words, calm words, reassuring, coming from her mouth. And a hand, her hand, pulling herself from Bradford's grasp and the other hand reaching for the silenced rifle and slamming the butt of it across Bradford's face, knocking him to the ground.

On the other side of the truck, a soldier reached for Francisco's body. Through the scope, Munroe set the mark for the man's forehead, let off a shot, and was gone from where she'd lain before the body crumpled on top of Francisco.

Touch him and die.

There was confusion now. Orders. Commands. The others dropped and found cover, searched out the direction of the shot. In the lapsed seconds of chaos, Munroe moved into the bush, silent, invisible, fast, the hunted now the hunter. Two more of the enemy moved toward Francisco's body. She fired two rounds that pierced body armor, then for good measure two more, each accurately aimed.

Touch him and die.

They knew this now, and their confusion segued to structure. She searched the faces and uniforms for the commander; she would find him and take his life from him the way he had taken Francisco's; nothing else mattered.

There was movement on the periphery. Shadows crept in the direction of where she'd left Bradford. The trail. The boat. Munroe paused. Concentration shifted from the commander to the path and back again until the decision to keep the way clear was forced. Each round let off a spit, found its mark, silenced, but in the stillness audible. Gunfire returned in her direction; the bullets kicked dirt inches from where she lay. She moved again, circled around, stopped on the edge of the clearing behind the truck, and began again to search out the commander. There, only yards away, Francisco's lifeless body watched with unseeing eyes, beckoned, and the world went silent.

Munroe crept toward him, oblivious to everything but the smile on his face and the power of his call. There was a staccato of gunfire from the direction of the shore and a rain of bullets over her head that took down two men behind her. She paused only to look back and then, feral and catlike, crouched again along the ground toward Francisco. She reached for him, could almost touch him, and then in the bush, there across the clearing in the line of sight beyond her hand, was a ghost of movement. She paused. Among those shadows was the commander, and he must die.

She drew away from Francisco and with patient relish cut off the commander's escape by taking out the tires on each black vehicle. And then, out of ammunition, she pulled the knife from Francisco's belt, left the rifle beside his body, and returned to the edge of the clearing to wait.

In the silence, adrenaline flowed, and with the focus of each passing minute, bloodlust heightened. Within the foliage across the clearing, shadows played against shadows until recognition formed: four of the enemy. One mattered, and she would have him.

She moved again, tracked them through the bush, closed her eyes and listened to the whispers of the landscape. Understood and smiled. They were circling, hunting for her. She would play the game of cat and mouse, eliminate the three, and take him down alone.

To hide, to hunt along the damp and dim of the rain-forest floor, was familiar, natural. The musk of living things permeated the air; it mixed with the inner cauldron of rage and fed the urge to strike, to kill. The knife was warm, an extended part of her body, and she stalked with patience, creating diversion to draw gunfire and deplete ammunition until their weapons were useless. And then, an apparition, she moved from the shadows long enough to kill before disappearing again.

Until there was only him.

He was there, waiting; she could feel his eyes and the figment of his breath along her spine. She was loud, careless, tempting as she moved through the bush, and then it came, the lunge from behind. She twisted to avoid the impact of his knife and in one drawn-out movement brought Francisco's blade across his neck. She forced the commander to the ground and, with fingers clenched in his hair, held his head, pulled the knife from his hand, and plunged his own blade into his throat. She jerked it around through tendon and veins, and when the crunch of his severed spinal column vibrated in her hand, the rush of euphoria flowed. She continued until his head separated from his body, held it high in gratified triumph, rose to her feet, and, trailing blood and fluid, carried it out of the forest.

For a quiet moment, Munroe stood over Francisco, droplets staining the ground at her feet, and then she struck out at the bodies that lay on him and near him, kicking in blind fury until he was free of the defilement of their touch. She knelt over him, dripping a mixture of sweat and blood onto his body, and in a picture of sacrificial offering placed the commander's head in front of open eyes that stared lifelessly into nothing. She reached for him, fingers shaking until they touched his forehead, pulled him close, cradled his shoulders, and closed his eyes. Then lifted her head to the sky and screamed.

It was primal, pain and rage, fury and pain again. Her body shook while tears that had not been shed for nearly a decade racked their way to the surface, and she buried her head in Francisco's chest.

LIGHT CAME SLOWLY into the fog that was in her mind, awareness brought first by the sound of Bradford's boots and then by his hand on her shoulder as he knelt beside her. Munroe raised her face to look at him, saw the carnage that surrounded them and the commander's head on the ground, and realized then for the first time what it was that she had done.

"We need to go," Bradford said.

Munroe cradled Francisco and said, "I'm not leaving him."

"Together we can carry him."

.   .   .

BRADFORD STARED OVER the ocean, hand to rudder, and glanced at the coordinates on the transponder. It had been three hours since they'd left the coast. They were running low on fuel, and as far as he could tell, there was nothing but ocean for miles to come.

He glanced at Munroe. She was seated between the benches, cross-legged, with Francisco in her arms and nothing but blankness on her face, the same as it had been since they'd shoved off from shore. She looked up for a half second, met his gaze, then returned to Francisco, and Bradford returned to the water, pushing back the crushing ache that came every time he stole a glance in her direction.

Nothing he'd read, none of the interviews he'd sat through in researching Munroe's past, could have prepared him for what she'd done. He understood now the fear others had described. She had been brutally efficient, accurate, had wasted no movement, misspent no energy, and she was fast, terrifyingly fast.

Bradford checked the coordinates again and then the horizon and saw it there, very faint, a black blemish against the blue, and he understood what it meant. He looked again at Munroe and then at Francisco and what little remained of his skull and the brain that had driven the genius of the man. What a waste. What a goddamn fucking waste.

The vastness of the ocean was dizzying, and over time the ship loomed large on the horizon, until finally they reached its bulk and Bradford brought the boat alongside. From the deck a crane swung over the water. Cables and sling lowered. Munroe sat motionless and gave no indication that she was aware of being shipside. Bradford knelt beside her and touched her hand; she looked up with such hollowness that it took his breath away. And then the fog in her eyes cleared and she turned toward the trawler, then back to him and pointed and said, "Hooks go there."

She bent over Francisco and kissed his forehead. *"When my enemies and foes came upon me to eat up my flesh, they stumbled and fell. Though wars should rise against me, in this will I be confident. . . ."* Her voice trailed from a mumble to silence, then she stood and went up the ladder on the side of the ship.

Bradford fought back the lump forming in his throat, moved quickly to secure the sling, grabbed an AKM, and followed her, his foot touching the first rung of the ladder seconds after she went over the top. There was a whir of motor as the deck crane began to hoist, and when the small boat was about eight feet out of the water, it stopped. He moved faster, his feet finding a rhythm against the steel until he reached the deck and was hit by panic.

CHAPTER 22

Munroe was fifteen feet ahead and stood facing a large man whose face Bradford couldn't see. Her mouth moved, and although Bradford couldn't hear the words, her eyes held the same empty glaze that had swept in when Francisco's body had dropped to the ground. Bradford watched her muscles tense and knew that if she went after the big guy, there would be another death, possibly two. He shouted her name, and her focus shifted slowly until she stared directly at him. Bradford maintained eye contact until the tension of the moment diffused, and then he turned toward the man, and when he did, a shock of recognition ran through him. He could see the same written on the other man's face.

Bradford nodded. "George."

Wheal said, "Miles."

And Munroe said, "Fuck."

And then she spoke again, the lucidity in the stream of words a stark contrast to her behavior of the past hours. "We're taking the ship to Douala," Munroe said to Wheal. "After that, you can have it back." And then to Bradford, "I'm going to the control deck. Have Wheal get the boat into the hold and then keep him away from me and from the ship controls. If he even twitches in the wrong direction, shoot him." And then she walked off.

There was five feet of silent space between the two men. Bradford stood with the rifle still pointed toward the deck; neither moved. Wheal stared down at him as if unsure whether Bradford would use the gun or how deep the shit pile was, until finally he broke the silence. "Want to tell me what the hell's going on?"

Bradford sighed, his shoulders slumped, and he nodded in the direction of the small boat still hanging over the ocean. "Take a look, and then I'll explain," he said.

Before Wheal had a chance to return to the crane controls, the trawler's engines kicked up and the ship began to move. Bradford glanced at the pilothouse and said, "Does she know what she's doing up there?" Wheal nodded, then brought the small boat over the deck and, like lowering a coffin into the grave, let it down into the hold.

Both men stood beside the boat. Wheal stared in silence and then with a heavy sigh turned and reached for a tarp. "I had a bad feeling about this," he said, and he opened the plastic and laid it over Francisco. His face twisted through a range of emotions and then hardened, became expressionless. He turned toward Bradford. "The explanation better be good, or I'm going to kill her."

Bradford described the events that had led to Beyard's death and the bloody aftermath that followed, and when he finished, the hold fell silent except for the sound of their breathing. Wheal said, "I'll take care of him, finish his business, do what I know he would have wanted." He walked toward the stairs. "I won't attempt to stop you from going to Douala—it's the easiest way to get you both the fuck off my ship. But I still hold her responsible."

Bradford ran a grimy hand through his hair and said, "George, whatever's going on in your head right now, don't engage her. You're both likely to end up dead." His back turned, Wheal waved him off with a gesture that could have been a middle finger, and as he stepped across the threshold, Bradford moved to the stairs. He needed to get to Munroe, get her sorted out, find out what the hell was wrong, and most of all keep Wheal out of sight. What a fucking nightmare.

He headed for the pilothouse, and when he entered it, Wheal was already there and Munroe was not. "Where is she?" Bradford said.

"Fuck if I know. If we're lucky, she jumped overboard."

Bradford left the pilothouse and took the stairs at a near run, paused long enough to confirm that Munroe wasn't anywhere on deck, and found the door to the interior. He opened it to silence, called her name, and received no response. He moved down the dark, narrow hallway, opening doors and flipping on room lights, going quickly from one to the next until he found the light switch for the hallway, slammed his fist against it, and when the darkness emptied, froze for a half second.

She lay on the floor at the end of the hall, her body partly through the threshold of a door. His throat closed, and he moved forward like someone running through deep water. He knelt beside her, checked her breathing and pulse; then his eyes rose to take in the room itself, and he whispered, *"Oh, shit."* The place breathed Francisco Beyard. Parts of his persona marked the room like a pen-scrawled signature, and whatever had driven her to enter it had not been strong enough to sustain her. As best he could tell, she had vomited before passing out.

He stared at the blood and mud and now the stomach juices that coated her skin and clothing, sighed deeply, stood, and went back through the bunkrooms searching for clothing that would fit, anything that didn't belong to Francisco. And then he carried her out of Francisco's room to the narrow hallway bathroom and with reverent tenderness sponged off the filth.

A BUNKROOM ON the trawler.

Munroe knew it by the familiar movement of a ship on calm water and the woody dankness of the air. Her eyelids were weighted, and she fought to open them, succeeded, and then, seeing nothing, closed them again in exhaustion. She was laid out flat with her arms to her sides, her head slightly elevated, her mouth dry. There were flashes of illumination against the blackness of her mind: the macabre sight of her reflection in the pilothouse windows; a walk down the hallway to Francisco's cabin to take a shower; the chessboard, the unmade bed, the fragrance of his presence; nausea and then darkness.

Time had passed. Maybe an hour. Or a day. Or a week. She struggled to lift a hand against the wall, to place the other against the side of the bed and create support to sit up, but found no strength, let go, and drifted back into the void.

It was light when she opened her eyes next, the source a low-wattage bedside lamp turned against the opposite wall. The room was unfamiliar—not Francisco's, not the holding cell—and her clothes were clean and foreign and without the stench of death. She shifted, and her eyes moved to take in the room.

Focus returned in small waves, and with awareness came tension, nausea, and the iron vise inside her chest that fractured each second and made life a waking death. In a wall niche was a bottle of water; she sat up and reached for it, emptied it in several long swallows, and then rested her forearms on her knees.

From the hall came the sound of footsteps, and the door opened. George Wheal entered carrying a tray of food, and he placed it on the narrow table between the bunks, gave a curt nod, and sat opposite so that their knees were nearly touching. "We're in Douala," he said. "I guess you'll want to get moving soon."

Munroe drew away until her back was against the wall, pulled her knees to her chest, and stared silently at the tray.

"Look," he said, "for what it's worth, the period you were here was the happiest I'd seen Francisco. If I know anything, I know he died content, at peace." Wheal paused as if calculating the weight of his words and then stood. "That doesn't change anything between you and me, but I owe it to Francisco to make sure that you know. He loved you, and it's what he would have wanted." Wheal opened the door, then looked back for a silent moment before he stepped out and shut it behind him.

The room went silent and then claustrophobic, and in an effort to hold on to sanity Munroe reached for the boots at the foot of the bunk, put them on, and laced them up. She struggled to stand; her vision folded inward to a pinprick of light, and she braced herself through the first wave of dizziness. Then she turned, leaned into the wall, and somehow one step at a time made it out the cabin door. She'd gone only a couple of feet when Bradford was beside her, arm around her shoulders holding her up, walking her forward.

Munroe moved in a daze, aware but not, body present and mind somewhere else, shut down. Sounds, sights, and smells filtered into her brain as if through gauzy film while Bradford ushered her through the motions and took care of logistics. They entered Douala at the southern edge of the port where Francisco's driver waited to take them into the city and, at Bradford's instruction, bypassed Francisco's flat for Akwa Palace, the crown jewel of the city's hotels, a place where one could almost forget what part of the world this was.

At the hotel-room door, awareness kicked in, and Munroe realized that Bradford intended for them to share the room. She stopped in the foyer, propped against the wall for support while Bradford entered and dropped his things on one of the chairs. He looked back to where she continued to stand.

"I'm staying here with you whether you like it or not," he said.

Munroe nodded and moved toward the closest bed and, with her legs still on the floor, tilted over onto the pillows. With her back to Bradford, she whispered, "We need to get tickets out of here, need to get to Houston."

"I'll take care of it tomorrow."

She wrapped an arm around a pillow and pulled it to her chest. "You're worried about leaving me?"

He walked to the edge of the bed and sat behind her, angled so that he could see the side of her face. "Very."

A long silence filled the space until Munroe said, "I play it over and over, and no matter what direction I take, there's nothing I could have done to save him."

"I know," he said, and he brushed a finger along her forehead.

"It doesn't make it any easier," she whispered. "Somehow it should, but it doesn't." She grasped the pillow tighter and pulled her knees to her chest, while tears spilled down her cheeks.

Bradford shifted to lie behind her, wrapped his arms around her, and drew her close.

The tears flowed faster, and Munroe shook with silent sobs until the shadows in the room deepened and the hush of evening settled, and there was nothing left to cry. And when the water of emotion had dried and all that remained was a hollow emptiness, she said, "You know, you're the first to live through what my demons are capable of doing."

His arms were still around her, and he whispered, "It wasn't without cause."

"That's not the point," she said.

"It's not the first time?"

"No."

"The scars?"

She nodded almost imperceptibly and said, "The missing years. You've wanted to know, haven't you?"

"Yes."

"You deserve to know," she said, and tilted her head to give him a pained, exhausted smile. "It starts with Francisco. I met him for the first time when I was fourteen."

It was completely dark by the time she'd finished a confession that encompassed nine years of buried secrets, embracing details even Logan didn't know. They lay on their backs and stared at the ceiling, engulfed in silence for a long while, and then Bradford turned his head toward her. "It's surprising you're still sane," he said.

"Sane?" She sighed. "There are days, months, sometimes even years that go by when I'm sure I've attained some state of normalcy, when I can look at myself in the mirror and really believe that somehow I'm like 'them'—those people out there who've lived normal lives and have no fucking clue what the dark side of humanity can do to a person's mind. And then there are days like today and yesterday, when it's obvious that the demons are still there, waiting in the background, taunting me."

She turned to face him. "Thank you," she said. "For saving my life in Mbini, for getting me out, getting me here."

And then, without waiting for a response, she let go and tumbled backward into the void, a mental freefall into the darkness of the abyss.

Bright sunshine streaming through day curtains was what woke her. Bradford was gone, the room was empty, and she was numb. Not the dead of internal shutdown or the muted silence of mental noise held at bay by adrenaline and distraction. There were no words or phrases or voices, no tension or anxiety, only acceptance, tranquillity; strange and unfamiliar.

She lay on the bed, arms behind her head, and breathed in each passing moment of peace, oblivious to time until Bradford walked in the door. He had entered quietly and, seeing her awake, moved directly to her.

He sat on the bed. "You okay?"

"Yeah," she said, and stretched, smiling. "Surprisingly good. How long was I under?"

"About seventeen hours. Didn't want to leave you, but we couldn't wait another day to get tickets." He dropped the documents on the bed. "Flight's tonight at nine."

"I need to contact Logan."

He nodded. "Business center will be open for a few more hours. First you need to eat."

It was strange, this process of conversing, interacting, eating, going through the motions of daily life without anxiety, without mental noise embossing itself onto synaptic activity and guiding reflex. It was calm, collected silence, and it remained that way through attempt after attempt to reach Logan, until after nearly two hours of intermittent dialing Munroe gave up and called Kate Breeden.

The conversation was brief, Munroe unwilling to discuss the assignment or the events of the past few days and Kate unaware of Logan's whereabouts, having also been unable to contact him. Munroe wanted the bike in Houston—for that she needed Logan—and the best she could do was provide Kate the flight-arrival information and hope the message eventually got to him.

While most people trying to locate Logan might have trouble reaching him by phone, the number Munroe used was known to few, was always carried and nearly certainly answered. There had been occasions in the past when Logan had dropped off the radar—each had been its own relative nightmare—and so Munroe heaved an internal sigh, reached for the tickets, realized Bradford had walked off with them, and then promised Kate she'd send the information by e-mail.

And there, waiting in the mailbox, unbelievable as it was, sat the final puzzle piece that transformed the present and gave context and meaning to everything that had taken place from the day Munroe accepted the assignment. She blinked now at the page, information tumbling in her mind like cotton cloth in a dryer: flashbacks, conversations, awareness, and understanding. She scrolled and reread:

To: Michael@race-or-die.com
From: Logan@race-or-die.com
Subject: I think you need to see this

Michael,

I have no way of getting in contact with you other than e-mail. The photos speak for themselves, although I'm not entirely sure what they mean. It's possible you're well aware of this already; I was not.

The reason for the attached: In spite of your instructions, Kate refused to release funding until I provided a complete inventory list. Her demands for this information went beyond odd behavior to intimidation and then threats of legal action, which I know had nothing to do with you although she used your name. For these and other reasons not worth getting into now, I placed Kate under surveillance.

If you need to reach me, I have a new number . . . see signature line below.

Munroe scrolled through photo after photo of Kate Breeden and Richard Burbank, each a snapshot in time that left no doubt their relationship went far beyond the tradition of lawyer-client privilege. There was a fragmented moment when Munroe's internal stillness became overwhelmed by rage and the piercing stab of betrayal, and it seemed that the newfound calm would dissipate into the ether. But there were no voices. There was no anxiety, no internal percussion, simply controlled anger and the knowledge that there was work to be done.

She dialed, and the relief she felt at hearing Logan's voice was obviously reciprocated on the other end of the line.

"You got my e-mail?" he asked.

"I did, and I need your help," she said. "I'm putting events into play, and I won't be back stateside for a bit. There's the possibility that when

I don't show up in Houston as Kate expects, she's going to run. I need to know where she is at all times. Can you handle that?"

"I've already got it covered."

"What about Richard Burbank?"

"Him, too."

"Instinct paid off, Logan. I owe you big time."

"Michael, what the hell is going on?"

Munroe sighed. "She set me up."

There was silence on the other end, followed by a stream of expletives, and when they ended, Munroe said, "Burbank used me as a cat's-paw, and Kate fed him the information to make it possible. Don't go anywhere. I've got a few things I need to take care of first, but I'll be seeing you in about a week."

"What's the plan? What are you going to do about Kate?"

"Trust me," she said, "you really don't want to know."

When Munroe exited the hotel, Bradford stood waiting with the taxi. They rode to the airport in silence, and after they had checked in and were standing in the terminal waiting for the flight to board, Bradford said, "Something's going on, and I'd like to know what it is."

Munroe rested her head against the wall, stared up at the ceiling, and let out a slow breath. "It goes against every instinct I have to talk about this with you," she said, and then she paused and turned toward him. "I'm not going to give you a lot, but you deserve at least something. I'll tell you what I can, and that's the best I can do."

"I'll take what I can get."

"I know now where the information leak is," she said. "It cuts deep and personal, and I need to deal with it on my own terms, in my own way." She paused. Sighed. "We have two days to get to Houston and put the information in front of the board." She turned to look at him. "It's on you, Miles. I won't be returning with you, won't be stateside until I sort through this—Paris will be good-bye."

Bradford struck the heel of his boot on the cement floor, repetitive dull taps that filled the silence, then slid down the wall into a squat, staring at nothing. "I'm not stupid enough to attempt to stand in your way," he said. "Even though it's what I feel I should do." He looked up. "I've just lived through two days of hell with you, Michael. To say that I'm concerned is the understatement of the year. You're not planning to go chuteless off Angel Falls, are you?"

Munroe shook her head and then smiled weakly. "I'm all right, Miles. Really, I am. I'll be back in Dallas in a few weeks—I promise I'll look you up. I owe you that." She held eye contact long enough to remain credible and then slid down the wall to the floor and sat beside him.

She had lied through omission, had conveniently left out the part where she planned to follow him to Houston and commit murder in cold blood.

CHAPTER 23

Paris, France

Munroe stalked the streets, collar turned up, hands tucked deep into the pockets of the ankle-length coat she'd procured off a departing passenger at the airport. Even in the sun, the difference between the equatorial summer night and the mild Parisian winter morning was about sixty degrees, and it would have been a relief to return to the warmth and comfort of the room she'd secured at the Park Hyatt.

She moved decisively in the direction of Place Pigalle, the city's chic red-light district famous for the Moulin Rouge, sex shops, and peep shows, its side streets and alleys notorious for so much more. The forces urging her onward were entirely her own; there were no voices, no anxiety, and the demons were silent. Her senses were overwhelmed by the thirst for revenge, and she paused for a moment and stood beside a wall, one leg kicked back against it for support while she studied passersby.

The intense focus on murder should have been disturbing, but she felt no conscience.

This was the abyss, that murky mental darkness she had so long held back one anxious breath at a time, though it wasn't dark. Here it was light and freedom. It was total control and power and peace. And enveloped in this goodness was the knowledge that she had finally become the monstrosity of Pieter Willem's making. His taunting laughter called out from the dead and was brushed aside as an inconvenient after-thought; all these years later he had won, and now she no longer cared.

Munroe thrust her hands deeper into the coat pockets and followed the sidewalk. Her eyes tracked random faces in the pedestrian crowd, her feet moved, and her mind churned in process and calculation. She crossed to rue Saint-Denis and spotted in a doorway, leaning against stone masonry as if unaware of solicitous glances paid by prospective clients, a body with a face that matched what she'd been searching for. He was a boy of seventeen or eighteen—prostitute, drug addict, child of the streets. Perfect alibi.

She walked a long diagonal path across the road and made eye con-tact; the boy straightened at her approach, his eyes sizing her up in a look disguised as interest. She was close enough now to breathe him in and allow the other senses to confirm what her eyes had already noted. Right height, right build, good facial features. Hair would need to be col-ored and shortened, but otherwise he would do. "I want you for a week," she said. "Who do I need to talk to?"

Taking the boy off the streets meant having to negotiate with thugs, and Munroe followed him down an alley and up narrow tenement steps with her right hand wrapped around the weapon she'd carried out of Cameroon. There were moments when tension filled the run-down room, when money changed hands and avarice appeared to control mental fac-ulties and a fight seemed inevitable, but in the end she stepped back into daylight without having to resort to threats or violence and with the boy trailing reticently behind.

She went as far as the end of the street, then turned and stopped. She grabbed his wrist and pulled him close, lifted his sleeves, searched for needle marks and bruises, found none; put her thumb to his chin and moved his head to the side, examining his skin. "What's your drug of choice?" she asked.

"I don't do drugs."

"I don't have fucking time to waste," she said. "It's not heroin, it's not meth. What is it? Crack? Coke? Prescriptions?"

He mumbled an affirmative.

"You have a dealer?"

He nodded, and she tossed him a phone. "Call him."

The boy's first name was Alain, and Munroe didn't catch his last, didn't care to, didn't need it. He was a breathing and functioning young male whom nobody would miss; it was all that mattered, and she'd be back to clean up this loose end long before the week expired.

Paying off the boy's hustlers had been for his peace of mind, not hers. She wanted him unafraid, comfortable, willingly following instructions. And they were simple: Remain at the Park Hyatt and run up as large a bill as possible—room service, Internet shopping sprees, anything he wished so long as for that one week he received no visitors and did not set foot outside the hotel. Every day he did this, his drugs would be delivered to the room by front-desk staff believing they were handling business documents, the instructions given them having been far more detailed and explicit than those she gave him.

When Munroe left the hotel, Alain was fast asleep, and she'd made sure he would remain that way for the final few hours she'd be moving about town leaving the last traceable threads of her existence. At the bank she deposited her passport, ID, and credit cards in a safe-deposit box and walked out the door with only the forged Spanish passport in the name of Miguel Díaz and twenty thousand dollars.

She purchased a laptop, burned several copies of Emily's recording to DVD, and sent two overnight to Logan for safekeeping. She stopped by a specialty electronics store to purchase harder-to-find items and then, after calling to confirm locations on Kate Breeden and Richard Burbank, left for the airport, where a charter waited to take her to London. From there the flight would route to Canada, and she would enter the United States on foot, then travel by road to Boston, where she would connect with a second charter and continue on to Houston.

Munroe spent the trip poring over documents she'd culled off the vastness of the Internet. Everything she knew about the Burbank assignment had passed through Kate Breeden, and as information was only as good as its source, everything was now suspect. Munroe read and jotted notes, her concentration broken only by the stops, starts, and connections of the journey. Time spent on the ground allowed her to follow threads and download additional files, and by the time the wheels of the last flight hit the tarmac in Houston, she knew exactly why Emily Burbank had been meant to die.

The eighteen-hour transit put Munroe on the ground a half day behind Miles Bradford and less than ten hours before the board of trustees was scheduled to meet. It was a narrow window of opportunity, and she counted on Burbank's greed and Kate's duplicity to hold them in place until after the board met.

From the airport Munroe caught a cab and stopped first at a pet store before heading downtown to the Alden, where a request at check-in netted the room adjacent to Breeden's. As of yesterday this was where Kate had been staying, and although a prior call to the front desk had confirmed that she hadn't checked out, it said nothing about her actual whereabouts. In an alcove off the lobby, Munroe switched from leather gloves to latex and dialed Breeden's room, let the phone ring, and after getting no response, took the elevator up.

In the dark interior of her own room, Munroe removed the eyehole from the door, replaced it with a camera that fed into the laptop, and then for ease of egress depressed the door latch with a strip of tape. Preparations made, she lay next to the door with the laptop at her side, and when her head touched the floor, exhaustion that had previously gone unnoticed settled in. How long had it been since she'd slept? Thirty-two hours, thirty-seven?

Through two hours of numbing silence, Munroe fought to keep alert, and now, at two in the morning, there was still no sign of Breeden. Based on Logan's surveillance photos, Munroe had been certain that Burbank wouldn't have Kate stay overnight, but still, choosing the hotel had been a gamble that might have done nothing other than waste a perfect opportunity. Munroe was waging an internal debate over the emergency recourse of contacting Logan for an update when the soft vibrations of footfalls alerted her to a presence, and a few seconds later Kate's profile filled the screen on the laptop.

Exhaustion was displaced by adrenaline, and Munroe was out the door, in the hallway, and standing behind Breeden with the weapon pressed into the woman's spine before she'd had a chance to open her door. "Hello, Kate," she said.

Breeden jumped slightly, put a hand on her chest, said, "Michael, you scared the bejesus out of me," and fumbled with the handle. Munroe opened the door and shoved Kate inside, pointed toward the bed, and said, "Sit."

Breeden remained standing. Slow and hesitant, she said, "No." And then, with a bark of nervous laughter, "What are you going to do? Kill me?"

Munroe slammed the back of her hand against Breeden's face, and the force of the blow knocked her to the bed. Kate looked up with shock in her eyes, and then with deliberation wiped a trickle of blood from her mouth. Munroe pressed the muzzle of the gun to Breeden's forehead and said, "Yes. I'm going to kill you. And the question you need to ask yourself is how much pain you're willing to endure before you die, because you know I'm certainly capable of inflicting it."

Munroe took a step back and tossed Breeden a roll of duct tape. "Around your ankles." When Kate had finished, Munroe pushed her backward so that she was in the center of the bed. She wrapped the tape between Breeden's ankles and then used it to anchor Breeden's feet to the bed frame. When she had finished, Munroe stepped back and said, "Fucking touch the tape and I'll put a bullet in your kneecap."

Breeden sat, hugged her knees, and a tear trailed down the side of her face. "Why are you doing this?" she said. "What is it that you want from me?"

Munroe ignored the questions and picked Breeden's purse up from the floor, fishing out the keys. "Which one goes to Richard Burbank's house?"

A look of pained innocence crossed Kate's face, and she said, "Why would you think *I've* got his keys?"

Munroe tossed an envelope onto the bed and watched for reaction as Breeden went through the eight-by-ten glossies. Breeden's fingers held the photos lightly, flipped through them nonchalantly, and then there it was, thumb clamped tightly to a photo and a second of hesitation, and then another and another until the masked calm was replaced by true pain, and Munroe took the photos back and stuffed them into the envelope.

Breeden said, "Michael, this isn't what it looks like . . . those photos. It's not what you think."

"Doesn't matter what I think," Munroe said. "It only matters what is. You fucking sold me out, Kate, to a man who cared less about his wife and daughter than he did about his Italian suits."

Breeden's face clouded over. She said, "What?" and Munroe held up the keys, jangled them. "You'll save me . . . what? A minute? Two minutes? Which key is to his house?"

"The square brown one," Breeden whispered.

Munroe laughed, hard and unfeeling. "I hope the betrayal was worth it." She grabbed Breeden's left wrist. Breeden struggled, and Munroe struck her again, then forced the wrist down onto the bed and, with the arm stretched out, wrapped the tape around it and anchored her to the side of the bed frame. Munroe took the other wrist and repeated the procedure so that Breeden was splayed like a crucifix. "So why'd you do it, Kate?" she said.

"It doesn't matter," Breeden said. Munroe snapped three leashes onto a choke chain, wrapped and knotted a length of one around Breeden's feet, and repeated the procedure with the others around the wrists, then ran them under the bed, tested them for tension, and slipped the choke over Breeden's head.

Kate's eyes grew wide, and Munroe said, "I'm not going to kill you yet."

Using a small penknife, she slit the taped anchors off Breeden's ankles and wrists, removed the tape from the bed and balled it up, then leaned over Breeden and tugged on the choke, causing Breeden to gasp and struggle for air. Munroe released the pressure. "This little guy is attached to your hands and feet. If you try to sit up, move your legs, or pull your arms, you'll die slowly, strangled by your own struggle. You understand?"

Breeden nodded, and Munroe said, "Good."

She released the clip on the gun and removed the bullets. Wiped them down, pressed them against Breeden's fingers, leaving a partial to solid print on each, and then returned them to the magazine. She could have gotten prints on the photos the same way, but provoking Breeden's reaction had been so much more rewarding.

Munroe searched through the closet, and Breeden said, "You're not going to be able to pull this off."

The sweet, sadistic smile of Pieter Willem spread across Munroe's face as she rifled through Breeden's clothing. "Oh, Kate," she said, "you know me so much better than that. Not only will I pull it off, I'm going to get away with it." She removed a shoulder-length blond wig from the case she carried and placed it solidly on her head. Then, still wearing the smirk, she took a bottle of perfume off the shelf, sprayed it on her neck and wrists, tugged a suit off a hanger, and grabbed a pair of Breeden's panty hose. "In fact, I can prove beyond reasonable doubt that I'm not even in the country."

Using the hose and some bathroom towels, Munroe padded her body to fit the suit. She dressed in front of Breeden, who kept her eyes mostly on the ceiling or shut. Breeden's breathing was calm and regular, and finally, in a near whisper, she said, "How bad could it have really been?"

Each word brought Munroe flashbacks of Francisco's body in a pool of blood, lifeless on the ground. She breathed in the rage and allowed it to consume her, tore off a strip of tape and placed it over Breeden's mouth, then jerked Breeden's right hand up from the bed and watched her eyes bulge as she struggled for air. After a moment Munroe placed the hand back on the bed and ran a finger along the inside of the choke to release the pressure, then patted Breeden's cheek. "For your sake," she said, "let's hope that things go well for me tonight."

She placed the laptop and equipment into Breeden's attaché case, picked out a purse, dumped Breeden's keys and wallet inside it, and, careful to leave no trace of her presence or identity, walked out of the room. She placed a Do Not Disturb sign on Breeden's door and then in her own room cleared it of any indication that she had been there.

RICHARD BURBANK'S HOME was an apartment that covered nearly the entire floor above his offices. Dressed as she was, Munroe didn't even garner a second look from night security when she entered the building. A card on Breeden's key ring took the elevator to the correct floor, and Munroe exited into a marble foyer that ended in a door opposite the elevator. The key card let her soundlessly into Burbank's home, and although the unit was dark, city lights filtering through large plate-glass windows provided more than enough illumination to guide her through the maze of furniture and carpeting. In the living room, Munroe stuffed a pair of Breeden's panties between the couch cushions and then followed voices to the far side of the apartment. She stood against the half-open office door and listened to one side of a phone conversation—Burbank and one of his many girlfriends, apparently.

She waited until the conversation had ended and then entered the room, weapon trained on the back of Burbank's head. If revenge were to be saccharine sweet, she would have killed him with her bare hands, staring into his eyes as he died slowly. Unfortunately, a bullet to the head was necessary for consistency.

Her steps were soundless, but the oversize clothes rustled, and without glancing up from his desk Burbank said, "Katie, is that you?"

"No, asshole," Munroe said. "Kate's dead, and you'll be with her shortly."

Burbank turned, facing into the muzzle of the gun.

Like the rest of the apartment, the office was nearly dark, and Burbank was a silhouette against the city lights, but even in the dimness Munroe could see the terror in his eyes. His hands trembled, and his eyes twitched nervously in the direction of the phone.

"Hand it to me," Munroe said.

Burbank gave her the phone and then, in a sudden shift to calm, put his palms out and said, "Look, you don't want to kill me. Whatever this is about, we can work through it. I can give you anything you want. I have connections, power—you know that. You want money? I'll give you money. I can set you up good, no more globe-trotting. Whatever it is you want, I can make it happen."

"Unless you're Jesus fucking Christ and can raise the dead, there's no way you can give me what I want."

Burbank's face went blank, and a second later his negotiator personality resurfaced. "You were never meant to get hurt. No one was supposed to be hurt. We should talk about this some more, work through it, see if we can't find those who were really to blame."

"Shut the fuck up," Munroe said. "You're making me sick." She placed a foot on his chair and pushed it away from the desk. "Stay seated and keep your hands and feet where I can see them." She flipped through the automated records on the phone and, not finding what she wanted, said, "We're calling Nchama. Give me his number."

Burbank's mouth dropped open, and he said, "What?"

"You heard me, you fucking bastard. Give. Me. Nchama's. Number."

Burbank sat without moving, and Munroe cursed inwardly, torn between the intense desire to inflict pain and the complications of fucking up the otherwise perfect forensics of Kate's would-be murder-suicide. "Last warning," she said. And when again he didn't move, she fired a shot into his left thigh.

Burbank screamed, lurched forward, and grabbed at his leg, and Munroe slapped a five-inch strip of tape across his mouth. "You want me to do that again?" she asked.

Eyes wide, fingers streaked with red, and grasping his leg, he shook his head vehemently.

"Good," she said. "I'm glad we're on the same page. Now get me the fucking number."

Burbank pointed toward the desk, and Munroe kicked the chair back toward it. "Keep your hands where I can see them and don't give me a reason to take out your other leg."

Burbank nodded and fumbled with the desk drawer.

"Stop," Munroe said.

He hesitated and then did as she'd instructed, placing his hands on the armrests.

Munroe stepped between Burbank and the desk, pushed him back again, and with the weapon trained on his chest used the other hand to open the drawer. She searched through it, then felt along the underside and located a small depression. She released it, and a hidden drawer sprang open. Munroe removed the handgun, checked the safety, and then slid it into the waistband at the small of her back. Then she nodded again in the direction of the desk. "Nchama's number," she said.

Whatever confidence Burbank had held in reserve was fast fading; Munroe could see it in his posture, in the way his hands shook, and in the tension in his face. He dug through a drawer, pulled out a notepad, and handed it to her. She motioned him away from the desk and to the floor, where, still clutching at his leg and moaning against the gag, he sat with his back to the wall.

With a sneer, Munroe came slowly after him, watched his eyes grow wide as she crouched down to his level. With the gun to his head and her eyes boring into his, she squeezed the wound on his thigh.

Burbank screamed under the gag, and then, when he had calmed slightly, Munroe said, "I will hurt you. I will hurt you badly if you are difficult. Do you understand me?"

He nodded.

She lowered the weapon, reached for the tape, and ripped it from his face.

He began to yell, and she shook her head.

Still crouched at eye level, she said, "You've read my dossier. You know what I'm capable of, and you know that I specialize in information. This means you also know that I'm not bluffing when I tell you that I know why you left Emily to rot in Africa." Her voice was low, monotonous, deadly. "Don't try to play innocent, because bullshit is only going to prolong your pain. I know what you've done, and I know why you've done it. What I *want* to know is what you told Nchama that caused him to hold Emily in Mongomo."

Through gritted teeth and halted breath, Burbank said, "That Emily was an impostor."

"And you ordered Nchama to kill her?"

"Not in those exact words."

Munroe prodded again at his thigh, and he swore.

"I didn't have to," he said. "Nchama said he'd taken care of it."

"She called you," Munroe said. "Nearly a year later, she talked with you. You knew she was alive, and you could have brought her home."

Burbank shrugged. "By that time it didn't matter anymore. Emily was pregnant, and Nchama never would have let her leave with the child."

"What you mean is that with her the soon-to-be-mother of his child, he wouldn't kill her like you wanted him to."

Burbank said nothing, and she saw the truth in his eyes.

"So he keeps her, alive but hidden. What is it that you hold over his head?" she asked. "What is he afraid of?"

Burbank gave no response, and Munroe smiled sweetly. "I haven't time to waste," she said, singsong and lilting. "It doesn't matter to *me* if you have all your fingers and toes. Does it matter to *you?*"

When he still said nothing, she placed the muzzle of the gun over his thumb, and when her index finger coiled for the trigger, Burbank said, "Video footage—a huge under-the-table deal that I threatened to take to his president."

There was no point in demanding he hand it over. Burbank surely kept copies. Munroe slapped the tape back across his mouth and said, "Fucking piece of scum." Then she stood, took the handset off his desk, and dialed.

She greeted Nchama in English and said, "I'm the one you've been hunting," and then for privacy she switched to Fang. "I took out your patrol and beheaded your commander. I am a phantom," she said, "and if I must, I will hunt you down and destroy you. Is the girl impostor alive?" Munroe received an affirmative and so shoved the phone in Burbank's face and again ripped off the strip of tape. "Tell him plans have changed," Munroe said. "That you need Emily returned to the United States."

Burbank managed to stammer only slightly as he spoke, and when he had finished, Munroe took the phone back and continued with Nchama in Fang. She bluffed through the remainder of the conversation as if she now had the information that Burbank held. In promising to control Burbank—to control the blackmail—she offered Nchama a way out. She twisted the promise into a threat should he fail to cooperate, and by the time the call ended, she was as certain as she could ever be that Emily and the children were free of Burbank's perfidy.

Munroe had no need for Richard Burbank now. He could die. Then Kate Breeden. That was the plan. Put a bullet in his brain. Then leave the photos, bullet casings, and Kate's undergarments and walk out into the night to take care of Breeden's suicide. For such short notice, the strategy was impressively flawless, and she stared at Burbank now, the whining, sniveling excuse for a man who had been the cause of so much pain.

She prepared to fire, but then she stopped. It could have been a minute or two, or ten, that she stood rigid, staring down at him while he

whined and shed crocodile tears. All the while, memory tapes of Pieter
Willem and Francisco Beyard danced inside her head, recollections of
one man overcoming the other. And she knew that Richard Burbank
wasn't worth it.

"Turn on your computer," she said finally.

Burbank stood again and hobbled to the desk, and then, with the
computer powering on, she tossed the extra DVD with Emily's footage
and the packet of photos on the desk. She shoved him into the office chair
and sat on the edge of the desk, where she could observe his expression
while she forced him to watch the entire length of footage.

Burbank's face betrayed no emotion throughout the viewing, and
if Munroe understood correctly, the wheels of his mind had kicked into
action, calculating the damage and planning spin and information control. If he lived, he would attempt to talk his way out of this, just as he'd
talked his way into Elizabeth's life and so many business deals thereaf-
ter, and so she waited until the footage ended.

Then, when the room had filled with silence, she said, "I don't have
to kill you, Richard. You're already dead."

Burbank looked into her face, surprise written clearly across his.

"You seem to be a little slow in catching on," she said. "So let me
help you." Munroe leaned forward so that her face was only inches from
his. "This morning Miles will take a copy of that footage to the board."
She paused and allowed the information to sink in. "Do I need to get
graphic, Richard? What will they do when the truth is known? How
much power will they allow you, Richard? How much control will you
retain? How much wealth?" She paused again. "You've lost it all. Gone.
Poof."

She waited for Burbank's reaction, read it in the creases around his
eyes, smiled Pieter Willem's sadistic smile, and beat her fist into her
chest in mock grief. "Poor Daddy Burbank. Lost his wife and lost his
daughter. Oh! The pain!

"You buried it well, Richard, your dirty little secret—shell companies and corporations behind corporations, all hiding the truth that your
wealth and power were nothing but a façade. You're broke, Richard.
You have nothing but debt. Everything you own, everything you have—
including Titan—belonged to Elizabeth and now belongs to Emily. And

with Emily missing, everything you retain is at the discretion of the board."

She smiled again and allowed Burbank to mull this over, then said, "Oh, I forgot to tell you. Your nightmare doesn't end with the board."

His face turned quickly toward hers. "How silly of me," she said. "But that would have been too easy for you and your smooth, glib tongue.

"Emily's footage and a thorough explanation outlining all this are also being sent to media outlets and law enforcement. The charade of your persona may possibly survive the news-shark feeding frenzy, but without the power and money granted by the board of trustees, I doubt you'll survive a courtroom.

"Motive is a powerful thing," she continued, "and I do believe yours has now been thoroughly documented. When you're arrested—and you *will* be arrested—your public defender is going to have his work cut out.

"No, Richard," she said, shaking her head, "I don't have to kill you. Death would be so much easier than what you have waiting. This is a revenge I will be able to enjoy every day for years to come."

She smiled. "Every night I will think of you, a soft white man with gang members, killers, and rapists as bedtime companions. I'll wake with a smile, knowing it's another day in the life of Poor Daddy Burbank, the bunkmate's bitch. Word will leak that you've gotten AIDS or hepatitis C, that you've grown older than your years, and that you're wasting away. Every bit of news will make mine a good day. And when you get out, *if* you ever do, I'll be waiting."

She paused again and whispered, "So far the fall, so great the degradation."

Munroe indicated the photo envelope she'd tossed on the desk. "Keep these as a memento, because once the shit hits the fan, memories are all you'll have." She stood, slid the silenced pistol into the far corner of the room, said, "Enjoy the rest of your fucking miserable life," then turned and walked out the door.

Munroe got as far as the kitchen before the stillness of the apartment was split by the unmistakable hiss of the weapon. She returned to the office and stood in the doorway only long enough to ascertain that Burbank had been successful. She removed the DVD from the computer and then went quickly down the hall, through Burbank's bedroom to his bathroom. She found a washcloth and soaked it, then repeated the procedure with a second, applying a generous amount of hand soap.

She returned to Burbank. Lifting his right hand with the damp cloth, she wiped it thoroughly, hand to wrist to forearm. She followed with the second washrag and for consistency did the same on the left. The soap and water would wash away enough of the trace powder to conceal the crime scene's silent truths.

Rags tossed into the attaché case, she moved back through the apartment and took the elevator down. Their encounter had veered far from the initial strategy, but her improvisation would suffice.

Her return to the hotel was on foot, cool air to clear her head, to think things through, to decide what the next step would be, but it wasn't until she was back inside Breeden's room staring at the body of the woman who had betrayed half a decade of friendship that she was certain.

Munroe said nothing to Breeden, merely stripped out of the suit and stepped into her own clothes, then released the gag, the bonds, and the choke from Kate's neck.

"Are you going to kill me now?" Breeden asked.

Munroe slipped the constraints and suit in with her equipment, turned toward the door, and said, "No."

"Is Richard dead?" Kate called out.

"Yes." Munroe said, and without looking back she walked into the hall, down the stairs, and into the darkened shadows of the city's steel-and-glass giants, mentally blinded, emotions coursing along a Geiger counter's range.

She had no direction, no motive, and no place to go.

epilogue

I-35, Austin to Dallas

From inside the helmet, the world's sounds took on a muted distance. There was that and the rush of wind and the vibration of power that rumbled through her body as the bike whined across the miles. Munroe was headed north, up from San Antonio and Texas's hill country, back into the flat of Dallas, where she was scheduled to meet with Miles Bradford later in the day.

She'd left him in Paris with the promise to look him up in a few weeks' time, and though the few had stretched into several, she knew that he knew by way of Logan that she was all right. She could have made the effort to see him when she'd first returned to Dallas but had needed the distance of time and space to purge the venom from her system and grieve Francisco's death.

More difficult was coming to terms with the decision to allow Breeden's treachery to go unpunished. It somehow seemed that in choosing to allow her own soul to go free, Francisco's memory had been betrayed, and there were still only a handful of days when Munroe hadn't considered tracking down Breeden and finishing what should—in the laws of the jungle—rightfully have been done that night.

After leaving the hotel, she'd wandered aimlessly, long past the rising of the sun and the chaos of the lunch crowd and far into the afternoon rush hour before finally making her way to the Greyhound station and catching the next bus to the Mexican border. She'd left the United States on foot and returned to Paris out of Monterrey, Mexico, the next evening.

In what was perhaps one of her life's only truly altruistic gestures, she'd taken Alain out of Paris to where the hustlers wouldn't find him and committed him to a lockdown rehab facility, with the promise of an apartment and job if he remained clean for six months. She held no illusions about recidivism rates and the odds of the boy's making it for the long term, but she'd given him a shot at a clean break. What he did with it was his own.

Munroe exited the freeway, turned off the access road, and rolled the bike into a parking lot adjacent to a twelve-story building. Capstone Consulting was located on the fifth floor, just one of the many midsize companies filling space in the North Dallas tower. But for the pair of muscle-bound bodies that exited the plate-glass doors of the office as she entered, Munroe would have seen no indication that the business was the mercenary outfit she knew it to be.

Bradford looked good, and his smile brought on a pang of guilt for having waited as long as she had to see him. Necessary business aside, this was closure, a proper way to conclude the strange bond forged between them, and so much better than the abrupt good-bye at Charles de Gaulle. After a few moments of small talk, he handed her a slip of paper and said, "Transferred to the accounts you specified, the full five million as per the contract."

She took the document and glanced over it.

"I assume you heard that Burbank's dead," Bradford said.

Munroe nodded and while skimming the page said, "Logan told me."

"Have you heard about Kate Breeden?"

She stopped and looked up. "No," she said. "I've been out of touch for a few weeks. What about her?"

"Let's sit," he said.

Munroe paused and after a brief hesitation took the chair that was to her right. Bradford sat opposite and swiveled so that he faced her directly. He was quiet for a moment and then leaned forward, elbows to knees. "Kate's been implicated in Richard's death."

The news came unexpectedly, and Munroe took a deep breath. She'd walked out of the Alden that night, turning her back on whatever revenge was to be had, not considering that in failing to carry out the original plan, that by allowing Kate to live, she'd left behind the details of a crime scene that still set Kate up for murder. Munroe imagined for a moment how easy it would have been to have gotten away with it all.

"It's still not certain that the DA is going to prosecute," Bradford said. "But she has been charged. According to my sources, they've got video surveillance of her entering and exiting Richard's building around his estimated time of death, her using her key card for the elevator, and her fingerprints and DNA are all over his place. The evidence is compelling.

"She denies killing him, of course, swears that she was set up, and she's pointed the finger in your direction. It's possible there will be a few people interested in talking to you." He paused for a moment. "There's a weapon involved that does raise questions, and I figured you'd want the heads-up."

"As far as I know," Munroe said, "Burbank died when I was in Paris. Wasn't it right after the board met?"

"Before."

She shrugged. "Either way. I shouldn't have any problem proving I was out of the country."

Miles nodded. He opened his mouth to say something and then stopped. He turned toward the window. "Look," he finally said, "I know it's not my place, but I think you deserve to know. For what it's worth, I don't think Kate intended to betray you. I've seen the photos, and the prosecution has seen the photos. To you and me, it looks like she was sleeping with the enemy. To them it looks like she came after him out of jealousy. But it goes deeper.

"Burbank was blackmailing her, and she was playing the lover's angle to try to mitigate the damage. I suspect even she didn't realize how deadly the information she gave him was."

Munroe stared at him for a moment and finally, unable to hide the waver in her voice, said, "Burbank was blackmailing Kate?"

Bradford nodded again, lips pressed together.

Another pause and she said, "How do you know this?"

"It hasn't been easy to piece together," he said. "I had a man on the inside when the call on Burbank's death came in, and for the sake of deniability let's just say I've had my ears open and leave it at that.

"It seemed wrong, you know, for a woman like Kate to betray you over a love affair, so I started digging." Bradford handed Munroe a slim folder. "I'm still calling in favors, but I believe that this is what Burbank had on her."

Munroe studied the pages, impressed by Bradford's ability to see through the redundant to what was key, following the threads that he'd taken—a trail through an evil so dark that Richard Burbank was clean by comparison. "These were Kate's clients?" she asked.

Bradford nodded. "She set up their corporate structures and kept them legal."

"You'd make a good analyst."

Bradford smiled a half smile. "Call it personal curiosity. And it does help to have worked so closely with Richard. I knew where a lot of his skeletons were buried, and I knew how to locate what he wanted to hide. I admit it's still a little sketchy, but it does tie together."

Munroe glanced at the folder in her hands. "You don't think she knew she was involved in this?"

Bradford shrugged. "She had to know something—how much is anyone's guess. You know better than I do that Kate is and has always been ruthless. *That* ruthless? Who's to say? Maybe one day you can ask her."

Munroe sighed. "In another lifetime."

Bradford said, "With Kate pointing the finger in your direction, *I* made it a point to pay her a visit. I gave her a copy of what you have there in your hands and told her she was an idiot for choosing clients who would rather chop her up in little pieces than have word of their activity spread. I may have also mentioned that I didn't want to hear her talking about you anymore."

Munroe gave a half grin of acknowledgment.

"That said," he continued, "if I'm right, based on Richard's notes, he'd already started tracking dirt on Kate before you took the assignment. I think she knew he had something but didn't know what until you arrived in Africa, because that's when he began holding her feet to the fire."

Munroe looked up at Bradford. "You know, it doesn't change the fact that she sold me out, but if he had this on her . . ." Munroe's voice trailed off. "Thank you. You didn't have to do it."

Bradford simply nodded in reply. The silence settled, and he said, "I've heard from Emily."

"How is she?"

"Alive—obviously—and doing surprisingly well. A complete turn-around in her situation." Bradford handed Munroe a DVD. "This was in among the stuff Burbank had on Kate."

"Let me guess," she said. "You found his blackmail stash, and that's what he was using on Nchama?"

Bradford chuckled. "Yeah. And it gives events context in a weird sort of way. Watching the footage, you'd think Nchama was being paid to finance an overthrow of the EG government."

Munroe shook her head, stared out the window, and whispered, "A man risks his life to save it from the greater fear."

Bradford nodded, said, "I'm returning to Equatorial Guinea at the end of the week in order to accompany Emily and the children home." He paused. "I wondered if you'd be interested in coming along. I could use the help."

"I appreciate the offer, but I think you can handle that one on your own."

"Well, from what I've heard, the country can be somewhat difficult to maneuver and the government difficult to deal with." He winked that irresistible wink of his. "Truthfully, I'd love to have you there."

"You'll do fine," she said. And what was left unspoken hung in the air.

When the silence grew awkward and stretched into minutes, Munroe stood and said, "I guess I'd better get going." Bradford stood and reached to shake her outstretched hand. She drew him close and hugged him tight. "It's hard to let you go," she whispered, then pulled back and turned to walk away.

"What about you?" he said. "What's next?"

She paused and looked over her shoulder. "Germany to tie up loose ends, then Morocco." And for the first time in a long time, she smiled. "There's someone I need to find."

acknowledgments

It would not have been possible to find the time, means, or motivation to write without the love and support of family, friends, and loved ones. Whether they were in my life permanently, sporadically, or for but a season, they touched me and now live on in the work that they helped to nurture.

There have also been many whose insights and direct contributions have improved the original into what it is now. To all of you, I say thank you, and specifically to Nico Hald for her attention to detail, and to my agent, Anne Hawkins, and editor, Sarah Knight, for their love of words and belief in my work.

Read on for an excerpt from *The Innocent,*
the next adventure starring Vanessa Michael Munroe.

*S*he moved in a crouch, blade between her teeth, all four limbs connected to the earth. She cocked her head, listened, then continued
through the undergrowth and past the body at her bare feet.

Along the jungle floor, shadows cast against shadows, playing tricks
with the light, and unnatural stillness replaced the buzz and chatter
of the canopy, as if nature held its breath while bearing witness to the
violence.

She paused at the whisper of air that alerted her to movement from
behind.

They'd been smart to track so silently.

She shifted, ready to face them when they came.

And they would come.

The knowledge brought with it a surge of adrenaline.

Euphoria followed.

Two emerged from the verdure, dressed in shoddy camouflage and
rubber shoes, carrying no firearms, only knives. They came steadily, circling, hunting, eyes glazed with bloodlust, lips turned up in snarls. They
wanted her dead, and so they must die.

She breathed deeply, focus pure, measuring the strength of the
threat. Awareness came in waves, a feral instinct that returned nuance

with radarlike clarity. Understanding their weakness, she launched forward for the first strike.

Connected.

A scream shattered the calm.

Off balance, the first attacker toppled, and in a fluid movement she twisted, pushing off his body to propel herself into the second man.

He shifted to avoid impact, and the twist of his neck met the slice of her outstretched blade.

He fell.

She landed in a crouch and without pause returned to the first. Hand to head. Knife to neck. Swift, through tendons and sinew.

The fight had taken only seconds, and now in the silence the kill was finished. She stood over the bodies, the sound of her own heartbeat loud in her ears, and after a moment of hesitation she swore. It had been too fast. Too easy.

Her chest heaved in hatred of the skills that kept her alive, skills that drove her to win, skills that inevitably brought death.

She dropped to her knees and there, for the first time, stared at the face of the nearest hunter. A vise of recognition gripped her heart. She fell forward onto the body.

His open eyes were green. His hair was blond, his face longingly familiar.

Her soul pounded a rhythm: Please not him. Not him. Not him.

In death, his eyes fixed a piercing accusation. She gaped in mute horror at the liquid life that had, in seeping from his neck, painted her skin crimson.

She couldn't breathe.

Dizzy. Suffocating. Nausea.

She found air. It came in a burning rush into collapsing lungs, a scream that started from the depths of her soul and ripped through her vocal cords, shattering the stillness, sending a flurry of beating wings through the canopy.

Head tilted upward, and with the primal shriek of rage and pain still rising, she opened her eyes. Not to the jungle roof but to her bedroom ceiling, patterned, whitewashed, and tinged with the color of dawn coming through the window.

Vanessa Munroe gasped. Curtains in the room rustled lightly. The call to prayer sounded from minarets across the city and her hand was still gripping the handle of a knife plunged into the other side of the king-size mattress.

Awareness settled, and she let go of the knife as if scalded, rolling off the bed in the same movement.

She stared.

The blade had struck twice and stood in silent witness to the increasing ferocity of the nightmares. The sheets were soaked with sweat. She glanced at her tank top and boxers. Drenched. And Noah, had he not had to leave for work early this morning, would have been dead.

CHAPTER 1

Casablanca, Morocco

At last, the crowd moved forward.

He picked up the duffel bag and slipped the strap over his shoulder. Aching and nauseous, he placed one deliberate foot in front of the other, part of the collective escape from transatlantic captivity—down the aisle, out the belly of the plane, along the Jetway and through the sunlit terminals of Mohammed V Airport.

Three days of little sleep had brought him here, three days and three lifetimes since that call in the wee hours that had, without warning, provided long-awaited news. He'd sat in the dark, rigid on the edge of the bed, searching his way through possibilities until, certain there was really only one option, he'd picked up the handset and placed the call to Morocco.

I need a favor.

Those had been his only words. No introduction, no explanation, only the plea.

"Tell me," she'd said.

"I'm coming to you."

And that was it. No good-bye, just his unspoken fear wrapped into those words and whispered into the night, and across the wires. He'd put down the phone and then, with palms sweating and hands shaking, sat in front of the computer and purchased a ticket.

He needed that favor and had flown halfway around the world to ask it.

Now, without thinking, he moved with the throng, while inside his head the words of entreaty came and went; rewound and started over; front to back, end to beginning, in the same perpetual loop that had not stopped since the call.

He slowed. Stood in front of a plate-glass window. Stared out over the naked runway while those behind him hurried past.

Even if he tried he could never count the number of airports and train stations that delineated his youth; a collection of visa stamps and endless moves that defined his life as one of eight siblings hopscotching the globe with cult-member parents, together forming a ragtag group of economy-class vagabonds.

Into the glass he whispered his name, strange as it was even to him. The sound drifted in a low and hushed tribute to the past that had brought him here, the past that refused to die no matter how long or how often buried.

Sherebiah Gospel Logan.

His name was Logan. *Only* Logan. *Always* Logan. And to those few who knew the rest, he blamed it on drugs and hippies, which was so much easier than trying to explain what most could never comprehend.

Desperation had compelled him here, to the one person who did understand, the one capable of burying the past for good. If she so chose. He needed that favor, needed her to say yes, and instead of arriving with something to barter, he'd come a beggar, hat in hand with nothing to offer but their shared bond and the secret dread that her answer would be no.

His eyes tracked the last of the thinning stream of passengers and the airline crew as they trailed luggage down the hall, and finally his feet again propelled him forward.

He moved through customs and the whole of the border crossing on autopilot, until he came at last to the waiting area, and there among the sea of faces he searched hers out. He passed over her once, twice, before finally spotting her with arms crossed and leaning into a column with a grin that said she'd been watching him for a while.

Vanessa. Michael Munroe. Best friend. Surrogate family. Personal savior.

She looked nothing like the battle-hardened woman who'd returned from Africa's west coast eight months ago, now nearly unrecognizable in flowing pants and delicate head scarf, everything about her soft and feminine and the opposite of what he'd expected to find. But seeing her, he could hope again.

He stood in place while she shoved off the pillar in his direction, her smirk indelible, slicing through the crowd nimble and catlike, her gray eyes not once breaking contact until she was within arm's length.

And then, in a movement that would have resulted in a broken nose for anyone else, she stretched out and tussled his blond hair, laughing that deep carefree laugh of hers that said she was genuinely happy to see him.

The inward rehearsal and stress that had consumed the last days was replaced by the possibility of hope. Logan grabbed her in a bear hug that she halfheartedly attempted to escape; he spun her full circle, and when he'd finally let go and there was a second of awkward silence, she tussled his hair again.

"Jesus, Logan," she said. "From the look on your face, you'd think you'd come to ask me to marry you."

He ran a hand through his hair to mitigate the damage, and unable to contain the ear-to-ear grin, said, "Maybe one day I will."

"You should be so lucky," she said drily, then with a light punch to the shoulder that held his bag, "That all you got?"

He nodded, the stupid grin still plastered to his face.

She smiled, hooked her arm in his and, shoulder to shoulder, nearly equal in height, led him away from the crowd, saying, "It's really good to see you."

The lilt of her voice, the uncharacteristic enthusiasm of her touch, gave him pause, and as they continued arm in arm, he turned to catch her eye. She grinned, impishly squeezed his biceps and then placed her head on his shoulder.

"You hungry?" she asked. "We've got a long trip ahead of us."

"I ate on the plane," he said, and then confused, he hesitated. "How long could it possibly take to get into Casablanca?"

"Not Casablanca," she said. "Tangier."

The last map of Morocco that he'd seen showed Tangier nearly two hundred miles northeast. He grasped for reasons. "You and Noah broke up?" he said.

Munroe shrugged and turned ever so slightly, so that she walked backward as she spoke. She flashed him another smile, and in that smile Logan saw a glimpse of the same, odd, telltale stupefaction that hadn't washed over her face in more than half a decade.

"Hard to call something that could never be whole, broken," she said. "But no, things haven't changed, we're still together."

She smiled yet again, and went back to walking side by side, but in the wake of this last, the burden Logan had come to share grew that much heavier.

He understood from that look what she'd not said with words, and he fought for composure, to prevent the shock of knowledge from escaping to his face. He kept beside her, matching her step for step across polished floors to the lower level, where they'd catch a train into the city.

Logan said, "Why the move to Tangier?"

"I like it there," she said.

Her words came blank and deadpan. No humor, no sincerity; her unusually indirect way of saying *none of your damn business*, and so he let it go for now. He'd find another way to probe the extent of the damage behind the smile, to come at it from a different direction, because both as friend and as supplicant, he had to know how hard he could push, how solid the chassis, how twisted the wreckage.

They reached Casa Voyageurs, the regional train station, and there, Munroe led him through the cool, high-domed terminal to the ticket counter where she segued into an exchange of Arabic.

Logan handed her his wallet and she pushed it back. "I've got it," she said. "This isn't breaking the bank."

Tickets in one hand, she took his hand in the other and moved beyond the clean and tidy interior, to the outside, to the tunnel and its confusing array of tracks to the train that would take them north. They were still walking the corridor to the first-class compartment when the car lurched and the train began a slow crawl out of the station.

Logan paused and, as he'd done so many times in years past, stood watching the platform shrink into the distance. Tracks and walls and city structures began to blur, and he turned toward the empty six-seat berth that Munroe had entered.

She sat beside the window with her head tilted back and eyes closed, so he dumped the bag on his assigned seat and took the spot opposite her. She opened her eyes a sliver and stretched so that her legs spanned the aisle, resting her feet between his knees.

Logan said, "I could have flown to Tangier, you know, saved you the trip down and back."

She nodded. "But I wanted to have the time alone with you," she said.

She'd handed him an opening, presented the opportunity to unburden himself and say in person what he'd flown across the Atlantic to say, but he couldn't. Not now. Not with her like this. He needed time to think.

He faltered and left the unasked "why" hanging in the air.

Munroe paused. It was a small hesitation, but enough that he understood she'd given notice. She was aware he'd parlayed the opening gambit and was willing to go along with him.

"Noah's there right now," she continued. "He's edgy, jealous." She turned her eyes back to meet his. "I didn't want you to have to face that right off the bat."

"Doesn't he know that I'm gay?"

She flashed a cheesy grin and crinkled her nose. "He knows. But he also knows that I love you."

"So that makes me a threat?" Logan said.

She nodded.

He sighed.

The only way his arrival could be deemed a threat was if something else wasn't right. Under ideal circumstances Logan would ask for details and she would tell; their conversation would flow in that bonded way of confidants that had defined their years together. But this wasn't ideal, not anything close to ideal.

They settled again into small talk, then gradually into silence as Logan, lulled by the peace of her presence, the rhythm of the wheels against the tracks, and fighting three days awake, drifted into the oblivion of sleep.

It was the subtle exchange of metal on metal that gradually pulled him back. According to the sun's path, hours had passed.

Dazed and disoriented, he turned to Munroe. She was smiling again, that odd telltale smile. She flipped the knife from her palm, her eyes never leaving his as she played the blade across her fingers.

Logan cursed silently, fighting the urge to stare at the weapon, and said, "Been a while since you've carried them."

She nodded, eyes still on his, still grinning, the steel continuing to play.

Logan leaned his head back and closed his eyes—his way of shutting out the pain of seeing her in this state. The knives and all that they symbolized spoke volumes to how far she had fallen.

THE SKY WAS DARK when they arrived in Tangier, Morocco's gateway Europe. Tangier Ville was the end of the line, and the station, with its clean and polished interior, was in turn its own gateway to nighttime streets that birthed life and motion into the humid air of Africa's northern coast.

Their destination in the eastern suburb of Malabata was close enough that they could have walked, but instead of footing it as Logan had expected, Munroe flagged a petit taxi. In the glow of the terminal's fluorescent lights she bartered with the driver over the rate, and Logan sensed disquiet in her haste.

The ride was but a few minutes, and the vehicle stopped in front of a three-story building that faced the ocean. The apartment block, like most of the others Logan had seen on the journey, was whitewashed, stacked, and topped with a flat rooftop that he knew to be as much a part of the living space as the rooms inside.

He stepped from the cab and sniffed the salt-tinged breeze.

Parked against the curb not far from the building entrance was a black BMW and Munroe swore quietly as she took note of it.

"He's already here," she said.

Logan lifted the strap of his bag to his shoulder. "I've wanted to meet him anyway," he said.

She stared at the car and after a long pause walked through the front door with Logan following close behind.

The stairs from the entrance led to a tiled mezzanine that ampli-
fied their footsteps, and they went up again, another half floor, stopping
in front of the only apartment on the landing. Munroe turned the key
and swung the oversized door wide to a deep and sparsely furnished living area.

"Home," she said with a flourish, and Logan grinned at the joke. Six
months in Morocco and she'd already jumped cities. For her there would
never be anything so permanent as home.

The apartment was quiet and dim, the silence made larger by high
ceilings, patterned floors, and a light current that billowed through open
windows into gauzy curtains. Footsteps echoed from the hall and Logan
turned in their direction as Noah entered the living room.

Noah Johnson, a Moroccan-raised American, had been a chance
encounter on Munroe's last assignment, an encounter that had eventually evolved into her latest and possibly final departure from the United
States.

Although Logan knew much of the man from pictures and conversations, this was the first time he'd seen him in person, and it was clear
why Munroe had taken such a liking to him. He was an easy six-foot-
plus, black hair, fair skin, and a rock climber's physique.

In a gesture proprietary and tender, Noah pulled Munroe close and
kissed her on the forehead, then extended his hand to Logan in greeting.

Munroe ran interpretation between Noah's rudimentary English and
Logan's broken French, and in the easy exchange Logan sensed a frac-
ture in the closeness the two had shared. He wondered as he stood there
now, making small talk through Munroe, what it must be like in Noah's
shoes, to helplessly watch the woman he loved withdraw emotionally, to
fear she would soon walk away, whilest extending a hand of friendship
to the man he suspected to be the cause.

Munroe returned Noah's kiss, said softly, "Let me show Logan
around. I'll be ready in twenty minutes," and with that took Logan's
hand and led him toward the hallway.

Three bedrooms and two bathrooms made up the bulk of the one-
level apartment, and a narrow staircase beyond the kitchen led to the
laundry and work area on the rooftop. Like so many places in the developing countries in which Logan had once lived, the apartment was bare

and rustic, the kitchen and bathrooms minimalistic, and as a whole the flat was without many of the standard fixtures found in even lower-income homes of the United States.

The brief tour ended at the guest bedroom and when Munroe had shown Logan what little he needed to know, she left to dress for the evening.

He turned off the light and in the dark dumped his bag on a chair.

The room was enveloped in the quiet of night, and in that quiet there was a form of peace. Here, alone in the dimness, he could think; he could process and plan and try to figure out how to dig his way out of a hole that had, in less than a moment of clarity, doubled in size. He'd come to Morocco focused on nothing more than begging for Munroe's help, a yes or no answer, and had instead been blindsided by the complex series of hoops he'd have to jump through to get it.

The sound of running water filtered across the hall, and in the street-light glow he sat on the bed, elbows to knees, methodically forcing calm; waiting.

A shift in the light under the bedroom door announced her presence before the footfalls. Logan lay back on the bed, hands behind his head, ready for the knock that came a second later.

She was stunning in silhouette, the loose and modest clothes replaced by a very short, figure-hugging dress that accentuated a long, lean, androgynous body and brandished sensuality. In heels, she had at least an inch over Noah's height, and together they would make a visually intimidating pair.

With a hug and then a house key placed in his palm, she was gone.

The front door echoed a thud and Logan rose from the bed to watch from the window as the BMW peeled away from the curb. He waited until he was certain they would not U-turn for a forgotten item, then headed toward the living room where he'd spotted a telephone.

A Conversation with Taylor Stevens

Q) Your debut thriller, The Informationist, *features a kick-ass heroine named Vanessa "Michael" Munroe who is getting some nice comps to Stieg Larsson's feisty protagonist Lisbeth Salander. How did you envision Munroe? Did you know when you first started writing the book that she would be such a strong, fierce character?*

A) From the beginning, when writing Munroe, I never viewed her in terms of strong or weak, good or evil, or even, in a sense, male or female. Initially, when thinking of her reactions to situations, I was drawn to the emotional conflict and skill of Jason Bourne, and the sensual confidence of Lara Croft, but these were gut feelings, nothing specific or tangible. So to me, Munroe has always been who she is as the natural result of her storied life, and I honestly didn't realize just how strong—and perhaps unusual—she is until feedback started coming in from early readers.

Q) What exactly is an "informationist" and how did you come up with the concept of the novel? Did you have an aha moment, or did the novel come together over time?

A) Everything about writing *The Informationist* unfolded backwards. When I started, I had no idea what I was doing. I had no plot, no characters, only the location in which the bulk of the story would be set, so the entire concept was definitely a slow evolution. On a personal level,

I've experienced the struggle of trying to adapt and survive after being thrust into a foreign society pretty much overnight, so putting Munroe on a path where acquiring information was innate and eventually turned into a career, seemed natural.

Q) You've set your thriller all over the world with a significant amount in Africa. Why the exotic setting?

A) I knew I would set the story in Equatorial Guinea before I knew anything else about writing, because I'd spent two years living there. Even having lived in other African countries didn't prepare me for what I experienced in Equatorial Guinea. When I first set out to write, I saw more potential in bringing the location to life for readers than in the story itself or the characters that might populate the book. Of course, I view it differently now, but that's where it started.

Q) You had a rather unusual upbringing. How did your early education, or lack thereof, affect your writing process?

A) Growing up in a religious cult, my education stopped when I was twelve, and although I've been able to teach myself a lot, with some things I'm still frozen in time. Contending with the reality of my educational gaps when entering the real world and facing the number of years it would take to play catch-up certainly propelled me to be the best writer I could possibly be, because there wasn't a Plan B or alternate career to fall back on.

Q) You've lived in a number of countries (and on several continents). Which is your favorite and why? What's the most exotic thing you've eaten?

A) Travel for me is like having children: how can you possibly pick a favorite? Every location has its own brand of special. As far as exotic foods, I guess the weirdest (that I'm aware of—sometimes you just don't want to know) was forest snails—not the same thing as escargot! Big chunks of rubber balloon.

Q) In The Informationist *Munroe has a knack for languages and an institutional understanding of different cultures—not to mention stellar knife skills. Do you share any of these talents with Munroe?*

A) Definitely not the knife skills—perhaps it's in part because of my own helplessness in self-defense that I created the counterweight in

Munroe—and abashedly, I only speak one language, so we'll have to rule out polyglot skills as well. But where we do share a trait is in my own absorption of English vocabulary. Having only a sixth grade education and no access to written material beyond cult-published propaganda literature until I was in my late twenties, it's still rather a mystery as to where my own bank of word knowledge comes from.

Q) The Informationist is the first in a series featuring Vanessa Munroe. Did you always see it this way, or did that develop after the first novel was fully drafted?

A) I think it was about halfway through *The Informationist*, when the characters had pretty much developed into who they are now, that I first realized that they were destined to live on in other stories.

Q) Take us through a typical day of writing. Do you write all at once or in spurts? Do you prefer to write in the morning or evening?

A) I am my most productive at night and into the wee morning hours. However, I'm responsible for two wonderful children, which means I'm up early in the morning in order to get them off to school, and since I don't function well without sleep, this also means I'm rarely able to access my most productive hours. Instead, I work around their schedule, and by work I mean mostly procrastinate until I realize that they'll be home from school any minute, at which time the noise level will return to filled-stadium loud, so I'd better actually put some words down. Sometimes the words are even worth keeping. That said, I do try to write every day, even weekends, and I set daily, weekly, and monthly goals, until I get a complete first draft. After that, crafting the story doesn't feel as much like work, and I tend to procrastinate less.

Q) Name one place you'd love to visit one day.

A) One? Just one? Okay. Bhutan.

Q) Where will Munroe's adventures take her next?

A) Certainly into South America, and into Europe again. I would like to take her to Russia, but for that I would need to develop a solid plot and I haven't gotten that far yet.

COMING SOON—the next adventure starring
Vanessa Michael Munroe

The Innocent
A Vanessa Michael Munroe Novel
by Taylor Stevens
$24.00 (Canada: $27.00)
978-0-307-71712-2

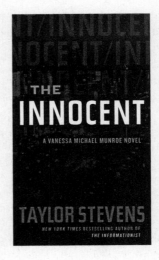